The unmanned ship was approached warily, the Messerschmitts being cautious of the guns it did not have. When they realized it was turretless, and therefore probably defenseless, their mood became more belligerent and they swung in for an easy kill.

"Mother ship two to mother ship one, my controller has fighters on his monitor. You better tell your guys to get his plane out of there."

Two of the Messerschmitts dove underneath the Aphrodite. Even if they did believe it was unarmed, they still weren't going to take any chances. Atkinson decided to take them on; hoping that the other German wouldn't attack at the same time.

As he dove under the robot's nose, they came up under its tail. All forward guns on his Fortress opened fire on the two fighters. One staggered from direct hits immediately but the other managed to start a line of cannon shells walking down the Aphrodite's belly. Then it evaporated in a searing flash.

From twenty-five thousand feet, it looked like a giant star shell going off. Though Lacey tried at once to contact Atkinson, everyone knew it would be in vain. . . .

JOHN-ALLEN PRICE

DOOMSDAY SHIP

ZEBRA BOOKS
KENSINGTON PUBLISHING CORP.

To Dr. Peter Duke, ex-Corsair driver of the Fleet Air Arm, and to those members of the Canadian Warplane Heritage, who helped me make this novel as accurate as it is.

ZEBRA BOOKS

are published by

KENSINGTON PUBLISHING CORP.
475 Park Avenue South
New York, N.Y. 10016

Printed in the United States of America

Chapter One
CONCLUDING REPORT
THE UNKNOWN

To: The Board of Sea Lords—The Admiralty.

On September fifteen, the Lancaster bombers of No. 617 squadron, Royal Air Force, successfully carried out their planned attack on the battleship *Tirpitz* as it lay in its anchorage in Kaa Fjord. Though only one aircraft out of the twenty-seven dispatched scored a direct hit, the 12,000 pound bomb did extensive damage to the forecastle and a one hundred and eighteen foot section abaft of the bows.

The longitudinal bulkheads beneath this section have been split open and both A and B turrets are inoperative. This damage has rendered the *Tirpitz* permanently unbattleworthy. It would take at least a year to return her to operational status and this is far longer than even the most pessimistic forecast has the European conflict lasting.

Intercepted Enigma radio traffic shows that Admiral Dönitz has ordered the *Tirpitz* towed to the port of Tromsö where it will form part of the coastal defences. Indications are that the move will be attempted at mid-October. Since Tromsö is within range of heavy bombers based in Scotland, the Royal Air Force should be allowed another strike to finish off the *Tirpitz*.

With the exception of the final coup de grace, this operation is concluded. No major surface threat to our North Atlantic and Arctic convoys remains and we can proceed with the redeployment of our major surface units to the Pacific theatre to assist in defeating the Japanese.

I have the honour to be Sir,
Your obedient Servant,
Lieutenant-Commander
Charles Wilfrid Cox R.N.
Intelligence Division
attached to the Fifth Sea Lord
Deputy Chief of Naval Staff

"Operations Centre, this is the Radar Room. We are plotting an unknown, high-speed target. Distance is seventy-three miles and closing. General direction, west-southwest."

"Understood, Radar Room. Do you have any other intruders on your screens? Does it look to you like an attack?"

"Negative, we have only the one. Its altitude is six thousand feet and its airspeed is three hundred and fifty knots. The unknown appears to be a single reconnaissance aircraft and not part of any organized attack force."

"Understood; we'll take care of it, Operations Centre, out. Leftenant, notify the captain of this development. He should either be in the officers' mess or his own quarters. Flight Director, what aircraft do we currently have airborne? Signals, standby to alert the destroyer screen."

"Sir, Flight Director here. There is just one plane still airborne, it's Commander Bradley. He's flying one of the new Fairey Fireflies."

The two-seat strike fighter orbited low and wide over its home base, the carrier HMS *Implacable*. Fuel permitting, it was Bradley's routine to be the last of his squadron to land. Now, as he watched his wingman taxi to the forward deck park, it came time for him to enter the pattern.

"Blue Stone Leader. Blue Stone Leader, this is Operations. We have a high-speed unknown approaching our position. Disengage from the landing pattern and proceed north-northwest to identify and intercept if necessary. The Flight Director will give you a precise vector and all pertinent information."

"But we've already been on a two-hour, anti-shipping rhubarb, sir," complained Bradley's Radio-Navigator, sitting in a second, separate cockpit. "Can't they send up some Seafires?"

"Not with the front half of the flight deck full of parked aircraft," said Bradley, "it will take at best several minutes for them to clear that jam. Who knows, this may be our chance to become heroes."

"What do you mean we? You'll be the hero, I'll be the assistant hero and assistant heroes don't get mentioned."

The landing gear and flaps had just been lowered and Bradley had to wait until they cycled completely before raising them. The Firefly roared over the carrier and rose into the cold, darkening sky. In spite

7

of the *Implacable*'s own gun defences, as well as those of her escorts, the lone fighter was the best answer for the intruder.

"Operations Centre to Signals, alert the *Scorpion* and the *Undaunted*. Tell them to prepare for a possible air attack on their port quarter. Radar, do you have an idea from where in Norway this unknown came?"

"We cannot give you an exact point of origin, sir. Our equipment doesn't have the range. The best I can give you is a swath of coastline from North Cape down to Tromsö."

"Can you identify the type of aircraft our visitor is? Three hundred and fifty knots is rather fast for the planes the Luftwaffe is known to have based in Norway."

"Whatever it is, it's definitely not a bomber or a seaplane. Not even one of the new Ju-188s is this fast. Our return echo is rather small, so it has to be a fighter and it has not slowed down since we first spotted it. So down here, our guess is this unknown is a jet."

"Flight Director! This is Operations! Double at once the number of Seafires you are preparing to launch. I'll tell the bridge to expedite the removal of planes from the deck park. We'd better alert our own gun crews. Leftenant, have you found the captain yet?"

"All hands rig for air attack. Gun crews to your battle stations. Repeat, all gun crews to your battle stations. Torpedo tube and depth charge crews may stand down. Fire Control Officer, let me know the moment the gun crews report in. Signals, make ready a message to the *Implacable* that HMS *Undaunted* is at full readiness."

In small groups, sailors fanned over the destroyer

to man the main turrets and anti-aircraft mounts that bristled along its superstructure. On the horizon off the *Undaunted*'s starboard side lay the aircraft carrier it was to protect, now turned into a dark silhouette by the low, early evening sun.

"I don't care if you have to push those ruddy aeroplanes off the side, just have the forward lift and the catapults clear. Yes, I realize I am stepping on your authority as Officer of the Watch but we may have just sent Commander Bradley to his death. The unknown we are tracking may well turn out to be a jet fighter. Its speed is a constant three hundred and fifty knots and it's maintaining the straightest course I have ever seen. Yes, we've notified him but what can you expect, he's Canadian and he's continuing anyway."

"If you don't mind my asking this, Commander, how can we catch up to a plane that's flying at over four hundred miles an hour when we can't do better than three hundred and twenty ourselves?" the radio-navigator politely asked.

"You forget, Les, that a Firefly can dive like a rocket-assisted brick. All we have to do is get above this intruder and drop onto his tail. We'll only be able to get one pass at him though I think that's all we can afford. The wing guns have only a burst or two left in them."

"Signals, transmit message to the *Implacable*. All gun crews at full readiness and add we can hear their fighter's engine. We have not yet sighted the unknown."

The Firefly passed the destroyer screen, climbing steeply. It was already at the intruder's altitude of six thousand feet; a minute and a half later it had gained another mile and leveled off at just under twelve thousand feet. Bradley swept the sky in front of and below him. Save for the wispy cloud layers spreading out from Norway, he saw nothing.

"Operations to Blue Stone Leader. You are fifteen miles from the intruder, at current closure rate you will intercept it in about a minute. Have you raised the intruder visually?"

"Negative, there's not even a sea gull up here," Bradley replied. "If what I'm out to stop is a fighter, then it won't be any bigger than fly shit at fifteen miles. I'll have to wait until it's closer, much closer. In the meantime, when can I expect to see some reinforcements?"

"Blue Stone, we have a sticky problem here. We must strike down some aeroplanes and move a few others. We won't have a single Seafire ready for launching for ten minutes. Do you understand the situation, Blue Stone Leader?"

"Understood, Operations, let me know when the distance has shrunk to five miles and I'll move into position."

"Could our home really be threatened by one, lone aircraft?" asked the radio-navigator.

"It sure as hell can," answered Bradley. "If you don't believe me then ask those in the American Navy who served on the carrier *Princeton*. It sank about three days ago in the Battle of Leyte Gulf after being hit by a single bomb. If what's coming is a Messerschmitt jet then it can accelerate past five hundred miles an hour. And if it evades us, I'm not sure the big guns on the ships below can turn fast enough to successfully track the bastard."

Seconds later the Firefly swung around, completely reversing its course, and tipped into a dive. Airspeed jumped at once to four hundred miles an hour. Several thousand feet in front of and below the two-seat fighter, a faint, pulsating glow moved underneath the lowermost cloud layer.

Bradley pushed his throttle to its gate stop; kicking his ship to better than four hundred and fifty miles an hour. It shot through the intervening layers until one thin veil remained. For a brief moment the red-hued mist enveloped the fighter, then scattered; leaving Bradley with an unobstructed view of the intruder.

He had calculated his dive correctly, he was almost on top of the tiny, swift but no longer unknown aircraft. It was small, much smaller than a fighter; its stub wings seemed out of place attached to the sleek, torpedo-like fuselage. Driving the miniature plane wasn't any propeller or turbojet engine. Mounted over its tail was a long, fire-sputtering tube. Bradley knew this could not be a jet fighter, even if he had never seen one before. It was another kind of weapon, a revenge weapon.

"Mother of Jesus, it's a V-1! Operations, the intruder isn't a manned aircraft at all. It's a buzz bomb! I've heard these little monsters are dangerous but I'm going to try to kill it in any event. I'm too close now so I'll let the distance open up a bit. Wish me luck, Blue Stone Leader, out."

The V-1 was less than a hundred yards in front of the Firefly. Bradley chopped the throttle as he brought his fighter out of its dive. Both actions reduced airspeed and allowed the robot to slowly creep ahead of him.

"HMS *Implacable* to *Undaunted* and *Scorpion*. Stand down your gun crews, repeat, stand down your gun crews. Our pilot has identified the unknown and will attempt to shoot it down. He should be appearing off your port quarters in the next forty seconds."

"Les, you'd better prepare for one hell of a bang," Bradley warned. "From what I've heard, there's about

11

eighteen hundred pounds of amatol riding inside this little bastard. So get things battened down at your end. Here goes the fireworks."

Bradley flipped away the guard plate from the gun button atop the control stick's circular grip. By now range had grown to two hundred yards, the optimum distance he knew Royal Air Force fighters used to combat the V-1s over England. The center dot of the gun sight's fixed aiming image almost covered the fleeing revenge weapon. It could scarcely be seen and yet Bradley could not miss. He felt his aircraft shake gently as the four cannons that comprised its main armament began firing. A moment later it was lashed as if caught in the middle of a hurricane.

The last few dozen 20mm shells converged on the V-1; ripping its sheet-steel skin, crippling its pulse jet power plant, rupturing its fuel tank and compressed air bottles. A fire started inside the narrow fuselage; the robot would have fallen into the sea like a comet had not its warhead finally detonated. At two hundred yards and four hundred miles an hour, there was not enough room or time to avoid the expanding fireball. The Firefly was swallowed at the same instant the shock wave slammed it about.

Four hundred miles an hour also meant the fighter was into and through the heart of the explosion in the following instant. It emerged slightly singed and flying on its back.

"Operations, this is Blue Stone Leader. I'm going to have some of the damnedest gun camera footage you'll ever see. I'll be coming in for a landing just as soon as I roll this aircraft right side up and slow her down."

"Understood, Blue Stone Leader but you're going to have to delay your landing for a little bit. In order to facilitate launching the Seafires, we've had to

12

move so many parked aircraft that there is no longer enough room on the flight deck for you to make a safe recovery."

ROYAL NAVY EMERGENCY
OPERATIONS CABLE

To: His Majesty's Ship *Implacable,* Commander Paul Bradley.

From: Admiralty Operations Centre, Intelligence Division.

Commander Bradley, you are hereby ordered to the Scapa Flow Naval Air Field at O-nine hundred hours tomorrow morning. Bring with you the Radio-Navigator you had at the time of the incident described in report TE-322 and all visual evidence of the aforementioned. This order supercedes all previous ones issued to you, commander, and carries the full weight of authority of the Fifth Sea Lord.

The gray-green and light blue Firefly arrived over Scapa Flow on time; only to have a lumbering Dakota hold it up on final. Except for a small oath, Bradley thought nothing more of the transport—until he was ordered to park next to it and saw that the officers who got off were clearly waiting for him to taxi in.

There were just two, a Royal Navy Leftenant-Commander and a tall and very pretty WREN leftenant with dark red hair. After a month of working up and operations on a cramped aircraft carrier, she was a most welcome sight.

Almost before the propeller had wound to a halt and the ground crew had folded the Firefly's wings, Bradley was rolling back the canopy and unbuckling

13

his shoulder harness. The two waiting officers came around to the trailing edge of the left wing and met Bradley as he climbed down.

The man who first greeted him looked to be his same age or slightly older. He stood several inches shorter, had sandy-colored hair and was not quite as robustly built as the more senior Canadian officer. Then again he didn't have to wrestle around seven-ton fighters on a daily basis.

"Good morning, Commander Bradley, I am Leftenant-Commander Charles Cox, Intelligence Division. And this is my aide and sole staff officer, Leftenant Constance Smythe."

Cox went on to explain where he and his staff came from and what they needed of Bradley and his radio-navigator. A special briefing room was prepared for them and the requested equipment set aside for their use. First Cox wanted to see the gun camera footage, then his questions would follow; but not before Bradley put in his own.

"What I'd like to know right off the bat is how come I flew out of the fire cloud upside down?" he asked, "it's the damnedest thing that has ever happened to me."

"For someone in the Fleet Air Arm it would be," Cox explained, "though for the Royal Air Force and American Army Air Force fighter pilots, who flew buzz bomb patrols over England, it was a rather common experience. At the distance you opened fire, you could not avoid the destruction of the missile. The moment you saw it you were in it. At the centre of the explosion a partial vacuum is created and the enormous propeller you have hanging on the Firefly, plus its seventeen hundred horsepower Griffon engine, creates a powerful torque which has the effect of twisting the aircraft onto its back. Now tell me,

14

how close did you come to the V-1?"

"When I first popped out of the clouds, I was about seventy-five yards behind it. Then I fell back to two hundred where I blew it out of the sky."

"Did you see any attaching lugs or rails on the topside of the fuselage or wings?"

"No, those all appeared to have smooth upper surfaces," Bradley answered. "Shouldn't those things be on the bottom of the fuselage? Where it is normally attached to the ramp?"

"Not if the missile were air-launched. Since the middle of September the Germans have been firing V-1s from modified Heinkel 111 and 177 bombers. So far they've launched about five hundred against Southampton and Portsmouth. Did you see any unusual markings or paint scheme? Any squadron code letters? Any numbers? Especially on the engine pipe or tail fin."

"There were some white stripes on the wing tips and forward fuselage. You can't see them in the gun camera footage because you have a dead tail-on view there. I saw them when I first jumped on the thing but I was too busy at the time to take real notice of them."

"Do you think you can recall them well enough now to describe the stripes to Leftenant Smythe here?" Cox asked; if he couldn't get a photograph then the next best alternative would have to suffice.

"Well, I'll give it a damn good try. Why?"

"Because before the war, Miss Smythe was an aspiring commercial artist. Go fetch your scratch pad, Connie. We're going to need that very special talent of yours."

While Constance worked with Bradley on producing a drawing; Cox went to question the assistant hero he had brought along. Cox did not get much out of the radio-navigator, save for a good description on what the inside of a fireball looks like. When he returned to Bradley, he got more of the information he needed to make a conclusion.

"Here's the view the Commander had of the V-1," said Constance, handing to Cox her first drawing. "As you can see, the stripes appear to extend from the tips down about one-third of the wingspan. On the fuselage, they run from the nose back to the wing juncture area. Here's an additional three-view drawing of Commander Bradley's V-1, based on what he has told me. Top view, front view and a side view. It should be obvious that they are not squadron or group markings but are for a completely different purpose."

"Yes, you're quite right," said Cox. "If anything, they remind me of the special markings I've seen on experimental aeroplanes and other vehicles. I think from this bit of information we can conclude that this V-1 was part of some test firing or launching. It could very well be that the Germans are planning to operationally deploy the V-1 in Norway."

"Why the hell would they do that?" Bradley observed. "There's nothing to shoot at from Norway. A V-1 isn't accurate enough to sink ships. This one appearing over the *Implacable*'s battle group was just a fluke."

"Small radio transmitters, spirited aboard ships by enemy agents could rectify the accuracy problem. They may also be planning to launch V-1s against Murmansk. If they were fired from the North Cape area the missiles would have just enough range to reach the port."

"But I didn't shoot this one down over Murmansk. I shot it down over the Norwegian Sea. Now how do

16

you jive that with your theory?"

"A missile doesn't have to be pointed in the right direction or at its intended target in order to test its range or launching equipment. In point of fact, it is best not to conduct such activities in the exact same area of deployment. Why tip-off the Russians to your plans?"

"True but the Russians don't really have the fighters to stop those things anyway. What are your plans going to be for the future of your investigation? Are you going to turn it over to someone else, or tip-off the Russians?"

"Ordinarily I would go back to the Intelligence Division with the information you have given me," Cox noted, "where we would decide by committee who to tell and what to do next, which of His Majesty's other armed services we would bring in and which of our allies we would inform. But things are different now. With all our battleships, heavy cruisers and fleet carriers being redeployed to the Far East, we are a little short of staff at Whitehall at the present time. My aide and I will have to handle this incident by ourselves. I've been empowered by the Board of Sea Lords to enlist the assistance of any of His Majesty's forces in the course of my investigation. When I have finished, I will report to the Fifth Sea Lord and maybe even to the full board itself. It wasn't like that in earlier days, but the Home Fleet and the North Atlantic are becoming a bit of a backwater area. The few major warships which are still assigned to the Home Fleet have been dry-docked and are undergoing modification and refitting for the Far East."

"I know, the *Implacable* will be returning to the Scapa Flow area by week's end for the same reason," said Bradley.

"Then I gather that means you'll soon be in the Pacific shooting down Zeroes?"

"No, not really. I'm going to be reassigned to work up new Corsair squadrons for the fighter carrier *Pursuer*. That should take a couple of weeks; it depends on the quality of the student pilots I will get, how many Corsairs the Royal Navy has on hand and whether or not the training carrier *Ravager* will be out of dry-dock on time. Maybe by the middle of December the squadrons will be ready and the *Pursuer* can sail for the Pacific. If you're going to continue this investigation by yourself, what will you do next?"

"I think Coastal Command can help me best at this stage," said Cox, collecting his notes and Constance's drawings. "They have a long-range, anti-submarine wing manned entirely by Norwegians. Its C.O. should be awfully interested in this turn of events. If not that unit, then it will have to be the Shetland Gang and their ferry service to Norway."

UNITED STATES ARMY AIR FORCES
EIGHTH AIR FORCE
INSPECTOR GENERAL'S OFFICE
DISCIPLINARY REPORT

To: Colonel Dennis P. Lacey, Fersfield, Norfolk.

From: Eighth Air Force Headquarters, High Wycombe.

Col. Lacey, this report is in regard to the extremely unprofessional behavior you and your Field Electronics Team have shown since your arrival in England. It is to the credit of the

18

local military police at Fersfield that your group did not jeopardize the security of Project Aphrodite.

Almost to a man, none of your team consistently displayed any of the manners or discipline that is normally expected of Army Air Force officers. This is all the more amazing because several of your men are experienced combat veterans. What follows is a list of the incidents known to have been perpetrated by members of your team and for which you, as commanding officer, must assume full responsibility.

One week after your arrival in England on August 25th, two of your team's pilots; Lt. Col. Frank Atkinson and Capt. Vincent Capollini buzzed the nearby 388th Bomb Group airfield at Knettishall. Because they were using one of the specially marked Aphrodite bombers, the base officer at Knettishall suspended all flying activities and ordered an evacuation of the field. When asked why they had pulled off the stunt, they claimed their watches had stopped and they needed to get the correct time from the clock on the control tower.

Two days later, after having an argument with the Operational Engineering Section over the reliability of certain electronic equipment; 2nd Lt. Andrew Martinez expressed his displeasure at the decision of the section head, Col. Duane Brogger, by throwing a tear gas canister into his quarters.

While Lieutenant Martinez was serving his sentence in the base stockade, it has been ascertained that certain unnamed members of your team were responsible for the removal of the propellers and tires from the O.E.S.'s personal aircraft, a B-25 Mitchell. These items were never found and replacements had to be purchased from a Royal Air Force Mitchell unit.

It is known that the next incident you yourself had a hand in. When Lt. General James H. Doolittle visited Fersfield on September 30th, you had your team's electronic specialists rig his staff car with remote control equipment of your own design. At the conclusion of his visit, you personally worked the controls that started up the car and drove it away while his driver had gone to open the front door on the station headquarters building. The general may have been impressed with your demonstration but base personnel were not.

In the last incident reported to us, you were directly involved. Your concern for safety should a mother ship lose control of an Aphrodite bomber is laudable. But measures have been taken to deal with such an event and you are neither condoned nor excused in your illegal acquisition of a Mark Five Hawker Tempest to shoot them down.

The aircraft in question, serial JN 799, has since been returned to the Royal Air Force fighter squadron which you won it from in a poker game. Because of these incidents, plus others which are not yet verified, your Field Electronics Team is hereby removed from operations in England.

Because you were never officially assigned to the Eighth Air Force, we cannot exercise anything beyond corporal sentences. But, rest

20

assured that a full report of your activities will be forwarded to your superiors at Muroc Air Base and they can deal with you. Your team is to report in two days' time to the Army embarkation facilities at Liverpool where you will eventually be shipped home.

Chapter Two
MISSION TO NORWAY
THE EMBARKATION BARRACKS

Leuchars, one of the smaller villages in county Fife, Scotland. Apart from its proximity to the sea and the River Eden, it had little to offer anyone, save for the odd angler and those looking for a Coastal Command airfield.

"Tower to Zed-Zebra, you are now cleared for takeoff. Be advised there is a build-up of overcast in the North Sea area from Denmark to Trondheim; however, Norway itself is clear."

The last operational Catalina at the base opened its throttles and waddled down the runway; flying boats never moved gracefully until they got into the air. With her departure, the entire wing was gone. PBYs and Mosquitos, were all out on what had suddenly become a maximum-effort mission. With the exception of the non-flyable aircraft and the communications hacks, Leuchars was now a very empty, very quiet base.

"I haven't seen such activity at a field since D-Day," said Cox. "How long will your wing be out?"

"It depends on the aircraft," said Wing Commander Holmen, talking to Cox though not looking at him. Instead his eyes were fixed on a retreating series of dots on the eastern horizon, C-Flight from his Catalina squadron. "The Mosquitos of Number three-three-four squadron will be gone for about two to three hours. They will only go as far as the Lofoten and Vesteralen Islands. I know your carrier reported that the rocket came from the North Cape-Tromsö region but I think the active search area really ought to be expanded.

"My PBYs will be gone much longer. Perhaps five or even six hours more. They're slower and they have much farther to go, but they alone have the endurance to reach North Cape, Sor Iya and return. They also have a lot more territory to cover. There are a half dozen major fjords between Tromsö and North Cape and a few more beyond North Cape which they will investigate as well. That's a lot of coastline and mountains to search, a lot of places for the Germans to blast out a base and install V-1 ski ramps."

"That is if they are ground-launched," Cox added. "We still don't know what the launch method was or is. If the V-1 was air-launched then any airfield which can take a Heinkel is the launching base."

"Fortunately there are few such air bases in northern Norway." Holmen went over to the map of his homeland displayed in his office. On it was marked every German military and intelligence installation in the conquered country. "There are four in the region and all except the one at Tromsö can take bombers. Banak and Alta are the largest. They were carved out of living mountains and I dare say there is no way of destroying them. Not even the Royal Air Force's Grand Slam bombs could do it.

"The last base is Kirkenes, right on the border with Russia. Since this one is under continual attack by Russian aircraft, it would not be the safest for such an operation. Still, if they want to hit Murmansk as you say they may, then Kirkenes would be the most optimum location."

"Commander Holmen, Commander Holmen, please report to the control tower at once. Aircraft P-Peter of Three-three-four squadron is making an emergency return."

"That's one of the problems of dispatching so many aeroplanes," Holmen noted. "There is bound to be one or two aborts. We'd better hurry on up."

P-Peter had a coolant leak in its left engine. The bright, white stream of glycol was visible at almost the same time as the Mosquito spewing it. The crippled fighter-bomber circled for a time over the Firth of Tay; jettisoning its bombs and firing its rockets into an empty beach before entering the circuit to Leuchars' longest runway.

The landing gear came down slowly, nearly thirty seconds longer than it normally took. The flaps were not lowered until the Mosquito was on final and landing speed stayed hot until the main gear hit the concrete. Crash vehicles surrounded it at the runway's far end; even if the crew wanted to taxi the rest of the way in, they could not. Holmen had also wanted to go down and see his men at the debriefing office but he could not. A new situation had developed which required his immediate attention.

"R-Robert to Odin Base, you said if we spotted anything suspicious we were to report it in. Well, we've got a gaggle of Heinkel 111s up here with us. It looks like they are all carrying tiny aeroplanes under their fuselages."

"Good God, this could be it," said Cox, "this could be what we're looking for. Have your men attack at once. Those bombers are probably going to launch their V-1s at some target in Scotland."

"Odin to R-Robert, how many ships do you have with you and have you been spotted yet?" In spite of Cox's urging, Holmen decided to go according to procedure. "You don't have to worry here, Commander Cox. I have yet to meet a Heinkel that can outrun a Mosquito. Is there any order you wish to add?"

"Yes, have your men return to base as soon as they're through. I want their gun camera film developed at the earliest possible moment."

"Odin, I only have my wingman with me. We estimate there are six to twelve Heinkels up here. Cloud cover is patchy and I don't think we've been spotted."

"Understood, R-Robert, attack formation at your opportunity. When you are finished, return to base at once. Good luck and good hunting, and bring back some fine pictures."

"R-Robert to S-Sugar, we are cleared to intercept. Enemy three o'clock low, distance, one kilometer. Tally-ho!"

The Mosquitos flew as a tight pair; with the wingman tucked in on the leader's left side. Suddenly, almost in unison, they rolled and fell into a dive. They roared through a hole, actually a tunnel, in the bright billowy overcast. The crews in the first trio of bombers did not notice the descending De Havillands until their heavy battery of cannons and machine guns began to sparkle.

R-Robert throttled back in order to keep the aircraft he had selected in his gun sight. His wingman continued on past the first formation to attack a second vee of Heinkels. They received the warning their squadron mates had not and gained just enough time to break ranks.

R-Robert's victim shuddered and began to twist desperately to avoid its doom. The twin, converging streams of .303-inch and 20 mm shells raked the Heinkel's center fuselage section and extensively glazed nose. Most of its crew were killed in the opening seconds of the attack. When almost one hundred pounds of high-explosive and incendiary rounds had been fired at the bomber, its fuselage disintegrated in a brief, powerful flash. Only its broad wings and tail remained, tumbling wildly toward the North Sea.

"R-Robert to S-Sugar, whatever these 111s are carrying is very dangerous. Keep a good distance when you fire."

"Roger, I have a good view of one of these little planes. They have it tucked under the starboard wing, between the engine and the fuselage. Here, I'll show you."

The lead Mosquito dipped a wing to watch its charge line up behind another black-green Heinkel. After only a second or two of firing, the German aircraft vanished in a similar explosion. Then they were alone. The other bombers had managed to find a cloud to hide in but they were still in the area; the Mosquitos' radio men could hear them talking to the other planes in their staffel.

The surprise attack now turned into a running battle. The Norwegians adopted the tactic of keeping under the overcast deck and waiting for the newly useless secret weapons to appear. They did not have to idle for too long, a perfect vee of tiny winged bombs fell through the clouds a half-mile away. R-Robert had the presence of mind to shoot some footage of them as they raced to the area and before climbing into the overcast.

Inside, he and his wingman caught fleeting glimpses of the bombers which had jettisoned the missiles. Eager for another kill, the wingman snapped out short bursts until his leader told him to knock it off.

"Stop firing at shadows, that's a sure way to get caught by vertigo. Let your radio man keep an eye on the enemy, you watch your flight instruments."

Their ASV radar, originally designed for surface search, was able to give the Mosquitos a range and rudimentary bearing on the Germans. But not height, and its other readings were too crude to be used for attempting interception. They had to follow and wait for a break in the clouds. A few moments later the hunters got what they needed.

The enveloping mists cleared away magically; leaving the lead Mosquito alone and bouncing in the prop wash of a Heinkel. It was close enough to fill the lead's view and the beauty of its splintered and swirled camouflage pattern transfixed him. The plane must have just been painted; what a pity it had to be destroyed. Then the gunner in the ventral gondola opened fire with a light machine gun and erased all regret from the Norwegians' thoughts.

A brief burst silenced the gunner. A much longer one chopped the bomber's right engine into a junk pile. The landing gear that shared the same nacelle fell out on its own accord and lastly, the right wing buckled.

"R-Robert to S-Sugar, where the hell are you?" the leader requested, banking his Mosquito in order to follow his second victim.

"S-Sugar here, I am on the tail of one of the other bombers. I think I hit him but he's still moving and fast for an old boat. If I can make another shot at him I'll have our next victory."

But R-Robert's second was also the last He-111 to go down. As they fled back to Europe, the increasingly dense overcast aided the Germans in evading the determined Coastal Command fighter-bombers. Each Mosquito made several more sightings apiece, though none was long enough to ensure the destruction of a Heinkel. After fifteen minutes of combat flying, the De Havillands found themselves running low on fuel and were forced to break off the engagement.

"How long will it take for your crews to return?" Cox asked, once R-Robert made his decision clear to Leuchars.

"They have gone far into the North Sea with their pursuit," said Holmen. "How long it takes them to return depends on what airspeed they select. At normal cruise they will need about an hour and a half to reach the coast and land."

"That plus another forty-five minutes to develop the film," Cox thought out loud. "A long time to wait for an answer. How I hate waiting."

"If you wish the answer now, you may talk to the crews over the radio. I know them, they will provide you with good descriptions of whatever the Heinkels were carrying."

"No, the Germans listen to our transmissions nearly as well as we listen to theirs. We can't take the chance and have the bastards put together what we're doing."

"You said almost the same words to me when you explained why my crews couldn't be told the exact reason for the mission," Holmen noted, then paraphrased. "'Because we cannot take the chance of having one of them captured and letting slip the truth.' Why must you intelligence people always think in such a way? You are even worse at this than your counterparts we have here for debriefing."

"It's called compartmentalization. Never let anyone know more than they need to in order to fulfill their task. That is especially true for those who are at risk. No matter how good your men are, they're in a rather perilous position when they fly over Nazi-occupied territory."

"I could say the same of your man, or I should say woman. If your aide is still alone with my photography staff, then she is indeed in very perilous territory. I think the most disruptive thing you could have done is to have brought a redhead onto this base."

"Why, what's the problem with having Leftenant Smythe here?" Cox asked, innocently. "She's the best photographic and general intelligence interpreter I have ever had on my staff. When they had to cut back on staffs at the Admiralty, I only asked to retain her and my secretary."

"If she had been a blonde or a brunette there would be no real problem," Holmen explained, "but a redhead! Such women are as uncommon in Norway as blondes are common. My men are absolutely fascinated with redheads and since we are in Scotland, that means the countryside is full of them. And if I know my men only half as well as I should, then I would say your aide has since been asked out by every man in Photography and has probably even received a few proposals."

"I don't think I need to worry about Connie. She's not some frail WAAF, she's an officer in His Majesty's Navy. Which means she has had to put up with some very ardent and sexually active naval officers who've spent months at sea and are eager for a liaison. She knows how to handle those hopeful, passionate lovers. Why, she ought to be given battle ribbons for her actions. But, I think I'd better go down and see her now. I mean, we really should have the chemicals that develop the cine film ready for when the Mosquitos return."

"A good idea, Commander," said Holmen, smiling wryly. "Here, you can use one of our phones."

"Ah, yes. Why don't you call them and tell them I'll be down."

Though she was a little pressed to dampen the enthusiasm of certain staff members, Cox found Connie handling the situation well enough when he arrived.

"If you men have enough idle time on your hands to make advances on my aide," he noted, "then I believe you have the time to prepare your film development tanks for a run. A couple of aeroplanes are due to return within the hour and I want their gun camera footage processed before their propellers stop turning. Now move."

"There are times I think you are actually capable of breathing fire," said Constance, while the Norwegians broke their circle of admiration and hurried off to the film labs. "You could have made a fine Sergeant Major with that baritone of yours."

"Perhaps, but with the tradition of naval officers in my family, I do not think they would have approved. It was hard enough to make them accept my choice of the Fleet Air Arm in the first place. Anyway, to return to the matter at hand, those planes that are due in have just finished shooting down some missile-carrying Heinkel 111s. Whether or not those missiles were V-1s will be answered by the gun camera film and the crews at debriefing. I want you and your scratch pad ready when they return, which should be in the next fifty minutes."

But the Mosquitos chose to use a higher than normal cruise setting, some forty miles an hour higher, and they were back in a little over half an hour. Cox grew slightly impatient with the pilots when they insisted on performing a number of victory rolls in order to let everyone at Leuchars know they had scored some kills.

"At least they are not Catalinas, Commander," said Holmen on observing Cox's displeasure. "Those big boats take five minutes to do a roll. And the way they flap, you would swear to God the wings are coming off."

"I just wish they would hurry up and come down. I've been waiting an hour for the answers they're carrying. I'll be waiting another hour to get them all. If they are not down in ten minutes, may I suggest you shoot them down?"

In a slightly altered form, Holmen relayed Cox's last statement to R-Robert and S-Sugar. Automatically they lowered their flaps and landing gear and swung obediently onto the runway. Just as their propellers stopped turning, the Photography service crews were removing the exposed film packs from the noses of the two Mosquitos.

"Now that's the oddest thing I have yet seen," said the pilot of R-Robert to his opposite number, climbing out of S-Sugar. "They always take care of the gun cameras last. Whatever we have done must have been important. I wonder if it has anything to do with that Navy intelligence officer we had at briefing this morning?"

Cox, as well as Constance and their commanding officer, stood waiting for the two Mosquito crews at the debriefing office. Beyond the usual questions of how many of the enemy they had sighted, the markings on the ships that were shot down, their camouflage patterns and the rest, came many more about the mysterious cargoes the Heinkels carried. Far more than normal and most bizarre of all was the WREN leftenant with a pad of drawing paper.

From the description the crews offered, Constance made several sketches of the missiles and the way they were mounted under the bombers. She allowed the men a chance to look them over and make changes; then talked privately with Cox and Holmen while the regular intelligence officers continued the debriefing.

"While I cannot definitely tell what the missiles are," Connie admitted, "I can tell you what they are not. These missiles are too small to be V-1s, they aren't equipped with pulse jet motors and they're on the wrong side of the aircraft. On a Heinkel 111, V-1s are always mounted on its port side with the pulse jet riding above the wing. Instead, these missiles are mounted on the starboard side and completely underneath the fuselage. As I said before, I'm not positive what they are though I'm willing to make a guess. The missiles are Henschel 293 guided rocket bombs."

Twenty minutes later, any lingering doubts about the identity of the weapons were dispelled by the newly processed gun camera film. As Constance and Holmen rewatched each reel of footage, Cox left the viewing room to make a few telephone calls. He returned several minutes later to find the two discussing what the missiles were to have been used on.

"From the point where the bombers were intercepted, their target was RA61," Cox informed, "a home-bound Arctic convoy. It is currently near the Shetland Islands. The German Navy has been making repeated attacks on it with some eighteen U-boats. None was particularly successful, so this was apparently the Luftwaffe's turn."

"But I have read reports that the Germans stopped using the Henschels after we found a way to jam all the radio frequencies they use to control them," said Holmen.

"Of course we jammed the channels. But the crafty bastards found a way around it and a rather ingenious one at that. I think Connie can explain it best."

She handed across to Holmen one of the sketches she had drawn from the Mosquito crews' descriptions. It had since been altered, given much more detail.

"As you can see, there is a conical-shaped drag body behind each wing tip. Originally they were used to limit the top speed the missile could achieve, which was around six hundred miles an hour. In the newest version, they have an additional function. A bobbin of thin steel wire is carried in each drag body, about eleven miles of it together with another ten miles in the mother ship.

"The commands transmitted along those wires cannot be jammed or interfered with. It's a simple and very reliable system, only the Germans gave it such a low priority status that it wasn't put into production until now."

"We should consider ourselves lucky it was not given a higher priority or placed in production sooner," said Holmen, "say about six months? If the Nazis had brought this version out in May, they probably would have had enough by June to cripple the Overlord invasion fleets."

"Exactly; I sometimes think that our leaders don't understand how lucky we have been and must continue to be in order to win this war," Cox observed. "It won't be won until the last U-boat is sunk, the last Messerschmitt is shot down and the last storm trooper is killed or captured. I know people who still think we're going to defeat the Germans by Christmas. And not just my countrymen but other Europeans and Americans as well. We must realize

33

that the war will not truly be decided until the final battle is over. Time and again history has shown that the most dangerous enemy is the one we think we've beaten."

"Which is why their last V-1 missile base must be found and destroyed," concluded Holmen, then, holding up Connie's sketch. "In the meantime, what should we do about this? Those Mosquito crews are very interested in why we paid so much attention to them. Shall we tell the truth or continue to keep them in the dark?"

"No, we don't have to do either," said Cox. "There is a third alternative, one which the Germans have been kind enough to provide. We tell your crews a little white lie about this latest version of the Henschel 293. We let on that it was the object of our interest. Indeed, their actions warrant an official commendation, perhaps even a medal? Having been a pilot myself, I know how a flashy bit of metal can quiet rumors and questions."

"That is not exactly what medals are given for, but I see your point, Commander. I can have the necessary letters written up immediately and forwarded to C-in-C, Coastal Command. I will have my secretary start them now and it would help matters immensely if you were to write a personal recommendation as well."

With Holmen gone shortly thereafter, there was little else for Cox to do except make a draft of the requested letter. Constance helped with its composition, though complained lightly that such services were not part of her job.

"I'm not here to take dictation," she reminded him. "I'm here to analyze photographs and raw intelligence. I'm here to advise and I should tell you that you were slightly wrong a minute ago when you said the wire-guided Henschel was the latest version of the missile. It actually isn't."

"You really don't have to correct me on such things. I believe the Americans refer to it as nitpicking. My wife practices a variation of it, though a less technical one."

"I prefer to call it, accuracy. Part of our profession is ascertaining technical minutiae, after all."

"Very well. Proceed, proceed," said Cox, resigning himself to getting another of his aide's long-winded lectures.

"The Henschel company is currently working on a much more advanced version of their 293 missile. It has been under development for some time and, because of the problems they've encountered, it will hopefully not be operational before the end of the war. This new version uses highly directional UHF radio beams for guidance and these aren't exactly as easy to jam as the earlier links.

"To control the missile, the company has produced a miniature television camera in cooperation with the research laboratories of the German Post Office. That camera measures only seven inches in diameter and sixteen inches long. It's a remarkable achievement and, once mounted in the nose of the Henschel 293, it will give the Germans an anti-shipping weapon of astounding accuracy.

"If you think what the earliest version of the 293 did to the Warspite and those cruisers during the Sicilian campaign was devastating, wait until you see what this model is capable of doing. It could be steered straight into the bridge or flown right down the barrel of a gun. And as an added advantage, the launching aircraft does not have to remain over the target once the missile is released. It can turn away, head for cloud cover or perform evasive maneuvers.

All because the missile operator sits in front of a receiver screen and has a pilot's-eye view of the weapon's flight."

"I certainly hope that one of His Majesty's ships doesn't have to be sunk in order to prove your point," Cox noted, once he was sure Constance had finished.

"Excuse me, sir, but are you Leftenant-Commander Cox?" inquired an airman rating, who appeared from nowhere and snapped out a fast salute as he spoke. The moment he received the merest glimmering of an affirmative, the airman jumped in with the message he was ordered to deliver. "Wing Commander Holmen says there has been a sudden development over Norway and you and your aide are to come at once to the control tower. I have a jeep waiting outside to drive you there."

The ride was a jarring, unnerving, journey, in spite of the fact that it never exceeded forty miles an hour. Cox felt relieved when the jeep skidded across the tarmac to a halt. He was alive and Constance took her elegantly long, painfully sharp, nails out of his shoulders.

"What drama do you have unfolding now?" Cox asked, once he reached the control tower. "Do your Mosquitos have another squadron of Heinkels at bay?"

"No, it's not them," said Holmen. "All the aircraft of Number Three-three-four squadron have already reached the operational limits of their endurance and are returning. They should all be back in the next forty-five minutes. This time it is my Catalinas that are the cause. One reports considerable air activity at Fortress Banak and another is heading into Alten Fjord on a hunch. They thought they saw something hiding there and decided to investigate. The Nazis don't have much left in the area and I told them what they probably saw was a shadow. Come over here, I'll show you where they are."

Of course unknown to Holmen, Cox was quite familiar with the area. Like a ganglia of nerve cells, Alten Fjord was no single arm of the sea but several. The most important wasn't the largest or the longest; it was the most remote. An inlet far removed from the ocean, sheltered by steep cliffs and jagged islands; Kaa Fjord.

"There isn't much left in here," Cox advised, "only a few destroyers and maybe a cruiser, the *Admiral Hipper*. The Royal Navy doesn't keep tabs on the traffic in Alten Fjord anymore. Not since the *Tirpitz* was towed to Tromsö harbour."

"M-Mother. Odin, this is M-Mother!" The transmission sounded weak and crackled with static. A combination of great distance and an active ionosphere; it was coming from near the Arctic Circle after all. "Sighting confirmed! We have the damnedest set of photographs you'll ever see."

A familiar comment, similar to one Cox had read in a report from a certain Canadian pilot. At his urging, Holmen requested the Catalina crew give an immediate report on what they thought the remote fjords held.

"Can't take the time to talk just now, Odin." Was the hasty reply. "We got a couple of 109s snapping at our tail. M-Mother, out."

"Messerschmitts?" said Cox. "But the bases in North Norway are used only by bombers and seaplanes."

"Well they have fighters stationed at them now," Holmen added, "probably to defend something very important. Such as your V-1 missile base. Unless my crew can outfox those 109s, there is going to be trouble."

The lumbering, bomber-sized, flying-boat had its Pratt and Whitney radials at full power. And yet, it could do no more than half the speed of the pursuing fighters. They were far down the fjord, out of machine gun range at the present time but not for long, as the PBY crew well realized and took steps to face.

The sliding hatches on the side blisters were rolled away and the beam guns swung into their firing positions. The tunnel machine gun was removed from its stowage rack and mounted in the open hatch at the base of the after flight deck. At the same instant the navigator crawled into the extreme nose to man the turret there. The pilots jettisoned the underwing bombs; they would now only create undue stress during violent maneuvers.

Two Me-109s made the first pass; opening fire the moment they were within range. Having no true tail guns, the PBY yawed from side to side so its waist gunners could unleash short bursts at the Messerschmitts. The slender fighters shot past its right wing tip float and climbed away, without scoring a single hit. A lone Messerschmitt closed to make the second pass, only to have the flying boat skid to the left and dive into another fjord.

One of the major branches of the Alten Fjord area, Long Fjord fully lived up to its name. The narrow dendrite of water was arrow straight and ran for several miles. It had barely enough room for a destroyer to fit in and even an aircraft would have trouble flying up its course. The Catalina was just able to claw its way through the fjord's mouth; less fortunate was the pursuing Messerschmitt.

At over three hundred miles an hour, the maneuver it made allowed no room for error. The pilot entered the turn a fraction of a second too late; what he needed was a few more feet to complete it when the fighter struck the vertical cliff face. With its wings nearly perpendicular to the water below, the Messerschmitt's nose and underbelly bore the full force of the impact. The propeller blades snapped off when they hit the steel-hard granite. The underwing radiators and fuselage bomb rack were the first items to be torn away as it scraped along the rock wall. The fuel tank had its bottom ripped apart by the jagged outcroppings; only one spark among the thousands being generated was needed to ignite its contents.

The fireball disintegrated what remained of the Messerschmitt; its fiercely burning wreckage scattered across the cliff and rolled or fell to the waters below. Seconds later, the three other fighters out of the flight it had originated from appeared at the mouth of the fjord.

Moving much slower than their comrade, they easily made the turn but had to form a single file line.

"Red Falcon One to Blue Falcon One, we have the intruder in Long Fjord. Take your schwarm over the high ground and cut his means of escape off, good luck."

To frustrate any more firing passes, the Catalina again slewed from one side to the next. In the restricted airspace above the fjord, it was a most effective maneuver, one that forced the Me-109s to stay behind the big amphibian. Neither could any of them manage a sustained burst. They all jockeyed for the best firing position and constantly got in each other's way. When finally the leader ordered the remaining fighters under his command to cease their attempts, or he would shoot them down, the PBY had begun to climb.

It rose to the left, after swinging as far to the right as was possible. To the crew it seemed like an eternity

39

for them to get above the fjord's wall. The seventeen-ton flying boat reared over the escarpment's edge, hanging, shaking; on the verge of a stall. To prevent their ship from falling out of the sky, the pilots pushed its nose down. And realized that they might have gone from frying pan to fire.

A neatly spaced quartette of Me-109s, Blue Falcon flight in a perfect formation, roared toward the PBY but held off firing. They dared not for risk of hitting their brothers immediately behind it. For one brief instant, all eight aircraft occupied the same airspace. They formed a cloud of metal in which none could possibly escape and yet all did. The pilots especially were amazed.

"M-Mother to Odin, we're still here, I think. If we can make it to the sea then we might be able to escape by hiding among the clouds. Wish us luck, out."

"Can your men do it?" Cox asked.

"They are the best ones to try," said Holmen. "Their pilot is Flight Lieutenant Christiansen. He's one of the oldest members of this wing and has pulled off such stunts before. I'm willing to bet he can do so again."

In eight separate directions the briefly entangled aircraft flew. Seven of them tried to end the confusion the encounter had caused and reform into an effective unit; one barreled across the barren mountains and dove for the head of a third fjord. This one faced the sea and had a gaping, mile wide mouth guarded by several islands.

The gray-green Catalina dropped inside the deep, water-filled chasm; accelerating past two hundred miles an hour in the process. The excessively high speed, for a flying boat, made the wing tip floats shake dangerously.

"It will tear them off their struts," warned the co-pilot; "Christiansen, we have to reduce our speed!"

"No, leave those alone," he ordered, slapping the co-pilot's hand away from the throttles. "I don't give a damn about the floats. They can be replaced, not us. That extra speed can mean the difference between our squeaking by and not."

Gradually at first, then dramatically, the fjord widened until its dark walls became obscured by low clouds. Ahead lay the island of Silden, to the left and a little farther out was its smaller neighbor, Loppa. Once past these two islands, the Catalina could lose its pursuers among the gathering clouds and darkening twilight. The crew felt confident they would; until a pair of Messerschmitts rounded the far side of Silden.

Unlike the last group of Me-109s, these had very familiar markings. They were recognized immediately, and too late, as the fighters that had made the first firing pass against the amphibian. This time their target was not maneuvering erratically and their gun sights had been given the proper wingspan reading. Far beyond the range of the Catalina's nose-mounted fifty, the Messerschmitts opened up with their heavy machine guns and twenty millimeter cannons.

The first shells tore the forward turret, as well as its hapless occupant, into non-operating wreckage. The rest walked up the gently sloping nose and through the cockpit before the tracer streams separated. One set continued down the fuselage's left side while the other hammered away at the right engine. In a few seconds it was all over; the Me-109s shot past the crippled, slowly sinking flying boat. Its course set and held by dead hands toward Silden.

Several hundred yards out the PBY touched the surface of the sea, only to bounce back into the air because of its boat-like hull. The second time it touched down was on the island's rocky shore line. What wasn't obliterated or burned in the subsequent crash and explosion lay mangled and scattered among the rocks. Save for the tail plane, little was even recognizable as having once been part of an airplane.

"I fear you've lost your wager, Commander," Cox concluded, after the many attempts to contact M-Mother had failed. "I'm afraid your man's luck has run out."

Holmen refused to believe what Cox said was true; until the PBY that surveyed Fortress Banak reported seeing a fireball and Me-109s milling around an island near Alten Fjord.

"I should have known a thing like this would happen," Holmen admitted, "when we got lucky earlier with those Heinkels. I should have realized then that fate has a way of evening out our fortunes. Both good and bad. Christiansen was a very popular man in the wing, men always liking being assigned to his crews. He is going to be missed."

"So's the information and photographs he would have brought back," Cox added, thinking of more practical matters. "At least your other ship has managed to escape. When do you estimate he will be returning?"

"Well, Zed-Zebra and the others who searched the region north of Tromsö must first refuel in the Shetland Islands before returning home. That plus flight time at normal cruise speed will mean another five or six hours. And don't ask me to have them fly any faster, because at higher fuel consumption rates they will end up in the Atlantic."

"Six hours," repeated Cox, checking his watch. "That means they won't start showing up till almost midnight. A lot of time to spend waiting or we can spend it working. Tell me, do you have any contacts with the Milord?''

"The Norwegian underground? Of course I do. And I also know the commanding officer of the Linge, Norwegian Army commandoes, and some top people in the Shetland Gang. Sometimes we help them ferry agents in and out of Norway. In fact we were to have helped them spirit a few agents from Sor Iya soon, but I do not think it will now be possible.

"Sor Iya is the outermost island of the group that guards Alten Fjord. It is remote, practically inaccessible and has never been occupied or conquered by the Germans. The Shetland Gang uses either a small fishing boat or one of my Catalinas when picking up Milord agents from Sor Iya. But, with such fighter activity in the Alten Fjord area, I am not going to risk one of my ships again. I'm afraid the gang will have to find another way to bring those people out.''

"I feel I may be able to help your friends with their transport problem,'' said Cox, smiling slightly. "Provided you can get me a secure line to the Atlantic Operations Centre in the Admiralty. And that the agents they want out may have information which will be useful to me.''

"Good, good. Let me talk to the Shetland Gang first. They usually don't tell me what type of information the agents are bringing in but they will if I ask them. I hope they have what you are looking for, Commander. From the feel of things, I think Adolf Hitler himself is in Norway. Building his last redoubt for the final battle. If you are needing any help in the future with this, just give me a call and I'm sure I can recruit a couple of dozen volunteers for you.''

*   *   *

"Okay men, select your accommodations. This'll be home for the next few days. Enjoy it while you can."

Enjoy it indeed. There was little in the way of pleasures at the Liverpool transit barracks; especially for a unit such as the one Colonel Dennis Lacey commanded and he knew it. Officers almost everyone of them, they had been assigned to facilities meant for enlisted men. It was the Eighth Air Force's way of giving the unwanted Field Electronics Team one last kick in the pants.

"I find it kinda ironic for us to get thrown in here, among the rats, after the way we first came to England," noted one of the team's more senior officers, Captain Vincent Capollini. "We fly in, top priority, on a C-54 straight from California. Now, we're getting shipped back in a Kaiser garbage scow some U-boat will probably torpedo to put it out of its misery."

"That's what we all like about you, Vince," said the chief electronics specialist, Second Lieutenant Andrew Martinez. "Your bright and sunny optimism."

"Aw shut up, Andy. If it weren't for you and your little prank of tossing that tear gas grenade into Colonel Duane's room, I bet we wouldn't be here."

"All right, let's not start fighting among ourselves," Lacey ordered, "that's just what Brogger would love to see. Let's not forget you and Frank didn't help matters much by buzzing Knettishall with one of the Aphrodite ships. And none of us made many friends by stripping the bastard's Mitchell and selling the parts to the Royal Air Force."

"I wish I could've been there," sighed Martinez, flopping down on one of the better bunks. "I used to

44

do those things to cars when I was young. We'd take the parts and sell them in the next county or Nevada."

"You were in jail at the time, Andy. A facility we'd better all stay out of if we want to get back to the states in time to be reassigned to the Pacific theater. I can safely say that we've screwed ourselves out of fighting the Germans, so let's play it straight for the next few days and maybe we'll have a chance at the Japanese."

Chapter Three
FREDERICK THE GREAT
ANOTHER CHANCE

"HMS *Venturer* to Shagbat One, we are approaching the rendezvous point. Our radar sweeps show no enemy aircraft or surface ships and we have no asdic contacts. If surface conditions are to your liking, we can make the transfer."

"Conditions are good enough for us to alight, *Venturer*. We are starting let-down procedures, Shagbat One, out."

With its pusher engine and sweptback wings, the Supermarine Walrus was a mixture of both things past and things to come. The biplane amphibian descended slowly toward a relatively calm, and for the moment empty, sea. From their vantage point, the pilot and his navigator could see a slim, dark shadow rise from the depths. Seconds later, the shadow's conning tower broke through the waves; HMS *Venturer* had arrived on time.

The Walrus's navigator withdrew from the bow position forward of the cockpit and prepared for landing. He took with him the Lewis gun and locked the cover over the open hatch. The pilot swung his aircraft over the submarine repeatedly; waiting for it to fire off a flare, so he could see in which direction the wind was blowing. When at last the tiny rocket hissed into the sky, the pilot found it would be best to land almost perpendicular to the *Venturer*'s position and elected to come down behind it, then catch up.

Even though its engine was all but shut off, the Walrus continued to glide along for a half a mile before its hull finally started to slap against the wave tops. The jarring collisions ended when the big amphibian lost most of its remaining airspeed and settled into the water.

Almost at once the pilot turned her around and taxied in for the *Venturer*. At thirty miles an hour, the Walrus threw out great sheets of spray that at times obscured her from view. The submarine's conning tower and deck were by now filling with crew. They manned its lone three-inch gun and prepared an inflatable life raft for use by their guests.

The Walrus slowed to match the speed of the *Venturer*. Its pilot lowered the mainwheels to improve handling and moved onto a parallel course with the boat. The navigator returned to the bow hatch, this time carrying a mooring line and the boat hook instead of a light machine gun.

On the second try, one of the gun detail caught the line. They secured it while the raft was launched and took on its passengers and crew. The two seamen had little need to use the provided oars. It was easier and more direct for them to haul the raft from the submarine to the pitching aircraft using the mooring line. The actual transfer of the three passengers plus their cargo proved more difficult.

Already narrow, the forward gun hatch was even more so with the navigator standing in it. Each passenger carried a back pack that first had to be removed before they squeezed through the hatch and crawled to the cockpit. The radio man helped them back to the rear of the cabin where they would stay for the duration of the flight.

In all it took ten minutes to complete the transfer; the last passenger had yet to disappear inside when the raft returned to the submarine. The gun crew cast-off the bow line and the Walrus swung around to face into the wind again.

"*Venturer* to Shagbat One, take good care of our guests. We've grown to like them and wouldn't want to hear of anything happening to them now that they're almost home."

"We understand, *Venturer*, but you have no reason to worry. We've done this service before, your guests will be in Scapa Flow in the next two hours. Shagbat One, out."

Hatches and landing gear were closed once more or retracted and the pod-mounted, Bristol Pegasus engine howled to take-off power. At first the Walrus moved sluggishly; its bow and underwing floats digging through the omnipresent, four foot swells. As speed rapidly increased, the amphibian began to plane across the surface. Only the wave tops and higher swells momentarily hindered it. Lift returned to the double set of wings, forcing the Walrus to rise above the water, eventually freeing it.

After the nearly mile-long run, the *Venturer*'s low profile had disappeared from view. The aircraft turned back to find the submarine once it gained a little more airspeed and altitude but the Royal Navy crew had worked fast. All that could be seen was the conning tower retreating beneath the waves and the foam caused by the blown ballast tanks. In a few hours the Milord agents would be at the end of their week-long journey. And what they could look forward to was an intensive debriefing session with their superiors and a team of Admiralty intelligence officers.

*   *   *

"Connie, have you completed developing those other rolls of film, or not?" Cox asked, raising his voice so it would carry through the thick, darkroom door.

"The final strip is still in the drying bin but the rest are ready," said Constance, allowing him inside. She switched on the room's normal lights once the door was locked. With all they had seen and heard in the last several hours, even the most trivial security procedure was now followed. "Unlike the first roll, which had only long-distance shots, these are mostly close-ups. This ship the Germans are hiding in Kaa Fjord is no longer going to look like a toy in a bathtub. With these we shall have a sense of some scale and detail."

"You're right. These should provide me with what I'm looking for," said Cox, stretching out one of the rolls and holding it up to a light. "Here, run this one through the enlarger first."

"But don't you want me to make a contact print first and then a set of standard prints of the good ones?"

"No, I'm afraid we don't have time for all that. I don't care if these are negatives, I need the answers they may hold now. Put it through, please?"

First the normal lights had to go out and then the red lights activated before the rolls could be properly viewed. In spite of the fact they were reverse images, the thirty-five millimeter stills showed remarkably clear details. From the crew men and nearby service boats, a sense of the warship's size could be made. The roll Cox had requested to see contained mostly bow shots of its powerful, dual-gunned forward turrets and bridge section. To him, they showed a ship of startling familiarity.

"Charles, you look as if you've just seen a ghost,"

Constance noted. "Have you?"

"No. No, not exactly. Just the sister ship of a ghost, in fact, two ghosts. Quick, show the others on the machine."

The succeeding rolls held shots of the amidships section and, finally, the stern. Instead of a set of turrets identical to those on the bows, mounted on the stern were a pair of long, braced, ski ramps. On one of them was a small, stub-winged aircraft. The V-1 base had been found.

"This confirms what the agents have been saying for the last ninety minutes," said Cox. "My God. Oh, my God."

"She looks like the *Tirpitz*," Constance remarked, "but I thought the Royal Air Force bombed her in the middle of last month? Didn't the Germans tow her away?"

"Yes, to the port of Tromsö but this isn't her. The *Tirpitz* is still at Tromsö, this is her sister ship."

"That's impossible, the only ship identical to the *Tirpitz* was the *Bismarck*. You, of all people, should know what happened to her. You were part of the strike the *Victorious* launched against her."

"I know, but as I said before, this is the sister of two ghosts," Cox repeated as he moved away from the enlarger; out of its halo of bright light. On returning, he spread a thin folder underneath the battleship's reversed image. "I obtained this from the naval intelligence library. It appears to be all that we have on this particular ship, until now. In 1938, the Germans laid down the keel of the third and last example of their Bismarck-class battleships. Launched late in 1941, they christened her *Frederick the Great*.

"Though assigned a crew at this time and given a pennant number, she never completed her outfitting at Kiel. By then the war effort dictated the production of more aeroplanes and tanks and Karl Dönitz had become grand admiral of the Kriegsmarine. Dönitz favoured U-boats over surface warships, especially major capital ships. The *Frederick the Great* languished in Kiel for the next three years. Only her secondary and anti-aircraft armament was installed. None of her main guns was ever manufactured; she had to make do with the spare turrets and guns made for her sister ships.

"The Royal Air Force kept up regular reconnaissance flights until the beginning of this year, to check on the battleship's status. They were dropped when the *Frederick the Great* was moved back onto the stocks where, so the Joint Intelligence Committee concluded, she was to be broken up. Now we know what really became of her. The last of her kind and yet the first of her kind. We may well be looking at the ship that will win the war for the Germans."

"Charles, how can a single ship possibly do that?" asked Constance, a little incredulous. "Look at all the planes and ships we have and those of our allies. Especially the Americans. How can one ship stand up to all that?"

"It's relatively easy, when all of those forces are scattered across the world. For a ten-day period back in 1941, a single ship seemed well on its way to bringing Britain to her knees. And look at what we had in Atlantic and Home waters to stop the *Bismarck* and look at where they are now. The *Hood*? Sunk. *Prince of Wales*? Sunk. *Repulse*? Sunk. *Barham*? Sunk. *Ark Royal*? Sunk. *The Warspite*? Badly damaged by your rocket bombs and still not back in service. The *Royal Sovereign* and others of her vintage? Turned over to the Russians so they wouldn't lay claim to an outrageous portion of the

Italian battle fleet. The surviving KG Five-class battleships have all either joined the Americans in the Pacific or are undergoing refit in dry dock for such service.

"The same is true for almost all of our Illustrious-class fleet carriers. Only two remain in Atlantic waters. The *Formidable* is laid up in Gibraltar with a complete machinery breakdown and the *Implacable* is currently limping back to Scapa Flow with severe weather damage to its forward hull. Neither of these two can be back in service before early next year. Even if they were not put out of action by their accidents, they would still be useless to us. Their sailing orders were for the Pacific. As of today, there are no major warships in Atlantic Waters that can stop the *Frederick the Great*."

"But surely we must have some forces," Constance maintained, in face of the facts. "This is only one ship."

"With four fifteen-inch guns, twelve six-inch guns and sixteen four-inch guns. The very best we can throw against it are some six-inch gun cruisers, destroyers and a few escort carriers. Not enough ships and not nearly enough planes to give any assurance that they can sink a battleship. And, if by some miracle, these meager forces do succeed in defending our Atlantic and Arctic convoys, it will not mean much. Those aren't the *Frederick the Great*'s main targets. The ski ramps on the stern give that away."

"Of course, V-1s aren't accurate enough to be used against shipping. The missiles need area targets but why launch them at our cities from a huge battleship, when the bombers they've been using are more effective."

"Quite right, don't think so chauvinistically that

52

our cities are the only important targets along the Atlantic Ocean," Cox reminded her.

"America?" The look in his eyes told Constance it was the truth. "It's so obvious."

"And so ingenious," Cox added. "The eastern seaboard of the United States has not seen a bombardment or any kind of hostile action since the War of 1812, when we had the poor taste to sack and burn their capital. The damage that will be done by the V-1s would be relatively minor. The psychological effects are incalculable. Never before in history has a missile-armed warship ever put to sea. If this one does, it may win the war."

"How then can she be stopped, Charles? Are you sure her targets are American cities?"

"While we don't have copies or illicit photographs of the battleship's sailing orders, we do have equally compelling information. One of those agents out there passed herself off as a girl of easy virtue in Alta, the town closest to Kaa Fjord. She took up with a Kriegsmarine officer who was part of the fire control staff on the *Tirpitz*. He was reassigned to the *Frederick the Great* on its arrival in Norway. Apparently he's been made part of the missile launching detail. On several occasions he has boasted to her that New York will be in flames by the end of the year and he will be responsible for it.

"As for stopping this ship, I don't know how we can do it. Not yet anyway. To make that decision, we're going to have to glean every scrap of information out of those agents and these photographs. I want blow ups of her main and secondary armaments, the radio and radar aerials on her superstructure, the ski ramps and all other modifications made to her for launching V-1s. In particular, these structures amidships and just before the X-turret position. I'll lay in more dark room supplies for you, Connie. I think you'd better forget about sleeping for the next day or so."

They all had to forget about the luxury of sleep. The already exhausted Milord agents, their superiors and the staff of Scapa Flow's naval intelligence library. Cox put himself in the center of the ceaseless beehive. His requisitioned office soon overflowed with photographs, maps, charts and reports and updates on all Allied and German operations. None of it came in any seeming order and he would let no one who entered the office study what he was doing long enough to comprehend it all—including Constance.

When she finally completed the last batch of photographs, she emerged from the dark room not knowing whether it was night or day outside; nor did she care. Cox had a cot set aside for her in the briefing room where the Norwegians were interrogated. It was small, uncomfortable and wobbled anytime someone sat on it. But to Constance, it looked too good to pass up. Even if it did mean sleeping in her uniform, something she normally hated to do.

Hours later, a seaman rating awoke her and asked what she would like for breakfast. While her stomach did growl for a meal more substantial than tea and stale biscuits, Constance first wanted to know where Cox was.

"Charles, they told me you've been in here all night," she said, swinging open his office door. "Did you manage to get some sleep or were you awake all that time?"

"Of course I slept," Cox replied, straightening his disheveled tie and jacket. "Right here, at the desk. Can't you see where I driveled on the blotter?"

"Oh, Charles, that's not a comfortable way to sleep."

"I know, I'm the one with the stiff neck. I'll sleep better on the flight back to London. The Dakota they're preparing for us is one of the old KLM Douglas sleepers we impressed. It still has the upper berths on board."

"You mean we're done? Do you have a plan?"

"We wouldn't be leaving if I didn't have a concrete proposal to make. Could you fetch me my shaving kit, Connie? I think before we go, we should refresh ourselves."

"And we should eat as well," said Constance. "I'll order you a couple of eggs and some rashers of bacon."

Cox waited for her to leave, then reached for the phone he had been using.

"Yes, do you have that secure line I wanted to the Admiralty? Good, put me through at once. Admiralty switchboard? This is Leftenant-Commander Charles Cox; is the Fifth Sea Lord in his office yet? No? Very well, who is? I want the highest ranking officer there. Yes, he'll do. I should say he'll do, connect me with his office. Override any other calls, what I have is highest priority. Hello, First Sea Lord's office? This is Leftenant-Commander Charles Cox. Intelligence Division, attached to the Fifth Sea Lord's staff. No, he isn't in right now. That is why I need to speak to the First Sea Lord. This is an 'Exeter'-priority message, thank you. Hello, Sir Cunningham?"

In Admiral Sir Andrew Cunningham, Cox found an eager and intently interested audience, one fully aware of the threat posed by the recent discovery. He immediately swept clean his afternoon appointments, as well as those of the other Sea Lords who were in London that day. To ensure they would arrive on time, Cunningham also ordered his personal staff car to meet Cox and Constance at the airport. It added a note of official urgency to their mission, but it was the final straw for the Fifth Sea Lord and he told Cox so when they met in the Admiralty Board Room.

"Why is it, that I must learn of the activities of my officers from either secondhand sources or the rumour mill?" he asked, then did not allow time for an answer. "You are part of my staff, Mr. Cox. Not part of the First Sea Lord's. You report to me, mister, not to him. I will not stand for such gross insubordination in my staff!"

"I did try to contact your office first, sir," Cox answered, finally. "But you weren't in and what I had to report was of extreme importance."

"That is of no matter, you should have waited for me to arrive. I was only a few minutes behind schedule."

"I'm afraid this information could not have waited. It may well affect the outcome of the war."

"I don't bloody well care if what you had was a report that the Germans had raised the *Bismarck* and re-equipped her. I am your immediate superior, mister."

"And I am his ultimate superior," said Sir Cunningham, on entering the board room. "And if circumstances require expediency, then Leftenant-Commander Cox may make his report to me. I do hope you two were not arguing over that particular point?"

Neither would admit that they were and the matter passed in light of more important topics. The First Sea Lord headed a procession of the other Sea Lords into the richly furnished board room. Virtually everything inside was an antique and by rights belonged in a museum. Taken together, they spoke of another time; another era in naval history. For a moment, the feeling overwhelmed Cox. He could scarcely remember taking his seat at the main table and the spell did not break until Sir Cunningham began the meeting.

"I am sorry to report that our civilian opposites and the Second Sea Lord could not attend this conference on such a short notice," he stated as the first order of business. "The civilian First Lord and the Secretary are in a meeting themselves, with the Prime Minister at Number Ten Downing Street. The Civil Lord is standing before Parliament to answer questions on service appropriations and the Second Sea Lord is delivering an address at the Portsmouth Naval College. They will be consulted later as to what is discussed here. However, we need to make decisions now with regard to what Leftenant-Commander Cox has to tell us."

Cox began at the beginning, with Bradley's sighting and destruction of the V-1. He progressed through the incidents the Norwegian Coastal Command Wing got involved in and concluded the first part of his report with the revelations by the Milord agents. For the next section, Cox produced some of their photographs, several diagrams and drawings.

"This, is the *Frederick the Great*," he said, displaying an artist's, his artist's, impression of the radically altered battleship. "The last of the line started by the *Bismarck* and the first missile-armed warship in history. As you can see, her after turrets have been replaced by V-1 ski ramps. The hangar, the catapult and cranes for the Arado floatplanes have also been removed. Apart from these, what remains of her original armament is unchanged.

"Her internal arrangements, we can only speculate on. But, with the absence of the after turrets, the shell hoists, the ammunition magazines and all the main and auxiliary machinery related to them, a very large stowage capacity is created. Enough for, we estimate, at least two hundred missiles. They would be stored in a disassembled state until needed. At that time, the components are brought to the surface, to this housing amidships, where the cranes and catapult were located. Here they are assembled and fueled, then moved through an internal passage to what we have christened the 'X house'.

"The function of it is similar to, we think, the 'square buildings' found at every V-1 launch site. It has a thick, armour-plated, outer casing but the interior is probably made of non-magnetic materials. Here the V-1 has its magnetic field aligned with the magnetic heading it is supposed to fly. The onboard compass would be adjusted to compensate for wind drift and the flight log mechanism set to control the missile's range. From this stage it's a short run on a track to one of the two ramps on the stern.

"Based on interrogations of personnel captured at overrun launching sites, I have deduced that the ship is capable of firing a missile every five minutes. Provided they have already assembled a sufficient stock of them."

The Sea Lords briefly interrupted Cox with questions he knew they would ask; what would be the targets of the ship-launched V-1s. Being more aware of the strategic situation and implications, the answer did not surprise them as much as it did Constance.

"And we must not overlook what will be the targets of this battleship's guns," added Cox, "it was something even I dismissed, at first. In the last twenty-four hours, information has surfaced which leads me to believe that the *Frederick the Great* has a two-fold purpose. It will be the flagship of a powerful battle group the Germans are assembling. The heavy cruiser *Prinz Eugen* is currently in Copenhagen, where it is preparing for a sortie. The report of her being involved in a collision with the cruiser *Leipzig* three weeks ago was a ruse to cover the activity. Even the photographs showing the two ships locked together were 'arranged.' The *Leipzig* was torpedoed a number of days earlier by a Soviet Navy IL-4 that defending fighters later shot down. It was an opportunity the Germans couldn't pass up. The other two ships destined for the group are supposed to be covering the evacuation of troops and civilians from Baltic ports. The heavy cruiser *Admiral Hipper* and the pocket battleship *Lützow*.

"They will join the *Prinz Eugen* in Copenhagen by the end of the week. Stocks of oil—fuel, diesel oil and ammunition have been accumulating in that port for months. Enough, just enough, to put those ships to sea for an extended period. Their eight and eleven-inch guns, combined with the reduced though still formidable armament of the *Frederick the Great*, can sink every operational ship in our Atlantic and Home Fleets. It would be suicide to allow any convoy onto the high seas. A single sighting by a U-boat would seal their fate. They wouldn't even be safe at their collection point. If the Kriegsmarine succeeds in deploying this group, they will win the battle for the North Atlantic, spread a panic through America that will resemble a plague, disrupt supplies to this country and Russia and, more importantly, to the Western and Mediterranean Fronts. In short, the Germans will be handed the best chance they've had since the summer of forty-one for winning this war."

Not everyone agreed with Cox's pessimistic forecast. Until, that is, the First Sea Lord made his views known.

"Those who do not wish to recognize the magnitude of this threat, show themselves to be fools and commit a great disservice to our country," said Sir Cunningham. "Mister Cox, would you be so kind as to give us a breakdown of the guns mounted by the German force?"

"If all four ships are employed, they will mount a total of four fifteen-inch guns, six eleven-inch guns, sixteen eight-inch guns, twenty six-inch guns and forty-six four-inch guns. To those, you can add the torpedo tubes on the cruisers and pocket battleship."

"Now do you see, gentlemen? Before we conclude this meeting, we must decide what to tell the First Lord and the Prime Minister. What to tell our Allies, particularly the Americans. And how we are going to stop the *Frederick the Great*, for this ship is the key to German success or failure. Once again, the future of the entire allied war effort rests on whether or not we can sink one lone warship. The convulsion caused by the *Bismarck*'s sortie will seem like a minor tempest in a tea pot, when compared to the damage this ship can cause. Mr. Cox, I will entertain ideas as to how we may sink her?"

But Cox found himself the last in line with ideas. Using their rank and imposing presence, the Sea Lords bullied their way past him to give their own. Naturally, the suggestions from each reflected their areas of expertise and prejudices. While all were professional, none of the plans had what was needed to succeed and everyone was all too eager to shoot down what the others would mention.

"We just finished launching our latest battleship," said the Third Sea Lord, "the *Vanguard*. She carries eight fifteen-inch guns. Surely, she'll be a match for *Frederick* here which carries half that number."

"Indeed she will be, in another year and a half," Sir Cunningham reminded him. "All the *Vanguard* has in place are those main guns. Her secondary and anti-aircraft armaments have not been installed, nor has any radar equipment, radios, electrical equipment or auxiliary machinery. She has only the barest of essentials and has yet to go on any sea trials or even to move under her own power. No, the *Vanguard* is simply out of the question."

"We do have the Nelson-class battleships and several battlecruisers in reserve," offered the Fourth Sea Lord. "If we return enough of them to service, we'll be able to deal most effectively with this German battle group."

"What, send World War One-vintage ships out to face a modern ship of the line?" questioned the Fifth Sea Lord, sarcastically. "That would be suicide. If *Frederick* is anything like her sisters, she'll be five to ten knots faster and have the latest in radar and range-finding equipment. And as for returning the Nelsons to service; why it would be easier to pull the *Anson* and the *Duke of York* out of dry-dock than to put them to sea once more."

"All right then, what is your idea?" asked the Fourth Sea Lord, issuing a challenge with his request.

"Sink the *Frederick the Great* with carrier aircraft. I reject Mr. Cox's observation that we have nothing in the Atlantic to stop her. We have a dozen or more escort carriers in operation. Surely we can assemble them into a task force powerful enough to sink a battleship. The Americans recently did it during the Battle of Leyte Gulf."

"I suggest you read the full report on that particular engagement," said Sir Cunningham. "The American 'jeep' carriers did not sink the *Musashi* as earlier claimed. They did indeed drive her and her sister ship, the *Yamato,* and the other Japanese battleships away from the invasion fleet. However, their aircraft were only a small part of the force which eventually sank her. It required the full air groups from the fleet carriers *Intrepid, Cabot, Franklin, Essex* and *Enterprise.* Almost five hundred aeroplanes and they needed five hours of continual air strikes to place the more than three dozen bombs and torpedoes that finally sent the *Musashi* to the bottom. The *Frederick the Great* is not likely to wait around so long.

"She enjoys a twelve-knot speed advantage over your escort carriers and can make or break-off engagements at will. The air crews on board are experienced in anti-submarine tactics, not in how to attack a fast and heavily armed dreadnought. Furthermore, most of their planes are not suitable for such strikes. No, if we're to stop this new threat it must be at her anchorage in Kaa Fjord and by the bombers of the Royal Air Force. If the *Frederick the Great* breaks out into the Atlantic, with or without those other ships, there will be no sure way of sinking her. Am I not right, Mr. Cox? She must be dealt with before leaving the fjord."

"In essence you are, Sir Cunningham, but not on the particulars. Oh, the battleship will be sunk where she now rests but not by the Royal Air Force. May I explain why and who we must get to do it?"

At last, someone in the room was showing a little courtesy. Sir Cunningham welcomed it even more than the information he needed to have.

"The first problem with the Royal Air Force are their bombers," began Cox, "there is only one squadron equipped with the specially modified Lancasters that can do the job. Number six-seventeen squadron, and currently they are preparing for a second strike at the *Tirpitz*. Because she's in Tromsö, they can reach her from bases in Scotland. The *Frederick the Great* is in the Alten Fjord area and that can only be reached from bases in Russia. Number six-seventeen used the Yagodnik airfield to launch their first attack on the *Tirpitz* this last September. Presently, the Russians show no interest in allowing another force of bombers to be stationed on their soil. Even if we were to obtain permission, it would only result in the loss of some very brave men and some vitally needed aircraft.

"One of the most important revelations made by Coastal Command's Norwegian Wing, was the build-up of defences in North Norway. At Alta, the closest Luftwaffe field to Kaa Fjord, the Ninth Fighter Group has recently been stationed. It has three full wings of Me-109s, one hundred and twenty aircraft. At Fortress Banak, north of Alta, there are two wings of Ju-88 night fighters. Additional light and medium anti-aircraft batteries have been installed in and around Kaa Fjord. Several destroyers and fleet torpedo boats have been given heavy anti-aircraft armaments and are being anchored at strategic locations along the length of Alten Fjord. It would be sheer suicide to send any kind of manned bomber through this gauntlet at any time."

"Then what do you propose we do, Mr. Cox?" asked the Fifth Sea Lord, growing angry with his staff member. "Use the X-class midget submarines? Even if we still had any in this theatre, the Germans would not fall for that trick once more."

"Or perhaps he wants us to organize some sort of suicide corps?" added the Third Sea Lord. "Something like the Japanese kamikazes the Americans are encountering."

"In a way, you're right, sir. But in our case, the planes will not be manned. They'll be flown by a new radio technology called remote guidance control. My aide explained it to me several days ago. What she said then was boring, today, it is essential to our success.

"Briefly, what she told me about was a new version of the Henschel anti-shipping missiles. The Germans have developed a television control system for it, capable of delivering the missile with astounding accuracy. Fortunately, due to production disruptions, this particular version will not be made. It would be the best weapon to use against the *Frederick the Great*. However, we have nothing like it in this country, either in use or under development. What we do have, is something far better. A weapon with a twenty thousand pound warhead, not a mere twelve hundred pounds. One that will ensure the destruction of a battleship with a single hit. An Eighth Air Force project called Aphrodite."

"What? You mean to bring the Americans in on this?" Cox's superior seemed ready to have an attack of apoplexy. Either that or attack Cox. "What we have here is a British show and we should keep it that way. Besides, those stripped-down B-17s and B-24s have caused nothing but trouble. Last August we had one crash into a wood in Suffolk and a week later another exploded over the Blyth estuary."

"Why not bring the Americans in?" said Sir Cunningham, "after all, it's their cities which *Frederick* will most likely bombard with V-1s. I concur with Mr. Cox, that we have nothing in our armed forces comparable to the Aphrodite program and that it offers us the best chance of stopping *Frederick*."

"But why work with the American Army Air Force?" maintained the Fifth Sea Lord. "They may be damned eager chaps, with regard to the war I mean, but in the past they've proven to be rather pushy and arrogant. Why can't we work with the U.S. Navy? They're involved with the program as well and our relationship is much better."

"Their Navy was involved with Aphrodite, though they aren't any longer. The bomber that blew-up over the Blyth estuary was a Navy Liberator and the pilot a Navy Lieutenant. In fact he was the son of a former American ambassador to our country and those points caused the U.S. Navy to drop out. As for our relationship with the Eighth Army Air Force, the situation is very much better than what you make it out to be.

"Captain Edward Terrell of our development section is meeting with remarkable cooperation at Bovingdon. I paid a visit there recently and he says work on his Disney bombs is proceeding smoothly. While we haven't always agreed on all points in the past, the relationship between our two services is most cordial. We can work closely together, provided no unnecessary friction is generated. Just how closely do you plan on having us work together, Mr. Cox?"

"Excuse me, Sir Cunningham, but we should turn this matter over to Operations Division," the Fourth Sea Lord interrupted. "I mean, we must follow established procedures."

"Not if they interfere with potential success and I feel we don't have the time for such formalities."

"Indeed we only have two weeks before *Frederick*, and with her, the rest of the battle group, weighs anchor," said Cox, regaining the floor. "And if that were not the case, we would still only have two weeks' time. At the end of that period the Arctic night will begin. Not true darkness but a twilight so dim no air attack will be possible. If we approve the basic plan I have here, I have deduced we can launch an attack in ten days' time. Most of the resources we must use are on hand and if we act immediately, we can keep this show under British control.

"My research of the Aphrodite project reveals that until recently, the Eighth Air Force bomb group in charge of it, had a team of experts from the States assigned to help them. Apparently there was some 'unnecessary friction' generated between the team and its host and the team is being sent back home. Currently, they are waiting in Liverpool for the next convoy to sail. They have no assignment and a few words with the Eighth's Commander-in-Chief, Lieutenant General James Doolittle, can change their situation. You are rather well acquainted with the General, aren't you, Sir Cunningham?"

"Connie? Collect your things, we're going to the airport. We must be in Liverpool within the hour."

Cox only stepped into his office for a moment, just long enough to issue his order and grab his Navy greatcoat.

"Charles, what's happening? Did the Sea Lords approve your plan?" Constance asked, looking up from her work.

"They did, after I explained the basic outline and we agreed on the details. Sir Cunningham put a call through to the First Lord and the Prime Minister at Ten Downing Street. They made the final approval and I have been placed in charge of the overall operation."

"You? But don't they turn over the actual execution of missions to the staff at Operations Division?" Her question wasn't incredulous or meant to be demeaning, she simply knew the limitations on what intelligence personnel could do.

"These are extraordinary times, Constance, they demand extraordinary decisions. I have been given command because it would take too long to fully brief someone else and because of my intimate knowledge of the situation. And I do know something of conducting operations. I was the first CO of the *Indomitable*'s torpedo squadron. We'd better hurry now, we'll be needing to make a stop before the airport."

The Admiralty motor pool furnished them with a standard staff car; Sir Cunningham was in need of his own. At the airfield, they had to wait while an aircraft was wheeled out and prepared for flight. That plus time spent in London's downtown traffic, meant Cox ended up far behind his original schedule. The clattering, old Avro Anson lifted off the runway at the time he had wanted to arrive in Liverpool. Once there, after an hour long cruise at the Anson's maximum speed, the first question Cox had was whether or not the elements of the latest U.S.-bound convoy had set sail; but no one could tell him for sure.

"Very well, I need to reach the American Army's transit barracks as quickly as possible. What type of transport do you have available at this field?" Cox inquired, asking his second question.

"Well if what you're doing is as important as you say it is," said the corporal manning the flight desk. "Then I'm sure the base commander will lend you his own car and personal driver. Here, let's see if I can't put you in touch with him."

Following the near-row with his immediate superior, Cox found the response from the Royal Air Force base commander quite incredible. Of course he could have the services of the car and driver.

"I remember when a chap in the Royal Navy did this for me," the base commander told Cox. "I always felt after it that I owed the Navy a favour. Lenny here, will take you anywhere you want to go. Before the war, he used to drive a taxicab in Liverpool."

The Army transit barracks looked shabby and forlorn; little to distinguish them from the rest of the city, except they were almost uninhabited. All who had been living inside were gone, only the staff remained.

"Gee, I'm sorry, Commander but there ain't nobody here anymore," said the MP sergeant at the main gate. "A state-side convoy has just set sail and everyone got passage back home. If you're lucky, sir, some of the ships may still be out in the harbor."

"Lenny, drive us to the Flag Officer's headquarters," Cox ordered, returning to the car. "I'm afraid we're too late. He's the only one who can help us now."

The flag officer for Liverpool was in his Operations room; an underground center where he could watch the movement of ships in his command area. Cox reached him just as the final transports of the America-bound convoy slid into the bay. Once beyond the boundaries of the command area, they would no longer be his problem. However, when Cox appeared, he found himself with another.

"The convoy will be out of my hands by the time it assembles off the Isle of Man," he explained. "What, precisely, do you want, Commander?"

"I need to locate a team of American airmen and return them and their equipment to this country. I was told at the transit barracks that everyone they were holding had obtained passage back to the States. Unfortunately the barracks' staff did not know which of the transports the men I'm looking for were placed on. I was hoping you might be able to tell me which one?"

"I am not some bloody cruise director or travel agent, Commander. Copies of all passenger manifests are kept by the captain of each ship and by the embarkation people, not me. In any case I will not order a ship to put about and return to port. To do so would hold up the entire convoy and place it in grave danger."

"Yes, Admiral, I know. I also realize that it will take almost half a day to bring the ship back to her dock and unload the airmen. I'm not asking you to do that, it would waste more time than we can afford. What I would like is the fastest warship you have in port right now. When my aide and I flew in, I saw a couple of 'J' class destroyers tied up. One of them will do."

"What?" The indignation rising in the flag officer's voice sounded faintly familiar to Cox. "Do you think this is some sort of rental office you can just barge into and order up a ship? Even if you had the rank that would enable you to make such an order, you're in the Fleet Air Arm. Why the hell do you want a destroyer?"

"I had hoped I wouldn't have to use this," said Cox, pulling an envelope out of his inside jacket pocket. "But I've really gone through enough arguments with superior officers for one day. Why is it that I must go outside my service to find the cooperation I need?"

While he lamented his current fate, the admiral opened the sturdy, white envelope addressed to Cox. It had a plain-looking wax seal and held a single-page letter with a few, short lines typed on it.

Dear Sir,

   You are to extend to the bearer of this document, Leftenant-Commander Charles Wilfrid Cox R.N., all due consideration and highest priority in executing his requests for equipment, personnel and all other services. He is acting in the interests of Great Britain and its western allies on a matter of critical importance. I cannot overemphasize the need for secrecy and expediency in handling his requests. Failure to do so or lack of cooperation will result in immediate corrective action.

Cordially Yours,
Winston S. Churchill

"Signals, make ready a message to the merchant-man *Steel Advocate Three* that we are coming alongside and to have Colonel Dennis Lacey report to the bridge."

For the past hour and a half, His Majesty's Ship *Javelin* had been plowing through the Irish Sea at its maximum speed of thirty-six knots. Now, on the northern horizon another blunt silhouette could be seen from its bridge. Like the others it had passed by earlier, this too was a liberty ship. Unlike the others, this was the one the destroyer had put to sea to catch.

"It's fortunate we're just on a ferry run," said the *Javelin's* captain. "Almost all of my gun crews were out on their shore leave when the Flag Officer alerted me. All I was able to recall were the crews for the two-pounder pompom and the half-inch anti-aircraft cannons."

"You only need a dozen or two men to operate those mountings," Cox noted. "Who else do you have on board?"

"Some of the torpedo tube crews and cooks. They can throw kippers at the U-boats if we sight any."

"Signals to Bridge, the *Steel Advocate* has acknowledged our transmission and wishes to know if we have someone who wants to come aboard to see Colonel Lacey."

"Yes, Signals, confirm we have someone who has orders for the Colonel and his team. Tell them to prepare to take on the lines for a breeches buoy transfer."

Once it came within range, the destroyer fired a series of rockets at the liberty ship; connecting the two vessels with the guy lines and hawsers needed for the breeches buoy. A few minutes later, Cox was swinging across the narrow strip of sea running between the ships. He arrived on the transport's deck shaken and chilled; the ground swells and late autumn cold conspired to make a normally unpleasant ride, excruciating.

"I feel as though I have just been on board a Fairey Swordfish that's had its ailerons shot away," said Cox, stepping out of the bird cage-shaped chair. "Has Colonel Lacey reported to the bridge yet?"

"Yeah, he's up there with the Captain, sir," replied the chief petty officer in charge of the buoy detail. "Boy, is he going to be in for a surprise. The last thing he'll expect to be bringing him orders is a Royal Navy officer."

The last thing Cox expected to see was someone who looked as young as Lacey did in a colonel's uniform. Dark-haired and still possessing the soft features of a boy; he must have been at least a year or two younger than Cox. And the chief petty officer was right, Lacey did register a mild shock when Cox walked onto the bridge.

"Permission to come aboard, sir?" he asked; the naval formalities had to come first and the liberty ship's lazy, rather grubby captain granted his consent to Cox. "Thank you, sir. Colonel Dennis Philip Lacey, I am Leftenant-Commander Charles Cox. I have orders for you and your Field Electronics Team, here. Is there someplace where we can discuss them with a little privacy?"

"Sure there is. You guys can use my cabin," the captain offered, "nobody'll bother you. Not even the clean-up crews on this tub bother to go inside. Just don't upset the atmosphere I've established in it, okay?"

Neither Cox nor Lacey tried to, or cared to, disturb the mess inside his quarters. All they wanted was to find a place where they could stand without stepping on something.

"I should've guessed it would be like this," said Cox. "Any captain who calls his command a 'tub' deserves to live in a trash heap. I've seen coal scuttles that were cleaner."

"Well, you're the last person I would have guessed would be bringing me orders," Lacey admitted, accepting a sealed envelope from the Leftenant-Commander. "I was expecting some Eighth Air Force type."

"Actually it shouldn't. You're going to be seeing a great many more blue uniforms in the near future."

Oh my God, we're going to be arrested by the Brits, Lacey thought, until he read his new orders. Unlike the ones Cox received, his were signed by the general commanding the Eighth Air Force, James H. Doolittle and not the First Lord of the Royal Navy and the Prime Minister of England.

"Now I know you and your team aren't actually under the General's command any more," said Cox, "in fact, you're in something of a limbo. You don't need to obey the orders of any senior Army officer while at sea. But if you would like to wait, I'm sure I can obtain some directly from your President."

"No, that won't be necessary." Lacey was impressed enough with the name on the orders, even if he didn't have to obey them. "But how come we're such a hot commodity all of a sudden? We left your country like a bunch of unwanted orphans. What's happened in the last few hours that has made us so needed?"

"I spent the better part of this morning, explaining why you are needed to the Sea Lords of the Admiralty. I don't want to go into all the details here. I can do so better, later. Back on the destroyer. All I can tell you for now is, what we do in the next two weeks will decide the battle for the Atlantic, the fate of our armies in Europe and of your east coast cities.

In short, the possible outcome of the entire war."

"What do you mean by 'back on the destroyer'?" asked Lacey. "I get the feeling I'm not going to be on this ship for much longer."

"I'm going to arrange for a mid-ocean transfer. You, your whole team and all your equipment and belongings will be shuttled over to the *Javelin* in the next hour. I don't know if it will be done by breeches buoy or by the *Javelin*'s power launch. It will take time so, perhaps, the buoy is out for moving so many people."

Two breeches buoy sets, however, were able to move the twelve-man Field Electronics Team, plus all their possessions and Cox, over to the Royal Navy destroyer in less time than it would have taken to ready the power launch and send the tiny craft out. It was safer as well, with securely tied cargo nets transferring the bulky cargoes at far less risk than manhandling them into a small boat.

Cox would be the last to make the trip. In the interim, Lacey introduced the other members of his team to the leftenant-commander. Only his most senior officers and the lone master sergeant had any combat experience. Like Lacey himself, the others were novices.

"Don't let the fact that we haven't seen any combat fool you," he said. "Those last three pilots were testing and ferrying B-17s from the Lockheed-Vega plant for almost a year before I got them. All of my electronics specialists have been working on state-of-the-art equipment for at least as long. Andy Martinez has been with me since the beginning of my assignment to Muroc."

"And what about you, Colonel?" asked Cox. "What is your background? Why are you the man in charge?''

"I've been told it's because of my knowledge of electronics but there are times I really wonder what the Army Air Force does see in me. Before the war, I was a California beach bum who ocasionally attended college. I only went because I loved to put together gizmos in the electrical engineering labs. When the Army found out, they put me in a uniform and sent me back to college to learn. Which I did and I developed some damn fine equipment but that's all I've ever done. I haven't had any operational experience until now and I sure as hell botched this chance up.''

"At least you showed ingenuity in your botching of your assignment. Ingenuity we must use in the next fourteen days if we are to succeed. Here, I think this trip across should be yours. I'll take the last one.''

The empty breeches buoy clattered back on the deck and Lacey was immediately thrust into its chair.

"I think I rode in something like this once at an amusement park,'' said Lacey as he was strapped down. "Was it any fun when you came over, Commander?''

"It was rather invigorating. It reminded me of the last time I flew a Swordfish torpedo-bomber, in fact.''

Like the rest of his team, Lacey was met when he reached the destroyer by its captain and Cox's aide. Unlike the rest, Constance retained him at the forward buoy station until Cox arrived. A wardroom had been set aside so Lacey could be briefed and only he would attend the meeting. His men were put to work moving their equipment below deck.

"How many people know about all this, Commander?'' Lacey asked, once Cox and Constance were finished.

"Beyond the three of us, there are the Sea Lords and the civilian Lords of the Admiralty. There is the Prime Minister, your General Doolittle and no doubt some trusted members on their staffs. And lastly, the Milord agents who supplied most of our information and their superiors. Too many for absolute secrecy, though surprisingly few when you consider the route this information took to come here. Apart from those agents, we three are the lowest-ranking officers in Britain to know of *Frederick*'s existence and the only ones who know the full extent of its dual mission. And that's the way the Admiralty, the Prime Minister and the commander of your Eighth Air Force would like it to remain. No one else on your team is to know of *Frederick*. Not while we're in training or at any time before we prepare our attack. Only then will everyone be brought together and told."

"My guys will probably beef about your blackout," Lacey admitted, "but they'll understand, I hope. If not, I'll have Frank Atkinson explain why and there should be enough work in the next two weeks to keep their minds off the question. I hope you realize that amount of time ain't a whole lot when you consider what we must do.

"We need many times the number of men I have in my team and a lot more equipment than what's in our special footlockers. We need B-17s and torpex, a test range similar to a fjord and a base at least as good as Fersfield. We need a mountain of spare parts to keep the Boeings in the air and a continuing source for state-of-the-art electronics. We're only carrying enough to make a good start. Since we can't work with the Eighth Air Force, can your Navy supply all those items?"

"Of course His Majesty's Fleet can," Cox maintained, "with a little ingenuity and some help from the Royal Air Force. It will take the *Javelin* around two hours to return us to Liverpool. I hope by the time we reach the dock, we'll have the answers to our problems. On this mission we need to land on the ground running. We may have two weeks but we cannot afford to waste even two waking hours."

Chapter Four
RETURN TO ENGLAND
THE FORTRESSES

At last light, the *Javelin* slid back into its dock space in the port of Liverpool. By the time it got ready to offload its special passengers, darkness had set in. The last waking hour was passing, and yet what Cox had in store for Lacey and his team was far from over.

"Hey, Colonel!" shouted Capollini, gaining his commanding officer's undivided attention. "About these trucks—are we gonna have to haul all this shit out of them when we get back to the transit barracks, or not?"

"I'm afraid we must, Vince," answered Lacey.

"Aw, Colonel, have a heart. What we did today weren't no leisure cruise. We're as tired as whores on a Friday night."

"I know you are. But it's either a little more work tonight, or tomorrow morning we'll have to fly back here and pick up our gear. We're not returning to the transit barracks, we're going to the airport."

He ordered Capollini back to his truck, then climbed into the cab of the convoy leader and told the driver to roll.

"That man certainly has a colorful vocabulary," noted Cox, squeezed in between Lacey and the driver. "Is he an officer or one of your enlisted ranks?"

"Vince is a captain; I only have three sergeants under my command. All the rest are officers."

"Are all the rest like him? I mean, in His Majesty's Navy, we're trained to be officers as well as gentlemen." Cox knew he was sounding stuffy and meant to be so. One of the delightful pleasures he found he could have in dealing with Americans was to goad them on their crudities and brutalization of the English language.

"In this man's army, we've been trained to fly B-17s. The only thing that makes us gentlemen is an act of Congress. If Capollini is a little rough around the edges, then he's entitled to be. A year ago he was ending his combat tour with the Twelfth Air Force in North Africa. He had one B-17 shot out from under him and brought in another on two engines."

"I stand corrected but not dissuaded from making future observations. Things would go much smoother if we both spoke the same version of the King's English."

"Well, Vince, did you get Dennis to tell where we're going?" inquired one of the other men in the truck Capollini entered, Lieutenant-Colonel Frank Atkinson.

"Yeah, we're going to the airport."

"I see, that really says a lot about our final destination. It could be anywhere in England or liberated Europe. Or maybe we're being sent back to the U.S., express? And here I thought you were good at ferreting out secrets. So far you haven't hit one on the head."

"Give me time, Frank, give me time, for crying out loud. This Royal Navy guy ain't no errand boy, I'll bet a month's pay on it. He's too high ranking and he came after us with a destroyer. You gotta be an admiral or something to give orders for a boat that big to sail."

"Not necessarily," Atkinson countered. "The destroyer may have been the only ship ready to go. And that lieutenant-commander may have been the only officer in this town who had the rank to run the ship."

"Then why did he have to bring that dish of an aide with him if he was just being an errand boy? And in case you didn't notice, he's in the Fleet Air Arm, not the Royal Navy proper so he can't captain a ship."

"I suppose you're right about that. I'm more interested in the guy's aide than in him. I think I knew her, or someone like her, when I was in this country on my last tour. It must have been on one of them forty-eight hour passes to London. I told you about those, didn't I . . ."

"Yeah, Frank, we've all heard your stories," said Lieutenant Martinez. "Why don't you tell them to us again? I need something boring to help me go to sleep."

The tiny, four-truck convoy moved through Liverpool unnoticed. There were countless similar processions every day, so one more, even at such a late hour, did not arouse many suspicions. Only at the airport did the insignificant line of vehicles stir up any real curiosity, when they rolled on to the flight line and stopped by the one aircraft still parked there, an R.A.F. Dakota.

Both the ground crew and the transport's crew assisted in transferring the gear and equipment from the trucks to the plane's hold. They grumbled a little once they found out that the passengers were Americans and Royal Navy personnel, not Royal Air Force. To top it off, none of the passengers would say what the flight was for or its specific destination. Not at least before the C-47 became airborne.

"Dennis, this will be our base for the next few weeks," said Cox, returning to their seats with a pilot's flight chart. "Blackburn. You wanted a base with facilities as good as those provided by the Eighth Air Force and I told you we needed one remote enough so we won't be bothered by anybody. Blackburn is perfect in both areas. It's in a rather remote section of Scotland's east coast, about ten miles outside of Aberdeen. The base is used by all British services to store obsolete aircraft and repair heavy bombers and patrol planes. It's not used for any operations but does have a large pool of skilled mechanics, engineers and other specialists from which we can draw our ground details."

"Fine, we have a base we can train at," said Lacey, "our first need has been answered. Now all we need to do is find a few dozen B-17s nobody wants; a nice, secluded test range where we can make our practice runs, get some volunteers to be our combat crews and since this base doesn't look like it's within range of our target, we need to find another which we can launch our attack from. Did I miss anything?"

"Yes, a few problems. What are we going to do for a fighter escort in the target area, for instance? But you needn't worry, the potential problems have all been identified and are being dealt with. Even as we're talking about them, in fact. Just wait and see what will be ready for us in a few hours' time."

To: Officer commanding the First Strategic Air
    Depot. Troston, Norfolk.
From: Lt. General James H. Doolittle, Eighth
    Air Force Headquarters. High Wycombe.
The First Sea Lord of the Royal Navy, Admiral Sir Andrew Cunningham, has recently

made a request to my office concerning long-range heavy aircraft. The Royal Navy is preparing its own weather reconnaissance service and has need of planes capable of making meteorological sorties over great distances. The Royal Air Force's Bomber and Coastal Commands have refused to part with any operational airplanes due to their mission needs but ours are not nearly as desperate.

Therefore, to aid the Royal Navy and further cooperation between our two services, all combat-expired B-17s you have in storage at your depot are to be turned over to a Lt. Commander Charles W. Cox who will arrive at Troston tomorrow morning. Accompanying him is a special team of Army Air Force officers who will be helping the Royal Navy establish their weather reconnaissance squadron. You are to give Lt. Commander Cox and his advisors every assistance in ferrying the B-17s to their destination and preparing the bombers for flight.

Landing at night, the team saw little of its new home; only a hangar and several floors of an officers quarters somewhere on base grounds. In the morning, they got a better look at the shabby airfield. Blackburn had the feeling in spite of the fact all the buildings were neatly maintained in the best Royal Air Force tradition. What caused it were the dozens of stored aircraft, parked in every corner of the field.

They had long grass growing around their landing gear, bird nests in the engine cowlings, degenerating paint schemes of various patterns and color combinations; a plastic film covered their canopies and windows and some even had their propellers removed. Most of the planes were Lockheed Hudsons and Venturas, together with a few Bristol Beauforts and Blenheims. At one time they formed the backbone of Coastal Command; now they had all been declared obsolete. The Royal Air Force had since replaced them with Beaufighters, Mosquitos and long-range, Consolidated Liberators.

"String up a few light bulbs and this place will really look like a used car lot," commented Lacey. "It's a damn shame we can't use some of those planes. But they just don't have the range or load capacity, even when stripped."

"The last item we have to worry about is finding suitable aeroplanes," said Cox. "Here are our orders for the day. They came in an hour or so before we woke up. It appears as though we've become the Royal Navy's weather reconnaissance squadron. At least officially. We are to proceed to the Eighth Air Force's First Strategic Air Depot to receive an unspecified number of Flying Fortress bombers."

"Well I hope that mean's we're going to get more than two and preferably more than twenty. We'll need as many to be both Aphrodite bombers and mother ships."

Like Blackburn, Troston was a base littered with airplanes. Only here most were not being held in storage but awaiting assignment to operational units. They also did not wear green and brown camouflage of the Royal Air Force; rather the olive drab or silver of the U.S. Army Air Force instead. So the R.A.F. Dakota which arrived around mid-morning was something of a curiosity, as was the fact that only two British officers came off the plane and they were in the Fleet Air Arm.

The Dakota had been ordered to the bomber side of the depot; where it parked amongst a row of brand new B-24s destined for operational units.

"I say, if we can manage it, why don't we use these aeroplanes?" Cox proposed to those members of Lacey's team standing beside him. "They claim the Liberator has a much bigger bomb load and better range than the Fortress."

"What! You want us to fly banana boats?" cried Atkinson, in an outraged disbelief which sounded almost serious. He turned and started gesturing at the nearest high-winged, twin-finned hulk. "This ain't no airplane! This is the box the B-17 comes in. They just stuck a pair of wings and some engines on it. A B-17 flies better than a B-24, it has more guns than a B-24 and it has more wing than a B-24."

"Frank, I think you'd better take a look at this," Capollini suggested.

"Not now, Vince. You think they build these things in a factory? They put 'em together here at air depots. I've seen WPA shit houses built better than these tubs."

"Frank, you really should look at this."

"All right, what?" Atkinson managed to say, before the howl of Pratt and Whitney Twin Wasps drowned him out.

A C-87, transport version of the B-24, skimmed over the Dakota's tail and roared down the flight line of its sister ships. It took nearly everyone by surprise; causing them to either duck or run for cover. All except Cox, who stayed to watch the impressive, if slightly illegal, air display. Near the end of its run, the Liberator disappeared from his view and did not reappear until it was climbing gracefully to gain altitude.

"You know, for a shit house with wings, I'd say that plane flies rather well," Cox noted.

"What the hell is going on down here?" asked

Lacey, returning to collect his team. "The sergeant and I could hear Frank's bitching all the way up at the hangar."

"He wants us to fly banana boats, Colonel," said Atkinson, maintaining his mock hysteria. "Now you know, no pilot has been able to make it out of one of these tubs after the crew has had to abandon it."

"Yes, we all know the Liberator has its problems. I don't think we need to worry about being switched. There isn't enough time to retrain us all and orders have already been cut for us to get B-17s. The sergeant is looking over and taking count of the Fortresses set aside for us. I say we should go help him."

Lacey didn't move to make any further suggestions to get his men moving. Atkinson and Capollini took the lead, with the team's three co-pilots close behind them. After spending more than a week away from their favorite mistress and the best toy a man could ever have, they were eager to reacquaint themselves. Following in their wake were Lacey, Cox and Constance.

"Actually, all I made was a suggestion that we could use the other bomber in place of the B-17," said Cox. "I didn't realize you Americans took such a serious liking to your aeroplanes. I haven't seen such loyalty since I was in a squadron that threatened to mutiny when it was due to switch from Swordfish to Albacores."

"Then you should understand the loyalty we show to the Fortress. She's the queen. She doesn't fly faster than any other bomber, or higher and farther but she's still the queen. She's the plane that made the Army Air Force what it is. An independent striking arm and not some adjunct to the Signal Corps or artillery. The B-17 was part of history before this war even started, something none of her contemporaries can claim. She's not the best bomber in the world, her big brother is that; the Flying Fortress is merely the greatest there ever will be.''

"The sergeant" Lacey had referred to was Master Sergeant James Herrmann. Beyond Capollini and Atkinson, he was the only one in the team to have any combat experience. They found him going through the B-17s scattered behind the hangars; the ones assigned to the Royal Navy.

Unlike the shiny, silver Liberators standing out in front, the Boeings were all old and mostly olive drab. They bore the signs and scars of operational use. The faded group markings and personal crew names, the patches covering all manner of shell and flak damage. Each bomber had a long line or box full of tiny, white bombs; representing the missions they had successfully completed. Also unlike the factory-fresh B-24s, the Fortresses were unarmed.

"Colonel, we got nineteen ships here," said Herrmann, showing Lacey a list of the planes, which he identified by their serial numbers and crew names. "And if this were North Africa in 'forty-three, I'd say we have a pretty good collection of bombers in top shape."

"Well, we're not at some Tunisian base but England," Lacey noted, in a less than profound observation. "And this is November of 'forty-four. So now what's the score?"

"We've been given junk, sir. At least five of these ships are not flyable and there are two others I would consider marginal. A small mountain of spare parts and some good mechanics should return them to flying condition in about eighteen hours. The other twelve Forts are basically sound. Reports from crew chiefs and the last pilots to fly them all say so, it's just that . . . What's wrong, Colonel? Is it something

I said?"

Lacey had crumpled the sheet Herrmann had given him into a small ball; even Cox could tell he wasn't pleased.

"No, it's not your fault, Jim. But twelve planes simply won't be enough. Not for both training and flying the mission. Perhaps with fourteen we might. Can you get those other two back into flying condition?"

"Colonel, I really think I should point something out to you," said Capollini, cutting in before the sergeant could answer. "This depot is within spitting distance of Fersfield. If we spend eighteen hours here, I'm damn sure 'Colonel Duane' will find out about us and then burn up half of this island to discover why we haven't left. If our operation is as secret as you're letting on it is, then we can't take the risk of him fucking it up."

"I say, this officer your man mentioned, he wouldn't actually set fire to an ally's country?" Cox asked.

"No, no, Vince was just using a slang term," Lacey explained. "What he means is a certain Colonel Brogger will scour the Eighth Air Force, and every other American outfit in England, until he gets an answer. He's an old West Point prick and we can't have him getting wind of us. Jim, are you sure you can't shave a few hours off your estimate?"

"I wish I could, Colonel, but that's the minimum amount of time it will take. With no meals or coffee breaks. And there's something else I should tell you, sir. None of these ships has any guns or turrets. Not even the good ones. They've all been stripped of combat equipment and while that is fine for the ones we're going to convert into Aphrodite bombers, what about the ones you want to use as mother ships?

Surely you want them to be armed and that's going to take time too."

"Jesus, it looks as though we've run into a God damn brick wall before we even reached first base," said Lacey; "this is going to delay us no end, unless we get some more orders. Or find alternatives . . ."

He turned and paced over to the nearest B-17. When he reached it, Lacey put out his hand and gently stroked a blade of one of its inboard propellers.

"Colonel, Dennis, why are so many planes needed?" Cox asked, following him across the apron.

"For training, mostly, and what we like to call 'operational insurance.' Making sure there are enough planes to fly the mission, no matter what mechanical malfunctions we may encounter. We'll need three B-17s to be mother ships, another three to be mission Aphrodites and nine more for the three practice runs each crew should make. That totals up to fifteen, leaving nine of the two dozen I had wanted to cover any technical screw-ups which may occur during the training period and the actual mission."

"Tell me, is it vital for us to expend B-17s on those practice flights? Could we not use other aeroplanes? Something twin-engined and considered obsolescent for example?"

"Of course, the Hudsons and other planes we saw back at Blackburn," said Lacey, catching on to Cox's idea. "The differences for the radio control operators won't be too great and my men are already experienced in remote flying. Yes, indeed they'll do. That solves one problem; I can cut the number of B-17s we'll need in half—down to the number we have on hand. But we still have to arm the mother ships. Sergeant, does Blackburn have the facilities to re-equip some of our Fortresses with gun turrets?"

"Sure, it's got the facilities," answered Herrmann, "but what it doesn't have are the turrets to do the re-equipping with. Where are we gonna scrounge them up, sir?"

"I have a few ideas on that, Sergeant, don't worry about it. Now show me which of these ships can fly."

Following a short inspection of the airworthy B-17s, Lacey met with those Ferry Command pilots who did not have much to do that afternoon. He finally picked eighteen of them, enough to give each Fortress he would take a set of pilots; including himself and the other officers of his team.

Fueled and suitably prepared for flight, the battered, worn bombers trundled off to the runway in pairs; a half dozen pairs in all. This guaranteed one pilot in each formation would know the final destination; none of the ferry pilots were told where they were going. Not even the co-pilot of Lacey's B-17 found out.

For the most part, the ferry pilots did not care to know. The chance to make a leisurely, cross-country flight into Scotland was enough for many of them. The two-ship formations were easy to fly, much better than the usual, three-ship vees. Three hours after they had departed Troston, the first pairs began to arrive at Blackburn.

The wing men followed their leaders down through the broken overcast, and in for landings at the base nestled among the rolling foothills of Aberdeen County. The leaders, Lacey's men, took precautions not to fly over the coastline or the city of Aberdeen itself. They flew in from the west, over the Grampian Mountains of central Scotland, and made straight-in approaches. Blackburn tower went along with the plan devised by Lacey and Cox and answered only to the code name of Peacock. They even covered over the name plate on the control tower's façade.

"Well, that's the last of 'em," said the officer in charge of the tower crew. "Once those two have switched off, the Dakota F for Freddy will alert us when they're ready for departure. I swear, this is more hush-hush activity than we've had here in months. Not since the Prime Minister's Liberator was flown in for an overhaul."

"Just who are these Yanks anyway, sir?" asked one of the enlisted men in the tower. "They blow in here in the middle of the night, led by some Royal Navy bloke and start taking over sleeping quarters, shops and hangars."

"I don't know but we're to give them full cooperation and not to ask questions or interfere with their activities. The base C.O. told me their orders and his came from the Air Ministry, Coastal Command headquarters, the Lords of the Admiralty, the American Eighth Army Air Force and the Prime Minister himself. They have clearances from just about everybody and God help the poor blighter who decides to give them a sticky time."

By following a different route, the R.A.F. Dakota that had flown Cox and Lacey to Troston arrived back at Blackburn ahead of the faster B-17s. To the ferry pilots and some of Lacey's men, it began to look as though the entire Royal Air Force had only one C-47.

"In a way your Captain Capollini is right," said Cox. "Currently there is a greater premium on transports in the RAF than on bombers. Many were lost in Operation Market Garden and the commanders on virtually every front in Europe are crying for more transports. In fact the situation is so desperate they're converting bombers into transports. I remember when, not very long ago, the situation required they do the exact opposite thing.''

"Yes, I know," answered Lacey as he strained to lift a small crate out of the back of their jeep. "Here, give me a hand with this. I know about a couple of Eighth Air Force B-24 groups which have been flying more gasoline and supplies to the continent than bombs. Which, if you ask Frank, is about all the banana boat is good for."

"This box is rather heavy, what do you have in it?"

"A present for these ferry pilots we used. Working at Muroc, I've learned that the best way to shut a man up is to stick an apple in his mouth, not to put a muzzle on it."

The "apples" turned out to be fifths of Scotch whiskey, rye and Russian vodka. They were handed out after everyone had boarded the transport and were eagerly accepted. The Dakota crew had its engines turning over before Lacey was ready to leave; they were running on a tight schedule and were making it known they did not want to be delayed by anyone.

"Some of that liquor you gave away was twelve years old," Cox noted, "and what wasn't twelve years old was ninety proof. Are you sure it's not a threat to our security to be mixing such potent spirits with even just a little knowledge of our activities?"

"Not in this case," said Lacey; "those guys don't know our full names, the name of our base or its exact location. They don't know where any of us really came from and have only been told the cover story. In an hour or two they'll be so smashed they won't remember clearly what little they do know. It's better to handle them this way than to just bundle the lot off in a C-47. They might start grumbling and the wrong people always seem to end up hearing it. Now I think we should go see what Martinez and the others have been able to set up."

Suitably armed with authority from Lacey, Cox and the base commander, Martinez had requisitioned one of Blackburn's largest hangars. They cleaned it out of Lancasters and its shops of Lancaster parts and hauled in the team's equipment. At last Cox and Constance got a chance to see what their footlockers held: a mountain of electronics that filled most of the available space.

To Cox it all looked the same. What difference was there between an oscilloscope and a television monitor? Constance, however, could see the differences her superior could not and devoured everything Lacey told her about the equipment his team used. Though there was one thing Cox did know, whatever the Americans had they would need more of; a lot more if *Frederick* was going to be eliminated. Fortunately, he had already taken steps to ensure a continuing supply.

"Yes, this is all very impressive," said Cox, trying not to show he was becoming bored with the eager, highly detailed descriptions Lacey and his electronics specialists were giving. "You should be happy to know that I've made arrangements with the Royal Air Force's experimental establishment at Boscombe Down and the BBC's television laboratories at Alexandra Palace to give you anything you may want. And you shouldn't worry as to whether or not their gadgetry is compatible with yours. They've been using American equipment for years."

"Oh really, why's that?" Lacey asked.

"Well, while your equipment may not always be the best in the world, you are a more reliable supplier than the Germans," Constance offered. "Could you tell me, Colonel, where and how you plan to install the directional aerials on your Aphrodite ships?"

"Please, I prefer you'd use Dennis."

"Yes, Dennis, and Constance. You can talk about all those little points later," advised Cox. "Right now we should be considering the answers to much larger questions. We have a base, we have B-17s, your men appear to have found the facilities adequate enough and several locations are being scouted for us to use as test ranges. But we still need to find out if your team can modify those Hudsons out there for remote control. We still need to find a way to re-arm some of the Fortresses without raising undue suspicion and we need to arrange a continual source of spare parts for them."

"Andy? How about it?" Lacey asked. "I know we haven't done much work on twin-engined aircraft recently but do you think you can adapt those old Lockheed Hudsons and Venturas to our control equipment?"

"What, those old things?" said Martinez. "Sure I can, Colonel. Hell, considering we'll have half the number of throttle linkages to set-up, it'll probably be a little easier to turn them into drones. But why, Colonel? Didn't you get enough B-17s outa the Air Force?"

"We got more than enough to fly the final mission. The trouble is, we don't have enough to train properly for it. Our target is situated in some very difficult terrain. It will take quite a bit of practice to learn how to fly over it and around it. The Germans selected the area partly because an air attack would be so difficult."

"Jeez, Colonel, you make it sound like this target would be suicidal to fly over. Is it some big headquarters?"

"Dennis, I think you've answered the first problem fully," Cox warned, "there's no need to say anything further on it. What are your solutions for the other two?"

"Ever hear of killing two birds with one stone?" Cox shook his head "no" but it didn't deter Lacey from proceeding with his suggestion. "Sergeant Herrmann saw to it that we brought back from Troston a fair quantity of spares which should meet our needs for the next few days. By then, if you agree, our operation should be paying off.

"It will work on a very simple principle. There are over fourteen hundred B-17s stationed on this island, divided among twenty-six heavy bomb groups and a number of special operations squadrons. Add to those the almost constant influx of new B-17s from the United States. So on any one day, there are hundreds of Forts making sorties of one kind or another. And at some point, Murphy's Law must take effect.

"I don't think you've heard of this one either, it's distinctly American. What it says is 'whatever can go wrong, will go wrong at the worst possible time.' At least one and perhaps several more will return to earth where they're not supposed to. If they're intact, more or less, if they haven't turned themselves into an acre of scrap metal surrounding a deep hole, then the wrecks can be salvaged and it's first come, first served."

"I hate to say it sounds rather bloodthirsty but it's also ingenious," Cox admitted. "The plan is damn well brilliant. No need to put through requests and have orders issued. We would not have to make up any cover stories or arouse suspicions as to why we need gun turrets for weather reconnaissance planes. All we have to do is arrive at the crash site before the

94

official salvage crews are sent from the nearest air depot. We have to be, how shall I put it, 'nimble.'"

"And I have the nimblest crew of scroungers and strippers in the entire Army Air Force," said Lacey, boasting a little. "If we can swipe the props and tires off a B-25 at some heavily guarded base, then we should be able to gut a few Fortresses that have made unscheduled stops in the English countryside. It won't take many to provide what we'll be needing. All we have to do is start a watch for these accidents. The more remote from U.S. air bases, the better."

"You know, time was when anybody even slightly criticized our gear, the colonel would jump all over him," Martinez whispered to Capollini. "You'll notice he didn't even snap at that Navy lady when she said the Germans have better equipment than ours. I kinda think he's taken a liking to her."

"I know, and she's taken a liking to him," Capollini replied. "God damn it. I was hoping Frank could work his charms on her and find out something about our mission. But not now. That look in her eyes, I've seen it before. He's gonna have to knock her down with a Sherman tank to just get her attention. Looks like I'll have to come up with another plan. Atkinson won't try to take away the colonel's girl. God damn it."

"C'mon, Mack, what's the matter with you? Why aren't you joining the party? I know we ain't got any girls but what the hell. There'll be plenty when we get off the plane and we'll be ready for them!"

The Dakota was less than an hour out of Blackburn and already the ferry pilots were consuming their presents. All except one, who preferred to remain separate from the others.

"Yeah, yeah," responded the loner, "thanks but no

thanks. I don't want to be stumbling off this Gooney Bird when we arrive at Troston. There's someone I have to see once I'm back."

"Oh, I get it. You got some hot little WAAF waiting for you, don't you?"

"No, I'll find myself a broad to share this with later. I want to see a guy I know named Brogger. He told me about some trouble he had recently and the people we just flew those Forts up for sound awful familiar. I think he'll be very interested in them."

Chapter Five
THE VOLUNTEERS
LOCH SEAFORTH

"Zed-Zebra to Blackburn Tower. We have passed your outer marker and are commencing our final approach. Please inform Commander Cox and his Americans that we will be arriving soon."

One of the problems that had been left unanswered by Lacey and Cox was who would they get to crew their B-17s and provide ground support. It remained unanswered until early on the second day of operations at Blackburn when a pair of Catalinas appeared over the base. The planes were familiar to Cox, as were some of the men who came out of them; especially the first one.

"Good to see you again, Commander Cox," said Holmen, descending from one of the side blisters on PBY Zed-Zebra. "I've brought with me the best men I can possibly afford to spare. If I were to allow any more to join this group, I'm afraid I wouldn't have enough qualified personnel to run my Catalina squadron. Here, let me introduce them to you; I hope they meet with your approval."

Commander Holmen brought with him men who had virtually every skill Lacey and Cox would need. Gunners, radio operators, flight engineers, co-pilots, navigators; everyone but bombardiers. Some thirty men, along with their belongings, had come packed into the two B-17-sized amphibians. Together with the twelve men of Lacey's team, they would form the crews for the three mother ships and the three pilot-flight engineer teams required by the Aphrodite bombers.

Though Cox eagerly accepted them all, Lacey was at first a little reluctant about their suitability.

"I understand your reasons, Colonel," said Holmen, "but let me assure you, my men are not only volunteers, they are veterans with long combat experience. Most have served in Bomber Command and other Coastal Command squadrons before coming to my wing. They know American aircraft quite well. Especially Consolidated's B-24 Liberator and PBY Catalina. Those are quite good aeroplanes."

"I know but I hope your men won't say such things around my men," advised Lacey. "They are quite fond of the queen, as everyone will soon find out. We'll be putting your men to work right away. We have thirteen days left, which leaves damn little time to spend socializing. If you'll bring your men over here, I'll show you why. My team is already hard at work."

Inside the newly Americanized hangar was a B-17 and one of Blackburn's many derelict Hudsons. As the latter was being prepared to fly once again, under remote guidance, the former was being outfitted to control it. Most of Lacey's team were divided between the two planes; those who weren't could be seen reading Hudson pilot manuals.

The appearance of so many men at the hangar's main entrance was a natural draw for attention. So much so it was scarcely necessary for Lacey to order his unit to gather and meet their future crew-mates.

"These men have all come from a Norwegian Coastal Command Wing," he said. "They have volunteered to join us and each is combat experienced. I'll let their CO, Wing Commander Holmen introduce them to you and then we can give them a tour of the facilities we just set up. If they're good enough to fly with us, they're reliable enough to see our equipment. They deserve that much."

They had also been cleared by Cox and the Royal Navy's Intelligence Division before Holmen was allowed to bring them to Blackburn. While he repeated his earlier introductions, and Lacey was preoccupied coming up with some for his own men, Cox slipped out of the hangar, in the company of an R.A.F. messenger. Several minutes later, he came back to find the Norwegians already divided into crews. Lacey was indeed serious about not wasting time. A pity such a smoothly flowing operation had to be interrupted but what Cox had would be of interest to both Lacey and Holmen.

"The Royal Navy has completed its search of all possible sites for our training range and has made its selection," he reported, "dependent of course upon our final decision. I've told the Operations Centre to prepare us a flight plan to the location. All we require now is an aeroplane. If a Fortress can be made ready then I suggest we use it."

One of the bare metal B-17s called "Careful Virgin" was selected. An ex-91st Bomb Group ship, it had the lowest number of flying hours and the least amount of combat damage of any of the twelve brought from Troston. The group's red tail plane and wing tips were still visible though somewhat worn. Because of its "newness," Careful Virgin was to be converted into a mother ship and had been the next in line to undergo the process, until Lacey had it towed to the flight line.

Leaving Atkinson in charge, he took with him

Cox, Constance, Holmen and, to actually fly the plane, Capollini and part of his newly formed Norwegian-American crew. With no gunners in the aft section, the four passengers found plenty of room to ride out the steep, fighter-like takeoff Capollini put the Fortress through.

"Aw, Colonel, have a heart," he responded after Lacey criticized him. "You wouldn't let me do it yesterday or at any time during the trip up. This is the best way to fly a Fort. When it's stripped down and ain't carrying no heavy loads of bombs or gas. Just take the co-pilot's seat and find out for yourself. You can practically feel every pound that's not there."

"Thanks, Vince but I'll try it later," said Lacey, "on the flight back. Right now I'm going to give the Royal Air Force and the Royal Navy back there a tour of the B-17. So just keep her straight and level and at five thousand feet. Once we reach our destination, you'll have plenty of chances for low-altitude high jinxs."

Lacey's tour began with the radio operator's compartment, where, so he explained, the Aphrodite controller would be located as well.

"It appears to me it would become rather cramped back here," said Cox, "what with two men and all this radio equipment already taking up so much space."

"Yes, it was one of the big areas of disagreement between myself and the officer who ran the Operational Engineering Section at Fersfield," Lacey admitted. "They put the controller in the nose, in the bombardier's old station. I say he's better back here, where he isn't so exposed and most of the plane's main electrical lines are located. As for a lot of this radio gear, it can't be used here in Europe. The low-frequency, Detrola receiver and half of the VHF channels are for use only in the United States. Yet, when aircraft are sent overseas, such equipment is still left in. Once we remove what we don't need, there will be enough room in this compartment for two men."

On the catwalk in the bomb bay, Lacey showed how the long-range "Tokyo" tanks would be installed. In the pilot's compartment, he also explained how the top turret worked and its installation directly behind the pilot seats. For the last part of the tour, he led the other passengers down into the nose section, where now only the navigator sat at his tiny chart table.

"It's really quite spacious," said Holmen, commenting on the amount of room available in the Fortress's nose. "I wish our Catalina's could have as much. It would reduce crew fatigue and make U-boat spotting very much easier."

"Well, it wasn't always this good and it won't be once we rearm these ships," warned Lacey; "up here used to be the bombardier's station. While we won't bring back his Norden bombsight, we will re-install the controls for the chin turret and remount the staggered, fifty-caliber cheek guns. Put all those weapons in here, together with their ammo supplies, feed chutes, catch boxes for the empty shells and it will get a little cramped."

"I can see why you would consider this position so exposed," said Constance, looking out the plexiglas nose. "Though it does have that one obvious advantage. You can watch the aircraft you're controlling . . ."

"What you've said is really a false advantage, Connie. Especially when you're at thirty thousand feet and your drone is at five hundred or so. It doesn't force the controller to rely on his instruments which, as troublesome as they sometimes are, must be the only things he is to use. And there's a more dangerous problem with stationing the Aphrodite Controller in the nose.

"Sitting here, with all his guidance equipment, he will take up so much space as to render the position next to defenceless. If there are no guns in the nose of a B-17, then the whole bomber is in grave danger, since the Luftwaffe likes head-on attacks. It really wouldn't be a problem if the Allies had air superiority where we're going, like over the V-1 sites the original Aphrodites were after, but they don't so we need the guns."

"Yes, I'm quite sure Leftenant Smythe understands your reasons," Cox interrupted, "no need to explain them any further. In fact I believe she already knew of your first reason. Do you see that dark shadow coming over the horizon? That's Lewis Island, part of the Outer Hebrides and the location of our training range. In a few moments, we should be able to discern its larger features. Most prominent among them will be an arm of the sea extending deep into the island. That will be our proposed range, it's called Loch Seaforth. Here, I'll borrow a map from the navigator and show you what it looks like."

Lewis Island itself lay west-northwest of the Scottish mainland and was separated from it by the North Minch Channel. At normal cruise speed, the Fortress took an hour to reach the island, then spent several more minutes circling over it in order to orientate the crew.

"Lacey to aircraft commander. Vince, I'm sending up the new navigator with the course we down here would like you to fly. This'll be your chance to perform some of those high jinxs you wanted. Please keep the navigator up there with you during the run, Vince. We're going to be holding a top level conference for a little while and we do not want to be disturbed, for any reason."

"Now we can talk freely," said Cox, after the Norwegian crawled through the hatchway and made for the cockpit. "Sorry for stopping you earlier, Dennis but we can't let slip anything about what or where our target is, no matter how innocent or generalized the remark."

"I'm going to be mighty relieved when this charade ends," Lacey admitted; "you must understand it is very difficult for me to withhold such information from my men. Ever since we were formed, I've almost always shared secrets with my team. They all have top security clearances from the Army Air Force and hell, they probably know a few secrets that would set your hair on end."

"No doubt, but you just said one reason why your men can't be told about the mission. Their clearances came from your service, not His Majesty's Navy. Believe me, Dennis, it really is better this way and I speak from experience. We're not in America, we're in a theatre of operations and even this far from the front there is still danger. And when there's danger, no matter how slight, it's always best to compart-mentalize, to clamp the lid on tight until we're ready."

"He said much the same thing to me, Colonel," Holmen offered, "around a week and a half ago. It was hard for me to accept as well, but I understood his reasons and I did. In case you're just finding it out, this is one of the problems a good commanding officer faces—often more times than he'd like to."

"All right, all right. You've both managed to convince me," said Lacey, "again. But I warn you,

Charlie. You're going to have to keep on me and catch my slips for the next week or so. An old habit is hard to break, especially for this commanding officer."

"Mission accepted," Cox managed to say, before the horizon spun and he was thrown against one side of the fuselage.

The centrifugal force generated by the sudden maneuver pinned everyone to the same side of the fuselage through the duration of the spin. When it ended, they slid off the wall and toward the nose where they were treated to a panoramic view of the rapidly approaching seascape.

"Did anybody break anything?" Lacey asked.

"A few bruises perhaps but nothing worse," Cox answered hesitantly. "At what altitude does your pilot plan to level us out? If we still have a whole aircraft, that is."

"Oh, somewhere between here and sea level, I hope."

For a mile the Fortress fell before Capollini decided it was time to end the first part of his demonstration on how to torture a bomber. The creaking mass of aluminum bottomed out of its dive a scant fifty feet above the deck, close enough to pick up salt spray from the choppy, foam-capped waves. Ahead lay Lewis Island's jagged, sheer coastline of sea cliffs and countless inlets.

Most of the openings were tiny bays hardly big enough to squeeze a boat into; but one was a mile wide canyon half filled with ocean, Loch Seaforth. Apart from a small village adjacent to its entrance, Seaforth was one of the most barren and uninhabited places on the island. And even the people in the nearby village took no notice of the low-flying B-17 approaching its entrance. A minute later the Boeing had disappeared from view and the last rumblings of thunder from its Cyclone engines were dying away.

"This is very much like the approach to Alten Fjord," Holmen remarked, "except at Alten there are more, and larger, islands guarding the mouth."

"There're also probably more guns guarding that entrance than this one," said Lacey.

"No, not really, Colonel. All the shore-based anti-aircraft batteries are in place around the anchorage at Kaa Fjord and the field at Alta. Other than mine fields, there are no coastal defences to speak about. At this point in your attack, you will have more to worry from Nazi fighters and destroyers outfitted as anti-aircraft cruisers. Those ships are to be anchored at various lengths of the fjord whenever an air attack is coming. Not all will be on station at any one time but enough will to make any attack a hard one."

Part way down its length, Seaforth widened and a desolate island rose from its placid waters. Their mirror-like surface was only disturbed by the turbulence from the bomber's propellers, until it neared the island. The four lines of ripples and wavelets died out as the B-17 clawed for altitude. Three hundred feet allowed it to barely scrape past the island's jagged summit. For an instant most of those riding in the nose thought the last rocky pinnacle was going to smash through the plexiglas. Once over the island, the Fortress settled back to its original, near zero-feet altitude.

Seaforth became irregular toward its end, narrowing drastically and then widening. Capollini wisely slowed his giant and climbed in preparation for the ordered turn. A sixty-foot high cliff seemed the only end to Loch Seaforth before the constraining canyon walls fell away and a slender ribbon of water grew out from either side.

By far the longer extension lay to the right, the direction in which the Fortress swung. Here it truly seemed as if the wing tips would be touching both walls. The passengers and crew of the bomber held their breaths for the last part of the run. All except Capollini, who was clearly enjoying himself, and Lacey, who trusted him. As a fitting finale to his demonstration, Capollini dove the B-17 at a small island and used the inertia generated to leap beyond the high walls at the loch's terminus.

"I say, that was quite exhilarating," Cox uttered, at last. "Whatever social manners your officer may lack, one thing is for certain, he's a damn good pilot. Are all of your flying officers as good as this one?"

"Atkinson is better," said Lacey, "and I'm nearly as good as Vince. Both of them have seen to that. The other three, O'Dell, Kretchmar and Lawson are all okay. They would have been our co-pilots but they'll now be the pilots for the Aphrodite ships. Any other comments?"

"Yes, could we go back and retrieve my stomach?" asked Constance.

"Your Navy has made an excellent choice," said Holmen. "It's smaller than the Alten Fjord-Kaa Fjord region but I still say you should use it. I don't think you will find a better duplicate anywhere else in the British Isles."

"It is rather small, Dennis," Constance added, "and I've read where radio control aeroplanes do not fly quite so well as manned aeroplanes. Their maneuvers tend to be crude. Could that not create problems for you here? I mean, we seemed barely able to fit into the loch just now."

"It looked much worse than it actually was. Still, it will be a problem though the drones we'll be using will have forty feet less wing than a B-17, which should help us."

"Could we go around again, Dennis?" Cox asked, surprising everyone. "That island in the loch's toe we dove at, I would like to see it again. Its location makes it a perfect stand-in for *Frederick*."

"Yes, I believe it does." Lacey moved back to the navigator's table and grabbed the intercom mike. "Hey, Vince. I've had a request down here for another go-around. Are you guys up to it?"

"Colonel, I feel as though I've just been laid by that little dish I had back in the States," Capollini explained, "so while I may be tired, I'm ready, willing and able to do it one more time. Hang on to your caps, here we go again."

"Commander Cox? Good morning, this is the Operations Centre. We have what should be good news for you, Commander. An American B-17 has gone down in North Wales. Reports indicate it may still be in one piece and there were no casualties. I suggest you ring up the Yanks staying with you and have them come over as well. This may be what you're looking for."

The telephone receiver had scarcely finished landing back in its cradle when Cox leaped out of bed. He washed briefly and dressed quickly; there would be time for a shave and a more thorough washing later. Somewhere in all his running about, Cox managed to get in a call to Lacey.

"What's up, Charlie?" he asked when the two officers met in the ground floor hallway. "On the phone, you made it sound like Christmas has come early this year."

"For us it has, your 'Murphy's Law' appears to work. Operations Centre has some very interesting information about a Fortress which has made an unscheduled landing. They promised to have all the information we need by the time we arrive.''

The B-17 had been on a night test flight when its electrical system failed completely. With no instruments, landing aids or radios, the crew felt helpless and decided to abandon the bomber. This they did over East Anglia and after thinking they had set it on course for the North Sea. In fact, it was on a westerly heading and flew erratically over central England until fuel starvation forced it down in the Berwyn Mountains, near the town of Corwen. Local air raid wardens heard the Boeing crash and a Royal Air Force unit was the first to arrive.

''Because of an inter-service communications problem,'' said Cox, ''aided of course by the staff here, the Eighth Air Force has yet to be told that one of their missing aircraft has been found. And they will not be told until we are through with it. How long do you believe it will take?''

''Depends on how much time we use getting down there,'' Lacey responded, ''and what we'll have to work with. Are there any bases in that region we can use?''

''Quite a number; the best would be Aberporth. It's not as close to the crash site as some others but it is still the best. It's a Royal Aircraft Establishment base. They test aircraft and all types of similar equipment; it's a bit like RAF Boscombe Down, only civilian. The facilities are first rate and its security is considered excellent. There are even a few captured German planes stored at the base.''

''If it can take a B-17, we'll use it. Let me call the rest of my team and get a Fort out on the flight line. I suppose I should leave most of them behind, to finish outfitting the mother ships with their electronics, and take some of the Norwegians instead.''

Lacey ended up taking only Atkinson and Sergeant Herrmann. He left Capollini in charge and said they would be back before nightfall, though he didn't know when. Together with the four largest Norwegians Lacey could find, an olive drab B-17 lifted away from Blackburn while most of the base was still stirring.

For all its secretiveness, Aberporth looked like any of the other Royal Air Force airfields dotting the English countryside, until one noticed it was the home for very few aircraft and several of those were in Luftwaffe markings. After a two hour flight from Scotland, Atkinson eased the B-17 into Aberporth's pattern and made a straight approach. No buzzing or mock bombing runs this time, perhaps more fun later but now it was purely business.

The Fortress taxied briskly down a motley line of aircraft and found a space in between the Anson transports, Harvard trainers and latest-model Focke-Wulf 190s. A delegation of base officers met the bomber's multi-national crew and escorted them to a squadron ready room. Along the way, they ran into more of Aberporth's unusual, though for some, familiar, residents.

"Hey, Colonel, look over here," Atkinson requested, "helicopters. I haven't seen any of them things since we left the States."

The pair sat inside a partially open hangar, their wingless fuselages and long, narrow rotor blades half-hidden by the shadows. They were Sikorsky R-4B Hoverflies, small, limited, rather primitive machines that nevertheless were superior to the earlier, one off, prototypes. They were the first production-line helicopters in aviation history.

"Tell me, Group Captain, what equipment will you make available to us?" asked Lacey.

"My superiors ordered me to hand you anything you may want," said the director of flight operations. "Even if that means giving you some of our captured German aircraft. Have you seen something you wish to use, Colonel?"

"Yes, those two eggbeaters over there. Back at my home base in California, they were found to be quite useful in many duties. One once rescued the pilot of a plane of ours that crashed in the Sierra foothills. If they can be equipped with cargo slings, they'll carry small payloads. Like, say, a power turret off a B-17?"

"I see what you mean. Those machines would also make the perfect way to transport your men to the crash site. It takes at least an hour to reach the site by foot and vehicle. I'll have home ground crews prepare the machines right away. What did you call them again? You used a term I never heard before."

The Royal Aircraft Establishment gave the new arrivals a quick briefing on where the unlucky B-17 had come down and what they could expect to find at the location. Then it was back to the flight line where the Sikorskys had since been pulled out of the hangar and readied.

Because each helicopter could only carry two passengers, the Norwegians were left behind on the first trip. Lacey and Cox went in one; Atkinson and Herrmann in the other. The rattling, vibrating machines took a mere fifteen minutes to reach the crash site, located in a valley of the Berwyn Mountains.

The Fortress had landed "roughly" according to the British, which meant one of its wings had been sheared off during the crash. What remained of the battered aircraft came to rest partly in a glade after plowing through a fair portion of the surrounding forest.

"In actuality, it's really quite a miracle that this much of your aeroplane survived intact," said the officer in charge at the site. "I was rather surprised at what we found when we reached here. If it had come down on the Salisbury Plain it might still be flyable."

"Yes, it's a pity it hadn't," Lacey responded, "but we'd still be salvaging her in any event. Have you ascertained whether or not the Fortress is safe to go in yet?"

"We've drained what fuel remained out of her tanks and, since it was only on a local flight, there are no bombs or live ammunition to remove. Yes, I'd say what's left of your bomber is reasonably safe to enter. If you care to know, the aeroplane's starboard wing is approximately one hundred and fifty feet back in the woods, wrapped around a giant oak."

Lacey ordered Atkinson to examine the severed wing while he took Cox and Sergeant Herrmann through the fuselage. They hunted for whatever could be salvaged; quickly building a list of what was and what wasn't. Herrmann ran through it when they returned to the cockpit.

"We got a basic 'F' model B-17 here, sir. Which means we're not going to get a chin turret nor any Cheyenne tail guns, fittings or gun sight. And we ain't going to get a ball turret either. It was ripped out by the crash and looks like a metal pancake. What we can strip off her is the top turret, all the armor plate, some of the electric motors and instruments. But there's a lot of things we can't use. A lot of systems were changed between the F and G model. The G has mostly all-electric and electronic systems. It's almost as if they were two completely different airplanes."

"Doesn't sound like this will be a very successful

outing," said Cox. "We will not and cannot obtain enough equipment from this wreck to make one of your B-17 mother ships battleworthy. I hope we shall be more successful in the future."

"Don't worry, we will," Lacey promised, uneasily. "You can't expect big things to happen in so short a time. Let's see what Frank has to say about the right wing. We'll take whatever we can get and leave. No matter how little that is, it will still help us."

Atkinson reported that nothing of use could be salvaged off the mangled wing. Not the propellers—they had been curled into bizarre shapes during the crash—or the engines, which were a different version of the Wright Cyclone, could be used. Several minutes later, the helicopters clattered back onto the scene with the Norwegians. Lacey put them to work at once removing the items he wanted.

"If you guys have enough fuel, I'd like you to stick around until we have a few things to transport," Lacey requested. "Did they give you cargo nets and slings back at your base?"

"Roger, Colonel, we were supplied with everything you mentioned," responded the more senior of the two helicopter pilots. "They informed us you have had some limited experience with transporting cargoes by these machines. I certainly hope so; we've only been flying the Hoverfly for the last two months. We're still learning what they are capable of and what they are not."

"Yes, why don't you stay here and I'll send over my most experienced officer in these things." Lacey turned and hurried back to the wreck where he collared Atkinson for the duty. "I know you don't know much more than me but you hung around those people at Muroc more often than I did. You must've picked up something along the way. If you

112

can't recall what to do, Frank, just do the most logical thing you can think of."

Herrmann already had the Norwegians working at detaching the top turret and removing the armor plate. The total weight of the plating was over a thousand pounds. The turret, with its machine guns, gun sight, gunner's seat and bicycle-like operating controls came in at around six hundred pounds. Together they were the heaviest items to be salvaged from the B-17, also the bulkiest. Everything else, the motors and instruments, were too small for the nets. They would have to be carried in the helicopters' cockpits. But not on the first trip; only a few had been removed by the time the Sikorskies were ready to fly back.

"We've jury-rigged these things as best we could, Colonel," said Atkinson, as Lacey inspected his work. "I did everything I can remember those guys at Muroc doing and then some. The pilots and I found a way to hook a safety release to the cargo net, so it can be triggered by a line we've run into the cockpit."

The helicopters had landed inside the glade and took up most of the available space. Their whirling rotor blades demanded it or they would decapitate a man as cleanly as a razor severing a flower's blossom from its stem. Lacey and Atkinson had only seen such an accident happen once; they were determined not to have it occur again.

After the nets had been loaded and rigged, they ordered everyone back to the tree line or the vicinity of the wrecked Fortress. Everyone except themselves.

"All I can tell you guys is to fly level and slow," Lacey advised. "Make all your turns wide and easy and fly no faster than fifty to sixty miles an hour. If you feel your loads start to swing like a yo-yo, or are dragging you to one side, then release them at once.

We can always find another turret and, if need be, we can weld old boiler plates onto our bombers."

"Understood, Colonel. But could you tell me what, exactly, a yo-yo is?" asked one of the pilots. "I don't think I ever heard of it before. Is it some kind of device?"

"No, it's really a kind of toy. It's based on the principle of the pendulum and centrifugal force. You see, you throw it from your hand and it comes back." To illustrate what he meant, Lacey flicked his wrist over and opened his hand as if he were throwing down something.

"You mean you bounce it off the ground and catch it?"

"No, you control the toy with a piece of string you wind up inside it."

"How do you control it when the string is inside?"

"No, no. The string isn't really inside, you see it's between the yo-yo and the . . . Well, it's . . . Well the string is . . . Never mind. Just get in your planes and get ready for takeoff. We'll direct you by hand signals." Then, once the two pilots were out of earshot, Lacey sighed, "Why couldn't they have asked me to explain something easy. Like a TV camera or the process of video transmission."

The lead helicopter was the first to switch-on. It carried the heavier armor plate sections and if it could fly, surely the other, hauling the lighter turret components, would. The main rotor blades vanished into a shimmering, silver disc and the frail machine rose on the cushion of powerful downwash they created.

For the first fifty feet, the lead Sikorsky climbed effortlessly; until the cargo net support cable became taut. Lacey motioned for the pilot to show his ascent as his aircraft took on the extra weight of the armor plate. The helicopter yawed slightly while he changed the trim and pitch of the rotor blades. Once the load had been accommodated, the Sikorsky continued to rise, climbing above the trees and heading slowly toward Aberporth.

A minute later the second helicopter lifted-off. Its lighter cargo swung a bit more than the other and turned in the slipstream. But it was able to climb a little faster and when last seen, was speeding off to catch its leader.

They were gone for nearly an hour. On their return, Lacey had everything else he felt his team could use removed from the wreck. This time there was no need for the cargo net and slings, just cockpit floor space. The compact electric motors for the cowl flaps, control surfaces, ball turret and a myriad of other systems; and the instruments from the cockpit were stowed as securely as was possible.

Again the helicopters carried no passengers: not because of weight restrictions; this time there wasn't enough room inside for anyone except the pilots. The machines departed for the third and last time, leaving all the men they had ferried in to take another way out.

"Does this mean we're going to have to walk, Colonel?" complained Atkinson, though not seriously. "I was told I wouldn't have to walk anywhere when I joined the Army Air Force. Hell, isn't that why they gave us these funny brown shoes instead of combat boots?"

"No, you know why they gave them to us," answered Lacey, "so we couldn't tell the difference when we were standing in shit. The officer in charge of the Royal Air Force detail says he has vehicles waiting a few hundred yards down that path over there. We don't have too far to walk. And most of it is downhill."

Downhill almost came to mean off a cliff as Lacey, Cox and their men ran, or tumbled, down an ever steeper incline. At the bottom they literally collided with one of the trucks that had brought in the R.A.F.

"Now I see why you wanted to use those vertical-landing machines," said Cox, once he had caught his breath. "My God, we very nearly killed ourselves just walking off this bloody hill. I hate to think what it would've been like to move a half ton of armour plate and a machine gun turret across it."

"I think the commander's right," agreed Atkinson, still gasping. "That mountain's a killer. I worked up more of a sweat coming down it than when I helped pry off that turret. Those helicopters were great, but why didn't you have them come back for us?"

"Because they couldn't," said Lacey, "they had reached their limit of flying hours for the day. The helicopter is still very much an experimental aircraft and it has a lot of limitations. They need twice as many man-hours of maintenance as a normal airplane. Those rotor heads need to be lubricated after every twenty or so flying hours. They're going to have to undergo much more development work before they become really practical. Let's go see which one of these trucks will drive us back to Aberporth."

They arrived at the Royal Aircraft Establishment exactly an hour after the helicopters had landed. All the equipment that had been salvaged off the wreck was laid next to the visiting Fortress. Stowing it all was wisely left to Lacey's crew and it took a little ingenuity to stuff the bulkier items inside the bomber.

Instead of removing one of the windows from a waist gun station, the bomb bay doors were opened and the prizes transferred through the door to the radio operator's compartment. The flat and curved armor plate sections proved easy to move and stow. The top turret had to be further dismantled. The machine guns, gun mounts and feed chutes were all removed before the plexiglas bird cage was squeezed through the narrow door.

The B-17 did not depart once the loading had been completed. The ground staff at Aberporth insisted on treating its crew and passengers to a late lunch before finally allowing them to leave.

"What do you expect we are going to find on our return to Blackburn?" Cox asked Lacey, after takeoff and the Fortress had climbed to cruise altitude.

"We'd better find three B-17s outfitted to act as mother ships or there will be hell to pay. Whether or not they're armed, we're going to start flying test runs tomorrow. I'll also expect to find several Hudsons ready to be expended as test ships. If I don't find those two things, I'm gonna light a fire under somebody's ass and make everyone pull an all-nighter."

"All-nighter? I suppose that's another one of your American slang terms. Does it mean what I believe it means? Working throughout the night to complete some task?"

"Yes, but it's really college slang and it means exactly what you said. It's something I rarely did when I was in school; since joining the Air Force it has become SOP."

Somewhere over the Grampian Range, Lacey and the others found out what, exactly, had been happening at Blackburn when they were intercepted by a scruffy-looking Lockheed Hudson apparently flying without a pilot.

The obsolescent patrol bomber dove on the cruising Fortress from behind, passing wide on its

117

left side and climbing out ahead of it. Next the Hudson circled around the Boeing, giving everyone a clear view of its empty cockpit, then slowly moved to take up a position on its left wing. The maneuver was not as smooth as a pilot could have made it; it lacked a certain finesse, but those who had no previous experience with radio control had just been given a vivid demonstration of its capabilities.

"How'd you like that, Colonel?" asked Capollini, the B-17 mother ship at last becoming visible; descending to join the formation. "Flies great, doesn't it?"

"Certainly does, how many drones have you prepared?" Lacey requested, keeping his own B-17 a safe distance from the pilotless aircraft.

"We got three ready to go and two more in the shop being outfitted. We also have all three mother ships ready to go. It got real easy to do after a while, until we started to run out of parts, that is."

"Don't worry over that, Vince. Commander Cox says there will soon be a shipment of electronics from Alexandra Palace. What you'd better start worrying about is how you are going to bring this drone down safely. I'm not about to let you waste one of these on some stunt."

"Oh the pilot's still in the Hudson, Colonel. He's back at the radio man's station. I'll tell you what you'd better start worrying about. That redheaded aide of the commander's is real steamed about you leaving today. She was madder than hell for a long time and don't bet on her being calmed down by the time you land either."

"God, no. After all the months I've spent with her you would think I wouldn't forget to tell her," sighed Cox. "It's my fault and it's really unforgivable."

"Well, it's not entirely your fault," said Lacey, "I

118

could've told her a lot easier than you could."

"Indeed now, how could you have when her room is on the same floor as mine? Not yours."

"Then perhaps it really is your fault. In any case I hope you can handle Connie. I really don't know her well enough to even try."

"Not quite, not quite. Connie isn't the type of person one can pull rank on or use the heavy stick of strict discipline to quiet. No, a naval procedure would be the best way to handle her. Rig for heavy seas and ride out the storm. Actually, I think what she's truly mad at is that we left her with the rest of your oversexed Yanks and those infatuated Norwegians. I'll explain it to you later."

"Lacey to crew, prepare for takeoff. The tower has given us final clearance. Lacey to Aphrodite Controller, make sure all your systems are on standby, Andy. I don't want to have another drone running off the runway because someone in the mother ship forgot to secure his controls."

Flight training was about to begin. And with all three mother ships and more than enough drones ready to go, today would be a maximum effort mission.

Lacey's B-17 was the first to depart. Nicknamed "Eight Ball's Revenge," the bomber carried virtually the same markings as Careful Virgin; bright red wing tips, tail fin bands and stabilizers. Only the unit identification letters and the squadron codes carried on the fuselage sides were different, the result of belonging to the same First Air Division but to different bomb groups inside it; in this case the 381st and 91st groups.

The third mother ship came from another air division and wore far plainer markings. "Fortress

Apache," also the third and last B-17 awaiting takeoff, had the simple, black tail fin square of the 100th Bomb Group, Third Air Division.

Eight Ball's Revenge thundered down the runway moments after Lacey gave his warning. At half-minute intervals following its departure, Careful Virgin and Fortress Apache lifted into the air as well. Climbing at a pre-set rate and flying at roughly the same speed, they began a ballet-like maneuver in order to join up. Each performed an identical, one hundred and eighty degree turn about ten seconds after the aircraft in front commenced its own.

All Lacey needed to do was reverse course and hold Eight Ball level; his wing men were required to work a little harder. Atkinson swung Careful Virgin under him and climbed onto Lacey's right wing. Capollini kept the nose of Fortress Apache ahead of the lead B-17 and made a slightly tighter turn than the other two. He pulled abreast of Lacey, then settled into his left wing position.

By the time the formation droned back over Blackburn, the second element of the mission was just lifting off. The three smaller Hudsons took off together, the runway's width providing enough room to make it possible. The trio spread their vee wider once they left the ground and started their climb out. At fifteen hundred feet, five hundred below the Fortresses and several hundred feet in front of them, the Lockheeds leveled off and separated even further.

"Mother Ship Leader to Drone Pilots. Standby to activate radio control systems. Lacey to Aphrodite Controller, Andy, check your equipment and report back on status. Lacey to Wing Men, have your Controllers check their equipment and report back to me on their status."

"Controller to Nose and Tail Gunners. I'm going to be taking command of our drone in the next few minutes. Report to me at once if you see anything unusual happening to it, everybody else you tell second. Controller to Lacey, television camera activated, all video systems are go. Flight control systems activated and all are go. Warhead arming systems remain on standby. Everything's go at this end, what's doing at the other end?"

For Martinez, the answer came through on the system display panel he was sitting at long before Lacey could tell him. A line of bright lights snapped on, matching the row he had activated. He was now in command of the Hudson and would fly it once he got word to unlock the controls.

"Lacey to Aphrodite controller, drone pilot reports all systems have been turned on. Everything is go at that end as well. You may take command of the aircraft after the pilot has bailed out. Lacey to Wing Men, status reports acknowledged. Contact the pilots of your individual drones and have your controllers prepare to take command."

In the space of a few seconds, all three pilots abandoned the Hudsons. The obsolescent patrol bombers wavered a bit when Martinez and the other two controllers unlocked the miniature joy stick, throttle levers and flap handles.

"Lacey to waist gunners, you can tell our passengers they are now free to wander wherever they want to for approximately the next hour, until we arrive at the test range when they'll have to get out of our way."

This time Constance made sure she got to go along. Because the nose was occupied by its gunner and the navigator, she and Cox had to ride out the takeoff in the waist section. Now, however, they had the run of the ship; though at first there was only one place either of them wanted to be: the radio operator's compartment.

"I must admit, even this fascinates me," said Cox, watching Martinez fly an aircraft several hundred feet below him. "Leftenant, would you be able to tell me something about this equipment you and Colonel Lacey developed?"

"Charles, don't bother him," admonished Constance. "I'll tell you what you want to know. Dennis told me quite a bit concerning what he and his men built."

"No reason for you to bother, ma'am," said Martinez, "I don't really have to work this hard. See."

He tapped one of the many buttons on his panel and activated the drone's auto-pilot. The flight controls were immediately locked into their current positions while all the systems that could affect the drone's performance now refused to respond to any command given them—at least until the auto-pilot was switched off.

"So long as I don't have to change course, I don't have to touch a thing," continued Martinez. "Ask me whatever you want, Commander. But I should tell you right off the bat that I didn't help the colonel develop anything. I just solved a few problems and put some of this stuff together."

Still, he knew the equipment well enough to answer all the questions Cox fired at him. No controls for landing the aircraft? None needed, who wanted to land a plane filled with twenty-five thousand pounds of volatile, high explosive? Is the television monitor the only way of observing the drone's flight? No, there was the information supplied by the radio altimeter, airspeed indicator and artificial horizon.

"These were instruments that the colonel either perfected or developed on his own," said Martinez, indicating the trio of gauges. "Of course they've all been around for some time but the colonel had to find a way to make them transmit their information to the controller. And he had to make them easy to install too. They give me more of a feeling that I'm really flying the plane. They're great even though we've had trouble because of them."

"Trouble? You mean technical malfunctions?" asked Cox.

"No, sir. I mean trouble, trouble. Those assholes we had to work with from the Eighth Air Force fought with us over using them. Well, I should say only one of those bastards fought us but he was the boss, Colonel Brogger. He simply refused to believe in them. We sweated blood working out their bugs back at Muroc and this bastard never let us install the equipment or even bench test it."

"Brogger? Oh yes, he was the officer you 'gave' a tear gas grenade to. A pity you were caught. Though you may not believe me, I do understand and appreciate your punitive retribution on an intransigent superior. I must admit I have a more sophisticated approach to settling a score, however."

"Sophisticated? Yeah, I suppose that's why you're a lieutenant-commander and I'm just a second lieutenant. And I don't suppose they threw you in jail at the end, either."

"No, but it would be safe to say there are those who would dearly love to lock me away," Cox admitted, before he was cut off.

"Lacey to controller, prepare for course change of about forty degrees north. I have been unable to locate our passengers, are they back there with you, Andy?"

"Sure thing, Colonel," said Martínez. "Why? Do you want them?"

"Yes, since you'll be busy for a little while have them come up here. They'll get a better view of the planes."

Because the recovered turret had yet to be installed, the flight deck had sufficient room to accommodate the two guests. By standing right behind the pilots' seats, Cox and Constance could peer out the aftermost cockpit windows.

"Now I have some idea as to what a formation containing hundreds of these bombers must look like," Cox noted, admiringly. "And here I used to think a handful of Swordfish was an impressive sight. This is quite amazing."

"Wait till we get the top turret put in and you'll really have a good view," said Lacey; "of course it will be partially blocked by the machine guns and the sight. Let's see, Lacey to navigator, have we reached the point?"

"Navigator here, fifteen seconds to turning point."

"Good. Lacey to wing men, execute turn, now. Frank will lead as planned. Lacey to controller, here we go."

Atkinson's B-17 broke first. Careful Virgin's wings barely tipped more than ten degrees from the horizon line and the barn door-sized rudder seemed to scarcely move. Still, the gentle bank produced the desired results as the Fortress slid through a shallow turn. The other two Boeing giants followed suit and all three moved smoothly, as if locked on sets of invisible rails. Their charges performed the same maneuver a little more erratically. Dipping and climbing, swaying and slipping, all except one.

"Nose Gunner to controller! Dive your aircraft at once! One of the other planes is not turning!"

The nose gunner did not complete his last sentence before Martinez reacted. He banged the joy stick forward and watched on the monitor as a shadow passed swiftly over his Hudson's cockpit. From the direction it came, even the fact that he had to work to avoid his drone's destruction, Martinez knew which of the other two had failed to respond. Careful Virgin's.

"Lacey to Atkinson, what the hell's going on over there? Your drone damn near rammed mine and Vince's."

"I don't know what's going on here, Colonel. None of us does. Least of all Davis, he's working like mad to make the plane respond to his gear but it's no go."

"All right, Frank, I'll see if I can't get you some help. Lacey to controller. Andy, have you been listening to this? Do you think you can help Davis find his problem?"

"Yeah, yeah, just as soon as I get my plane leveled out. If I don't we'll have one gone for sure."

"Lacey to waist and tail gunners. Track that Hudson that failed to turn and report if it makes any changes."

It didn't. The twin-engined bomber continued to fly on serenely and, at a cruising speed of two hundred miles an hour, quickly became a tiny silhouette against the far clouds. Soon it would be out of sight and winging blindly into the North Atlantic.

"Frank, you'd better go after it or it'll fly beyond control range," Lacey warned. "I will give you five minutes to regain control before I order the plane destroyed."

After acknowledging his commander's last message, Atkinson banked his Fortress, more steeply this time, and climbed over the other two B-17s. He re-set the mixture controls while his co-pilot increased propeller rpm to the desired levels; then he grabbed the triple-runged throttle quadrant and added power. Brief plumes of dark smoke shot out the engine exhaust stacks and the bomber bolted off in pursuit of its errant charge.

"Lacey to Stanmoor Leader, we have an apparent runaway on our hands. The mother ship has gone to get it but recovery is doubtful. How many aircraft are with you?"

"Stanmoor Leader, here. I have four aircraft including my own. How many do you need?"

"Only one will be necessary, Stanmoor Leader. Your target is a Lockheed Hudson, coded CY-X. You may take up position but do not open fire until I give permission. Lacey to Atkinson, how is the recovery going?"

"Nowhere, Colonel. This plane hasn't moved an inch since we started tryin'. I've had the crew check our equipment here and Lieutenant Davis says everything in this plane is working fine. So the problem is in the drone."

"Which means it is either something simple, like a loose connection, or something complex, like a total system breakdown," Lacey mentioned to the guests in the cockpit. "Lacey to Atkinson, break off your attempt to regain control. I'm going to have the fighters come in and destroy the plane."

"Aw, come on, Colonel. We haven't tried everything yet. Let me try tapping it with my wing tip."

"No way, Frank, that's one risk I'm not going to let you take. You can't fix every machine by just kicking it. Now break off, I'm ordering the Brits to shoot down your drone. Lacey to Stanmoor Leader, you may proceed."

Before flight training was set to begin, Lacey had contacted all the fighter squadrons and operational training units in Scotland to provide an escort. Nothing special but he just wanted to make sure that any local flights or sorties would be on call, in case of an emergency—such as this one.

Stanmoor flight was from one of the Royal Air Force's OTU's. Equipped with Mark Fives and early-model Mark Nine spitfires, the unit was the last stage a fledgling fighter pilot went through prior to being assigned to a front line squadron. The four aircraft had been on their way to a gunnery range when Lacey first alerted them. Now they were holding position far to the right of the B-17s; orbiting slowly about a thousand yards out.

For the first seconds following Lacey's command, nothing appeared to happen to the fighters. Suddenly, the outermost pair broke formation as they wheeled around and shot past the bombers; banking steeply to show off their slim fuselages and classic, elliptical wings.

Atkinson also broke formation; just as sharply but with a little reluctance, he swung his Fortress away from the drone, abandoning its fate to the pair of incoming Spitfires.

"Stanmoor Leader to Stanmoor Two, I feel as though I've already shot down my quota of aeroplanes. You may have this one. I'm giving you a chance most students don't receive. So don't muck it up, just shoot the plane down."

Leader and wing man changed positions, the student charged ahead and, overeager as they always are, started firing before he computed his lead or estimated his range.

"No, no, no! You've just made every mistake a neophyte could make! Now come around and try it again. And next time be sure to use your cannons as well as your machine guns."

Next time the wing man did enough things right to send his streams of shells and bullets sparkling along the Hudson's deep-bellied fuselage. The stricken bomber began to waver unsteadily and lose altitude but it did not fall. On the third pass, a long burst mangled its left engine and finally, sliding off on its wing, the drone plummeted toward the Hebrides Sea.

Chapter Six
DISCOVERY
THE SECOND OPERATION

Reduced to being a mere observer frustrated Atkinson to no end. He hovered around the other two B-17s while they made their test runs, then hurried off to inspect the results once the last drone was flown up Loch Seaforth and successfully slammed against the target island.

"Should he not have asked for permission before leaving?" Cox inquired. "In the Fleet Air Arm we had to."

"I'm willing to overlook it this time," said Lacey, "though not if he buzzes any villages or airfields on the way home. He needs, and his whole crew probably needs, to blow off steam. I'd rather have them be insubordinate now and beat up some remote island than go off base tonight and wreck some bar. Everything will be okay by tomorrow, when we fly our next mission."

Less than twelve hours later, a cold front swept over the British Isles, grounding even the sea gulls. Neither the Eighth Air Force nor the Royal Air Force's Bomber Command flew any of their scheduled missions for the next two days. Only the odd anti-submarine flight and lone weather reconnaissance sortie would lift into the gray overcast and subject themselves to the buffeting of the front's storm cells. Ironically, the blizzard and zero visibility over most of Great Britain was to help in the effort to rearm the team's B-17s, when they combined with a little bad luck to force down a pair of Fortresses on an island in the Inner Hebrides.

"Yes, Commander, I happen to have a report on the incident right here," responded the officer in charge of the Operations center. He then proceeded to root noisily through a desk file, making Cox hang on for a nearly infuriating length of time. "Here we go, Commander. The two planes involved were part of a group being ferried in from Iceland. They had been delayed there for a couple of days and were eager to leave. The formation departed under marginal conditions, which soon deteriorated. Some turned back but most continued on, though by the time what remained reached England, they had become completely lost.

"Only one of the bombers managed to land at the designated ferry point. The rest sat down at fields all around Scotland and Northern Ireland. One developed engine trouble before finding a base to land at and had to use a bog on Eigg Island. Another of the Fortresses heard its distress calls and tried to land to pick up the crew. However, it too became mired in the same bog."

"Has the Army Air Force been informed about all this?" Cox asked; "what's become of those crews?"

"The bomber crews hiked to a farm close by and now they are being housed at the island's Coast Guard station until the local ferry arrives. The Eighth Air Force has not been informed as to what's happened nor will it be prior to that ferry reaching the mainland. Those were your standing orders, weren't they, sir?"

"Correct, correct. Now, find out if there's an

airfield or any sort of landing facilities on the island and what kind of transport will be available to us. Ring me back when you have all that. As before, don't worry about the Americans staying with me, I'll ring them."

In between his hurried attempts to wash and dress as quickly as possible, Cox got the return call he expected from the Operations center. It was not exactly what he had wanted to hear. Eigg Island was a primitive place, no airfield or even a landing strip and no vehicles to speak of. Just a few animal-drawn carts and wagons. Getting to the stranded Boeings would be fairly hard, removing the needed items would be next to impossible.

Still, Cox had proved in the past that he was resourceful and feverishly worked out some ideas to answer the problems; at least he hoped they would. Somewhere in the middle of it all, he forgot about calling Lacey before heading down to see him. However, Cox did remember to stop by Constance's room to let her know what would be happening that day, unlike the last time, only to find her quarters empty.

"Frightfully neat," he observed, taking in the crisply made bed and spotless bathroom. She must be down in the officer's mess, he thought, then ran for the stairway.

At the first floor landing, Cox stopped momentarily to pull the wrinkles out of his jacket. By accident he hit the exit door with his elbow, which knocked it open a few inches and allowed him a limited view of the hall outside. From the far end, he heard another door open and click shut. Then it opened again and a pair of heavy feet bounded down the hall for a short distance.

"Here, honey, you forgot these," said a hushed,

familiar voice. "I think they're the last things we would like my men to find lying around my room."

Cox managed a brief glimpse out the door and immediately identified the couple. At first he wanted to barge out on them but thought of a different, much better plan. He retreated away from the exit, back into the shadows by the staircase. There Cox waited for the door to fully open and begin to close before acting.

"Leftenant Smythe?" It was all he needed to say.

Constance nearly jumped out of the uniform she was loosely wearing. She gave a startled cry, then tried to start speaking for several seconds but her words came out in a broken, hesitant manner—not quite the way she wanted.

"Leftenant Smythe," Cox repeated, walking up to his aide and running through his fingers the nylon stockings she was clutching. "I believe you're out of uniform. Could you please explain to me why I caught you coming out of Colonel Lacey's room just now?"

"We were a bit late in rising this morning," Constance explained. "And . . . I love him, Charles. I love him more dearly than I have ever loved anyone else. I've never met a man quite like Dennis, he's so very special to me. You like him too, Charles, I know you do."

"That goes without saying. I would even admit I'm a little envious of him. The way he can command his unit so casually and yet so effectively. Connie, I hope you realize the kind of trouble this behavior can land you in?"

"I'll still do my job just as well as before, Charles. No one beyond us need ever find out, so long as I am covered. And I quite distinctly recall the many times last year I had to cover for you when you were courting your wife."

"Yes, indeed. All right," Cox relented. He too remembered the potentially embarrassing incidents which Constance helped to hide from their superiors. "Anyway, I should've known you would fall in love with a man like Dennis. You're about the only woman I know whose forte is technology. It simply stands to reason you'd be drawn to a man who talks more of cathode ray tubes and guidance systems than of romance and passion. It never did work on you."

"Why talk about something that you can show so much better? I realized I loved him when the hours I spent talking with him seemed to pass like minutes. I kissed him first and from there we couldn't stop."

"Sounds to me like the current line about Americans being oversexed is rather true."

"I don't think I would want him to be any other way," Constance admitted, "though I do say his eagerness will sometimes hinder things. That's why I'm late coming out of his room today. I told Dennis I wanted to leave at six o'clock but he insisted on making love to me first. I didn't have the heart or the will to refuse him."

"Indeed now, what exactly did you tell him?"

"All I said was I wanted him to knock me up at six. Which he did but then he started to make love to me right away and I couldn't stop him. Did I say anything wrong to him, Charles?"

"Not that I can ascertain," noted Cox. "It must have been something you did. Perhaps I will try to find out when I talk to him, though not right away."

"Charles, you wouldn't! Would you?"

"Oh but I should; as your commanding officer, I am the nearest thing you have on this base to a father. And a father must look after his charges and a commanding officer must tell them there may be an

133

operation today, this time you won't be left behind. I suggest you hurry on to your room and dress properly. While you may be in love, you are still an officer in His Majesty's Navy."

Cox found Lacey in the middle of taking a shower. At least he would get a thorough washing today. Above the hiss of the water streams, Cox was able to communicate the basics of his latest developments.

"You mean there are two Forts down on that island?" Lacey asked, ending his shower so he could hear the response better. "What condition are they in?"

"The first one apparently made a wheels-up landing and the other a letter-perfect touchdown only to sink into the bog after it came to a halt. Neither is very badly damaged, in fact both could fly again if they could be pulled out of the mire intact and onto dry land."

"Here, Charlie, hand me a towel. If what you're telling me is true, then we'd better get moving if we're to salvage anything. Never underestimate what the Army Corps of Engineers can do."

"Yes, we in the British Isles are well aware of what your engineers are capable of doing," said Cox stepping back a little, so Lacey could have the room he needed once he came out of the shower. "But short of building a complete runway, these aircraft cannot be removed. They're in the middle of a peat bog, not some farmer's field. The only solid ground is a narrow road that cuts through the area and some of the larger stream beds. The whole island is rather primitive and not even the most rudimentary airstrip exists."

"Then how do you propose we get to it?" asked Lacey, at last making his exit from the shower. "By boat?"

"You almost have it right. We'll go in by flying boat. I've put a message through to Wing Commander Holmen, seeing if we can't use one of his Catalina aircraft for today. If this rotten weather really does start to break, that is."

By sunrise, the weather system that had remained over England for the last forty-eight hours was on its way out. A weak, distant sun broke through the deteriorating cloud cover and, by mid-morning, so did a gray-green mottled PBY from Leuchars.

It stayed at Blackburn only long enough to take on additional fuel and a dozen extra passengers. Then it was off again for a leisurely, one hour flight to one of the lesser islands among the Inner Hebrides. Once over Eigg Island itself, the Catalina did not have to search the mushroom-shaped rock long to find the downed B-17s.

From fifteen hundred feet, the two bright silver Fortresses did not appear to be damaged. Only at a closer, near tree top altitude could the curled propeller blades and wrinkled skin on one of the bombers be seen.

"That's the one that belly landed," said Lacey, pointing it out to the other passengers who were using the same side blister to view the crash scene. "You can see the single, deep furrow its fuselage made when it came in. Those surface wrinkles probably means there's structural damage. I don't think that Fort can ever fly again."

"How long will it take you to remove what you need from those two planes?" Cox asked.

"Depends on what there is to work with once we get down. But, with the crew we already have here, it shouldn't take us any longer than the rest of today. Only, how are we going to move everything off the island once we've gathered it all together?"

"No need to worry, I have contacted someone who has promised me he will be sending us help shortly. At least I hope so."

The Catalina made one more pass over the crash site before heading east to find the island's Coast Guard station and a calm patch of sea to land on. A single power launch came out to greet the big amphibian. It needed to make several trips to bring in the entire team Lacey and Cox had brought along. Worse yet, there were only a few bicycles and horse-drawn carts for transport to the site. The improbable caravan that was formed seemed to take longer to reach the bog than it took the PBY to originally fly to the island.

On the ground, the two Fortresses were a most impressive sight. Factory fresh, there was not a mark on them apart from their national insignia, the serial number on the tail fin and the olive drab anti-glare panels. No painted wing tips or tail planes, no squadron codes or division symbols. The bombers were pure, their bare metal surfaces almost glowed in the mid-morning sun. Nothing on them had been touched, not by the Coast Guard personnel who came to watch over the planes or the civilians drawn to the area; even the doors were still open.

For a half hour Lacey, Capollini and all the Norwegians they brought along with them climbed through the two B-17s. Taking stock of what they could use and planning how to remove it all. Cox and Constance preferred to wait on the road, the one piece of truly solid, dry ground in the entire area.

"I now see why you suggested we wear our flying boots instead of our regular shoes," said Lacey, returning to the carts. "It's like trying to walk on top of a mud slide out there. Which leads me to ask, why aren't you two out helping us?"

"We are helping you, Dennis," Cox protested. "We're worrying about when that aid I was promised will arrive."

"I hope it comes soon. While we've got the tools to remove what we need, this kind of transport is useless. They aren't sturdy enough to carry the armor plate or large enough for the really bulky items, like props."

"You mean propellers? You mean you're going to actually remove the propellers from these aircraft?"

"Just the ones from the Fort that made the more normal landing," Lacey explained, "the others are useless. Hell, we'd take the engines if we could but they're too heavy to move. I'm sure they'd sink anything into the bog we would use to carry them."

"Charles, Dennis, I think I hear something approaching us. It sounds like an aeroplane but not any I've heard."

The throbbing noise seemed to beat the air itself. One could almost feel the source draw near as well as hear it. Gradually, the sounds of more than one machine became discernible and Lacey at last could identify what Cox had been able to call in.

"The director of flight operations at RAE Aberporth, has turned over to us their complete development flight of Sikorsky R-4 Hoverflies," said Cox. "That's six machines in all. Though I have worries as to how many of them have actually made the long flight from North Wales."

Like giant dragonflies, the two helicopters darted over the bog and dropped down to closely inspect the mired B-17s. Their now deafening clatter caused the horses to bolt and carry off with them the carts and their owners. Even some of the civilians scattered at the sight of the strange, fearsome-looking machines. Using hand signals, Cox and Lacey guided them to landings on the crude, irregular dirt road.

"Did you see how those farmers ran when the helicopters appeared?" Cox asked, once their engines were shut off.

"Yes; who knows, we may have found another role for this bird," said Lacey, "crowd control. Okay, you've solved the problem at this end but what about getting the stuff to Blackburn? I hope you don't think these things can fly all the way across Scotland, dangling a thousand pounds or so of deadweight under them."

"I know they can't. You yourself told me they could not. So I made arrangements with the Royal Aircraft Establishment for additional transport. I couldn't obtain anything from either His Majesty's Navy or the Royal Air Force on such a short notice. Dakotas are in such a premium that even training squadron aircraft are used on operations. So I've had to do with something less but not a lot less. Let's go see from the pilots if 'Annie' is on time."

During the trip from Aberporth, Annie carried spares for the Sikorskies in case they were to break down, not an infrequent incident with what was still a very experimental aircraft. Before heading on to the mainland RAF base they would all use, she had to pay a call at the crash site; according to Cox's orders.

"I'll admit she isn't the most advanced aeroplane in the world," he noted, when the transport made its appearance. "She is very reliable, as the Germans have found out."

To her former masters in the Luftwaffe, she was known as Iron Annie but to her new English owners, the Junkers trimotor was simply called "Annie." Heralded by the steady, deep rumble of its three BMW radials, the Ju-52 sedately pounced on the site. The boxy, angular-winged giant floated in over the B-17s; for a moment it made everyone who didn't know of its arrival think the Germans were going to invade. Those who had guns were ready to fire, until Cox and Lacey stopped them.

"Jeez, Colonel, how was I to know?" Capollini asked, climbing off the B-17 wing he was going to use as a firing platform. "How come you guys didn't get a Gooney Bird? Why do you have to use a kraut plane?"

"Believe it or not, it was easier to get the Junkers than a C-47," Lacey explained. "Perhaps I should let Commander Cox tell you the whys and hows. He's the one who coordinated all this in the first place."

The Ju-52 made one more pass before departing for the RAF base, where the other four helicopters of Aberporth's development flight were preparing to join the operation.

"Considering the type of reception that Nazi tin-box almost got here," said Capollini, still holding onto his forty-five automatic. "I hope someone has told that RAF base to expect it. They got lots bigger guns than this."

"No need to worry, Captain, the station is well aware of its impending arrival," Cox answered, "though I doubt it was all that necessary. I recall how the Royal Air Force managed to obtain its first flyable example of the Focke-Wulf 190. It landed at their Pembrey field after its pilot mistook it for a similar Luftwaffe channel coast base. The duty flying control officer at Pembrey in turn mistook the Focke-Wulf for a Hawker Hurricane and allowed it to land normally. He didn't realize what had happened until the ground crew put in a request for a detail of security guards."

"Will you put away your gun, Vince," Lacey ordered, finally. "You're more of a danger playing with that than when you play with a B-17. Now let's start working on these two. I've decided we're going to remove the armor plating first. Except for the ball turret, they will be the heaviest loads we'll have. And the most difficult ones to move out of this swamp."

The individual sections weren't the largest items to be removed from the Fortresses but because of their high weight, they caused anyone handling them to sink up to their knees in the soft earth. It took the strong, hefty Norwegians an hour to move the sections a mere fifty-odd yards to the road where cargo nets were spread out and waiting.

This time the helicopter pilots did have some experience, however limited, in moving heavy items. They lifted off smoothly, slowing down when their aircraft took on the extra one thousand pounds of deadweight apiece. Once the pilots were sure their loads were being securely carried, the Hoverflies turned gently and moved east; gaining speed and altitude.

Next would come the gun turrets, Lacey put his crew to work removing them before the helicopters had disappeared. Each bomber would yield a top turret and a chin turret, the one on the wrecked Fortress had miraculously escaped damage during the crash, but only one could give a ball turret. Provided a way was found to salvage it.

"You see, Colonel, the Fort sank after it came to a stop," Capollini explained, "by nearly two feet. A few inches more and the tips of the propeller blades

140

will be touching ground. Which is fine for when we get around to stripping them props but not now with this here turret.

"Take a look under there, Colonel, it's halfway in the ground already. If this ship settles any deeper, we're gonna have to sink a mine shaft to get it out."

Lacey had to bend to his knees in order to get a good view of the bottom turret. Like all the others, it was minus its guns for ferry purposes. Very little of the metal and glass sphere could actually be seen; what hadn't been pushed into the bog was inside the bomber. Pinned, trapped between a thirty ton airplane and the ground, it looked impossible to rescue.

"Couldn't you say, remove it from inside the plane?" Cox ventured. "It would be the simplest way."

"Well, first there's all the support equipment right above the turret," said Lacey, "though we're going to be needing it anyway, it will have to be removed before we try to pull the turret inside. And once we've done so, how do you propose we get it out of the fuselage? The crew access door is too small, so are the waist gun hatches. You can't move it forward to the bomb bay either, the radio compartment doors are too small as well."

"I see, you'd have to rip the bloody fuselage open just to remove it. I don't think the Eighth Air Force would like that very much. What about the other bomber? You yourself said it would never fly again. I don't think it would matter much if we ripped that one apart to salvage its lower turret."

"No, it didn't survive the crash like the chin or top turrets did. While it's still relatively intact, it's been greatly compressed. I don't think you'll fit anyone bigger than a midget inside. No, this is the one we have to have, Vince; what kind of shovels do we have?"

"We've got those collapsable spades, Colonel. But hell, they won't do for digging this turret out. Their blades ain't big enough and this ground is nine-tenths water and one-tenth mud. What we need is one of them machines with a scoop on the back."

"What you could use are coal shovels," Cox suggested. "I'm willing to wager that nearly every farmer on this island has one, or something very much like it. They use them to clean out barns and horse stalls. I think we should enlist the Coast Guard personnel to help gather them. The locals will be much more willing to cooperate with people they know."

Capollini's statement regarding the soil's composition was only slightly exaggerated. While they waited for the shovels to be collected, Lacey organized some of the Norwegians to begin excavation work. Try as they might, they could not get a significant start on the watery, sponge-like earth. Lacey stopped them before they wore out.

"God damn, this must be the dirtiest job out here," Lacey observed, the lower half of his body now covered with mud. "I think this stuff is freezing to me."

"Indeed it is," said Cox, keeping a respectful distance from his friend. "Why then, are you in command of the detail? Why not your Captain? In His Majesty's Fleet, senior-ranking officers rarely assume the most unpleasant duties."

"Maybe that's why you've lost so many ships? Anyway, I know a little bit about this type of thing, Vince doesn't. My roommate in college was a

142

construction engineer. And this job will have its own rewards. You may not understand this, but I have to even the score with Vince after that stunt of his a few days ago. The one with the Hudson? Just sit back, I have it all arranged."

Several minutes later, the coast guardsmen returned carrying the long-handled, wide-bladed shovels. In less than half an hour Lacey's crew had dug a shallow, vee-shaped trench under the ball turret, removing a sizeable amount of water-saturated peat. He had them make the trench with a tapered end in the direction he wanted to move the turret. At the same time, he ordered Capollini to complete dismantling its support equipment and certain other items.

"What is he doing in there?" Cox asked, pointing at the familiar figure huddled inside the lower turret.

"He's taking out the gun sight and the controls that turn the turret," Lacey answered. "We don't want them to get damaged when we manhandle this thing across the swamp. If he's inside, that mean's he's nearly done."

Lacey knelt down beside the cramped ball of glass and steel and tapped on it to gain the occupant's attention.

"Hey, Vince, how's it doing? You through yet or not?"

"Yeah almost, Colonel. I'll be out of here in a minute. The only things holding this up are the external bolts and the safety wire."

"Good, just what I wanted." Lacey's voice became smooth and menacingly sly, he reached up and banged the side of the fuselage, three times then once. An instant later, the turret's access door was slammed shut and locked. "I hope you like the trip, Vince.

143

Hang on."

As Lacey stepped back, two of the Norwegians came forward and began to unscrew the outside bolts holding the turret in the massive, steel yoke. When they were removed, only the safety cable remained. All through the operation, Capollini shouted and protested the way Lacey had tricked him.

"This ain't fair! You let me out of here, you son-of-a-bitch, sir! Tell those goons to let me out right now! What's going to happen to my back when this thing falls? Aw, come on, Colonel, have a heart."

A repeat of the same four-part signal, a lever was thrown and the bulky sphere landed with a moist thud on the peat bog. Before it came to rest, the Norwegians were pushing it out from under the bomber. The turret cleared the fuselage by a mere inch or two and rolled, a little stubbornly at first, up the trench's gentle incline.

From there it was relatively easy to keep the sphere rolling across the soggy terrain. It had to be kept moving, for if the turret were to stop for any reason, its great weight would cause it to sink and be nearly impossible to budge.

"Roll it faster, you guys," Lacey urged, keeping pace with the detail. "Roll it faster. We're going to be needing that momentum when we reach the road and we have to get it over the embankment. How's it going, Vince?"

"You know damn well how it's going, Colonel." A little muffled, a little jumbled but Capollini's protests still came through clearly. "This thing ain't got no seat belt, you know. It ain't fair for you to trap me like this. You didn't play according to the rules."

"Since when are there rules for committing practical jokes? Apart from not landing the victim in trouble or using any of his dead relatives. You're just pissed that you didn't think up of something as good as this."

It was good, even Cox had a hearty laugh at Capollini's expense as he was bounced along toward the road. Only Constance felt some sympathy toward the captain; helping him out of the turret while all the others got in one more laugh before another pair of helicopters appeared.

They were not the same ones as the first two; those at the moment had just delivered their payloads and were still being refueled. Because of this, the pilots flying the R-4s had absolutely no experience with the operation being conducted below. It took some time until they realized that all the hand signals from the officers on the road were meant for them.

". . . And in the future, if you guys take this long to land again, I'll ask the Royal Navy to shoot you down," said Lacey, drawing to the conclusion of his briefing. "You can pass that on to the other pilots in your unit. Now man your planes and remember, even though you'll be taking off with little more than half of your machine's maximum load, it will still create a great deal of drag. Take things slowly and you'll be okay."

For their first mission, Lacey gave the novice pilots relatively light cargoes. One would carry the ball turret and the second, the massive yoke and other support equipment. Some of the smaller, more delicate items would be transported in their cockpits; all the rest, as usual, went in the nets.

The helicopters rose faster than the previous pair and their loads swung a little more but they were safely off. The most difficult recovery had been successfully completed. While what remained wouldn't be much easier, they would prove a lot cleaner to salvage.

In spite of the relative ease, the operation slowed down. Exhaustion and only one helicopter from the third flight arriving were the main causes. As Cox had earlier feared, breakdowns were starting to happen.

"Dennis, I think these men need a rest," he suggested to Lacey. "Exposure to this raw weather is having a greater effect than I had originally calculated. The men are tired, hungry, cold and soaked to the skin."

"So am I, damn it. But we all need to keep working. It's still early in the afternoon and already the shadows are starting to lengthen. And, what the hell is that?"

What Lacey called attention to was a faint, distant droning. He and Cox moved out from under the undamaged B-17's nose and scanned the horizon. They both knew it was too early for the helicopters to show up again. Whatever it was, it had to be something else.

"It's definitely one aircraft," Cox discerned. "Perhaps it's a Coastal Command flight? I believe that base the Hoverflies are using has several Wellington squadrons at it."

"No, correct me if I'm wrong but a Wellington is a twin-engined bomber. What we're hearing isn't a multi-engined airplane, it's single-engined. Which means either a trainer or a fighter. Hey, Vince, what can you see?"

Relatively speaking, Capollini held the area's high ground. He now stood in the open hole where the undamaged B-17's top turret used to be. His view was unobstructed by everything except the bomber's

146

massive tail fin. Capollini made a quick scan and immediately locked on to a remote, tiny silhouette rapidly approaching from the Atlantic Ocean.

"I got it, Colonel," he said, "it's coming out of the southwest. I'd say its altitude is one thousand feet and dropping. Whoever it is, he seems interested in us."

"How far away is he, Vince? Can you identify his nationality or the type of plane he's flying?"

"It's a fighter, radial-engined and a big one. I can't tell what country he's from but you'll be able to ask him soon. He's really barreling in."

Seconds later, the big radial fighter was easily identified as the biggest radial-engined fighter of the war. The Republic P-47 Thunderbolt, in U.S. Army Air Force markings. More visible were its bizarre unit colors. The massive cowling of the seven-ton fighter was covered with red, white and blue stripes. Black and white D-Day invasion stripes wrapped around the center section of each wing and the fuselage behind the canopy. The last most obvious touches were the bright yellow wing tips and tail plane bands.

"Get inside, Vince!" Lacey shouted, once he recognized and recalled what the markings meant. "Duck inside the plane God damnit! I'll join you there."

Lacey hid underneath the Fortress's left wing as the Republic fighter made its first pass. Cox found his behavior rather like that of a child hiding from an angry parent seeking to punish him. It would almost be funny if it were not for Lacey acting so serious about remaining unseen. Cox tried to ask him why but he moved too fast to be cornered and questioned. As soon as the Thunderbolt had flown by, he leaped to the forward crew access hatch and lifted himself inside.

"Dennis, why on earth are you playing hide and seek?" Cox was finally able to inquire, from his position under the still open hatch; he could see both Lacey and Capollini huddled inside the bomber's cockpit. "I mean, that's only one fighter up there. He is either lost or on a training flight. He's just curious about us."

"Don't bet on it," said Lacey, "that Jug isn't from a fighter group or some training outfit. It's from the Fifth Emergency Rescue Squadron. It's not curious, it's out here specifically to find these planes. Maybe we made a mistake not telling the Eighth Air Force a little more about what happened. They're going to have a lot of questions as to why the Royal Air Force is out here stripping these Forts. They will have even more questions if that pilot spots two Army Air Force officers helping them. That is why we are hiding, get the picture, Charlie?"

"I believe so; what shall we out here do?"

"Smile and wave. And once that fighter is gone, we all work our asses off. We can in fact get started now; tell Connie to go to the Coast Guard station and collect the PBY crew. Because of this discovery, we're going to have to change our plans."

The P-47 returned for a second, then a third pass. Each time it came in lower and slower than previously. For a minute Cox thought its pilot was sizing up the area for an attempted landing but on the start of a fourth pass the Thunderbolt pointed its blunt nose into the sky and roared away. As soon as they were sure it had departed, Lacey and Capollini emerged from the B-17 with their salvaging plans considerably altered.

"We can expect to see the Eighth Air Force back again in a few hours," Lacey told the assembled team. "I want us to be long gone when they do. Unfortunately, that means we're all going to have to work harder and we won't be able to take everything we'd like to.

"The next set of helicopters is due to arrive in ten or fifteen minutes. I want the two chin turrets and the remaining top turret to be ready to go. Following that, I think we'll only have enough time for one more helicopter sortie. They will take out the four propellers from this ship and maybe a few other things. After they leave, anything else we want we're going to have to carry out ourselves. Now back to work and don't feel too sorry for yourselves; we'll be getting some more help soon."

The next set of Hoverflies was in reality the first pair, with the most experienced pilots. They were the best for flying out the heavy cargoes. One of the helicopters would carry the chin turrets, minus their aft fairings, which would be carried by the other, along with the last top turret and its ancillary equipment.

Constance got back with the Catalina crew in time to see the two machines depart. She brought every member except for the pilot, who said he had more important duties.

"He refused to leave his aircraft unattended," Constance relayed to Lacey. "He said that was his first duty and claimed he could help us better by staying there."

"I suppose it's true but how the hell can he help us by sitting out in that plane on his butt?"

"He didn't precisely tell me what he would do, though he did say if you and Charles can take care of

149

the large parts on your own, he'll arrange transport for the smaller ones."

There were countless smaller items Lacey wanted to take. Electric motors mostly, for operation of the turrets, cowl flaps, de-icers, flight instruments, supercharger controls and pumps for hydraulic fluid, fuel and oil. Those plus the other pieces of equipment, such as gun sights and the flight instruments themselves, ranged in weight from just a few ounces to over a hundred pounds. Following the exhaustive removal of the undamaged Fortress's propellers, they were the only things left to salvage. Fortunately, the team did not have to remove the more than two dozen fifty caliber machine guns the bombers would have been carrying if they had been on anything other than a ferry flight to England.

Once the last flight of helicopters departed, each with a pair of twelve-foot diameter propellers dangling beneath it, Lacey put the team to work prying from the B-17s whatever they could carry, or load into a horse-drawn cart; some farmers had been persuaded to return after they were assured that the predatory-like machines would not come back again.

"Vince, how long has it been since that Thunderbolt was here?" Lacey asked.

"About two hours and nine minutes ago, Colonel. Why? Do you think it's time we should be leaving?"

"High time we should be leaving, Vince." Lacey turned to face the bombers and waved until he got Cox's attention. "Commander, bring the men who are out there with you to the road here. It's time for us to go. Unless you'd like to stick around and do a lot of explaining to the Eighth Air Force when they show up."

The half-dozen or so Norwegians still working on

the B-17s were quickly collected and brought to the spot where Lacey was supervising the loading of the carts. They came carrying all the tools the team had used and the last pieces of equipment to be salvaged.

By cart and bicycle, mostly bicycle, the tired, dirty crew started down the winding trail to the island's Coast Guard station. Only two carts were in the convoy and since they were piled high with the heavier items, they only carried two passengers apiece; Lacey and Constance in one and Capollini and Cox in the other.

"Jesus, but that was back-breaking work," said Capollini, trying to find the most comfortable riding position, and failing. "Not even them helicopters made it easy."

"I suppose that means you are as tired as a whore on Friday night?" Cox offered.

"No, but I'd sure like to have one. Right now I'd love to have a nice, hot bath, a steak this thick with onions and a woman with big yams to knock up."

"You certainly bring things down to the essentials, don't you? But why do you want a woman just to wake up? Being married, I do know of other activities that are infinitely more pleasurable than spoiling someone's rest."

"So do I, man. I mean, Commander. I don't think we're operating with the same understanding, sir. When I say knocked up, I mean what you're meaning. About them other pleasures I mean. If we want to wake up a girl, we wake her up. If we want to knock her up, we zip off our pants, hop in bed and plow away."

"I see, I see quite clearly now," Cox said reflectively and smiling lasciviously. "That explains everything Connie told me this morning."

151

"Are you talking about your big redhead? Hey, is there something going on between her and the Colonel?" Now it was Capollini's turn to wear a lustful grin.

"In His Majesty's Fleet, we never discuss a brother officer's romantic liaisons unless it affects his duties."

"Yeah but Colonel Lacey ain't in your Navy, he's in my Air Force. So, how about it, Commander?"

"Leftenant Smythe does happen to be in 'my Navy' as you put it and I wouldn't like to say anything which may hurt her. I like her too much to do that."

"Ah, yes. This time I see," Capollini alluded, still beaming his smile. "You're jealous of him, aren't you?"

"Nothing could be further from the truth," Cox said stridently, almost making it an order. Though he had to put up with suggestions of illicit affairs between him and Constance, they still made him angry and unguarded. "In point of fact, I'm rather impressed by what he's done."

"Thanks, Commander, you just answered my question."

For the remainder of the trip down to the Coast Guard station, Cox was mostly silent. Being outfoxed by a mere Army Air Force captain was frustrating to no end but he didn't want to admit it. Lacey and Constance also said little to each other, though for a different reason. They were afraid of their driver picking up a stray bit of dialogue and repeating it to one of the other men in the team; very much unlike Cox and Capollini in the cart following them.

As they neared the station, and the tiny collection of buildings which comprised the island's one true village, a familiar chorus of sounds greeted them. The deep roar and sputtering of Pratt and Whitney radials. They were coughing to life, idling, being run-up and used to taxi around the harbor. It was far too much for just one aircraft to make.

"I haven't heard such a symphony since almost a fortnight ago," said Cox, listening attentively. "Not since Leuchars. Tell me, Captain, did Consolidated ever manufacture a six-engine Catalina?"

"I don't think so. They have built a big, four-engined boat called the Coronado but I think the U.S. Navy has kept all of them. Sounds to me like there's a whole B-24 base out there; what do you think?"

"Highly impossible, no matter how good your Corps of Engineers are, they can't build a bomber base on water."

A few hundred feet farther on and they saw the answer. Instead of one PBY there were four, all from Coastal Command's Norwegian Wing. Far from sitting on his butt, the pilot of the original PBY had been quite busy.

The Norwegians all held an informal reunion down at the station's landing. As much as they hated to, Cox and Lacey had to break it up if everything they had salvaged was to be loaded and the Catalinas gone before the Eighth Air Force arrived.

"You know, for a time I was thinking we would have problems putting all our men and every piece of equipment we removed into one plane," Lacey admitted; "I have no idea what the load-carrying capacity of a PBY is. We may have had to leave someone behind. In fact, we may have had to all stay behind in order to get this stuff out."

"Dennis, would you have actually left us here,

stranded us, if these extra aeroplanes had not arrived?" Cox asked, "probably to stay until next morning?"

"Well you guys would have had to stay. Vince and I would've left, unless we could've borrowed from the Norwegians some RAF uniforms."

The other three Canadians had originally been on anti-submarine patrol flights when contacted. They received permission from Holmen to abort their planned missions and flew across Scotland to Eigg Island. Four aircraft were more than enough to ensure that everyone and everything they dragged out of the crash site would find a seat or a space in one of their holds. Still, with only the one power launch from the Coast Guard station to shuttle all the people and equipment out to the flying boats, it took time to complete the operation.

Some of the weightier items nearly sank the small boat, so did the piling of one too many hefty Norwegians into the frail craft. To ease its burden somewhat, several life rafts were inflated and used to transfer some of the men. The sun hung almost behind the island when the PBYs turned their engines over and departed. A few minutes later, after the harbor waters had calmed and the amphibians were a formation of retreating silhouettes on the eastern horizon, a float-equipped Noorduyn Norseman, in U.S. Army Air Force olive drab and D-Day invasion stripes, puttered onto the scene.

All things considered, the operation had been a success, but not enough of a success to make all three mother ships viable combat aircraft once more. One still needed a chin turret and two required ball turrets. Everything else, armor plate, tail gun equipment, intercom and electrical gear, waist and cheek guns had been installed. Even the machine guns for the absent turrets were laid aside, ready. Only the turrets themselves remained to be obtained. One or two more operations, a few more downed B-17s in reasonable shape and Lacey's plan would be a complete success. However, fortunes were soon to change, necessitating a drastic alteration in operations.

Chapter Seven
CHANGE OF PLANS
THE SNATCH

"It doesn't look as though we can continue in our current way any longer, Dennis," said Cox, laying in front of Lacey the latest forecast from the weather office. "If this report out of Meteorology is even remotely correct, the south of England can expect to be hit with a low-pressure centre in thirty-six hours time. That means more blizzards and storms like they had last weekend and this time it will probably continue for a full week. We have only nine days left before we must launch our attack. Training is going along much better now that we have a fully operational Fortress but it would be best if we had all three."

"I understand that last bit better than you do," Lacey pointed out, while scanning the forecast. "We must teach these Norwegians not just to fly in formation but to fight in formation as well. And you're right, we can't do that with one B-17. We only need a few more turrets to make the other Forts combat-ready and I'm all for sticking with the plan we've been using. It got us eighty percent of what we need so far; all we have to do is wait a little while longer and it will get us the rest."

"Quite frankly, I don't feel we have the time to wait. In the twelve hours since our last salvaging operation, not one Fortress has come down in anywhere near an intact state or far enough away from Eighth Air Force bases for us to use. Your original plan has worked fine but the situation has changed and we can no longer afford to be so passive. We need to be elastic and respond, Dennis. Don't pull a 'Monty' on us."

"Pull a Monty?" repeated Lacey; now he was curious. Whereas before, he had been getting a little angry with Cox's suggestion that his brilliant strategy was somehow going to fail. "What the hell does that mean?"

"It's a British colloquialism, or a slang word to use your term. It's rather derisive and originally came from the Royal Army. It refers to the way General Bernard Montgomery always operates 'according to plan.' No matter what may occur or what the Germans may do, he always has his forces follow exhaustively drawn up plans which, if he must, he will have rewritten to accommodate the situation. Of course this means he usually doesn't exploit any sudden advantage fate may present to him or deal effectively with a reverse before the losses mount up. Don't make his mistakes. The truly good commanders are, as I just said, elastic and respond quickly."

From their office in the requisitioned hangar, Cox and Lacey could see Blackburn's flight line and runways. Among the aircraft using them was Eight Ball's Revenge; Lacey's B-17 and so far the only one to be fully armed. It was returning from a gunnery training flight; so were the target-tow Harvards chugging through the pattern behind it, with Frank Atkinson and his crew inside.

"Let's get Frank in here," Lacey suggested, "right after he parks my 'Seventeen. Ever since we went to that air depot in Troston, he's been cooking up some hare-brained scheme to raid it for the spare parts we need. He says it's like a candy store waiting to be picked. I think he just wants to risk his damn-fool neck again, but if the plan has merit we should use it. A good commander always uses a good plan, no matter who came up with it."

In its original form, Atkinson's plan was simply not workable. It hinged on taking a British C-47 and painting it to resemble one in the U.S. Army Air Force and nothing had changed from the previous day, when the shortage of Dakotas forced Cox to borrow a captured Ju-52.

"And how long would it be before someone at Troston becomes curious about this Dak which arrived unannounced and is busily being loaded with all kinds of parts?" Cox inquired. "Certainly not long, I believe. The aircraft will have to remain on the ground for a much shorter time than you would have it. And preferably not in broad daylight. It is tempting to say they'll be too busy to notice you but if you interrupt the smooth flow of flight operations, no matter how busy, you will be noticed. During off-hours, especially into the evening, it will be much easier though eventually someone will come around to find out why you've landed."

"What do you suggest we do instead of just landing and ransacking the candy store?" asked Lacey.

"Thirty-six hours will give me more than enough time to obtain orders allowing some of us onto that base. Myself and Leftenant Smythe, for instance. And perhaps Colonel Lacey here can be our nondescript escort, maybe we should make him a Leftenant so nobody will really pay him much notice. We can gather the parts we want and, instead of trying to take them through the main gate, we drive to the flight line and load everything into the aircraft we'll be using. Though I've never participated in anything like this, I believe the plan is logical. The big question is, which aircraft can we use?"

"God damn, why didn't I think of this before," said Atkinson to himself; then, to the others in the office. "Hey you guys, why don't we use one of these planes?"

Atkinson hopped off Lacey's desk and went over to the windows where he pointed out the second line of a half dozen B-17s standing beside the hangar.

Unlike those in the first row, they were not destined to be either mother ships or Aphrodite drones, unless an accident was to happen. They had the most flying hours and the most combat scars. They were being held in reserve and, since the ferry flight to Blackburn, the bombers were slowly returning to a semi-derelict state.

"We take one of them," Atkinson continued, "mark it up to look like an assembly ship or a target tow hack. Those planes are always flying around on some little hop, whether official or unofficial. Why, I remember the time I and some of my friends took up a couple of WAAFs for a nighttime joyride in one. We had a little fire start in the number four engine and that made us put down at Gatwick. Our arrival caused quite a stir and one of them WAAFs was so scared, we had to get 'er drunk before she'd go back in the plane."

"How amusing," said Cox, who distinctly wasn't. "But tell me, what, precisely is an assembly ship?"

"It's a war weary bomber," Lacey answered, "much like the ones we have out here. Probably these Forts would've been made assembly ships if we hadn't taken them. The Eighth Air Force uses assembly ships to make sure that formations gather properly and join the attack force at the right points. Every bomb group has one; they're stripped of all combat equipment and painted in very bright color schemes. They're covered with stripes or dots or squares of usually white, red and yellow. The planes have to be the gaudiest things flying but you can spot them a mile off."

"I gather that's principally why they're used. Tell me, how long would it take us to paint up one of our reserve bombers to look like an assembly ship?"

"Well, Frank, how about it? You're the one who came up with the idea in the first place."

"If we got the paint shop at this base to start working on it now, we'd probably have it ready by tomorrow morning," said Atkinson, "and then it would take only a few hours for us to install some heavy-duty winches in the bomb bay. That's where we'll load in the turrets and keep 'em when we fly out."

"Now you have a much better plan," said Cox, "one that can work. How long do you estimate it will take to load all three turrets?"

"No more than ten or fifteen minutes, a whole lot less time than I originally thought we'd use. If it all goes right, we'll be off and away before anybody even comes around to check on us."

An olive drab Fortress from the same unit as Lacey's Eight Ball's Revenge was selected. In part because it had one of the lowest overall amount of flying hours among the reserve B-17s but mostly because Atkinson knew what the 381st Bomb Group's assembly ship looked like.

The Boeing was towed to the base's repair and maintenance facilities where it cut in on a line of Coastal Command Liberators waiting to have their weathered camouflage redone. First a crew went over it, cleaning off the accumulated slush and snow; only then was the Fortress brought inside and placed in a drying room prior to being repainted.

"It's a procedure we have to do with every aircraft during bad weather," the shop's chief explained. "Paint don't adhere too well to a wet surface. Well now, can you two give me an idea as to how you'd like her painted?"

Lacey and Atkinson did better than that. They handed over a three-view drawing Constance had done from Atkinson's description. Since it was just a pencil sketch, he had to tell the chief what the colors would be.

"Except for the wing tips, you paint the outer half of each wing, white," said Atkinson, "the wing tips you leave red. Paint the rest of the tail surfaces red. The rudder, the elevators, everything. And then add white dots to the whole tail fin. Paint a white, two-foot wide stripe around each engine cowling and the nose. On the rest of the fuselage, from the cockpit area to the tail gunner's position, paint white dots just like the ones on the tail fin. Understand the scheme now?"

"I think I do. What are you going to use this aeroplane for? If you don't mind my asking."

"Yes, but we can't be too specific," said Lacey. "We're going to use it to sneak into an air base."

"What! In a plane painted up like a ruddy clown?"

The only chance Lacey, Cox and Constance had of seeing the finished product was early the following day, from the air.

At first light, one of Blackburn's communications hacks, an Avro Anson, was readied to take them to southern England. They received word of the paint shop completing the task while boarding the transport. Cox said they did not have the time to waste inspecting the bomber but did allow the Anson to circle the base after it had rattled off the ground.

"You're right, it's positively dazzling!" Constance said to Lacey. "It can be seen a mile away."

"That's the whole idea," he responded. "I still wish we could've examined the results at a closer range. You never did fully explain why we couldn't take the time to do so. We don't need to show up at Troston for hours."

"True, old boy, but we still have a schedule to keep," said Cox; "I think you'll understand why once we're down."

At the sedate cruise speed of one hundred and twenty miles an hour, it took the Anson a little less than three hours to reach the airfield outside of Cambridge in the south of England. Instead of the usual staff car or jeep, a Royal Navy truck was waiting for them on landing. And instead of driving immediately to the Eighth Air Force Air Depot, Cox made a detour to a small village in East Anglia. To Constance, the countryside gradually grew familiar.

"I've been here before," she commented. "I know this road and that town up ahead. You cheeky bastard."

Cox merely smiled at Constance; it was all he could do to keep from laughing. Lacey had to do a little prodding in order to get one of them to answer.

"Do you see that house there on the left?" Constance asked him, pointing to a small, neatly kept cottage among a row of such buildings. "It was once a summer home for Charles's family. Now he has his wife there."

"It's only a temporary move, until the V-1s and V-2s raining down on London are stopped," Cox explained and then he stopped the truck and climbed out.

"You sly dog," said Lacey, following him. "No wonder you didn't want us to spend any more time in Blackburn than we had to. We weren't going on any schedule but your own. You lecherous, sly dog."

"Here, these are the keys to the truck. I suggest that you come back by around fifteen hundred hours to pick me up, so we can arrive at Troston by sixteen hundred hours. Or would you prefer I say pick me up at three o'clock so we can reach our destination by four?"

"I understand the last one better, I was never much for using military time. Okay, Charlie, but what are Leftenant Smythe and I to do for the next four hours?"

"I had planned for that as well." Cox pulled from his greatcoat pocket a folded slip of paper and pressed it into Lacey's hand. "This is the address of a country hotel a mile outside this village. The people who run it have been family friends for decades and before I married Anne, we used it quite often for our, well, sojourns. For some time I've known about you and Constance and I think you two will find it to your liking. Just mention my name to the people at the front desk and that I recommended them and everything should be okay. I'm not only a sly dog, I'm a discreet one."

"Somehow, I expected you would react this way. You're not the typical top brass type who would rant and rave and want to throw the book at me."

"Oh I admit that I did have those feelings at first. But later I admired you. You have no idea how many men have tried to win Constance. I came to the conclusion she would only let a special, superior man have her. Well, she thinks she has found that superior man and I feel she has as well."

They parted before reaching the opposite side of the road. Cox was still fumbling to open the main gate when a slim, dark-haired woman came hurtling down the walk. Though she could not match the height or weight of her husband, Anne Cox was still able to nearly pull him over the fence when she embraced him.

"Hmmm, maybe I ought to trade Charlie one tall redhead for one short brunette," Lacey said reflectively, as he viewed the proceedings from the truck's cab. "Not unless all Englishwomen greet the men they love in a similar way."

"We do, but I hope you'll never have to leave me for as long as he had to leave her in order to find out," said Constance. "I know it will be impossible but I want to be with you always. I just don't know what I would do if I were without you for any great length of time."

"Well, all I can truly promise you, Connie, is that you won't have to be without me for at least the next four hours."

At exactly three o'clock, Lacey and Constance were back in front of the cottage waiting impatiently for Cox to appear. As much as he didn't want to, Lacey used the truck's horn to hurry along the parting of his friend and wife.

"For a guy who once told me we couldn't afford to waste two waking hours, you sure set a good example," he humorously chided Cox when he climbed on board.

"Since we spent so many non-waking hours on this operation, I feel we have earned the right to spend a few at a more pleasurable activity," Cox explained, "especially when a lull in the operation allows it."

It took them a little longer than the planned hour

to navigate their way through the bleak, East Anglia countryside. The snow dumped on the land by previous storms was now either melting off or turning into a brown sugar slush, making the winding country lanes difficult to pass. Road conditions improved greatly when they reached the vicinity of the Troston Air Depot. Before coming into view of the base, Lacey stopped the truck so Cox could change seats with him and he could change rank.

"Here, Connie, help me get my birds off and replaced with these bars," said Lacey, removing both his winter coat and jacket. "And hurry, I don't really care to freeze to death."

The tiny, silver eagles were removed from the shoulder straps of each garment and single, silver bars pinned in their place. It took little more than a minute to make the changes and yet Lacey was already well chilled.

"Just goes to prove us California-types can't take cold weather," he explained, teeth chattering. He fished through the deep pockets of his coat, eventually producing a pair of plain, black-rimmed glasses. "These will be the final addition to my disguise. There, how do I look?"

"Like someone I don't know," said Constance. "It makes you look like some meek little labour MP."

"I'd prefer to say a mild-mannered reporter. I think I know what you mean by MP and I hate politicians."

"All right, mild-mannered reporter, time to see if our story and your disguise works," Cox interrupted. "There's Troston's main gate. Look official, you two."

At mid-afternoon the vehicle traffic into the Air Depot had diminished considerably from the morning peak. Cox found it easy to insert himself into the weak flow and pulled to a halt at the sentry station.

"Aren't you guys a little far away from the water?" asked the Military Police sergeant at the gate.

"In England you're never far away from the water," Cox answered. "I am Leftenant-Commander Charles Cox of His Majesty's Fleet. This is my aide, Leftenant Constance Smythe and that is the escort officer your headquarters assigned to us, Leftenant Lacey."

"Okay, Commander, what's your business here?"

"Leftenant-Commander Cox and his aide have come down from Scotland to tour this base and one of our B-17 bomb groups," Lacey blurted out. "He's in command of a special Royal Navy weather reconnaissance squadron. We gave him some B-17s about a week ago and now he's down to observe our operations and get some spares. Here are the orders allowing them onto this base."

Clumsily, Lacey handed the orders across the cab to the sergeant who gave them a cursory look.

"These come from your Navy, Commander, not the Eighth Air Force. But I do see you have them countersigned by someone at High Wycombe. General James Doolittle; when you guys want something you go right to the top, don't you?"

"Yes, we find it saves immensely on time spent gaining cooperation," said Cox. "Are we free to go, Sergeant?"

"Yeah, sure thing. Just make sure you get the right papers for your spares from the warehouse foreman, the on-duty aviation supply officer and the base security office before you bring them through the front gate. Okay, sir?"

"Yes, Sergeant, I believe I have it. Could you now tell me how I may reach that part of your base where you store spare parts for B-17 Fortresses?"

The sergeant ended up giving his directions twice. First to Cox and then to Constance, who wrote them down. Being much larger than the town whose name it borrowed, Troston was an easy place to get lost in if one didn't have exactly the right directions.

"I can't believe we'd have to obtain authorization from three offices to have the turrets we need released to us," said Cox, once they were past the main gate. "And I suppose all those papers have to be in triplicate as well? I've never heard of a military service which functioned differently."

"Afraid so," Lacey responded. "We'd be here till doomsday trying to get what we want through legal channels. And doomsday may come a whole lot sooner if we don't have everything we need to stop that Nazi battlewagon."

"How odd you should say that. I recall the air duty officer on the *Victorious* saying much the same to us just before we went out to attack the *Bismarck*."

"I knew you were in a Swordfish squadron but I didn't know you saw action against the *Bismarck*."

"There's quite a bit about me you don't know. At least that time I had the opportunity to shoot back. My first encounter with German dreadnoughts was far different. Look, I think that's our destination up ahead."

"Building Fourteen-A? Yes, that's the one," said Lacey, looking over Constance's notes. "A word from the wise, Charlie. In this kind of mission we call our destination, the target. It makes it more fun, you'll see. This will almost be like combat, with all of the exhilaration and none of the terror."

Cox felt his stomach begin to tie itself up and his palms grow damp with sweat. There was fear, but Lacey was right, that nagging little terror of being killed did not surface. In fact after the opening minutes, Cox found himself enjoying the furtive action and played along with Lacey.

The plan was to obtain some blank shipment forms from the aviation supply office and give themselves the turrets they needed. All that had to be done was divert the office room staff long enough for Lacey to lift the forms. While Cox drew the attention of the supply officer, Constance struck up a conversation with his harried, WAAF secretary.

"You think it's easy working for Yanks? I wouldn't wish this job on anyone," she confided to Constance. "Oh, a few of them are nice but those aren't many. Not enough to make up for the others who think they can buy a night in bed with you. You remember what I say, that wimpy little Leftenant escorting you, I've seen the look he has in his eyes before. He'll be making a play for your affections, you wait and see."

With her last statements, the secretary lowered her voice to almost a whisper and turned her back on Lacey. He could not have asked her to be more cooperative. Later, in the truck, the three created their own shipping orders.

"Dennis, these forms have serial numbers," Cox observed, when he first compared the stolen blank with the ones filled out by the aviation supply officer for assorted spare parts. "That means, sooner or later, someone is going to realize the one you lifted is missing and will institute a search."

"I know, that's why I took one from the bottom of the stack," said Lacey. "I only hope they don't go through the whole thing before this day is out. Now that we have a sample of this guy's handwriting and a blank form, who among us would like to try forging our new shipping orders?"

"I think we would obtain the best results if Connie

did it. I noticed the on-duty supply officer I spoke to was left-handed, and so is she. Also, Connie once told me that when she was in art school, she could make fairly good copies of Turner landscapes, right down to his signature. I never thought we'd have to make use of her rather illegal talent but these are the times that demand extraordinary actions.''

First she had to make several time consuming practice copies before attempting to work on the blank form. Rather than sit and wait and draw attention to themselves, Cox drove the truck around the base until the bogus orders for the items they truly needed were finished.

The warehouse where all B-17 armament was stored was two blocks and one check point down from the destination on the original orders. For a few seconds, Cox feared they would be found out but all the Military Policemen wanted to know was where the truck was going and what it would be collecting.

''That information will be sent on to the base security office,'' Lacey told him afterwards. ''They won't ask the warehouse supervisor to confirm our shipment until we go to the office to get their release for what we have. Of course we're not going to carry this charade that far.''

The actual taking of the turrets was something of an anti-climax. They just drove up to the warehouse, showed the foreman the shipping order and had the crated turrets loaded into the truck by a detail from the warehouse staff. The only excitement came when the foreman took a little longer than normal to fill out his confirmation order, and when the M.P.s back at the check point asked the trio where they were going.

''Could you direct us to the officer's mess?'' Lacey requested while Cox fumbled around for an answer.

"It's been ages since any of us last ate."

Troston's officer's cafeteria fronted on the runways and from that vantage point, Lacey, Cox and Constance could watch the base's air traffic fall off to a mere trickle of incoming flights. Soon, only their lights could be seen.

"The night's as black as a grave," said Constance, "and there's no moon out. How are we going to identify our aircraft when it finally comes in?"

"The runway marker lights will illuminate it somewhat and then there'll be the signal," Lacey answered. "Frank will wave a light from the cockpit when he's moving down the taxi strip and we'll respond by flashing our headlights at him."

"You mean waving a light like that aircraft is doing?"

"Holy shit!" Lacey almost ripped the cuff off his shirt as he attempted to read his watch. "Jesus Christ, he's twenty minutes early, this could really fuck things up. C'mon let's get going before he attracts someone else's attention."

They left their trays at the table and bolted through the cafeteria doors; causing a minor stir of their own. Outside they could see the Fortress more clearly, its dazzling paint scheme still eye-catching even in the dim light.

"Dennis, I think those other people in the mess have taken notice of the manner in which we left," Cox warned.

"Have they? Well to hell with them, we'll be gone in fifteen minutes and they'll still be wondering what happened."

"Shouldn't you be coming in the cab? I mean, standing on the running board while a . . ."

"No, damn it, just get the truck moving. I can watch where the Fort is going better from out here."

Fortunately, Atkinson had begun signalling early. He was just turning from runway to taxi strip when Cox got the truck in gear and gunned it away from the parking lot. Lacey did everything but climb onto the roof of the cab in an effort to keep the B-17 in sight. Shouting directions to Cox, he managed to steer him to the bomber side of the field. Of the long line of B-24s that stood there approximately a week ago, only a few remained. The flight line was slowly being filled with factory-fresh B-17Gs; some were probably the sister ships of the two Lacey had stripped on Eigg Island.

Atkinson was part way down the taxi strip as Cox threaded a path between the parked bombers and broke onto the flight line. He flashed his headlights at the fake assembly ship, getting the pre-arranged response from its cockpit. The wavering beam blinked a few times and went out. At least communications was intact.

"Frank had better have a good reason for jumping the schedule or I'll leave him here," Lacey promised, "and he'd better be keeping to the rest of the plan."

When the Fortress turned onto the flight line tarmac, its number two propeller appeared frozen and feathered. According to plan, Atkinson identified himself as the assembly ship from the 381st Bomb Group and alerted Troston tower that he had engine trouble. So far, in spite of it being launched prematurely, the operation was going along almost normally.

"Dennis, another vehicle is approaching us," Cox warned.

"Damn it, the day you count on 'em to be lazy, the bastards become eager beavers. It looks like some repair crew, don't worry, I'll handle them. You take care of loading the crates, you know the routine as

171

well as I, and make sure you ask Frank what the fuck is going on."

Cox continued out to the bomber once it had come to a stop on the tarmac. Number one, three and four engines were throttled back to idling speed; the bomb bay doors opened up and several crew men jumped out the rear access door.

They came forward and signalled Cox to turn the truck around and back it into the niche between the fuselage and the number two engine. In the meantime, Lacey had cut off the base repair crew and was busily persuading them that their services weren't needed.

"No, nobody ordered us to come out here," he explained, "no one had to. My men and I are from the Three Eighty-first Bomb Group and that's our assembly ship out there. We saw it was in trouble when it landed and it just so happens that we came here to pick-up a load of spare parts."

"I see," replied the sergeant in charge of the repair crew. Throughout most of Lacey's answer, his attention was focussed on the stricken B-17. From a distance, the maneuver Cox was executing looked like a normal procedure and nobody could see the Royal Navy lettering on the truck sides. Still, the sergeant wasn't entirely satisfied with what Lacey told him. "But why are you guys all the way up here; Troston is a long way from your home and Hitcham is much closer."

"I know, but the Fourth Air Depot is a little short of spare parts for B-17Fs. And besides, this place has better food than either Hitcham or Ridgewell."

"Okay, leftenant, I get the picture. May I suggest, sir, when you get out there, that you have the pilots switch off their engines. It'll be safer and easier on your men," the sergeant advised, then later, after

Lacey had started back. "Food's better here, huh? Jeez, they must be catching the rats and eating 'em at his base."

Lacey waited until the repair crew moved off before breaking into a run. He reached the Fortress and found the operation half over. One of the ball turrets had already been stowed and the other was being hoisted into the bomb bay. If no further foul-ups occurred, the loading would be finished in five to ten minutes.

"Did you find out why they arrived so damn early?" Lacey shouted, even inside the truck's cab, he had to raise his voice so Cox would hear him.

"As a matter of fact, yes. I asked Mr. Atkinson what the fuck was going on and he replied that he had to come in now or cancel the operation. It seems as though the Royal Air Force is attempting one more nightly outing before the weather closes in. If Mr. Atkinson had tried to keep to the original schedule, he might have blundered into some Lancaster or Halifax. And to add to that, there's an intruder alert for the south of England."

"We should have planned for those two problems," Lacey admitted. "This is what happens when you do not have the time for proper planning."

Suddenly someone banged repeatedly on the driver's door, it was Sergeant Herrmann; loading had been completed.

"Hi ya, Colonel," he said, saluting. "We're all through back here. We're closing the bomb bay doors now. You guys better get this truck outa here if we're gonna leave."

"Looks like we're the ones who are fouling up things now," said Cox, engaging the ignition. "Are you going to come along for the ride?"

"Might as well. I'd just be wasting more of our

173

time climbing out of this thing."

With that, the truck pulled away from the idling B-17. It drove a dozen or more yards down the tarmac then turned in toward the flight line. Cox parked the truck under the wing of a Liberator and abandoned it there. By the time he and Lacey exited the cab, Atkinson had the Fortress's number two engine restarted. If traffic remained light and nobody got curious as to how quickly the plane's engine trouble was fixed, they would be leaving Troston in the next few minutes.

"Dennis, Dennis, that truckload of mechanics you shooed away. They've been stopped by a Military Police jeep."

By the far end of the hangar row, on a service-access road, the headlights of both vehicles could be seen. While Cox stared intently at them, Lacey barely gave them a glance.

"Don't pay 'em any attention," he advised, "they're probably just shooting the breeze. Concentrate on the Fort instead. We only have a hundred feet or so to go before we reach it. Less if Frank will taxi a little faster."

"I'll wager that they may be discussing us. I would not put it past them. Our hasty departure from the cafeteria may have just piqued someone's interest and led them to make a report. We've already had one near-disaster befall us; such things usually occur in threes."

Damn it, why did he have to go and say that? Lacey thought, the comment making him hesitate and miss his stride. A moment later he froze completely as a searchlight swept across the bomber-lined tarmac and locked on the two, solitary figures. It made Cox's heart skip a beat as well.

"Run! Run, God damn it or we'll end up in the

174

base stockade for sure!" Lacey shouted, dragging Cox by the shoulder and breaking into a deer-like sprint to the Fortress. In spite of his initial lag, Cox soon caught up with Lacey and, as they circled around the bomber's tail, cut inside him and reached the open access door first.

"Charles, what on earth are you two doing?" Constance asked, unaware of what was happening outside. "Have you and Dennis been in some kind of schoolboy race?"

"No, we're on the lam from the law," gasped Lacey, being helped—actually dragged—by one of the Norwegians to the bulkhead dividing the aft fuselage from the radio compartment. Though winded, he quickly scrambled over to the left waist hatch and watched the Military Police jeep try to cut-off the B-17 at the taxiway, and fail.

"This station's security forces may well be wise to us," Cox explained to Constance. "I don't believe they have deduced our operation, but they're awfully curious about us."

"And they may want to stop this plane from taking off," Lacey added. "I'd better go forward and talk to the cockpit."

Because of the operation's importance, the very best pilots in the team were used; Atkinson and Capollini. Except for Sergeant Herrmann, who acted as flight engineer, everyone else in the crew was Norwegian; which meant the navigator, radio operator and gunners. Lacey only went as far forward as the radio compartment. In order to make room for the turrets, the catwalk through the bomb bay had been removed.

"Let me speak to the flight deck," he ordered, indicating to the operator that he wanted a microphone and a headset. "Vince? This is Dennis, what's

175

going on up there?"

"Plenty, what the hell did you guys do, Colonel? Rob a bank? The tower's asking us to stop and allow MPs to come aboard and search the ship. What'll we do, Colonel? Let them in or try to takeoff?"

"Stick to our plan and get this Fort off the ground. Traffic's light so there's no problem with safety. Just stall the tower for as long as you can. Tell them you got radio trouble or something. The success of this mission is in your hands now, don't let us down."

"It's do or die time, Frank," Capollini advised, switching off the intercom. "The Colonel says damn the torpedoes and full speed ahead. What shall I tell the tower?"

"Bullshit them, Vince," Atkinson ordered, "heaven knows you're good at it. All I need is enough time to line up on a clear runway and open the throttles. This is an electric moment, don't spoil it for me."

"That's it! Now I know how to bullshit 'em." As Capollini reached for the command transmitter controls, he ran his free hand over the recognition and landing light toggles; flipping them from one position to the next. When he picked up the microphone to respond to the tower, he raked his thumbnail across the fine mesh screen protecting its diaphragm. The resulting noise closely resembled a heavy, interfering static. "Tower, this is Ridgewell Nine-six-three. You will have to repeat your last message. We are experiencing an electrical malfunction. Please repeat your message slowly and clearly so we can understand."

"That should keep 'em busy for the next few moments," said Atkinson. "Let's get Jim Herrmann up here and really make your malfunction look realistic."

When the sergeant appeared, Atkinson directed

him to the electrical panel on the left side of the cockpit; showing him the toggle switches and dimmers for the position and formation lights.

"You've seen electrical failures in airplanes before, Sergeant. Just get behind me and fake one. I'll tell you why, later. Now get cracking."

"Ridgewell Nine-six-three, this is Troston Tower. Military Police report that persons unknown have apparently climbed aboard your aircraft. You are requested to stop so that they may make a search. Do you understand, Ridgewell? Troston Tower, out."

"Now the real fun begins," Capollini observed slyly, prior to keying the mike. "Troston Tower, the situation is getting worse here but our flight engineer says he can have it fixed by the time we are airborne. We wish to report that a vehicle is pursuing us too closely. In your last transmission, I believe you said something about MPs. Tell them to get out here and take him off our tail."

Capollini had barely ended his message when he burst out laughing. It was a few seconds before he could speak.

"They must be pulling their hair out in that tower," he managed at last to say. "They gotta be having fits."

"I'm going to have a fit right now," Atkinson warned, "look what's up ahead of us. God damn it."

Less than a hundred yards in front of the B-17 was the beginning of Troston's primary runway. Also at about the same distance was a communications hack of the First Air Wing; a Douglas A-20 Havoc seconded from an operational unit and stripped of its olive drab paint. The bare metal fuselage and tail glinted brightly in the Fortress's landing lights, when they weren't blinking out.

"Knock it off with those landing lights for a little

while, Vince. I wanna be able to see this. Even if that A-20 were to start his takeoff roll now, I can't use the same runway. I'd probably fly into him somewhere during our climb outs. Is there any traffic on the other runways?"

"No, both alternates are clear. Looks like the Colonel was right this time. Traffic is very light. I don't see anything starting up on the hangar aprons either."

"Then hang on to your socks, we're going on a little trip," said Atkinson, "take the throttles, Vince and help me with the brakes."

The B-17 had to be slowed as it neared the active runway. Capollini eased back the throttles then quickly reached down and released the tail wheel lock at the base of the center control pedestal. Atkinson used flaps as well as brakes to slow the bomber to an acceptable speed. They both jumped on their pedals at the start of the turn while Atkinson swung the rudder and Capollini juggled the outboard engine throttles to steer the ship onto the runway.

Instead of stopping, the Fortress rolled across the concrete and continued down the taxi strip on the opposite side. Taking the Military Police, tower personnel and everyone else in the B-17 by surprise.

"What on earth are the pilots doing?" Cox demanded from Lacey. "We just passed over a runway we could have used."

"Not with that A-20 sitting on it," he said, pointing at the now dimly illuminated machine visible through the right waist hatch. "We would have had to stop and wait for it to clear the field, giving the MPs more than enough time to board us. What Frank and Vince are doing is fine, they're cutting through the fighter side of the field to reach one of the unused runways."

In place of bulky Fortresses and Liberators, Troston's other half held the slim, graceful shapes of North American D-model Mustangs; together with a smattering of Lightnings and Thunderbolts. Two rows of the brand new fighters stood on the tarmac. A few others were scattered among the hangars and maintenance shops. Those nearest the paint shop had their group markings and squadron codes freshly applied.

"Troston Tower to Ridgewell Nine-six-three. The vehicle behind you is a Military Police vehicle. Repeat, *is* a Military Police vehicle." A certain level of frustration was becoming evident in the controller's voice. "You are to go no farther on the taxiway you are now travelling. You are to stop and allow your aircraft to be inspected. Do you understand these orders, Ridgewell? Troston Tower, out."

"This'll drive 'em right up the wall," Capollini predicted as he gave his response. "Troston Tower, this is Ridgewell Nine-six-three. We did not fully understand your last transmission but we are working on the electrical problem and should have it fixed soon. We will let you know when it's done. In the meantime, we are moving on to the primary alternate runway because of obstructions on the main."

Whatever the controller's response was, he did not transmit it. Instead, he tried to contact the errant Fortress by using the colored signal lights, though by that time, the bomber was almost underneath the control tower.

It taxied rapidly down the fighter-filled tarmac, the Military Police jeep still in hot pursuit. From around the end hangar, another jeep with a gyrating red light appeared.

"I think they're going to try to cut us off," Capollini observed. "Mother of mercy, is this the end of Rico?"

"Not by a long shot, they're not smart enough to blockade the taxiway," said Atkinson, "look at them. They're coming out to stop us. Standby to slow the ship down, we're going to make another turn."

In order to keep the blocks of incoming fighters separated, each row was split in half at the tarmac's midpoint. The gap produced was just large enough to thread a B-17 through, provided Atkinson could reach it before the oncoming jeep did.

As the Fortress slowed, the trailing jeep began to catch up. And when it turned left, the two Military Police units found themselves on a collision course. They both veered wildly in the same direction, toward the runways, setting up another collision until the oncoming jeep veered once more and careened toward the outermost line of parked fighters.

It crashed against the corner Mustang, sliding sideways into the left wing; the jeep would have eventually flipped over if the plane wasn't there to stop it. The force of the impact rocked the P-51 back a few inches and mangled its wing's leading edge and bent the left landing gear strut.

"Jesus Christ, I hope those guys didn't get hurt bad," Capollini admitted, glancing back at the accident.

"And I hope they are," said Atkinson. "They try to save a two-bit jeep and end up wrecking a fifty-five thousand dollar airplane. They deserve every fracture and laceration they've received. Where's the jeep that was following us?"

"Sitting in the mud, off the edge of the tarmac. I think the MPs in it are going to help the others who crashed. Looks like we're in the clear."

"We're not in the clear until we get off this field and out of range of their anti-aircraft guns. Standby to slow the plane again to make a turn."

Another turn later the B-17 was back on a taxi strip, heading toward an unused runway. The tower kept flashing red lights at it; until Atkinson and Capollini had it lined up for takeoff and the runway lights went out.

"Jesus Christ, what the hell are we going to do, Frank? If we try the other runways, their lights will go out too."

"The other runway lights are already out," Atkinson noted. "All the approach and perimeter lights are being shut down as well. So are the tower lights, hangar lights, everything. Do you suppose there's a power failure?"

"Troston Tower to Ridgewell Nine-six-three! If you can hear me, kill your engines and abandon your aircraft at once! Luftwaffe aircraft are in our area and we can expect to be under air attack at any moment. This field is being closed—again, abandon your aircraft!"

A solid clunk followed the controller's warning. He had left his carrier wave open and dropped his headset as he ran from his station. Above the rumble of the Fortress's Wright Cyclones, the mounting wail of an air raid siren could be heard. The passengers and crew of the bomber were now alone, even their pursuers had left.

"No, leave those throttles where they are," Atkinson ordered, brushing Capollini's hand away from the ladder-shaped quadrant of levers. "We're not abandoning this ship. We're getting outta here. Prepare for takeoff."

"Frank, we can't take the risk. What if we all get

killed? What'll happen to this operation the Colonel and the Commander are planning? We're out to stop something you know, something that could change the whole war."

"If it's that big there'll be others to replace us. Guess what will happen if we all get caught and our cover is blown? That's worse than dying."

"Okay, Frank, I give in," said Capollini, throwing up his hands. "But I still say this is a damn big risk. Preparing for takeoff. Brakes, set. Flaps, full up."

"Trim tabs set at zero position," Atkinson responded, reaching down to the trim wheels at the base of the center pedestal. "Set propeller controls to High RPM. Mixture controls to full rich and turbos to takeoff manifold pressure."

"Done, Frank. Cowl flaps are open and locked. Fuel boost pumps are on. How are the gyros?"

"Horizon gyro is uncaged. Directional gyro set to magnetic compass heading. Sergeant, as soon as we're airborne, I'll be ordering you to turn off all our exterior lights. Releasing brakes now, standby to lock tail wheel."

As Capollini freed the parking brakes, he grabbed the tail wheel lock and engaged it. The few feet the bomber had travelled in the time between the two actions was enough to straighten out the wheel. Atkinson wrapped his hand around the center rung of the throttle quadrant and began adding power to the engines; gradually and to one side at a time.

The B-17's rumble changed to a flat howl and its entire airframe vibrated slightly, as if it could not absorb the increasing power. With no runway lights, Atkinson and Capollini gingerly worked the flight controls to keep the bomber in the center of the runway's dim outline.

"Airspeed, eighty," Capollini read off, "tail

should be coming up soon. Frank, something just shot across the face of the moon, did you . . ."

"Yes, I caught it, I'm tracking it now. Watch the runway, Vince. I don't want to take my eyes off our friend. Sergeant, reduce the cockpit lighting to minimum levels."

Herrmann deftly reached forward, under Atkinson's left arm, and hit the switches on the extreme left of the front instrument panel. The soft but harsh glare caused by the side fluorescent lights died when they blinked out. Only the overhead fluorescent remained on; it had to if the pilots were to see their controls. When the tail came up, the rudder became effective and Capollini no longer had to tell Atkinson which throttles to juggle in order to maintain the Fortress's direction. At a hundred and ten miles an hour, the main wheels skipped once and the bomber was airborne.

"All exterior lights, off, now!" Atkinson roared, "gear up, Vince. I don't care what our altitude is, gear up!"

The powerful landing lights, the position lights, the formation lights and pulsating, anti-collision strobes all snapped out within a few seconds of each other. From being a constellation of light, the B-17 transformed itself into a nucleus of darkness nearly as black as the night itself.

"Where's our friend?" Capollini asked, nervously. "Even with our lights off, he still knows where we are."

"And I know where he is, dead ahead of us and about a thousand feet higher. He hasn't opened fire, so he has to be one of them souped-up intruder bombers, not a night fighter. But I'll bet he still has tail gunners and they'll try to get us once we pass behind him."

Now Capollini could see the oncoming intruder. At close range, its black undersurfaces were too dark and in the faint moonlight, the slim, familiar shape of a Ju-88 was discerned. More visible were its pencil-thin, white crosses on the lower wing surfaces and blue exhaust flames. Aft of the extensively glazed, insect head-shaped nose, was the bomb bay; its doors opening so the Junkers could begin its attack on Troston.

"Gear's up, Frank. Airspeed's getting near one-forty, shouldn't you be reducing power?"

"No, not yet," said Atkinson, "and don't you turn off the turbos or the booster pumps either. It's been so long since I've seen a kraut, I almost forgot we were fighting them and this one isn't getting away from me. I'm going to play a little game of chicken with him. Give me a maximum left bank but keep her on course."

"You may want him but you're draggin' the rest of us along and risking our necks as well," Capollini responded, swinging his control wheel in unison with Atkinson. "You can only get away with saying 'I' in a fighter."

As the Fortress's left wing dipped farther below the horizon line, its desire to turn in that direction increased. Prodigious amounts of rudder and ailerons had to be used to keep it tracking straight. Rate of climb fell off also but it couldn't be helped. The engines were already straining at their limits. Still, the B-17 continued to gain altitude. Closing on the other bomber, their wings nearly perpendicular to each other.

The maneuver did not go unnoticed by the Junkers crew. They quickly realized that the Boeing's intent was to slice their wing off with its own and reacted at the moment when Atkinson and Capollini were sure they would collide. The Ju-88 reared and banked steeply to avoid doom and in the same instant, its pilot lost the horizon.

"Well, if we haven't hit the bastard now, we never will," commented Atkinson. "Let's ease her into a left turn and see if anything's happened to the base."

With the Fortress already in a seventy degree bank, all that had to be done was reduce control forces holding it in the bank and allow the plane to follow its natural inclinations. The response was immediate, almost as if the B-17's desire to turn grew with each passing second. Atkinson and Capollini guided her through the maneuver, decreasing the angle of bank until the wings were level and they were heading back to Troston.

"There he is!" shouted Capollini, almost poking out Atkinson's eye with his finger. "My God, it looks like he's spinning. He's out of control, we did hit him."

"No, that's not the result of any collision. That's vertigo, and he doesn't have the altitude to recover."

In trying to escape its doom, the Ju-88 had sealed it. The bomber twisted through the second revolution of its spin, then a third and, part way through a fourth, slammed into the ground; its bomb and fuel loads exploding together in a brief, intense fireball. All of Troston was illuminated by the flash, as was the Fortress that caused it.

"Well, after fifty missions over Europe, I finally get my first Kraut," said Atkinson, almost gleefully.

"Yeah, but we nearly went down with him," Capollini observed. "If I've said this to you once, Frank, I've said it a thousand times. You take too many risks. And the colonel will be telling you the same thing, too. Just as soon as he can crawl to the intercom."

* * *

Escaping Troston wasn't the end of their troubles. Until the B-17 reached the border with Scotland, it had to fly through a rising cloud of Royal Air Force Lancasters and Halifaxes. Mosquito night fighters intercepted it several times and, after nearly shooting it down, would elect to escort the wayward American bomber while waiting for Fighter Command to alert them to other, possible intruders. Passengers and crew all breathed a little easier when it set down at Edinburgh for a refueling stop. In little more than an hour, they would be home.

Like every other airfield in England, except R.A.F. Bomber Command airfields, traffic was light, practically nonexistent. So the appearance of another U.S. Army Air Force aircraft at an exclusively British base drew Lacey's attention.

"I never realized your Air Force operated any Mitchells in my country," Cox observed, while he and the rest waited for the B-17 to have its tanks topped off. "I only thought we did. The Royal Air Force, I mean."

"You're right, the Eighth Air Force never did," said Capollini, "but a Twelfth Air Force unit was stationed here for a few months. It was the Three-tenth Bomb Group, my outfit shared a base with them at one time. They never flew any missions from England and left for North Africa by the end of 'forty-two. Some derelicts stayed behind and were taken over by the Eighth for use as VIP transports and station hacks; this has to be one of them."

"It sure looked familiar when we first taxied in here," Atkinson added, "however, that tie-down area is so far away, it's difficult to tell. The colonel will have a better look and he'll find out where the B-25 came from."

Lacey did; all he had to do was check the medium bomber's markings and ask at the flight desk who got off it. He came charging back to the Fortress as the fuel browsers departed, out of breath. The B-25 was all too familiar.

"Let's get this ship out of here, now!" he shouted, still wheezing. "Before someone who shouldn't finds out about us."

"God damn it, I knew I saw that Mitchell before," swore Atkinson. "It's Colonel Brogger, isn't it?"

"You hit the nail right on the head. And from what the flight desk people said, he's looking for us. C'mon, everybody back on board the plane now. I'll explain it all to you later, Charlie, when we're back in the air."

Chapter Eight
TRAINING CONCLUDES
THE UNWANTED ARRIVAL

The name of Colonel Duane Brogger was of course not unknown to Cox. Lacey and the members of his team, had made enough references to Brogger in the last several days for Cox to gain some knowledge of the man. Lacey only needed to fill in the blank spots and give all the details of what he learned at the flight desk.

"This man sounds like my first squadron C.O.," Cox noted, at the conclusion of the briefing. "One of the few fortunate things about the sinking of the *Glorious* was that he went down with her."

"What a terrible fate to wish on a guy," said Lacey, "sometimes you're as bad as us, Charlie. But at least you have an idea as to how much we hate this prick and why he can be such a threat to the security of our operation. What he's out for is pure vindictiveness."

"How can such a high-ranking officer get away with such activities? More importantly, how can he be stopped?"

"Brogger is the head of an elite unit and as such, he can pretty much write his own orders. How do we stop him? Well, we could have General Doolittle order him to knock it off. The problem is, those orders will not be effective until they reach him and they might not for a couple of days. We could do that but I don't want to.

"Everyone in my team, myself included, has been wanting to get even with that son-of-a-bitch since he had us kicked out of England. Now, thanks to you, we have a chance and we won't have to face disciplinary actions for what we do, because of the secrecy of our mission."

"Sounds to my line you're going to abuse the services of His Majesty's Navy," said Cox, smiling slightly.

"I may even resort to a little blackmail. If you were in my situation, would you do anything different?"

"I certainly wouldn't resort to blackmail. Especially when I know how willing these representatives of His Majesty's Navy are in aiding you." Cox indicated both himself and Constance. "Provided your actions do not hinder our plans."

"Colonel Duane may hinder us but he won't delay us," Lacey promised. "Our training is almost over. Tomorrow should see the completion of its most critical phase—if we get the turrets we're carrying mounted on the bombers in time."

Blackburn's armory crews were put to work the moment the B-17 returned. They worked throughout the night rearming the two uncompleted mother ships. By first light, when the rest of the base was awakening, they had finished their task. All the mother ships were at last fully armed, fully operational and ready for combat. Or at least, for the full-scale dress rehearsal Lacey was planning.

"Mother ship leader to formation, we are now in the test range area. The target-towing flights have reported in and should be appearing soon. Have your Aphrodite controllers check over their drones, attack runs are commencing now. Lacey to Martinez, you may begin."

Bristling with machine guns and gun turrets, the bombers finally resembled what they were called. Their gunners swung their weapons about alertly, menacingly; waiting for the arrival of the "enemy." Far below the trio of Fortresses, nearly two miles below them and hidden by broken overcast, were their drones. Bouncing along in a similar, though more widely spaced formation, until the center aircraft, a Lockheed Ventura, dropped its nose and dove toward Loch Seaforth.

"Controller to pilot, drone away. She's on course and everything looks okay."

"Right waist to pilot, I have incoming aeroplanes. Four o'clock high and crossing to our twelve o'clock position. There's three of them and they look like Harvards."

Atkinson's top turret gunner spotted the aircraft at the same time as Lacey's right waist; nevertheless, Lacey spread the alert to his wing men, then to the rest of his crew.

"And this time, try to fire shorter bursts," he added, "especially those of you manning the turrets. You've got twin fifties there, not single weapons and your weight of fire is twice as much. So take it easy you guys and conserve your ammunition supplies."

Except for individual code letters, all three Harvards wore identical color schemes. As did the dozen that were following them. Today was to be a maximum-effort mission for the gunnery training squadron as well; unfortunately depriving the operational training units in their north Scotland area of the day's air-to-air weapons practice.

The yellow and black-striped trainers unreeled their target sleeves as they approached the Fortresses; deploying them fully by the time they were ready to

190

attack. The inboard Harvard, the one closest to the bombers, broke first and headed in alone. The remaining two held off a few seconds longer then attacked as a pair.

"Lacey to gunners, bandits twelve o'clock high. One lone ship and one pair. They will pass to either side of us. Keep your eyes open for others. Don't concentrate on these, they're just the beginning."

Cheek guns, chin and top turrets on all three Fortresses opened fire on the sleeves as the towing aircraft passed safely overhead. The top turrets tracked and continued to fire at the targets throughout the initial attack, being joined toward the end by the waist and tail guns. Afterwards, Lacey only had a few moments to criticize his gunners and find out about the drone.

"You concentrated too much fire on the single, lead target," he told them. "You didn't give enough attention to the two ships coming in behind it. You left it up to Capollini to deal with them and if they'd been real, they could've overwhelmed him. Top turret, this goes especially for you. You have the best position in the whole airplane—use it to everyone's advantage, including the formation's. Lacey to controller, Andy, how's it going?"

"The drone is about halfway down the loch, Colonel. I'm skimming it over that center island now. In less than a minute, we'll be coming up on the turn. So far, it's fine."

"Capollini to flight, two bandits, nine o'clock high and closing. Look lively, they're less than a thousand yards out."

The Harvards were practicing old Luftwaffe tactics on the B-17s. Head-on attacks mostly, either by themselves or in rapid succession or in combination with attacks from other quarters; usually from the sides or below. Never a side attack by itself or a tail attack at any time. The bomber's relatively high maximum speed, compared to either a two hundred mile an hour trainer or a four hundred mile an hour fighter, precluded a fast pass from that quarter, as the Germans had early and painfully found out.

Attacks were carried out by single ships or formations of up to four aircraft. Mass attacks by squadron-sized waves were not carried out. It would take too much time to assemble enough Harvards and, with each trainer dragging a steel cable hundreds of feet long plus the tow sleeve through the air, it was far too dangerous to bring so many aircraft together in a tight formation. Even with the smaller units, close calls happened; usually the cables came close to shearing the tail fin from one of the B-17s.

And the Fortresses were trying out tactics of their own. Yawing slightly from side to side once the attack had commenced and making formation turns to spoil impending ones. None of which could be done if Lacey's three-ship command were part of a thousand-plane raid over Europe.

For an hour the intense, mock battle was fought until the last of the drones was successfully splattered against the target island.

"I would like to thank you, Colonel, for the workout you've given my men," said the commander of the gunnery squadron. "This was quite a bit different from the normal routine they're used to. It was quite a challenge, really, and I hope we met your expectations."

"The thanks should come from us, archer leader," Lacey replied. "Your outfit gave us a very realistic exercise. Everything but the cannon shells and the swastikas."

"Our pleasure entirely, Colonel. I wish I could stay

up here and chit-chat with you further but we exhausted most of our petrol on this outing and we'd better leave before we all become glider pilots. Cheerio, Colonel and good-luck."

The Harvards struggling to maintain their position over the lead B-17's left wing broke and climbed away from the now relaxed, and more open formation of bombers. They turned and flew off in the opposite direction, rapidly shrinking to dark specks joining a cluster of similar objects.

"In a way, I'm glad the show is finally over," Cox admitted, coming up to the flight deck for the first time since the Fortresses arrived over the target area. "We received a message about ten minutes ago from an RAF base on the Scottish coast south of Aberdeen. They were 'scouted' just recently by a Mitchell in Army Air Force colours. Your warning net has worked; it looks as though you correctly guessed Colonel Brogger's plan."

"It wasn't difficult. Which is not to say that the asshole's stupid," said Lacey, "just that he's doing what I would be doing in a more obvious way. Scan all the airfields for B-17s and land at the ones you see any. Only I would've used an airplane other than my own personal ship. I had hoped he would have started on the western side of Scotland. We could've gotten a day or two more if he had. Not that we need it, mind you. Just, well, it's likely to be a hot time at Blackburn when we arrive."

"Yes, it's something I'm sure you wouldn't miss for the world. What shall we do, Dennis?"

"Call Blackburn, let them know he's in the area. And have them send out a station hack to pick us up at the alternate landing field. With Brogger so close to Blackburn, I doubt he's going to overlook it."

He didn't. Cox barely had time to transmit Lacey's

message. He was busy talking to his wing men, before their home field was buzzed by an Army Air Force Mitchell. Almost immediately, it asked for permission to land.

"Stall him, Constance," Cox ordered, "stall him until we arrive there. Inform the base commander as to the gravity of the situation and I'm sure he will help you. Have that utility plane launched as soon as possible; also, that Fortress we used last night. What is its progress in the paint shop?"

"The last report I had said it was almost stripped of its new paint scheme," Constance noted, instinctively ducking as the B-25 made another low pass by Blackburn's control tower. "It should be finished, Charles, why do you want to know?"

"Because it can now be part of our deception plan. Have it sent back through the shop and repainted in Royal Air Force, Coastal Command colours. If this Colonel Brogger wishes to see one of our weather reconnaissance ships, then he will. What a pity it won't be finished."

The alternate landing field was an R.A.F. base outside the city of Inverness, on the Firth of Inverness. Used by both operational training units and Coastal Command patrol squadrons, it was more than big enough to take in and hide three B-17s. The same Avro Anson that took Cox and Lacey south to begin their most recent operation arrived to take them back to Blackburn.

"What about us, Colonel?" asked Capollini, as they boarded the light transport. "What are the rest of us gonna use to return home? Our thumbs?"

"No, their trucks," said Lacey. "The base transport officer will be here in a few minutes with some of his trucks and drivers. They'll get you back to Blackburn, though it'll be well after nightfall by the time

194

they do it. Which should coincide nicely with our plans. You're in charge, Frank, get everyone home safely; you're all going to have a lot of work to do tonight. Good-luck.''

Lacey ducked through the small, oval doorway in the Anson's right side and slammed the hatch shut. The pilot fed a little power to the idling engines and released the brakes; the Avro responded by scooting off the tarmac and back to the runway. Cox found he almost had to punch Lacey to make him turn away from the window.

"The earth is not going to open up and swallow them all," he told him, "you've left your men before, Dennis."

"I know, but not out in the middle of nowhere," Lacey explained. "I don't know exactly why I feel this way. Everyone of those men is a combat veteran. They've seen everything, I've seen zip. And yet, I get the feeling that I'm abandoning a bunch of orphans along the road."

"It's another sign of being a good commander. If you didn't feel anything over leaving your men alone, I'd have worries about you, Dennis. They should be fine; this is not enemy territory, after all. Now tell me a few more things about this Colonel Brogger we're going to meet."

For the half-hour flight across eastern Scotland to Blackburn, Lacey filled him in as much as he could about Brogger and the possible entourage he'd have with him. Perhaps he overdid it a little, Cox returned expecting to find a fire-breathing monster in khaki. In reality, he saw a mean-faced little man who reminded him of one of his former headmasters; together with a blubbery, rotund aide, Captain LeRoy March.

"That's the spineless wimp I told you about,"

Lacey observed, while their aircraft was still taxiing in toward the flight line. "The colonel's yes-man. That's also an American team, let me see if I can explain it to you."

"No need, it's really self-explanatory. Look, there's Constance. It seems she survived him, let's see if we can."

Cox and Lacey waited until the Anson was stopped and shut down before exiting. Though Cox led the way, it was Lacey who first spoke to Brogger.

"Vell, Herr Colonel, ve meet again," he said, in a clipped, clichéd German accent.

"Somehow, I expected you would say something like that," Brogger responded, making a short, perfunctory salute.

"Colonel Brogger, I am Leftenant-Commander Charles Cox, of His Majesty's Fleet." Cox snapped out a grander, more measured salute than either of the two colonels. Even if he already had a healthy dislike for the man, he thought he should at least begin the encounter civilly. "I am the commanding officer of the Very-Long Range Weather Reconnaissance Squadron. I trust you've already met my aide, Leftenant Smythe. To what do we owe the honour of your visit?"

"Perhaps you can tell me that in addition to my name?" said Brogger. "You seem to have known I would be coming."

By God, this man really is sharp, thought Cox, taken aback by his deduction. What a stupid slip to have made, let's see if I can cover it. "Not at all, Colonel. Mister Lacey here, pointed you out to me when we taxied in. It was very easy for him to identify you. I can't tell you what he's told me about you, we're in mixed company."

"I can just guess, which leads me to the reason why

I'm here, Leftenant-Commander Cox. It's Colonel Lacey and his team. I thought I had managed to banish them back to America; now, I find them up here in Scotland working on another secret project. At least some of them are. Where are the rest? Especially Lieutenant-Colonel Atkinson and Captain Capollini?"

"They are out flying missions on behalf of His Majesty's Navy. Until we can establish a trained cadre of Royal Navy personnel, missions will have to be flown by a mixture of Royal Air Force and American Army Air Force crews."

"Yes, that was one of the things I noticed in the limited inspection your aide allowed me to make. Except for her and yourself, I have not seen a single officer or enlisted man from your Navy. This outfit seems to be entirely manned and run by the RAF and, in particular, by Colonel Lacey's gang."

"Oh, there's a few more of us around," Cox offered, lying openly but successfully. "You just haven't seen them yet. How limited was your inspection?"

"Very. Your aide didn't allow me inside the hangar or into any of the B-17s outside it. She threatened to have me arrested if I did and she restricted the rest of my people to the plane, the flight desk and the mess hall. She even put guards on them."

Lacey managed to stifle his laugh but the resulting gargle that leaked out brought an angry glare from Brogger and, a little later, a coy wink from Constance; which completely broke Lacey's resolve.

His knees started to buckle and he nearly fell to the ground laughing. Lacey was able to turn away from the group and hung on one of the Anson's propellers, laughing himself silly while the others either secretly envied him or publicly chastised him.

"Enjoy your guffaws while you can, Colonel," Brogger advised, "they'll be the last you'll have on this island."

"I gather that means you've come here principally to locate Colonel Lacey?" Cox asked, making the supreme effort to refrain from laughing as well. "I know you haven't come all the way up here simply to further Anglo-American relations."

"My reasons do have to do with Colonel Lacey and his team of misfits. They were removed from duty in the Eighth Air Force because of some very serious incidents. They are a disgrace to their uniforms, as their leader has just demonstrated; they were being sent home to be disciplined and I was disturbed to learn about a week ago that they were still in England. Now, I am shocked to discover that not only are they still here but they're involved in an operation in which the pride and prestige of the U.S. Army Air Force is at stake."

"As if they were the only important things at stake here," Lacey muttered, a little louder than he wanted to.

"Quiet, Dennis, don't give him any ideas," Cox warned. "Since you've found them, what do you want to do now, Colonel Brogger?"

"Have his 'gentlemen' removed from this operation and more suitable Army Air Force representatives put in their place. I will institute an investigation as to how these, of all people, were selected for so secretive an operation. And, I would like to know exactly what is going on at this base. The veil of secrecy is drawn very tightly around it: why? Is it because of the nature of your operation, which I doubt. Or is it because Colonel Lacey did not wish to have the Eighth Air Force discover that he and his men had remained in England?"

The last part of Brogger's response had been directed at Lacey, but it was Cox who registered, however momentarily, the greatest shock. It was as if he had seen an impending apocalypse while for Lacey, the battle lines were drawn.

My God, this man is planning to ruin everything just to settle a personal score, Cox thought, trying to regain his calmness before speaking. "I can assure you, Colonel Brogger, that His Majesty's Navy is so far satisfied with the work of Colonel Lacey and his men. They've held up their end rather well. As for the secrecy surrounding this operation, it is quite legal and officially sanctioned."

"Oh really. Well, if that is true, then it certainly is a little odd to keep confidential the operation of a mere weather reconnaissance squadron. And I have seen very little at this base to indicate it is even operating. Look over there, at your hangar.

"None of the B-17s lined up beside it is painted in British markings. All eight are still in American markings. Eight? You did say Capollini and Atkinson were out flying missions. Where are the other two? Not unless your men are such amazing pilots that they can fly two aircraft apiece?"

"Glad to see you can still count, Duane," Lacey answered, knowing fully how it violated military courtesy and how it would anger Brogger.

"Quite right, Colonel, two aircraft are on missions," Cox quickly interjected. "A third one unfortunately crashed in Inverness County and the fourth is currently in the paint shop. Would you care to see it?"

It at least got the confrontation off dead center and in out of the cold. The Fortress was in the midst of getting its first layers of non-reflective white paint applied to its fuselage sides and undersurfaces. Cox did not wish to stop or interfere with the procedure, which naturally meant that the plane could not be inspected. Instead, he bullshitted his way through the tour.

"The aeroplane will not receive its Navy serial number until the painting is completed. Only then will it be officially accepted into His Majesty's Fleet. And only when we have enough planes and enough trained men will this squadron be formed and become part of the Fleet Air Arm."

"How interesting," said Brogger, in a way that told the others he knew he was being given a snow job. "May I speak to you in private for a moment? No, Captain, I want to be alone with Leftenant-Commander Cox. You stay here with Colonel Lacey and the commander's aide."

With that snap, Brogger's shadow retreated from the observation room's entrance and moved back over to Lacey and Constance. But not before they were able to say a few hushed words to each other.

"Dennis, I'm worried," Constance admitted. "This man seems capable of doing anything. He could send you away and destroy everything we've accomplished."

"I'm worried, too. I hope Charlie doesn't play into his hands," Lacey managed to say, before Captain March returned. "Well, LeRoy, nice to see you again. Tell me, have you blended in with any good wallpaper lately?"

Outside the observation room was a long hall with doors to various offices along the opposite side. Here, insulated still further from the noise of the painting room, Cox and Brogger were able to talk in quieter levels.

"Now we can speak frankly, leftenant-commander," said Brogger. "I know you're not giving me the whole story. Something more than just the working up of a weather recon unit is going on here. I've gathered a number of reports of recent incidents involving B-17s. Some crash-landed ones have been found stripped of much of their combat equipment. Including two on an island not far from here, where an air-sea rescue plane observed Royal Air Force personnel actually stripping the bombers. The most recent incident appears to be an attempt by someone to steal more combat equipment from one of our air depots. They still don't really know what went on there last night. A plane crashed on the base but they don't know if it was the B-17 or a German night intruder that happened to be attacking the base at the time."

"I hope you don't think my unit had anything to do with these incidents," Cox observed, letting a little incredulousness creep into his voice.

"With all due respect to your ability to command, if Colonel Lacey is involved then he's really running things."

"I suppose you're basing that assumption on his activities at Fersfield? Where you, as the most senior officer from the Eighth Air Force's Operational Engineering Section, should have been in command?"

"Okay, leftenant-commander, let me lay all my cards on the table." Brogger's voice was rapidly losing its smoothness. Cox's put down was apparently closer to the truth than his. "Whatever is going on at this base, whether it is officially sanctioned or some hare-brained scheme Colonel Lacey is responsible for, it will have a direct impact on the pride and prestige of the United States Army Air Force. Colonel Lacey and his 'unit' are not worthy of that responsibility. I insist that an official

Eighth Air Force unit take over from them and that an investigation be launched by the Army into how on earth Lacey was chosen to be part of this operation."

"No need to launch an investigation, that much at least I will tell you," Cox offered. "I chose them. And my choice was approved of by the Board of Sea Lords at the Admiralty. It will not be changed or revoked at this late date to please you. No doubt the 'official' Eighth Air Force unit you'd like to replace them with is one of your own, drawn from the Three-eighty-eighth Bomb Group and the OES. My squadron must become operational in the next seven days and nothing, most especially your demands, shall interfere with that."

"I didn't realize that the debut of a weather reconnaissance squadron is to have such an important effect on the Royal Navy's war effort. Or should I say yours and Colonel Lacey's war effort. Perhaps the Admiralty should conduct an investigation as well as the Eighth's Inspector General's Office. Perhaps things here are not quite official as you claim they are? I didn't want to believe you were in collusion with Colonel Lacey but you leave me no choice. From what I've seen and heard, you're just like him, Leftenant-Commander Cox. Just like him."

"If you think you've just delivered an insult, Colonel Brogger, you're wrong. After watching Dennis work for this past week, I take it as a compliment that you've found me similar to him."

"Dennis is it? I should've known," said Brogger, his face breaking into a smirk. His suspicions had just been confirmed. "If you'll excuse me, I'll collect my aide. You can keep me out of your hangar and away from your planes. But there are areas of this base you have no control over and you can't confine me the same way you confined my flight crew. Believe me, I'll find what I need to put you away; good day."

Cox waited until Brogger towed March out of the observation room before entering. Naturally, Lacey and Constance were eager to speak to him, though for different reasons.

"I figured from the way they left you had handled them pretty well," said Lacey. "What I want to talk to you about is this . . . That paint job has given me an idea; we should paint the Aphrodites an overall white so we can see them better. Not unless you think we'll be running into snow storms over Norway?"

"We'll have to ask the Meteorology Staff about that but I suppose it's a good idea," Cox replied, a little distracted. "I don't really think I handled Brogger so well. He doesn't know a scrap about our real mission; what the twit does think is we're conducting some sort of private operation. Without the knowledge of my Navy or your Air Force. He says he's going to take the information he'll gather and turn it over to your Inspector General's Office and the Admiralty."

"Of course the prick would go to the inspector general. They're old West Point chums and the inspector general is high enough to cause us real trouble, yet not high enough to know what our real mission is. How about the Admiralty, Charlie? Is there anyone there who can cause us trouble?"

"No doubt; the Admiralty is a rather big place. A virtual rabbit warren that's expanded far beyond the original building built in 1722. I've made my share of enemies since I went to work there, about two years ago. And since only the Civilian Lords and Sea Lords know the full extent of our mission, Brogger will find someone in that labyrinth who would love to crucify me."

"I don't believe they'd go that far but if they do, just remember, it'll only hurt when the nails actually go in. A moment ago you said something about information. What kind of information?"

"The kind that Brogger said he would go out and start collecting. Why do you ask? I personally didn't put much validity in his threat."

"Because as I told you before, while he may be an asshole, he's not stupid," Lacey reminded Cox. "He'll be able to get plenty of evidence against us. Even if he can't get into our planes or hangar. I say we watch him and see where he goes."

One of the paint shop's offices had a large window facing the control tower and main flight line. Amongst a sea of blue uniforms, a pair of khaki ones were easy to spot.

"There they are," warned Constance, singling out the two distant figures. "They're moving away from the flight line. Toward the base armoury it appears. But why go there? Blackburn is just a maintenance facility, not a front-line base. Why, we've made more use of the armoury since we've been here than anyone else."

"You've just answered your own question, Connie," said Lacey. "Colonel Duane will find out that we've been flying gunnery training missions and that at least three of our planes have been armed. Get on the phone and contact the armory, let's head 'em off at the pass."

Brogger found the staff there to be remarkably close-mouthed during his friendly, later pointed, questioning. He couldn't even get them to say if any of Lacey's men had been over to collect ammunition for firing range practice.

"Wouldn't know 'bout that, governor," replied the

sergeant in charge. "You'd have to ask the blokes at the target range 'bout the Yanks taking in practice. Don't you chaps use Colt Forty-fives? I don't think we store that kind of ammunition here. They'd have to bring their own."

By the time Brogger left, Cox and Lacey had set themselves up in another vantage point to watch his movements.

"Now, he's heading toward the petrol dump," said Cox, "not the gun butts like you claimed he would. I'll wager he's going to ask them how many flights we've made and how many aircraft we sent up each time."

"That's it, Charlie, you're learning. What's the number for the fuel dump?"

"I believe it's three-one-two. They have a fair distance to walk; I think you have sufficient time to ring Connie and find out if she's reached Inverness?"

"Well I don't," Lacey observed, waiting patiently for the switchboard to notice he had picked up the phone. "I swear, this is the only country whose telephone system is designed to make wrong calls. Yes, three-one-two, please."

It took time but Brogger slowly realized he was being watched and outmaneuvered. Every answer he got was the same, evasive and non-specific. Anywhere he wanted to go, he knew someone could call ahead and coach the staff on the right kind of useless information to give; except for one place.

"What do you mean he's going to the dump?" Lacey responded, a little incredulous. "He's been to the dump."

"No, not the petrol dump, the other dump."

"You mean the bomb dump? But we don't have one, this isn't an operational air base."

"I know, I mean the other, other dump. Where all

205

the scrap and junk is thrown," said Cox, getting exasperated himself. "The trash heap. It's an interesting switch in tactics but could Colonel Brogger find anything there to use against us?"

"He damn well can if he keeps his eyes open. I think this situation demands closer scrutiny."

Soon there were two sets of officers scrounging through Blackburn's garbage site. The hulks of wrecked aircraft and vehicles, junked engines, worn out or damaged equipment of all kinds lay scattered around the facility; together with discarded boxes and other shipping materials.

Cox and Lacey found the battered fuselage of a Lockheed Hudson to be the best vantage point they could use. It had the cleanest—relatively cleanest—interior and was still sitting upright; most of the other wrecks were lying on their sides. Unlike virtually all the other Hudsons at Blackburn, the one they selected still had its egg-shaped, dorsal turret and its windows were not covered with an obscuring film. Probably because most of them were already broken or shattered.

"All this is garbage, just garbage," complained Captain March, uttering his most profound observation of the day. "It makes me depressed just to be here. What could we possibly find here that will be of use to us?"

"Plenty, but so far 'we' are not searching for it," snapped Brogger, "only I am. Get down here and get your hands dirty, March. Your enthusiasm for this work may determine whether or not you continue as my aide."

"If you'll lie down and look this way, you can watch them through the plexiglass nose and side windows," said Lacey, himself lying on the right side of the cockpit floor and peering out the forward access hatch.

Cox knelt down beside the hatch but refrained from actually lying on the wet, rusting floor like Lacey.

"Thank you, I can see quite well from here," he answered. "Thus far, they have poked through everything they've come across. Except for the wrecks of vehicles and aircraft. Do they know what they're looking for?"

"Not exactly, but they'll know it when they find it and . . . I think they just have, Jesus H. Christ. I thought I ordered those crates to be broken up."

Brogger and March practically blundered into the pair of large, wooden crates which were clearly marked as containing sperry ball turrets for the B-17G Flying Fortress. A few feet farther on they found the crate for a chin turret. While his aide wondered aloud about where they had come from, Brogger almost at once correctly guessed their origin.

"They came from that air depot that was raided last night," he said, "Troston. I knew Lacey was responsible for it. It's just the kind of overgrown, childish prank he'd enjoy. Come, help me rip out the boards that the data blocks and serial numbers are printed on. No, you idiot, don't use your hands! Use one of those old pipes or some other piece of junk."

"Well, it looks like your orders are going to be finally carried out," noted Cox. "Unfortunately, it's being done by the wrong people. Will what they're collecting be enough to ruin our operation?"

"If they can get it to the inspector general's office, it sure as hell can," Lacey said, gloomily. "Which leaves us with only two options. One, we shoot down their plane when they takeoff tomorrow and two, we clear out. Now. All essential training has been completed, perhaps only a few more gunnery flights have to be made. Surely our operational base can handle that? Wherever it is?"

"The Scapa Flow airfields. I had hoped to surprise all of you with it but it looks as though my fun has been spoiled by this asshole."

"Don't worry, you can join in on ours. Which will start as soon as we can sneak out of this wreck."

While Brogger and March broke up the crates to obtain the planks they wanted, Cox and Lacey crept out of the Hudson and back to their hangar, which they promptly began to strip.

"The flight crews will return here in about ninety minutes," Lacey told the assembled ground crews. "By then I want us to have a good head start on them. Everything we brought with us we must take with us. I'm sorry we have to leave this way, I would've liked it to be longer and more formal. But the local situation has changed and it could get hot if we stay here. I would like you to know that both Leftenant-Commander Cox and myself have greatly appreciated your work for us, you have much to be proud of. And now, let's get cracking."

Lacey, together with Herrmann and his other sergeants, packed away all the electronic equipment in the hangar shops. Cox, later joined by Constance, gathered up everything from the hangar's offices. What they didn't need was burned, what was, they filed in large briefcases. At the end, they handcuffed them to their wrists.

The flight crews arrived shortly after nightfall. There were orders waiting for them at the gate, telling them to drive straight on to the hangar. The crews were tired, hungry and then astonished at what they found inside.

"Jeez, Colonel, what's going on?" asked Capollini, "have the Germans landed or something?

What's the score?"

"No, I told you who's landed, and he's out to hang our butts," Lacey answered, breaking away from his work detail to fill in his returning men. "And the score is Lions—one, Christians—nothing. Though our side hasn't come to bat yet."

"When will we come to bat, Colonel?" Atkinson asked this time. "In the next war? It looks as though we're running out with our tails between our legs."

"We're just obeying the words of a famous Englishman who said, 'he who fights and runs away lives to fight another day.' I can't remember who said it, perhaps Commander Cox can tell you. At any rate, there's a larger battle awaiting us and we can't afford to waste time fighting with Colonel Duane. We're moving on to our operational base. Planes, equipment, personal belongings, everything we need will be flown out tonight. Of course that means we'll have to divert Brogger's attention for a while. Frank, I'm sure you and Andy can come up with something. Whatever it is, make it nasty and that's an order."

But first Lacey sent all to their quarters to pack their baggage. As they filtered back, he put them to work dismantling the last of their electronics shops and preparing the B-17s for flight. They were busy until nearly midnight, when the last items were loaded into the awaiting bombers.

"Colonel Brogger, his aide and his flight crew all retired approximately two hours ago," Cox reported, to a hastily called briefing in the darkened hangar. "As per our instructions, they were assigned to quarters on the edge of the base perimeter. About as far removed from this hangar as was possible. Before going to bed, the colonel dispatched a wire to the Eighth Air Force's Inspector General's Office. He appears to be quite smug that he has us right where

209

he wants us."

"Good, that's exactly what we should want him to think," said Lacey, smiling maliciously. "Frank, have you surveyed the area?"

"Yeah, Colonel and it's perfect for what I have in mind." Atkinson wore the same smile as Lacey and, as he spoke, he produced a rough diagram of what he saw. "They stuck 'em all in a quonset hut and there's an air raid shelter and some anti-aircraft guns nearby. The base commander said he'll give us anything we want and Lieutenant Martinez has gone to him with a shopping list."

"Since we're asking for it all, what are 'we' planning to do with it?" Cox requested.

"Stage a fake air raid. They'll hear our planes take off no matter what corner of the base they're stuck in. If we can set off a few explosions and fire those guns, together with our departure, we'll make 'em think there's a real air raid underway and keep their heads down."

"Not if you can't persuade them to leave their building. It has been my experience in air raids that people often do not leave the imagined safety of buildings for the real safety of underground shelters."

"Don't worry, Commander, we'll make them move. Martinez has come up with a nice variation of that tear gas bit he pulled earlier on Brogger."

"Fine, good work, Frank," offered Lacey, "now for you, Sergeant. What's the situation with the aircraft?"

"All nine birds are ready to go, Colonel," said Herrmann, with a touch of pride. "Even the ones that haven't been flown since we brought them here were still in good shape. Captain Capollini is making the final checks. Do you want him to bring in the flight crews?"

"Yes, tell Vince to bring in the other pilots, the flight engineers and Sergeants Schmanski and Grey," Lacey ordered, once Herrmann had disappeared. "We are going to fly out all nine Fortresses at once, which means that each plane will only have one pilot. But that shouldn't make the situation too risky, each plane will also have a man qualified to be flight engineer on board. It's easier to fly a Fortress with a pilot and flight engineer than with just two pilots. We'll divide the planes into three-ship flights and, since we only have three navigators, we'll give one to each flight. The time is four minutes to twelve, you guys. If everything goes right, we will commence operations at one o'clock. That's zero-one hundred hours for you real military types."

Capollini brought with him the Aphrodite drone pilots, the mother ship co-pilots, the flight engineers from both groups and the other two sergeants who were part of the original Field Electronics Team. They received the briefest of briefings Lacey could manage and they all emerged from the hangar some five minutes later to join the rest milling around its main doors.

Almost at once the forty-odd men divided themselves into four or five-man crews and fanned out along the line of Fortresses. In the middle of the rush, Martinez drove up with the base commander. He had done much better than expected.

"My chaps who work the anti-aircraft guns, haven't had a decent exercise in months," the commander explained, "and neither have my fire fighting crews in nearly as long—not since one of these clapped-out Hudsons had to crash land on its ferry flight up. Anyway, your man's idea will give me the perfect opportunity to stage a big show. We'll make your send-off something to remember. People will think the Jerries really are attacking."

In less than the allotted hour, enough units were in place to begin the deception. Most of Blackburn's anti-aircraft guns had been manned, a team from its armory had laid a few explosive charges near Brogger's quarters and Martinez found enough Very pistol flares for his plan to work.

"Isn't his plan a trifle dangerous?" Cox warned, as he and several others watched Martinez sneak off to the isolated row of quonset huts.

"I know those flares can give someone a bad burn but I don't give a damn," said Lacey. "I ordered them to be nasty and, damn it, that's what I want."

"Oh I'm not worried about those inside the building; you misunderstand. I'm worried about Lieutenant Martinez. With that curved roof, one slip and he could fall."

A base fire truck stood waiting for Martinez on the opposite side of the huts. The firemen had already set up one of their ladders against the building where Brogger and his entourage were sleeping. It could be easily distinguished from the other quonset huts by the fact that its chimney pipe was trailing a plume of smoke while the others were noticeably dormant.

Martinez almost had to do a balancing act as he walked down the top of the hut's curved exterior. He knelt beside the chimney when he reached it and began to carefully pry off the cone-shaped rain cover. Rust had nearly sealed it to the pipe but after several tugs the cover finally gave and by twisting it, Martinez got it to rise. He hurried the process toward the end, not caring what noise the contraption made, and eagerly threw it away. The built-up heat in the cover had been rapidly cooking his hands, even through his insulated flying gloves.

It was still in mid-air when the wail of air raid sirens started to grow in the distance. Martinez was behind his schedule and he didn't need to check his wristwatch to know it. Still, he then unzipped his flight jacket. He reached inside and grabbed handfuls of shotgun shell-sized flares; he dumped them down the hot chimney pipe he now straddled as quickly as he could. Of all people, Martinez knew he had only half a minute before the anti-aircraft guns and the first of the charges would be detonated. After all, he was in on the planning.

"Colonel? Colonel Brogger, it sounds like there's an air raid," said Captain March, fearfully. "What should we do, sir? Should we go to the air raid shelter?"

"Roll over and go back to sleep," Brogger growled, half awake. "It's probably just a test or something. What the hell could the Luftwaffe find here to bomb?"

A sudden, window-jarring explosion brought everyone who was sleeping, or trying to sleep, fully awake. A second followed immediately and much closer to home. The potbellied stove, which had been providing the room's only heat, turned into a boiling fireball. It was as bright as a sun and spit out hot, incendiary missiles that ricochetted about the hut. For those falling out of bed and scrambling for an exit, it was as if a phosphorus bomb had fallen through the roof.

"There, he's off the top," said Cox, tracking Martinez back to the ladder. "I believe I can hear the engines of the first Fortresses turning over. The fire truck can return your man to the flight line; I really think we should be leaving."

"No, I want to see this through," answered Lacey. "my formation won't be starting up for several minutes."

Someone finally got to the hut's front door and broke it down; there wasn't time for the formality of opening it. They came out stumbling or crawling, ill-dressed for the cold weather and being chased by multi-colored Very flares. A second charge was detonated in a nearby stand of trees and base anti-aircraft guns began firing at non-existent intruders. Cox and Lacey counted those who emerged from the quonset hut and assured themselves everyone in Brogger's entourage had escaped to the air raid shelter.

Martinez returned to the spectator area rather than make the fire fighting crew drive him to the flight line. They had a real blaze to extinguish. The assembled officers climbed into their jeeps and left; just as Capollini flew out the first B-17.

Its thunder, combined with the unending moan of the air raid sirens and the steady pounding from the adjacent Bofors guns, convinced those huddling in the shelter that a true attack was under way.

"This has to be because of Lacey," Brogger concluded, "him and that Royal Navy type. They were planning something and the Germans got wind of it. Whatever it was, we'll find it in ruins when this raid is over."

"When do you think this raid will be over, sir?" March asked. "I think I was hit by a hot piece of shrapnel and it hurts. And what isn't hurting is freezing."

"Shut up, March, we're all in the same boat. A little pain will be good for you. You'll get a medal out of it, I'll see to that. And Lacey will find himself facing a court-martial. I'll see to that too."

For more than an hour the "attack" went on. The firing of anti-aircraft guns, the roar of airplane engines and sporadic bomb blasts filled the air with a clamorous din until the all-clear sounded. Brogger and his men were found in the shelter by rescue crews and were taken to the base hospital to be treated for first and second-degree burns and severe frostbite. It was mid-morning by the time any of them were released.

Only then did they find that the air raid had been a staged exercise. And only when Brogger went to the flight line, did he find the Fortresses gone and the hangar he couldn't get into the day before standing empty. It seems as though Lacey volunteered his men to be the "raiding force," so the base commander explained, and when the exercise ended, they did not return and no one had the faintest idea where they disappeared to.

Chapter Nine
SCAPA FLOW
THE ICARUS CRISIS

Ironically, the last aircraft to be ferried to the Scapa Flow Air Base were the most important ones. The mother ships, following their night in Inverness under armed guard, were collected and flown to their new home in the Orkney Islands north of Scotland. When they arrived over the Royal Navy's legendary fleet anchorage, Lacey saw there were a pair of visitors taxiing to his corner of the field.

"Hey, Colonel, those are Corsairs," Capollini radioed. "We haven't seen any of them since the gyrenes buzzed Muroc."

"I bet it's some of Charlie's friends," said Lacey, "they've probably dropped in to see him. And if you'll allow me to drop out of formation first, Vince, I should be able to meet them right after he does."

Normally, the left wing man would be the first to break away and enter the last leg of the landing pattern. This time, it was the lead ship that fell out, almost dove out, and requested permission to land. Since the bombers had already entered the downwind leg, it only took a few minutes for Lacey to set his Fortress down and turn off the active runway.

By then the two blue and green mottled Corsairs had parked but were not yet stopped. The propellers still ticked over while their wings were folded into stowage position. Lacey swung in beside them as their engines died and the propellers windmilled to a halt.

In between the steps he had to take to shut down his own plane, he watched the Corsair pilots dismount theirs. Out of the nearest fighter climbed a great bear of a man. He was at least six inches taller than Cox, who met him on the ground. Lacey couldn't believe anyone that large could fit into the typical fighter cockpit.

"Jesus Christ, they must have to use a shoehorn to fit him in there," he said, mostly to himself.

"Sometimes they have a tinsman fit little bulges to the sides of the cockpit, sir," noted Lacey's co-pilot. "Do you think they have anything to do with our mission?"

"I don't know. You guys are under my command but it's Commander Cox's show. I'll find out what's going on just as soon as we get out of here. All right, engine instruments have settled to neutral positions. AC power switches, off. Battery and master switches, off. Let's lock up the flight controls and then we can leave."

When his crew hit the ground, they were naturally drawn to the Navy fighter pilots. So much so, Lacey had to practically shoo them away in order for him to meet them. Both the bear and the other pilot wore the same number of stripes on their sleeves but while the latter came from the Royal Navy, the first was of the Royal Canadian Navy.

"Gentlemen, I'd like you to meet Colonel Dennis Lacey of the United States Army Air Force," said Cox, who was to do most of the talking. "And Colonel, this is Commander Mark Rotherham of His Majesty's Fleet and this is Commander Paul Bradley of His Majesty's Canadian Navy. If there's a place where we can talk in private, I suggest we go there."

Lacey's office was still unfinished but was the only one big enough to accommodate all four men, plus Constance.

"Dennis, do you recall those unanswered problems we had a week ago?" Cox continued, then he went on to answer his question. "Well, these two officers will take care of one of those problems. Commander Bradley is in charge of a newly formed Corsair squadron for the fighter carrier *Pursuer*. Commander Rotherham is in charge of the Navy's Corsair Operational Training Unit, currently embarked on the training carrier *Ravager*. Both the unit and the carrier will now be upgraded to operational. They will provide our escort over the Alten Fjord area."

"I was wondering how you would handle that problem," said Lacey. "I was beginning to think I would be flying a suicide mission. How many fighters will you have altogether?"

"Each of our squadrons will have twenty-four, combat-ready Corsairs," Rotherham answered, "plus spare aeroplanes."

"That makes forty-eight in total," Cox quickly added. "Now I know that doesn't sound like much, Dennis, considering what the Luftwaffe is supposed to have at their Alta Air Base. But, recent intelligence reports show the situation to be a little different. I only wish all the reports I have here were as good. Connie?"

Only then did Lacey notice she was wearing a briefcase handcuffed to her wrist. It was the same one Constance wore throughout most of the previous night. But he knew it had been emptied when they arrived at Scapa Flow and the contents placed in a safe. What she took from it now were different and completely new report folders. There were far fewer than the previous armful and also something Lacey had never seen before; a round, flat, metal canister.

"These have come from the continent in the last week," Cox began, dividing the reports into two groups. "The first has to do with fighter strength at Alta. Number six-seventeen squadron is carrying out diversionary raids against the crippled battleship *Tirpitz*. The last one was on November twenty-ninth and it has had its desired effect. A wing of the Ninth Fighter Group's Messerschmitts has recently been transferred south to Tromsö. This means that the squadron will have to switch back to pure night attacks and there will be fewer fighters for us to deal with. Those remaining at Alta have had problems with the sub-Arctic climate. As much as forty percent may be unserviceable at any one time, which further puts the odds in our favour.

"This next report has to do with the anti-aircraft defences inside Kaa Fjord. Because they believe that the *Frederick the Great* has still not been discovered, the Germans have removed some of the flak batteries guarding it. About a third are being transferred, mostly heavy-calibre guns, south to Tromsö once again. The *Frederick the Great* sets sail in less than one week; obviously the Germans feel that no attack by heavy, land-based bombers can be mounted in so short a time, and that the principal threat is now carrier-based air attack and there is the limit of the good news."

Cox put aside the first set of reports and concentrated on the second, much larger, pile.

"Here now the news we can least afford to hear. This first one concerns the battle group that was to put to sea with *Frederick*. The heavy cruiser, *Admiral Hipper*, will not be part of it. Severe boiler troubles have been keeping her in port most of the time and it appears as though the Germans really do need major warships to cover their evacuation of Baltic ports. So, the *Hipper* will remain behind and her place in the group shall be given to the pocket battleship *Admiral Scheer.*

"Which means that the battle group will comprise the missile battleship, *Frederick the Great,* the pocket battleships *Lützow* and *Admiral Scheer* and the heavy cruiser *Prinz Eugen.* Together they will mount a total of four fifteen-inch guns, twelve eleven-inch guns, eight eight-inch guns, twenty-eight six-inch guns and forty four-inch guns. The *Lützow,* the *Scheer* and the *Prinz Eugen* also mount a considerable number of torpedo tubes. Nearly thirty in all. In total, it means that the danger posed by this force to our shipping has greatly increased and this is only the beginning.

"We have here a late report from Germany on *Frederick*'s anti-aircraft armament. Her four-inch and thirty-seven millimeter guns have been given both optical sights and gun-laying radar, further increasing the effectiveness of her already formidable aircraft defences. Night and poor weather conditions will no longer be an aid to attacking planes, such as when the *Ark Royal*'s Swordfish made their twilight attack on the *Bismarck.*

"This is another late report from Germany, detailing some of the construction changes made to the *Frederick the Great* in light of operational experience with the *Bismarck* and the *Tirpitz.* The rudders are now protected from torpedo strikes by a set of armoured 'vanes' that extend from either side of the stern. An emergency retractable rudder is also provided just forward of the propeller shafts. The number of watertight compartments has been increased to nearly a thousand below the armour deck level. The Kriegsmarine has borrowed an idea from the French Navy. A thick, black gum called ebonite mousée fills several of the more strategically placed compartments. These rather novel modifications reduce *Frederick*'s vulnerability to torpedo damage to practically nil. In light of what happened to the *Bismarck*, *Scharnhorst* and *Tirpitz*, they should only have been expected.

"I have saved the most ominous for last. These four reports all concern developments in German biological and chemical warfare and in their development. The Germans have developed a new, extremely lethal, nerve gas. Too costly for use in SS concentration camps, this gas, called T-four, has been turned over to the military. In particular, the Kriegsmarine.

"Other labs have been building specialized canisters, for the transportation and dispersion of anthrax, cholera and pneumonic plague cultures. These canisters can be placed inside the hollow shell of a one thousand pound bomb or in the warhead of a V-1 missile. Whether or not the production facilities for the gas or the canisters can be destroyed is a moot question for us. Shipments of some three hundred V-1 warheads left those facilities for Norway. They arrived at Alta approximately three days ago."

"You have one more file on your desk, Charlie," Lacey noted, hesitantly. "Dare I ask what's in it?"

"This is not exactly a report, Dennis, it happens to be a study. Done on the quick by a team of medical experts at a college whose name and location aren't important. But their conclusions are. I thought the havoc caused by V-1s with just normal, explosive warheads, would be sufficient to cause a panic. These new 'plague missiles' would surely do that and more, perhaps even unravel the very fabric of society in the region they will afflict. The experts conclude it would take less than ten of them to start an epidemic in a city the size of New York, Boston or Washington. Perhaps three dozen to start an epidemic over a larger area, say the heavily industrialized, northeast corner of New Jersey. And maybe as few as three or four to start an outbreak in a smaller location, like the Norfolk Navy yards or the giant Republic factory in Farmingdale, Long Island.

"The Germans have chosen their diseases well. Pneumonic plague and cholera agents are fast-acting, spread rapidly and are difficult to eradicate. The same can be said of anthrax, though it affects livestock more than people. Fighting the outbreaks will be almost futile. In a few days, the *Frederick the Great* will have started a dozen. The United States has not enough medical personnel or vaccine stockpiles to deal with so many. And the nerve gas, or just the threat of its use, will greatly hamper any endeavour. The end result could be a pandemic, spreading from the east coast across most of North America. The Germans have chosen correctly and estimated correctly, that we have nothing equal to this weapon to threaten them with. We, the Allies, have ignored the dangers posed by chemical and biological weapons and now we shall pay for it.

"A week ago, the Sea Lords felt my conclusions were a bit too 'melodramatic.' They're bang on, if anything."

Cox let the last page of the study slip from his fingers; then he closed its heavy folder and laid it on top of all the other negative documents. Several seconds went by before anyone else in the room spoke up.

"What's in the canister, Commander Cox?" asked Bradley, his voice almost shattering the death-like silence.

"Oh yes, this. It appears as though the Milord agents still in Alta have been doubly lucky. This is ciné film of some recent V-1 launchings done by the *Frederick the Great*. Connie, did that projector and screen I ordered earlier arrive yet?"

"I believe they have," Constance responded. "I'm not quite sure. Let me go check your office. If they have, I'll be needing someone to help me fetch them. They'll be rather bulky and quite heavy."

Naturally, Lacey volunteered ahead of the rest and quickly followed Constance out the door.

"Yes, with your strong arms and broad shoulders, I should think you'd do," she said, in jest.

"You should know, you're the one who keeps complimenting me on them, among other endowments." When they reached the second office, Constance had to stop and sort out which key on her chain would open its door. As she bowed her head to examine the keys, Lacey also bent slightly and planted a fast, soft kiss on the exposed nape of her neck.

"Dennis, really! Your men can see us! What will they think if they catch their commanding officer kissing a subordinate?"

"That I'm a lucky bastard," Lacey answered, "also a horny one. I haven't been with you for days, Connie, we've been doing so much running around lately. With things settling down, I think we can see each other tonight."

"We shouldn't right away, Dennis. Be brave, have a stiff upper lip. After all, it's only been about two and a half days since we last made love."

"Ah yes, I see you've been counting the days as well," Lacey managed to say, before Constance unlocked the door and pulled him inside the empty office; where she embraced him and kissed him.

"The truth is I've been counting the hours," she admitted, still holding onto Lacey. "Darling, it's just as hard for me. You must understand, I know you do. This is a trying time, events command attention and for now, this must do."

She kissed him again, a little longer and then they separated. The equipment Cox ordered had arrived in the office. Lacey grabbed the projector and Constance took the screen. He got to the door first and opened it; on the other side he found Atkinson and Capollini. Both were wearing ear-to-ear, shit-eating grins; so he had been seen.

"Hi, Colonel," Capollini purred, "what're you up to?"

"Collecting some movie equipment, Vince, and we must be leaving. We're late as it is. Oh, you and Frank go over and check out the electronic lab Martinez has set up across the hangar. We only need one, for the Aphrodite drones, since the mother ships have already been outfitted. I would be doing it myself, but my meeting is far from over."

Constance followed Lacey out and they almost made it back to his office, when Atkinson fired off an innocent question Lacey knew he would have to answer carefully.

"Colonel, what are you going to be showing?"

"I don't know, though Commander Cox said something about showing a Donald Duck cartoon before the feature."

"Donald Duck my ass," said Atkinson, once Lacey and Constance had disappeared inside. "That's the last thing I'd believe."

"Yeah, everyone in the team knows that the colonel wouldn't sit still for Donald Duck, he's a Bugs Bunny man."

"Oh shut up, Vince. I thought you were going to

unravel this mystery in a couple of days. It's been a week now and you haven't done anything more than what I could've done."

"Aw have a heart, Frank," Capollini protested, "look at what we've done in that time. If we haven't been flying B-17s, we've been working on them. If we haven't been working on them, we've been stripping parts off of other B-17s to make ours flyable. And if we haven't been doing that, we've been stealing those parts.

"Half the stuff we did in the last week was illegal enough to land us in Leavenworth—if we had been caught and that's just it, we haven't. We got clean away every time and you know as well as I, them kinda odds ain't natural. In all the stunts I pulled in North Africa, I never batted a thousand. Not like this. Which means we have some pretty big guardian angels looking after us. Which means our mission is big, damn big. Not a mere sub pen or a V-1 base like what you thought. But something that can affect the whole war."

"Okay, I get the picture," said Atkinson, throwing up his hands. "A secret like that is going to be buried deep. But now we're at a new base and I'm willing to bet there's some people here who could tell you a few things about our mission. So get friendly with the natives and stop talking to the Norwegians."

"Those two, they never miss a chance," Lacey observed, once safely in his office. "Dig for every little clue."

"What, you mean Frank and Vincent?" Constance asked.

"Who else? The rest of my team are as curious as the next man. It's just that, those guys scrounge for every little innocent clue. They ought to be in intelligence. Frank and Vince are smarter than any

G-2 man I've ever met. They might even be as good as Charlie. Charlie? What the hell is going on here?"

The desk Cox had been using, Lacey's desk, was empty. All the reports, Constance's briefcase and the film canister were being locked inside the office safe by Cox.

"I'm afraid we must postpone the other half of our meeting," he informed. "We'll view the film and discuss the Corsair squadrons later. A problem has developed and we're needed."

"What problem? Has *Frederick* decided to leave her lair ahead of schedule?"

"No, nothing quite so critical though it does concern a ship, with potentially serious consequences. A ship in an outbound Arctic convoy has caught fire. It can't be put out and the crew has abandoned ship. The Admiralty just called and asked us to look over the situation. We may be the only people who can safely destroy that ship."

"Why can't the Royal Navy sink it, with torpedoes or gunfire? How come they laid the job on us?"

"Believe me, Dennis, if it could be done any other way, the Admiralty wouldn't bother us. They know this will delay us but you said we had completed all essential training. This ship must be totally destroyed and not merely sunk. None of its cargo must be allowed to escape and the Admiralty claims that our operation is the only safe, sure way to do so. And I must agree with them. The ship in question is the fleet tanker *Icarus* and she's carrying around two hundred thousand gallons of aviation fuel.

"The Fleet Air Arm is sending over to us a Mark One Avenger torpedo-bomber. It won't be as comfortable as an Avro Anson or a Dakota. But it will transport us to the scene and back a lot faster. Gentlemen, I suggest you go and collect your parachutes. Connie, we'd better have some brought out for us."

The Avenger that taxied across the field was not a true torpedo-bomber but rather one modified into a seven-seat transport, for carrier on-board delivery. Its massive, single-gun dorsal turret was replaced with a streamlined extension of the plane's greenhouse canopy. Apart from that, it was little different from the other Avengers based at Scapa Flow. It wore the same camouflage of gray-green mottled top surfaces and sky green undersides and carried the same squadron codes.

For about a minute, the Avenger parked, idling, in front of the American-occupied hangar while its passengers trickled out and piled inside. Constance was the last to climb in, after trying in vain to locate a pair of pants to wear instead of her skirt. A small crowd managed to collect before the torpedo-bomber left; in it were Atkinson and Capollini.

"Where the hell's he going now?" Capollini asked, referring primarily to Lacey.

"I don't know," said Atkinson, "but they're all going. The colonel, the commander, Connie and those two friends of the commander. Whatever's happening must be big; maybe we're finally going to get to the bottom of all this."

"Shit, I hope not. That would spoil all my fun."

Once the tower cleared it, the Avenger thundered off the active runway and swung over the Scapa Flow fleet anchorage. It selected a west-southwest course and climbed to five thousand feet. As the plane settled into level flight, for approximately the next half hour, Cox produced a map and gave a fuller explanation of the situation to Lacey and Constance.

"Here is where the *Icarus* is currently located," he said, pointing to a large pencil mark on the very familiar map. "About twenty-five miles off the Outer Hebrides. Near the Flannan Islands and this, of course, is Lewis Island.

"The *Icarus* was part of an outward bound, Arctic convoy. Four hours ago, a fire broke out in its engine room. It spread quickly and though the crew was able to eventually contain it below decks, they realized it could not be put out. At great risk, two of the convoy's escorts came alongside and evacuated the crew. Since then the tanker has been drifting, in moderate seas and surrounded by a ring of destroyers and frigates."

"How far away are those warships staying?" Lacey asked.

"They have orders to maintain a distance of eight to ten miles. Both our Navies have had experience with ships in similar circumstances and they have damaged, even sunk, vessels that were closer than that. I believe the latest incident happened to the U.S. Navy. During the Philippine landings, a kamikaze plane dove into an ammunition ship, what resulted was rather devastating."

"Eight miles? Couldn't the destroyers use their big guns to blow-up the tanker? Or torpedoes?"

"I see you don't know much about naval weaponry," Cox noted. "Eight miles is beyond the range of torpedoes and anything below cruiser-sized guns. And we can't tell an aircraft to carry out rocket, torpedo or dive bombing attacks either. They'd never survive the detonation of the fuel which, if such weapons were used, would not be completely consumed. The Sea Lords reached the conclusion that that can only be assured if we use one of your Aphrodite bombers."

"And this time I'll agree with them as well," admitted Lacey. "It will take time though, to prepare any Aphrodites. I only hope we can wait that long."

Exactly a half hour later, a pair of warships passed underneath the Avenger. On either side, more could be seen hovering in the distance. Directly ahead lay the tanker *Icarus*. Only a slight haze of smoke hung over it and there were no visible flames. The ship did list slightly to one side and several of its life boat davits were empty. The life boats themselves bobbed about in the sea near the tanker; empty, their passengers long since removed by the surrounding destroyers and frigates.

The torpedo-bomber gave the *Icarus* a wide berth, coming no closer than four or five miles on its initial pass. The extended, greenhouse canopy allowed the passengers an excellent, though distant, view of the stricken ship.

"Here, Dennis, use these if you want a better look at her," said Cox, handing to Lacey a pair of binoculars.

"Oh I don't think I can get a better view of her than what I already have," he responded, pointing the glasses at Constance. "No, these don't improve things."

"Not her, Dennis. I mean her, her."

Lacey's prank embarrassed Constance, frustrated Cox but made Bradley laugh jovially. Which in turn elicited a caustic comment from Rotherham.

"Why must you 'North Americans' always add levity to even the most serious of situations?"

"Because that's the only way you can win a war," Lacey answered, finally turning the binoculars on the ship. "Now let's see . . . Charlie, does this plane still have a gun camera?"

"I don't know, it may still. I'll ask the pilot. Why do you wish to know that?"

229

"A little movie footage would be great to show my men. It'll make the briefing go much faster."

The gun camera was one of the other items to have been removed besides the dorsal turret. However, another aircraft, a Seafire this time, was quickly dispatched from Scapa Flow. In fact it arrived over the scene, filmed it and returned to the Orkney Island's base ahead of the Avenger.

Lacey's hastily called briefing produced the expected clamor of excitement among the mother ship crews and the Aphrodite drone teams. Only one voice was heard complaining about the sudden call, Capollini's.

"This ain't fair," he groused, "I didn't have enough time. Ain't fair at all. I was just getting some hot leads."

"Why don't you tell it to the colonel?" Atkinson suggested, "I'm sure he'll delay the operation until you can find out what it is."

"Thanks, Frank, I should've known I wouldn't get no sympathy outta you. You're probably glad that you don't have to risk any of your money on a bet."

The auditorium quieted down when Cox and Lacey appeared. Moments after they began the briefing, it was apparent that the main operation was not going to be discussed. It produced a noticeable letdown in the assembled personnel, except of course for Capollini. Soon the auditorium lights were dimmed and a short, ninety-second film shown.

"This is our target," Lacey continued, standing to one side of the screen. "The tanker *Icarus*. Part of a convoy bound for Russia, she caught fire some hours ago and had to be abandoned by her crew. The Royal Navy wants her destroyed but there's a problem; her cargo is two hundred thousand gallons of av gas. It's too risky to use normal weapons against her. The

230

ship or planes employed might be lost as well and the total destruction of her cargo would not be ensured. I emphasize that this tanker must be completely destroyed, wiped off the face of the earth. And frankly there's no better way to do that than to dive one of our drones into her."

Lacey's plan was to use two drones, the second would be operational insurance. The oldest pair of B-17s were taken in hand and outfitted with the full range of guidance and control systems. Once that job was done, the bombers were handed over to some Royal Navy armory teams. They, under Lacey and Atkinson's direction, loaded each drone with ten thousand pounds of torpex high explosive. Some seven and a half tons less than the maximum amount permissible but it would still take hours to safely load.

Cox was reduced to merely watching the proceedings, the latter from a safe distance, listening to reports on the *Icarus*'s condition and worrying if the situation would remain the same or suddenly go critical. At least Capollini got something better to do with his time. He checked out the two mother ships assigned to the operation. Naturally they were Lacey's and Atkinson's.

"C'mon, Charlie. It's nearly midnight and it's time for us to get some sleep," Lacey suggested, when he stopped by Cox's office. Cox sat behind his desk, facing the window instead of the door. When he didn't stir or respond, Lacey stepped up and was ready to prod him; until it became apparent that he was asleep. "Well I'll be damned."

"Dennis, what's going on in here?" Constance asked, appearing in the doorway. "What are you two discussing?"

"Nothing, he's dead to the world."

"Oh no, this happened the last time we were up here." She came around to the opposite side of the desk and checked on Cox herself. "Dennis, we must do something."

"Wake him up. I was about to do it when you came."

"Easier said than done. He sleeps quite soundly. Why not pick him up and take him back to his quarters?"

"Connie, you know this base better than I do," Lacey protested, "that's more than a mile away. I'd bust a gasket or something carrying him that far."

"Not really. I have a jeep waiting outside."

"That's better, at least I'll only strain something. Here, lock these things away and grab his hat and coat. I'll figure out a way to lift him."

Lacey scooped up the files on Cox's desk and handed them to Constance. Then he pulled Cox out from behind the desk and rotated his chair so he would have enough room to move the inert figure. Lacey kneeled in front of Cox and threw him over his right shoulder. With great effort he straightened up and turned slowly. For a few moments, Cox mumbled something unintelligible and seemed ready to stir from his sleep. But the attempt was futile and he was snoring lightly again by the time Constance returned to Lacey's side.

"Poor Charles, this day really has been trying for him," she sympathized, placing Cox's cap on his head.

"Trying for him?" Lacey repeated, incredulously. "Hell, I was the one out today flying B-17s, wiring them with radio controls and showing how to load them with explosives. All he had to do was plan and worry."

"You forgot to mention greeting those Fleet Air

Arm commanders and then seeing them off," Constance added, poking a little fun at his complaint. "Don't be too jealous of him, Dennis. After all, he's going to be spending this night alone. Whereas you shall have company."

Loading of the Aphrodites continued through the night, until just before dawn; when Martinez and the other electronics specialists returned to complete the wiring of the arming and detonation circuits. Lacey appeared to make the final checks on all the systems in each plane and to give their pilot-flight engineer teams one more briefing.

"Commander Cox says the basic situation hasn't changed much. The tanker is still afloat, still burning and has drifted a little closer to Lewis Island. But it can't go on forever, eventually she'll either sink or explode on her own.

"Now the mother ships will take off first, followed by the lead drone. Number two will remain here on the ground, engines idling, as a backup. It'll be safer that way, for if the first one succeeds, you'd have to either abandon the second in flight or try landing it back here. Which, with five tons of torpex on board, would be a little hairy. Good luck and don't do anything stupid; this isn't the big one."

The runways at Scapa Flow were wide enough and long enough to allow Lacey and Atkinson to make a formation takeoff. Not only did it save time over single-ship departures, and later formationing maneuvers, it was also a most impressive display of Army Air Force air power. The sound of eight Wright Cyclones howling in unison and the sight of two Boeing giants lifting off together, caused more than a few heads to turn. By comparison, the takeoff of the first Aphrodite was something of an anti-

233

climax, though some people did notice that all traffic was suspended during the drone's departure and the other one was held at a remote corner of the field.

"Mother ship leader to Aphrodite pilot, level off at five thousand feet and activate all radio control systems. Lacey to Aphrodite controller, check out your equipment, standby to take command. Lacey to crew, operations are about to begin. Gunners, you know the routine. Can anybody tell me where Commander Cox has gotten to?"

Once again, Cox was along for the ride and, as had become the norm, he sat behind Martinez; watching him take over the flying of a plane far below them. This time however, there was a slight change in the procedure. When full command had been transferred to Martinez, and after the gunners confirmed that the drone crew had bailed out, he raised the guard plates on an isolated trio of toggle switches and flipped them.

"Aphrodite controller to pilot. Primary detonator, on. Secondary detonator, on. Igniter defeat has been deactivated. The drone is now armed, everything is go, Colonel."

"Roger, Andy, change course twenty degrees to the right. Maintain altitude and increase cruise speed to one hundred and sixty miles an hour."

Martinez unlocked the flight controls and fed them the slight movements needed to swing the unmanned Fortress onto a new heading. It looked as if he were scarcely working. Cox of course knew differently.

"My aide may know more about this than I do but it still fascinates me," he admitted. "It's really quite amazing. I just wonder if this will be the way future wars are fought."

"No, I doubt it, Commander," said Martinez. "No matter how much we improve this gear, there's one problem we can never overcome. There's only so many frequencies we can use. Why just to control the three drones we do have uses up most of them. And a drone just can't be flown like a regular plane. Here, try it for yourself."

Cox had been wondering when he would get a crack at flying one of the drones. He was starting to think he would have to make a blatant suggestion or order it. Martinez engaged the auto-pilot and moved out to allow Cox in. He gave him a few pointers on how to handle the controls, then told him it was his airplane.

Cox grabbed the joy stick firmly and hit the auto-pilot switch. The unlocked flight controls immediately began to float; he tried to correct for the natural tendencies and ended up with the Aphrodite wallowing about the sky.

"Lacey to controller, what the hell's going on back there? The gunners say something's wrong with the drone?"

"No, nothing's wrong with her, Colonel. I've just let Commander Cox take control of her. He's finding out it's not like flying a normal plane."

"I'll say it's not," Cox added. "You have to completely divorce your actions from what you're feeling. It's not like normal flying at all. I'm responding to the movements of the plane I'm in and not the one I'm flying."

"Yeah, it'll take some getting used to, Commander," said Martinez, "but don't worry, you'll have plenty of time. It will be twenty minutes before I have to do anything."

As his stay at the controls wore on, Cox's skill at flying the drone improved. He became acquainted with its touchy sensitivity, the rather limited field of view the television monitor gave him and the fact that he didn't need to use, didn't have any, rudder pedals to make a turn or hold the B-17 on a straight course. Gradually, he got proficient enough to make a few rudimentary maneuvers; climbs, dives and simple turns. Near the end of his time, Cox was able to make a complete, three hundred and sixty degree turn with a shallow climb thrown in.

"Nice work, sir," Martinez offered. "Now make four, ninety degree, right turns and lock her back on course."

Cox responded with his most polished handling yet. The B-17 banked cleanly to the right, no skidding or erratic wing dipping, levelled off and flew on that course for approximately half a minute. Then the maneuver was repeated for a second time, then a third; then, nothing. The Fortress just stopped answering to Cox's commands and flew off on a south-southeast heading. At first he didn't realize that something had gone wrong; neither did Martinez until he heard Cox banging the joy stick from one side to the other.

"Controller to pilot, Colonel, we got a problem! The drone ain't under our control no more! Commander Cox was making ninety degree turns and all of a sudden she decided to stop making them. She's flying away to the south at about six thousand feet."

"Check all your controls and systems, Andy. Make sure the fault isn't up here, with us. Leader to wing man, Frank, we have some trouble here. Stay with us for now but alert Scapa Flow and tell 'em to move your drone onto the runway."

Lacey broke formation with a steep, left turn and dove to increase his speed. Atkinson followed, repeating the same moves and eventually coming back to his original position on Lacey's right wing

236

tip. By that time Martinez had started to run a frenzied diagnosis of his equipment.

With Cox still sitting in the operator's seat, he pulled off the console's back panel and panned a flashlight beam through its interior. On finding no obvious shorts or burned-out vacuum tubes, Martinez asked for Cox to try each of the flight controls and switches.

"I have a response from the throttles," he observed. "The airspeed has just gone up by ten miles an hour. Has anything happened at that end, Leftenant?"

"No, sir, not a spark or a fizzle."

"Do you want me to try the arming toggles?"

"No, they don't have anything to do with the flight systems," said Martinez. "I'll try the leads and the connections to the antennas. See if any of them are loose."

None was. In frustration Martinez went on to check the power lines. Eventually he concluded that nothing in the mother ship, nothing he could correct, was malfunctioning.

"It must've been the rush job we had to do on wiring up the drones," said Lacey, after Martinez made his final report. "I'll have the pilot and flight engineer on the second Aphrodite make a check before they abandon it."

"Yeah but what are we going to do about this one in the meantime, Colonel? Commander Cox says she'll still respond to the throttles. Why don't we just cut power and let her crash?"

"Because she's in level flight and will only start gliding if you kill her engines. You know how well a B-17 can glide, Andy. It could go on for miles before finally crashing. If it's still working, take a good look at your monitor screen. That's the coast of Scotland ahead of us. I don't think Commander Cox would appreciate our drone coming down somewhere in his country. No, I'm going to have it destroyed in mid-air. Keep on top of the situation and let me know if anything changes.

"Leader to wing man, order your drone to takeoff. Have the crew check over the flight control systems before they bail out. It's your show now, Frank, good luck."

Atkinson said the same to Lacey then peeled his Fortress away like a fighter. For a moment Lacey held his own bomber level. He waited for the turbulence caused by Atkinson's departure to die down prior to diving after his errant charge.

The drone held steady to the last course Cox had set it on. Guided by a frozen, electronic hand, nothing bothered it. Even when another B-17 dropped onto its wing.

"Perhaps we could try 'tapping it with our wing tip'?" Cox suggested, paraphrasing an idea he heard someone mention during an earlier, similar situation.

"Hell no, not even Frank would risk a stunt like that with a plane in this state," said Lacey. "One good tap could blow both our planes to kingdom come. A good burst of cannon shells will do the same thing and I have just the people for the job. Lacey to Stanmoor leader, I see by the schedule, you're up on another gunnery training flight this morning. How many neophytes are with you?"

"Stanmoor Leader, here, I have two aircraft with me. Are you having another problem like the last one?"

"I'm afraid so, it's similar but not exactly alike. This particular drone is 'hot,' it's dangerous and that's all I can tell you about it. We'll be needing a good marksman, do you happen to have one?"

"I believe so, give me your altitude, heading and approximate location and I'll join you as soon as possible."

"Mother ship two to Aphrodite pilot, we have you in sight. Standby to activate all radio control systems and check out the wiring on the flight systems especially. The colonel thinks the problem that made the first drone fuck up on us was in there. All I can say is, if yours fucks up too, we're all going to have egg on our faces. That goes especially for our Royal Navy buddy and I don't want to let down a guy who's given us a second chance."

"Got'cha, mother ship two. We don't want to let down the commander, either. We'll go over those circuits with a magnifying glass, a fine-tooth comb if we have one."

The two bombers approached each other on a collision course; fortunately, more than a mile in altitude separated them. Atkinson let the Aphrodite slide underneath him before coming around to the same course it was flying. Both his controller and the pilot-flight engineer team went over the electronics that would soon be flying the drone.

The Spitfires rendezvoused with Lacey far above and behind his drone. Struggling to keep pace with the slow giant, they had to drop their flaps in order to pull their speed down. Stanmoor leader held the closest position to the B-17's left wing tip; his two students bobbed and weaved in their stations on his left wing.

"What I need from you is some top, long-range shooting," Lacey told Stanmoor leader. "I don't want your guys to get any closer than one thousand yards. As I said before, that ship down there is hot and dangerous."

"I see, couldn't you tell me just a bit more about

why this plane is so dangerous? It's not for me, mind you. It's for my men, so they'll understand the situation better."

"Sorry I can't oblige you. But you will see what I mean when that B-17 is hit and I want solid hits on the fuselage. No shot out engines or chewed up wings. I don't want her going out of control and crashing, got it?"

"Understood, I'm sure my men are equal to the task. Stanmoor leader, out."

Once he explained the situation as best he could, Stanmoor leader unleashed his charges on the drone. The outermost Spitfire dove after the bomber first; opening fire with its 20 mm cannons when the gun sight said it was in range. Because of Lacey's requirement, the fighter's battery of .303-inch machine guns were silent. And because the sight's span dial had been improperly set, the eagerly hammered out burst of cannon shells went wide of its intended target.

"Mother ship two to mother ship leader, we have control of our Aphrodite and we have armed its warhead. How's it going with yours?"

"I got hold of some Spitfires but they haven't destroyed it yet," Lacey replied. "What's your ETA, Frank?"

"At current speed, my time to target will be twenty minutes. If you get done in time, c'mon up and watch the fireworks, Colonel."

The second wing man opened fire too late and had to break off after pumping only a handful of shells through the B-17's tail fin. The first one made a return pass, getting hits on the number four engine until Lacey spoke up.

"Knock that off, Stanmoor three!" he shouted, barely giving his co-pilot time to switch to the fighter frequency. "I told you no hits on the engines or wings. Now disengage and let the other guy try again. If he's unlucky, you can have a third chance."

He was. Stanmoor two did everything correctly, lined up the target properly, poured a burst into the fuselage but nothing happened. The unmanned Fortress flew on serenely, a little worse for wear. Stanmoor Three had his third chance and he wasn't going to let it slip away like the others.

"Mother ship two to containment leader, we are approaching the target area. Withdraw your warships to the maximum possible radius. We will circle the area and we'll let you know when we are beginning the run. Stand by to put your fingers in your ears, this is going to be one hell of a bang."

"Colonel, that Spitfire is in a very steep dive," said Lacey's co-pilot, "in fact he will not pull out . . ."

". . . Until he's underneath the ship," Lacey completed, "sorry about that but you're right. Stanmoor leader, what the hell's going on with your man?"

"I don't know, though he may be feeling somewhat frustrated over not downing your robot plane."

"Well stop him damn it or he'll down more than a runaway B-17. He's already too close to open fire."

It was too late. The Spitfire bottomed out of its dive and reared onto its tail, climbing toward the bomber's underbelly. His cannons had barely started to spit their shells when the Fortress was torn, shattered by an intense white flash. The expanding cloud of wreckage, and the still climbing Spitfire, were consumed by the fireball the initial explosion had become. A powerful shock wave preceded it, rocking the remaining B-17 and Spitfires. They overflew the point of destruction and by the time they turned back to view the results, the flames had spent themselves.

"Mother ship two to containment leader, we are ready for our run. We will make it from the west and we'll attempt to hit the tanker broadside. I suggest you put your ships on battle stations and put your fingers in your ears."

"My God, there's nothing left," Cox observed. He had come forward to the cockpit and was crouched beside Lacey.

"No, a few things will be found," Lacey corrected, "engine cylinders and some twisted scraps of metal, that may be identified as tail feathers or wing tips. And some larger pieces from the Spitfire. At least that dumb son-of-a-bitch never knew what hit him. Jesus Christ!"

Off to the left, on the northwestern horizon, a new sun rose from the sea. Far brighter than the old one, it flared into being silently and became a boiling red giant as the Fortress and its escort were hit by the shock wave. It was a sharp crack followed by a deep, sustained rumble. Not nearly so bad as the previous, ear-numbing thunderclap but, given the distance involved, more powerful and awesome. The *Icarus* had ceased to exist.

If the first blast left them speechless, this one stunned them. No one in Lacey's crew uttered a sound or made a conscious move during the life of the new, artificially-created, sun. If the B-17 had gone into a dive, Lacey would probably not have recovered it.

"I'll wager they heard that all over Scotland and saw it as far away as the continent," Cox finally said.

"That, is what happens when you mix one B-17, ten thousand pounds of torpex and two hundred

242

thousand gallons of aviation gasoline together," said
Lacey, trying to be nonchalant about it. "Just wait
till you see what happens when we mix twenty-five
thousand pounds with your target. Even if it's not a
direct hit, it could still bring the mountains
themselves down upon it."

Chapter Ten
BRIEFING
THE MISSION BEGINS

Of course Cox immediately hushed Lacey up with his traditional warning. However, the damage had been done. Both the co-pilot and the flight engineer heard his incautious remark. When the B-17 returned to Scapa Flow, Lacey noted they were met by Capollini, once they had completed their post-flight procedures and briefings. And Capollini met with Atkinson, once he had completed his.

"Those two, I'm going to have to put a stop to this," Lacey observed, indicating to Constance, the semi-clandestine meeting his top officers were holding under the wing of a Fortress. "As I said before, they don't miss a thing. Charlie, how long will it take for those Corsair squadrons to get here? I know we didn't finish our meeting with their COs but I do know that's one of the reasons why they came."

"They'll be in Scapa Flow by early afternoon," Cox informed, stepping up to the office windows.

"What? Hell they're only down in Cornwall, at your Culdrose training station. At cruise speed, those Corsairs could be here in two hours and it's not even noon yet."

"They happen to be bringing their homes with them. The carriers *Pursuer* and *Ravager*. They, and their escorts, will drop anchor in Scapa Flow by noon tomorrow. Pilots of the embarked squadrons will be brought here and, with your men, be fully briefed on the situation and our operation. Until then, you must surely know of something to keep your men busy."

"For the afternoon I do," said Lacey, "some of this base's Avengers will tow targets for us. We need more formation, air-to-air gunnery. Everything else we've done enough training for but that can't last forever."

"Only as long as there is daylight. Which, in this second week of November, is becoming a precious commodity. While I know it's not your style, Dennis, you could order them to shut-up for the next twenty-four hours. It may sound harsh but in the past, I have seen it work most effectively."

"Well, you're right. It's not my style and it wouldn't sit well with my men. My team is no squadron of average Joes, they are highly experienced, highly skilled men. Too experienced to put up with military bullshit, especially Atkinson and Capollini. They call me colonel even when I'm not around and the only reason for that is, they think I'm good enough to be respected. Otherwise, it would be 'Colonel' to my face and 'asshole' behind my back. You haven't forgotten Colonel Brogger, have you?

"Respect for a military superior is a tenuous thing, you should know that. It doesn't take much to destroy it. Oh sure those guys would still obey my orders but they wouldn't be inspired. And maybe the only reason why we've come as far as we have, is because they were inspired."

"How then do you propose to deal with your men?" asked Constance. "You can't plead with them, Dennis. You're their commanding officer, you're not one of them. Even I know a commanding officer can't always be popular with his men."

"Yes, though you don't have to be blunt about it," Lacey maintained, "there are subtler ways to get the message across. I'll have to corner one of those two alone and hammer it in. After the gunnery mission would be the best time, right now they're going to be too busy preparing for it."

Lacey chose Capollini to pounce on; catching him on his way back to his quarters. Capollini couldn't resist the chance to grab a ride and it was not until he got in the jeep, that he realized his commanding officer had another motive for making the offer.

"I know you're putting together the pieces of what we're doing," Lacey informed him. "And right now, we're getting down to the wire. Whether or not you're getting close is something I can't say. The important point is we are and we can't afford to have you snooping around."

"Are you asking me to stop?" Capollini inquired.

"Yes. I know that's like asking a duck to lay off June bugs but I am. What we're doing is critical to the war. We've taken too many risks with its secrecy already and now that we're so close, I don't want anymore. This isn't like Muroc, where we were in the safety of the United States. We're in a theater of operations."

"Aw, Colonel, North Africa was a theater of operations and we never jeopardized any mission we ever found out about. Including the big Ploesti raids."

"This is bigger than Ploesti. It will be the most important operation launched from England since Overlord."

"How can what a couple of B-17s do be as big as D-Day? That changed the whole course of the war."

"What we're part of could change the course of history itself," warned Lacey. "Bigger than anything you've ever encountered. Except one. Except one. Do you remember the New Mexico project you uncovered once?"

"Sure I do. What guy from Long Island wouldn't be interested in a project called Manhattan? Hey, you're not telling me that what we're on is as big as that?"

"It's bigger. The uranium-bomb project is months away from completion. What we are part of is ready to go now. Do I need to elaborate any further?"

"No, not if what we're on is bigger than the Manhattan Project," Capollini responded, his face draining of color. "I'll back off this time, Colonel. I don't want to know until you're ready to tell me. When might that be?"

"Very soon, Vince. Within the next twenty-four hours, you will be told all you need to know."

Capollini was dropped off at the main door of the building where all the team's officers were housed; whether they were British, American, Norwegians, male or female. He did not stay there for long. Just enough time to pick up a small blackboard and head out the back door. His destination was the barracks where the team's enlisted men had been placed and were currently resting from the latest sortie.

"All right you guys, c'mon gather 'round!" Capollini shouted, getting their attention. "This is the time to place your bets. I got the low down from the colonel; our mission starts tomorrow, so let's see your money."

He set the blackboard on a table and, while the Americans and Norwegians obeyed his request, he erased several of the entries.

"Hey, Captain, that was my idea you just scrubbed," said Herrmann, "what's going on? Did the colonel tell you what our mission is?"

"If he had, I wouldn't be taking bets and if he did, the colonel wouldn't be a colonel. He didn't tell me exactly what it was but I know how big it is. It ain't no sub pen, or V-1 launchers, or Gestapo headquarters, or mine entrance, or bomber base. What we're going to do is change the whole damn war, so it has to be one of these.

"The research labs at Telemark, the guns of Trondeness or a German battleship hiding in a fjord."

"How can them things change the war, Vince?"

"Easy. The Telemark labs were a top priority target for a long time with the Royal Air Force. They made heavy water and did other things in atomic research. These guys said they were sabotaged by the underground a year ago but they could be in operation again. The guns at Trondeness are a coastal defence battery, there's three of them and they have nineteen and a half-inch bores. They're the biggest guns the Germans have ever built, they can lob a one ton shell over thirty miles. German battleships mount either fifteen or eleven-inch guns and can do a lot of damage to convoys or, like the Trondeness battery, an invasion fleet."

"Invasion? Did I hear you right, Captain?" asked one of the Norwegians.

"You sure did," said Capollini, then, making a formal announcement. "Gentlemen, we're going to be the spearhead of the invasion of Norway!"

"Gentlemen, be seated," Cox instructed, after he and the other commanding officers reached the front stage. In an auditorium built for several times the number, less than one hundred men occupied it. They were almost evenly divided between the Army Air Force/Royal Air Force team Lacey commanded and the pilots of the two Fleet Air Arm Corsair squadrons. Beyond them, only the captains of the *Ravager* and *Pursuer* were present. Cox continued his presentation, once they all took their seats. "For the last ten days, you have been operating, training, in great secrecy. Whether you were originally working up for operations in the Pacific, flying patrols over the North Sea or heading home for 'reassignment,' you were uprooted and given a new mission to prepare for. You had to learn carrier operations under Arctic conditions, how to crew a B-17 and how to fly remotely controlled aircraft across difficult terrain. On top of that, you had to turn your commands into operational entities. You were told as little as possible about your mission. I know that rankled some of you but it had to be, though not anymore."

At the wave of his hand, the auditorium lights came down and a slide projector threw an image on the screen behind him. To all save a tiny handful of the gathered, the warship shown was a complete unknown. Cox picked up a pointer, identified the ship and began to explain her history, the changes made to her and the threat the *Frederick the Great* posed to the Allies.

Following that, he gave a brief outline of the attack they were to launch against the battleship and then turned the briefing over to the other, operational commanders. Lacey covered the routes his unit would fly, both to the Alten Fjord area and the return trip to their refueling station in the Shetland Islands. Commanders Bradley and Rotherham came up next and explained how their squadrons would escort the mother ships, the Aphrodite drones and suppress flak defences in the target area. Last was Cox, back to end the briefing. As in the beginning, he motioned for the room lights to dim.

"Lest you people underestimate the power of *Frederick*, I have decided to show you this. It was gained at great cost and hardship and I hope you appreciate it." This time a movie projector came on and ran a jumpy, unedited film of the battleship's latest weapons' trials. Throughout, Cox kept up a running narration. "Agents of the underground shot this a week and a half ago. The *Frederick the Great* has been moved to the entrance of Kaa Fjord, where its main guns were fired at test missiles launched . . ."

In the first part of the film, the ship's forward turrets were trained to the left; at the Brattholm Islands on the opposite side of Alten Fjord. Their fifteen-inch guns were elevated slightly and fired at the rocks. Singly, later in unison, they fired some twenty shells in all, before being swung back to their rest positions.

". . . There is not a ship in the Atlantic that can stand up to those guns. Not even another battleship, if we had any of those ready to sail and we don't. Her secondary armament is the equivalent of a cruiser's main guns and anti-aircraft guns, the size of a destroyer's. In this next shot, you'll see the missiles they tested. Part of the reason why *Frederick* was moved from her mooring location was to give those missiles the distance they needed to rise above the fjord's high walls."

The scene shifted to the battleship's stern. A set of hangar-like doors opened on the "X house" and a pair of stub-winged V-1s were pushed out on cradles. They each followed a separate line of tracks to one of the two ski ramps. The handling crews quickly slid the missiles onto the ramps and hooked to each a power umbilical. Then they ran for a hatchway and closed the door behind them.

The shot ended before the missile pulse jets had started. In the next one, the V-1 farthest from the camera was already firing; a faint jet of flame could be seen erupting from its tail pipe. The second came to life as the first was enveloped by a cloud of steam. A moment later it rode off the launcher on a long, white plume of gases. The piston that propelled it up the ramp, fell away from the V-1's underbelly and hit the water like one of *Frederick*'s fifteen-inch shells. The camera panned to follow the missile's flight but swung back to catch the launch of the second. When they both cleared the fjord's walls the film ended and when the auditorium lights were switched on, Cox was still standing. Waiting to give the final word.

"As it so often happens, we are what war comes down to. A handful of untried men and equipment, about to be committed to a desperate battle, upon whose outcome the fate of nations and perhaps even civilization itself will be decided. I know this to be true, not just from reading history but from being part of it. Three and a half years ago, I was in your place. Part of a torpedo strike the carrier *Victorious* was about to launch against the *Bismarck,* one of the sister ships of the *Frederick the Great.*

"We failed that time but, fortunately, there were others who didn't and today, the *Bismarck* rests on the bottom of the Atlantic. The situation is now a different and much more desperate one. We are the only force that has been trained to stop this ship and if we fail, there is no one to take our place. Even if there were, they wouldn't have the time. If we are not successful, if the *Frederick the Great* emerges un-damaged, she will raise anchor in twenty-four hours and set sail for the North Atlantic. Through planning and luck, she is precisely the right weapon, in the right place, at the right moment in time.

251

Together with the last pocket battleships and heavy cruisers of the Kriegsmarine, she will wield more power than any other naval force in history.

"Gentlemen, we are in a unique position. In the next few days, our actions will change the course of world events. We shall hold the fate of millions in what we do or fail to do. Based on what I have seen and heard, I don't think they could be in any better hands. The best of luck to you all, see you over Norway."

The *Pursuer* and *Ravager* weighed anchor by nightfall, as soon as their pilots had returned from the air base. They departed with their destroyer escorts to join, and eventually outdistance, a Russia-bound convoy.

At the Scapa Flow air base, there was also activity related to the operation. First, Capollini had to go around and collect his money from the losers and payoff the winners. To those who balked, he responded, "We bet on what we would blow-up, not on what the outcome would be. You makes your bets and you takes your chances. You lost, so pay up."

Eventually he made almost two thousand dollars; later came the more important activities. The three B-17s earmarked to be Aphrodite drones, were flown out to another, more remote, airfield in the Orkney Islands. Used mostly for training flights and the occasional patrol mission, it was now turned over to the U.S. Army Air Force and some Royal Navy armory teams. Here the drones would be equipped with their electronics and loaded with torpex; which would come from a combat store ship, moored to a nearby pier.

Everyone in Lacey's original team and many of the Norwegians either flew with the B-17s or followed them in a Royal Navy Dakota. Other duties forced

Cox and Constance to stay behind. Except for the remaining Norwegians, they were alone until the Dakota returned at last light.

"I left the armory teams in charge of loading the explosives," said Lacey. "They got experience with the other two drones though not in placing a full load on board."

"Then shouldn't you have stayed behind to help them?" Cox asked. "I mean, what if they improperly secure the explosives and they later shift in flight? We could have another disaster on our hands."

"Hell, it will take them until tomorrow morning to load the first ten thousand pounds. And there's another fifteen thousand pounds after that. I only hope your supply ship has enough torpex to fill all three drones. We used up twenty thousand pounds of the stuff yesterday."

"Oh there's no need to worry. That ship is carrying a month's production of torpex. Some one hundred thousand pounds in all. I had hoped we would have enough to outfit a reserve drone but now, it looks like we'll have to go with the first three, whatever their problems."

"There won't be any," Lacey maintained. "We'll give the systems a proper check out this time. And then check the check out. Why don't you come with us tomorrow and see for yourself?"

Cox did. The day's few duties could be handled by Constance and there was more than enough room on the Dakota to take him along; most mother ship personnel stayed to give their aircraft thorough examinations as well.

The airfield was on Hoy Island, one of the south Orkneys that formed the Scapa Flow lagoon. A simple, one runway station, the incoming Dakota would be its only traffic for the day and, beyond the three drones, would be the only aircraft on the field.

Lacey, together with Martinez and his other electronics specialists, Davis and Mueller; went from Fortress to Fortress, seeing if anything had changed during the night. Cox followed Lacey around like a shadow. Though when it came time for the specialists to be assigned, he chose to accompany Martinez on his inspection of the lead drone's electronics. Lacey, in turn, went off to instruct the armory teams on loading the remaining seven and a half tons of torpex. Hours later, they met each other while wandering around the bombers.

"I see you've run out of things to pass the time," said Lacey, confronting Cox behind one of the drones.

"Yes, Lieutenant Martinez was starting on the exacting, circuit by circuit check. Connie might have liked it but that was really too detailed for me. Besides, Martinez mentioned he preferred to do such work in solitude. How is your work proceeding with the armory teams?"

"They don't need me anymore, a few pointers and they got the idea. I've been spending most of my time just watching their operations at each bomber. They're loading more than a thousand pounds of explosives an hour, they'll be done by around six o'clock this afternoon. I'm ready to crawl out of my skin—I wish the mission were starting now."

"So does everyone else but a commander feels it the most," Cox observed. "Even I do and I'll be little better than an observer tomorrow."

"What's it like to attack a battleship, Charlie? I've never seen one in the flesh, or maybe I should say in the steel?"

"Yes, that would be better. I don't care how much the aircraft carrier has eclipsed the battleship, they're still frightening to behold. They're like great, ugly gray monsters. Too big to be kept smart and clean, too big to move as fast as they do and too big for you to think they can be stopped, though perhaps I'm being a little prejudiced.

"My first assignment was to the carrier *Glorious*, to its Swordfish squadron. By June of 1940, I had flown exactly six combat ops and we were covering the evacuation of Norway. On the fourth of June, I was scheduled to fly a reconnaissance sortie. That, however, was scratched. Some RAF Hurricanes had escaped and were doing the impossible, like landing aboard a carrier with no training or arrester hooks. They all made it down safely and just as we were stowing the last, the battle cruisers *Scharnhorst* and *Gneisenau* appeared on the horizon behind us.

"What followed really wasn't much of a battle. We only had two destroyers with us and would have had to turn into the wind to launch any aircraft. Instead we tried to outrun two of the fastest warships in the German fleet. A half hour after they spotted us, the battle cruisers opened fire. In fifty minutes they sank both of our escorts and the *Glorious* had to be abandoned. She sank an hour later and we were in the water for two days before a Norwegian ship picked us up."

"I suppose after that came your *Bismarck* encounter," said Lacey, recalling what Cox mentioned at the briefing.

"Yes, a year less a month after the *Glorious* went down, I was on a brand new carrier, the *Victorious*. We were taking Hurricanes to Malta, again Hurricanes, when the *Bismarck* and the *Prinz Eugen* broke into the North Atlantic. We dropped the fighters off at Gibraltar and returned to the Atlantic, with only fifteen embarked aeroplanes. We managed to launch a single strike at around midnight, scoring a lone torpedo hit that did nothing to hinder the *Bismarck*. It was up to the *Ark Royal* to cripple her and allow His Majesty's battleships to sink her. Thus a second chance to sink a German battleship had slipped by me."

"What? Don't tell me you actually wanted to face a battlewagon?"

"Not exactly. My father wanted me to," Cox admitted. "He said it to me when I received my wings and each time I went to sea. 'Go and sink a battleship, my son.'"

"Sounds to me like your father is trying to live your life. Why the hell doesn't he go out and sink his own?"

"Oh but he tried to, once. Back during the last war. Both my father and my grandfather were in His Majesty's Navy then. They were both at the Battle of Jutland. One was a junior officer on the fleet's flagship, the other was captain of one of His Majesty's latest battle cruisers. At one point in the battle, I could tell you exactly where and when, the cruiser took several hits and exploded. No survivors.

"My father was wounded in a later action and invalided out of the service at the end of the war. He was determined that his son would follow in the family tradition and also avenge that loss. And I did, up to a point. He took a dim view of me joining the Fleet Air Arm, though he reconciled himself to the fact that air power would dominate naval warfare. Then came the war and my—air power's—failure to sink the *Scharnhorst*, *Gneisenau* and *Bismarck*."

"Hell, he can't blame you because some frail, old biplanes couldn't sink those ships," Lacey snapped, "it isn't fair. Your father should have been like my father."

"No, he doesn't really blame me, just my choice. After the *Bismarck,* he said he would settle for a Japanese battleship but even that eluded me. With my combat experience, I was elevated to command the torpedo squadron of a new carrier, the *Indomitable.* However, during her workup in the West Indies, the *Indomitable* ran aground off Jamaica. In addition to her damage, I suffered two broken legs. By the time I came out of the hospital, this posting in Intelligence was about the only one open to me."

"Couldn't your friends have helped you? You old warhorse types always have a friend in the right place."

"Yes, one could have," said Cox. "I had one very good friend. Ed Esmonde, he was my squadron commander while on the *Victorious* and he helped me obtain my command on the *Indomitable.* The week I emerged from the hospital, he received the DSO at Buckingham Palace. A week later, he was written up for the Victoria Cross, posthumously.

"The Germans called it 'Operation Cerberus.' The channel dash of the *Scharnhorst, Gneisenau* and *Prinz Eugen.* It was a daring plan, launched in bad weather and right under our noses. It took us completely by surprise. We didn't detect the ships until they were past Dover, our response was muddled and ineffective. A lot of little strikes, none of which did any damage. Esmonde led an attack by six Swordfish, not one of them returned.

"After that, the doctors found my legs hadn't mended too well. They had been broken in several places and were judged to be not strong enough to withstand combat flying."

"Couldn't they have put steel pins in your legs?" Lacey asked. "Before the war, Frank was going to follow his father and become a doctor. I think he almost finished med school. He told me once about a new operation where they stick steel pins in your bones to strengthen them."

"I suppose, but there came a sudden need for combat-experienced officers in the Intelligence Division. At the time, it was that or become a flight instructor, which would not have pleased my father at all. At least Intelligence allowed me to stay in the war if not, on occasion, the front lines."

"Sounds to me like your family has some kind of death wish for its men. Either come home wearing your shield or carried on it."

"No, it's not quite like that," Cox corrected. "What my family has is a tradition of naval service. It can be traced all the way back to Nelson's fleet. I don't think someone who comes from a non-military background can truly understand this tradition. You gave yourself away the first time we met and you just repeated the prime phrase a minute ago. Before the war. Before the war, Frank Atkinson wanted to be a doctor. Before the war, you were a college bum . . ."

"Beach bum." Now it was Lacey's turn to do a little correcting. "Before the war, I was a beach bum."

". . . Very well, you were a beach bum. And before the war, Constance was a commercial artist. You know what I was before the war? A sub-lieutenant. This was my home and profession, it is and will be after the war. The rest of you will most likely go back to your civilian pursuits. I can't blame you but the Fleet is my life. I love it and not just because my family ordained it."

"You only wish your father would understand your choice better," Lacey surmised. "Well, perhaps after this is over he will. Your hand won't sink the

Frederick the Great but your plan sure will. I'm betting my life it will."

By six o'clock that evening, the armory teams had finished loading the drones and Lacey had supervised the wiring of their arming systems. When all work on the planes was over, a detachment of Royal Marines moved in and surrounded them. The same thing was done to the mother ships at the Scapa Flow air base. No one, save for authorized personnel, would be allowed to approach either set of Boeings until an hour before dawn on the following morning; when the crews and fuel trucks would arrive.

To most people on Lacey's team, that marked the start of their mission but in fact, it began just after midnight. Hundreds of miles to the north, closer to Norway than to Scotland, the aircraft carriers *Pursuer* and *Ravager* broke away from the convoy they had only recently overtaken and set course due east. When the mother ship and Aphrodite crews at last woke up, their planes were fueled and readied and their escorts were three hundred miles off the north Norwegian coast.

"Now that's odd," Cox observed, when Lacey first entered the briefing room, actually the electronics shop, of their hangar. "Dennis, where's Constance? I thought she'd be coming with you?"

"No, she left the cafeteria ahead of me," Lacey answered. "I thought she'd be here, waiting for me with you. She's carrying some of our maps in her briefcase. She'd better get here quick or I'll send a patrol out for her."

The minor mystery, and crisis, cleared as Constance arrived just before the crews. Lacey repeated what he had said two days earlier, in the general briefing. This time, he went into more specific detail about the drones; how they would take off, their altitude and where they would rendezvous with the mother ships. He also gave out the cruise altitudes for the mother ship and drone flights, their cruise speeds, latest weather reports, latest reports on enemy activity and when they could expect to pick up their escorts. Then he officially concluded the briefing though there were still two duties for him to perform before it was really over.

"Vince, Frank, let's gather up here," Lacey suggested. "It's time for us to choose the order of attack. Connie, if you'll do us the honor?"

As the command pilots clustered together, Constance stepped into their midst and removed her cap. Lacey pulled three numbered strips of paper from one of his jacket pockets and dropped them in it. While the rest of the mother ship crews were free to go, they all hung back; waiting to see which of them would have the first crack at sinking the *Frederick the Great*.

"Go ahead, Connie, mix them up and then hold your cap high but not too high. After all, Vince does have to select as well."

When Constance was finished, Lacey reached in before the others. "Rank does have its privileges," he explained.

"But that don't mean you always get the best position," Capollini noted, a moment later. Lacey had drawn third place.

Next it was Atkinson and he drew first place; leaving Capollini to take second. Only then did the crews leave to pick up their flying gear. All except Lacey, who stayed behind to say good-bye to Constance; this was his other duty.

"Are you sure you won't come with me to the squadron ready room?" he asked. "We could have another fifteen or twenty minutes together if you do."

"No, Dennis, I told you why I don't want to," said Constance, clasping one of his hands. "It would remind me of how I last saw my fiancé. The first time I ever went to the field to see him off on a mission and he never came back. Oh please, darling, you must understand, this is the way I want to remember you. I'll watch you from the control tower, okay?"

It would have to do; Lacey didn't have the time to make any further arguments; not if he wanted to catch a truck to the ready room. He embraced Constance and gave her a long final kiss before he had to depart.

As events turned out, Lacey almost did miss the last vehicle to leave. He also held it up at the squadron ready room, hoping against her firm stand that Constance would show.

"We'd better move, Dennis," Cox suggested, not quite making it an order. "The other crews are already at their planes. If Constance didn't want to come here, she won't. She is most likely in the control tower by now."

"Yeah, I know and there are so many WRENs working in that tower, I'll never know which one is her. Okay, let's get moving, that battleship won't wait forever."

They were driven back to the tarmac in front of their hangar. Lacey made up for the time he used by having his co-pilot do half of the external check. Once this most preliminary of procedures was done, the eleven-man crew plus their passenger piled inside the Fortress.

"Lacey to crew, standby for check. Co-pilot?"

"Flight controls unlocked. Aileron locking pin stowed."

"Nose gunner?"

"Chin turret gun sight stowed. Machine guns locked."

"Navigator?"

"All charts and navigation equipment stowed. Left cheek gun locked and stowed, right cheek gun locked and stowed."

"Flight engineer?"

"Upper turret switches, off. Guns locked in aft position. Fuel transfer valve and switch, off. Hydraulic fluid supply tank, full. All bomb bay fuel tanks are full. Tank filler caps are secure. Bomb rack selectors, off."

"Radio operator?"

"All radio equipment has been pre-flighted. IFF, instrument landing and navigation aids are in working order."

"Aphrodite controller?"

"Remote guidance systems checked and ready. Drone flight controls are locked."

"Ball turret gunner?"

"Ball turret switches, off. Guns locked in aft position. Ball turret hatch locked and secure."

"Waist gunners?"

"Left waist gun locked and stowed. Right waist gun locked and stowed."

"Tail gunner?"

"Tail gun position empty. Tail guns locked, I think."

"You think they're locked?" Lacey noted, sharply. "Hell, get back there and make sure they are."

"Colonel, they are locked," said the co-pilot. "I tested them from the outside and they are."

"Okay, cancel that last order. Lacey to crew, standby for engine start. We're going through the check list. Fuel transfer valves and switch?"

"Fuel transfer switch, off," answered the co-pilot, who would do the check with Lacey. "Fuel transfer valves, off."

"Intercoolers?"

"Intercooler controls, cold."

"Gyro instruments are uncaged." Lacey was able to do this one himself. "Fuel shut-off switches?"

"Fuel shut-off switches, open."

"Landing gear switch?"

"Landing gear switch, neutral. Switch guard in place."

"Cowl flaps?"

"Cowl flap levers, open." To make sure they responded, the co-pilot looked out the right side of the cockpit while Lacey glanced out the left. "Cowl flaps open right."

"Cowl flaps open left," said Lacey, then he reached over and reset the cowl controls himself. "Cowl flaps levers, locked. Turbosuperchargers?"

"Turbo levers, off."

"Mixture controls?"

"Mixture controls set on idle cut-off."

"Throttles?"

"Throttles, closed, now moving them forward a crack."

"Propeller controls?"

"Setting propeller controls to high RPM position."

"Automatic pilot?"

"Auto pilot switches, off."

"De-icing systems?"

"Wing de-icer control valve, off. Propeller anti-icer controls, off. Propeller anti-icer switch, off."

"Cabin heat, off. Generators, off." Lacey could, had to in fact, do these two checks himself. The controls were on his side of the cockpit wall. Next he leaned out his window and ordered: "Fire guards clear left."

"Fire guards clear right," shouted the co-pilot.

"Activate the master switch, I'll handle the battery and inverter tests," said Lacey; again he had to take care of these himself because of their location. He also tested the plane's alarm bells and asked the crew if they could be heard. "Okay, thanks, Commander. The alarms are operating. Hydraulic fluid pump is on automatic and the hydraulic pressure gauges read seven hundred pounds across the board. Set parking brakes."

"Parking brakes, locked. Wheel chocks in place."

"Fuel booster pumps?"

"Fuel booster pumps, on. Fuel pressure gauges are registering nine pounds apiece."

"Carburetor air cleaners?"

"Carburetor air cleaners, on."

"Fuel quantity?"

"All four wing tanks are full. Together with those bomb bay tanks, we have enough fuel to stay up for an entire day, if we need to."

"And we might just have to. Lacey to crew, we are starting engines. Switch fire extinguisher to left outboard engine. Rotate number one propeller."

The last order was to the fire guards. By hand, they pulled the first of the bomber's four, twelve-foot diameter props through three complete revolutions. When finished, they backed off and collected their fire extinguishers.

"Standing by to start number one engine," the co-pilot informed Lacey.

"Ignition switches are on. Start number one."

In the extreme right corner of the instrument panel, were the engine start and meshing switches. As the co-pilot hit and held down the first toggle, he worked the priming pump on his side of the cockpit wall.

"Mesh number one," Lacey ordered, once twelve seconds had passed.

The co-pilot pushed down the adjacent mesh toggle and, as the propeller began to tick over, Lacey flipped the number one ignition switch to both. The engine responded by firing up perfectly. The propeller snapped as the initial jets of smoke rumbled out the exhaust stacks, then it vanished into a soft, silver blur.

Immediately the co-pilot released the start and meshing switches. Lacey slid the number one mixture lever from idle cut-off to auto rich and made note of the oil pressure gauge.

"Oil pressure at sixty pounds and building. Engine is idling at one thousand rpm and oil temperature is climbing. Switch fire extinguisher to left inboard engine. Rotate number two propeller."

For the other three engines and on the other two mother ships, the starting procedure was repeated until a dozen Wright Cyclones were purring in unison.

"Lacey to tower, have you any word from Hoy Island?"

"Yes, sir, the Hoy Island Air Station reports that your other flight has completed its check outs and they're ready to switch-on at your order."

"Lacey to tower, tell them to start engines and prepare for takeoff. Do we have permission to taxi to the runway?"

"Permission granted. As the base has been closed to all traffic, you need not make any further transmissions. Wind and weather conditions have not changed since our last issue. You have the full run of the field, tower out."

The drone crews had been taken directly to Hoy Island after the briefing. Their plane ride consumed enough time to put them ten minutes behind the mother ship crews. While they were still moving down to the runway, the mother ships completed their magneto and engine run-up checks.

"Mother ship one to Aphrodite one. We are ready to lift-off. What is your current status?"

"We are just starting our own checks. We'll be ready in a few minutes, Colonel. See you over Scapa Flow."

The time difference was now going to be an advantage. It would take approximately ten minutes for the mother ships to climb out, do their post-takeoff procedures and swing over Hoy Island. The drones would not have to wait, orbit and waste valuable gas while they got themselves organized. Nor was any to be wasted making the drones climb to some high cruise altitude or gather in formation. Not even the mother ships would formate until later. As each came over Hoy Island, they picked up their drone on takeoff and together, circled the Scapa Flow lagoon.

"Mother ship one to Aphrodite one. All systems are go at this end. Turn due north and prepare to bail out. We are taking command. Mother ship one to mother ship flight. Your status reports are acknowledged, prepare to take command of your drones."

Trailing above and behind their charges, Lacey and his wing men circled around the almost empty fleet anchorage. Below were a few motor torpedo boats, waiting to pick up those who would bail out.

First Lacey, then Atkinson and Capollini, swung their Fortresses onto a northerly heading; following their drones and taking control of them. As the lead Aphrodite neared the opposite shore line, two parachutes blossomed out of its nose hatch. A second pair dropped from the B-17 behind it and, by the time the first were hitting the water, a third set had appeared. The drones were now unmanned.

"Aphrodite controller to pilot. Primary detonator, on. Secondary detonator, on. Igniter defeat has been deactivated. The drone is armed, Colonel, everything is go."

"Mother ship one to mother ship flight. Report on the status of your drones and take up your positions. Mother ship one to Scapa Flow tower, send message to escort command that we have departed on time."

At last the mother ships gathered. Atkinson, in Careful Virgin, and Capollini, in Fortress Apache, slid alongside the wing tips of Lacey's Eight Ball's Revenge. The drones were also rearranged, from a line astern to a line abreast formation. It was rather crude and not nearly as tight when compared to the perfect vee their mother ships could maintain. But the guidance systems that controlled were not quite as skilled as a pair of human hands. And besides, who wanted to take the risk of bumping together two of the most powerful bombs ever built.

"Squadron, attention!" barked the exec, the moment Bradley entered the flying ready room. His pilots responded to the order and stood ramrod straight until he told them to rest. For an hour they had been waiting while Bradley went to the ship's radio center. Some suggested they rename it the lounge room for all the readying they were doing. Now, with Bradley back, there was hope for some action.

"Gentlemen, at nine minutes past the hour, the attack element of our operation departed from Scapa Flow," he announced, which brought an immediate cheer; only to be followed by a little grumbling when he explained how long it would take them to reach the rendezvous point. "At current cruise speed, those B-17s will be here in three hours time."

"What will we do until then, sir?" asked one of his pilots. "Watch movies? We're ready to go now."

"You may all be eager but this squadron isn't anywhere near ready and won't be so for several hours. This operation will be your baptism of fire; beyond myself, only our squadron exec has had any combat experience. I intend for as few things to go wrong as possible. We'll have a general briefing now, then go to the hangar deck to personally supervise the loading of our aircraft and finally back here for our operational briefing. Doug, may I have them now?"

The squadron exec handed to Bradley a pair of large, balsa wood models, just liberated from the ship's cafeteria. One was a replica of the *Pursuer*'s latest aircraft, the F4U Corsair; complete in the Southeast Asian Command markings the real fighters still carried. The other was of its principal antagonist, the Messerschmitt 109.

"I don't think you need any introduction to this airplane," Bradley started, holding up the latter model. "Or for you Brits, this aeroplane. In spite of the appearance of the Focke-Wulf, she is still the preeminent fighter in the Luftwaffe. Lately, some of you have been saying disparaging things about the Messerschmitt. About her age, her performance and her general worth as a combat fighter. That's a good way to get yourself killed, underrating your opponent.

"I don't care if this airplane's design is five years older than the Corsair's or that it doesn't carry as many guns or fly as fast. Take a very hard look at these planes."

Bradley held up the F4U model for comparison. Both had been built to the same scale and one difference was quickly apparent, the size of each.

"The full combat weight of an Me-109 is seventy-five hundred pounds," he continued, "more than half a ton less than an empty Corsair. More than two and a half tons less than a loaded one. The M.E. has a lower wing loading than our fighter and can outmaneuver it. If any of you attempt to turn or roll with a '109 you can expect to be shot down. If by chance you are not, you can expect to deal with me when you get back here and then you may wish that you had been shot down.

"Use the Corsair's strong points. She can out-climb and out-dive almost every other fighter, she has the same engine as the Thunderbolt and weighs a ton less. We'll have to use the same tactics that we would've used in the Pacific against the Japanese. Dive and climb and for God's sake don't get suckered into a dogfight. If you do, just dive again or out-run it. The only real maneuver I want to see any of you making is a half roll when you enter your dives. I've told all of you a dozen times, simply nosing over won't get the aircraft in a steep enough angle of attack.

"Now this may sound like I'm leading you by the hand into combat. In a sense I am. Like Leftenant-Commander Cox, I was once out there where you are. And I saw too many good pilots, and friends, die

269

because they made some foolish mistake they were warned not to do and forgot. Perhaps on some other mission I can afford to lose a few of you but not on this one. Every aircraft is vitally needed; that's why we're carrying four additional fighters at the expense of some spares. We can't lose any to either human or mechanical faults; that's the main reason why we're going to the hangar deck. Each of us is going to be personally responsible for the condition of our own aircraft, smug combat veterans included."

"Commander Cox? Could you come back here for a minute? We have something you should urgently see."

It was the tail gunner who made the request; he came into the radio compartment toting a portable oxygen bottle; the mother ships had been climbing to their combat altitude for the past half-hour and everyone was by now on oxygen.

"What? Is it serious?" Cox asked, waking up after being asleep for less than ten minutes. "Is it an attack?"

"No, no attack but we feel it is very serious."

"Have you told Colonel Lacey about it?"

"No, we feel you should see it before the colonel is told. Come, I think you will understand why."

Cox was slightly irritated that he, and not Lacey, had to take care of a problem apparently concerning the airplane, yet it also interested him. As he got up, he pulled his mask line from one of the cabin regulators and attached it to his own portable tank. On entering the waist section, the situation at first looked normal to Cox. One of the gunners was being attended to by the others; he had either forgotten to or not reached his oxygen supply in time and was being revived. It took a moment for Cox to realize there had

270

been a slight increase in the number of gunners and to remember what Wing Commander Holmen had said about red hair and its rarity among Norwegians.

"Cons . . . Leftenant Smythe! What the hell is the meaning of this?" Cox thundered, though his mask muffled his rage a little.

Still, Constance's grogginess evaporated when he barked, though she did have to be helped to her feet.

"I knew that baritone of yours would come in useful again," were her first, slurred words. "It's better than the smelling salts and oxygen they gave me."

"Let's skip the esoteric observations for now. I want an answer to why you have imperiled this operation? Do you realize you can be court-martialed for disobeying orders?"

"I have not imperiled this operation. I have compelling reasons to be here and I may even be of help to you. And I didn't disobey any orders. No one specifically told me I could not be on this mission."

"I was not talking about specific orders," said Cox, correcting himself. "There are general regulations against women in combat. You know them as well as I."

"I happen to know them better and they're quite vague. If they were strictly enforced, not a single WREN would be in England," Constance noted, "you know that as well as I."

"All right, all right. Why didn't you ask either Dennis or myself for permission to come along? One of us may have said yes?"

"I don't think either of you would have. And I knew if I did ask and you refused me, you would've both been waiting for me to sneak on board. So I didn't and you weren't. Don't you know how much I love both you and Dennis? I just couldn't let you go."

"And don't you know how much Dennis loves you? As aircraft commander, he would be fully within his right to turn this plane around and head back for base. That is how you have imperiled this mission."

"If Dennis finds out about me," Constance added.

"Yes, if Dennis finds out," Cox agreed, before he realized what he had agreed to. "Wait a minute, what exactly are you suggesting? That we not tell him?"

"As aircraft commander, he's not about to come strolling through this section of the plane. He's isolated in the cockpit, you yourself said it was like being in a separate world up there. He won't come back here unless he has a reason to. Let's not give him one, Charles, please? I want to be with him and on the other hand, I don't want him to worry about me. That is what could imperil this mission."

"Of course you're right. Damn it how I hate it when someone sees what is right before I do."

"Let me explain it better. Dennis is the man I love and I want to spend the rest of my life with him. And you've been more than just my superior and a good friend. You've been the father I lost and the older brother I never had. You said that yourself, once."

"Yes, indeed. Well as your commanding officer, I would still like to press charges against you. As your father, I would like to take you across my knee and give you a right good tanning. As your brother, I would like to slap a parachute on your back and boot you out the door. And as your friend, all I can say is, welcome aboard."

If it were not for the high altitude, and the need for the oxygen masks, Constance would've kissed him. Instead, Cox had to settle for a tender, sisterly hug.

"Thank you, Charles," she said, during the embrace. "I don't know what I would've done if I had lost both of you. You each mean so much to me."

"You're right for these times, Constance. You're an extraordinary, unconventional woman. I only hope Dennis knows what he's in for when he marries you. Now tell me, how did you sneak on board this aircraft?"

"It was simple, I hid in there." Constance pointed aft, to the tail gunner's position. "On previous flights, I noticed it wasn't always checked from the inside. The crew often made an external test of the guns to see if they were locked and left it at that. So last night I set aside this flying suit, the boots and other items and I also came out to the aircraft and hid an oxygen mask and cylinder. Perhaps I should've also taken along an altimeter. I didn't know how high we had gone and passed out before I put the mask on."

"That is when we heard a thump, Commander, and we went back to look," the tail gunner interrupted. "We dragged her out and gave her oxygen and decided to go to you first. Instead of the colonel."

"Pilot to crew." Now it was the tail gunner's turn to be interrupted. The sound of Lacey's voice gave Constance a scare, until she realized it was a message on the intercom. "We have reached our combat altitude of twenty-five thousand feet and we are in touch with the aircraft carriers *Pursuer* and *Ravager*. They will be launching our first group of escorts shortly. Pilot to Aphrodite controller, I want a report on her status."

The *Pursuer* was the first of the carriers to turn into the wind. Its, Bradley's, squadron would provide escort for the opening part of the attack. Later, the *Ravager*'s squadron would supplement and then supersede Bradley as his aircraft ran out of ammunition and low on fuel. Or, if needed, they could be committed earlier.

Because of her short flight deck, only sixteen of her Corsairs were spotted topside; the remaining eight would be brought up as soon as the deck was cleared. In the lead ship was, of course, Bradley.

"*Pursuer* lead to *Pursuer* squadron, we have been contacted by the Americans. If you have all gone through the oil dilution procedure, we can start engines. Now I'm going to take you by the hand again, I'm not letting any of you foul an engine at this stage. Standby to run down the checklist, we'll take it one step at a time. Before we begin, make sure that the deck handling crew is rotating your propeller by hand, at least four revolutions.

"Ignition switch, off. Mixture control, idle cut-off. Fuel selector to reserve standpipe. Cowl flaps, full open. Propeller control to takeoff setting. Carburetor air control, direct. Supercharger control, neutral. Open starter breech, insert a Type E cartridge and make sure it's a Type E. Close breech and lock. Close access door and lock. Open throttle one inch. Battery switch, on. Water injection switch, on and hold for a count of five. Instrument switch, on. Auxiliary fuel pump, on. Primer switch, on and hold for a count of five.

"Shift Mixture control to auto rich. Auxiliary fuel pump, off. Ignition switch to both. Starter switch, on. Primer switch, on and hold until engine is turning over."

A sharp crack and a wisp of smoke issued from the cowling of each Corsair. Their propellers jerked and windmilled slowly as further explosions rattled their exhaust stacks. Within half a minute, all the aircraft on the flight deck had fired up and their engines were running smoothly. The tiny escort carrier shook from the combined thunder of the sixteen Double Wasp radials; which, when totalled, had almost four times the horsepower of the ship's turbines. If they needed to, they could push the ship along on their own.

"*Pursuer* leader to *Pursuer* squadron, check your temperatures and pressures, your generator and radios. *Pursuer* leader to Able flight, spread and lock wings. Do your engine and accessory checks, standby for takeoff."

The first flight was positioned abreast of the carrier's island and in a loose formation. The remaining dozen were squeezed in on the last third of the flight deck; only a foot or two separating them. Only when the first group was away, could they come out and spread their wings.

With his preliminary checks on engine performance over, Bradley reached for a lever by the left side of the seat and threw it forward. His wing man and the other element in his flight followed suit. The four aircraft lowered their upraised wings like giant butterflies readying for flight. When they were fully spread, Bradley pulled and turned a handle beside the folding lever. One at the wing joints, a set of red closing doors snapped shut; the wing hinge pins had been inserted and locked in place.

"Bradley to air director, wings down and locked. Engine warm-up and magneto tests completed. Request permission to taxi forward and prepare to takeoff."

Both he and his wing man moved a little farther down the flight deck and, obeying the plane handler's instructions, positioned their fighters alongside each other. They had less than three hundred feet of deck to get airborne in; an impossible task for a fully loaded Corsair but then again, there

275

was a constant, fifty-knot headwind.

"*Pursuer* leader to *Pursuer* squadron, I can't take off with each of you, so you're going to have to do this checklist yourselves when you get out here. Lock your arrester hook up. Move your mixture control to auto rich. Propeller control to maximum RPM. Close cowl flaps by one third. Close intercooler flaps. Open oil cooler flaps. Set rudder trim six degrees right. Set aileron trim six degrees down, right wing. Set elevator trim one degree, nose up. Wing flaps, thirty degrees. Tail wheel, unlocked. Check your canopy release safety pins, your cylinder head and oil temperatures, before you signal that you're ready to advance throttle. Remember that you will stall going over the edge. Go easy and rendezvous with me at two thousand feet."

When Bradley gave his signal, the handler twirled his upraised fingers and continued to do so until the engine was bellowing at the appropriate din and the tail was rising off the deck. Then he pointed out to sea and dropped to his knees. Bradley released the brakes on his straining fighter and jammed the throttle against the gate stop.

A moment later and the Corsair would probably have nosed over. Instead it waddled at the start of its roll, which ended as the tail rose, and sank from sight as it cleared the deck. Indeed the fighter did stall, falling half the ship's height before the wings filled with lift. It reappeared with its landing gear and flaps cycling up. Once the Corsair was clear, it banked to the left.

Bradley's wing man followed a few seconds later, then the other element of his flight. The remaining twelve fighters came forward in pairs. They spread their wings, did their magneto tests and moved to takeoff position. Which, as there became fewer aircraft on the flight deck, was rolled back until the last ones were able to make their takeoffs down almost the full length of the carrier. Unlike the others, they didn't stall when they got in the air.

The succeeding Corsairs got into formation on either side or behind Bradley. Again he led his charges through a checklist, this one for post-takeoff procedures. They made a single pass over the *Pursuer* in their neatly spaced flights. On her lift could be seen two of the eight Corsairs being held on the hangar deck. In a half hour they too would be off. By that time, Bradley and the first two-thirds of his squadron would have rendezvoused with Lacey's mother ships. They as well would be approaching the north Norwegian coast and, at a distance of one hundred miles, appearing on German radar. The battle of Alten Fjord was about to begin.

Chapter Eleven

THE BATTLE OF ALTEN FJORD
CONCLUDING REPORT

"Mother ship lead, this is *Thrasher*. You have just appeared on our radar. As of yet, there is no German activity apart from normal traffic and we have not yet picked up your escort."

"Mother ship one, this is *Pursuer* leader. Don't worry, we're out here. We're at angels nineteen and climbing. We should be appearing off your left wing in the next three minutes."

With the carriers almost two hundred miles off the Norwegian coast, their radar and operation centers could not yet take an active part in the attack. Until they could, if they could, another command post would have to provide early warning and fighter direction. Any ship would do provided it had air search radar and a well-equipped radio room. But a surface ship so close to enemy territory was too vulnerable to detection and attack. His Majesty's submarine *Thrasher* was not.

Its casing was continuously awash and only the uppermost part of the conning tower was above the wave crests. The boat lay just forty miles off the outer islands guarding Alten Fjord. Far enough away to avoid coastal patrols, yet near enough for its radar to cover any air activity at Alta of Fortress Banak.

"Mother ship lead, this is *Thrasher*. We have

picked up your escort. We count sixteen ships and they're two thousand feet below you. German air activity is still normal. You will not register on their air defence net until you are one hundred miles from the coast. At their final altitude, your second flight will not appear on radar until they are approaching Sor Iya Island."

"He just said South Island Island," Lacey's co-pilot noted. "In Norwegian, Iya means island. Look, there are the fighters! Colonel, are you sure sixteen will be enough to protect us?"

"It should until the Germans figure out what we're doing," offered Lacey, "by then we should have more than twice that number. There's eight more on the *Pursuer* and two dozen on the *Ravager*."

The Corsairs banked steeply over the Fortresses and continued climbing for another two thousand feet before levelling out. With their cruise speed fifty miles an hour faster than the bombers' cruise speed, they began to make slow, graceful S-turns to keep their station above the B-17s.

"Mother ship one to *Pursuer* leader, glad you could make it. I hope your friends will be able to join us later. When will the escort for the Aphrodites arrive?"

"They will be taking off in the next ten minutes. Since they don't have to climb as high or come as far, they should arrive before we enter the German air defence net. My exec is leading them so don't worry, they'll be here."

And with only half the number of aircraft, it would also take less time for the second wave the *Pursuer* launched to form. On the *Ravager*, their first Corsairs were being brought topside. If everything went right, they would be appearing just when they were needed the most.

"Mother ship lead, this is *Thrasher*. You're ten minutes from piercing German radar. We have your second group of escorts on the screen, they are overtaking your other flight."

"Mother ship one to *Pursuer* leader, we're going to be detected any minute now. Bring your aircraft in, as close as you possibly can. I want us to appear as a single, large blip on their screens. I know flying at our lower cruise speed may foul your engines so we'll try to add a little more to help you. Mother ship one to mother ship flight, boost airspeed by twenty miles an hour. Lacey to controller, boost your drone's airspeed by twenty miles an hour."

After their last pass over the Fortresses, Bradley's squadron swung out wide; wider than they had at any other time. As they came around well behind them, the Corsairs closed ranks and slowed down. From an altitude two thousand feet higher, they descended to approximately one hundred feet above Lacey's flight. Carefully, they slid in over the tail fins of the B-17s and settled on top of them.

"*Pursuer* leader to *Pursuer* squadron, we are entering a combat zone. Time to arm aircraft. De-activate safeties and charge wing guns . . ."

Bradley reached under the left corner of the main instrument panel and twisted a pair of knobs then pushed each in. The breeches of the wing guns were now closed and live shells had been inserted in the firing chambers.

". . . Gun camera, on. Master armament switch, on. Outboard guns, armed. Centre guns, armed. Inboard guns, armed. Gun sight, on and select the brightness of your cross hairs."

Bradley's flight sat almost on top of the cockpit to Lacey's Fortress. The flights on either side of him stationed themselves in a similar fashion over

Atkinson and Capollini. The fourth flight nestled in between their bombers and behind Lacey's. Together they formed a tight nucleus of silver and blue aircraft, gliding through a near cloudless sky. A few minutes later, the formation crossed an invisible line and entered the German air defence net.

"Lacey to Cox, Charlie, are you on the line?"

"I'm here, Dennis. Back in the waist section. Has anything happened up there?"

"I think something has but I can't tell. We should be on German radar but the submarine hasn't seen any response to us. With such an important target to protect, I thought the Luftwaffe would be swarming after us the moment we were picked up?"

"They would be if we were a huge attack force," Cox answered. "On their screens, we probably look like a weather or general reconnaissance sortie. And our presence is not a surprise to them. We've probably been tracked since we climbed out of Scapa Flow. They won't try intercepting us until it looks as though we're heading toward Alten Fjord. Remember, the Catalina wasn't attacked until after it came out of Kaa Fjord. Cooperation between the Luftwaffe and the Kriegsmarine has always been a problem, some say it even caused the Germans to lose a few ships."

As events developed, it didn't take long for a threat to appear. And when it did, it was an entirely unexpected one.

"Mother ship lead, this is *Thrasher*. We have a German aeroplane on the screen that may give you trouble. It's at approximately the same altitude as your other flight and if it keeps to its current heading, it will pass very close to them."

"Roger, *Thrasher*, do you have any identity on this plane? Is it a fighter or a bomber?"

"It looks to be a bomber, either a Heinkel 111 or a Junkers 88. From its heading and direction, it is probably on a reconnaissance or anti-submarine sortie. There is now forty-five miles separating them. At their respective airspeeds, they will close to visual range in six minutes."

"Okay, *Thrasher*, we'll handle it. Keep your eye on those fighter bases. Mother ship one to *Pursuer* leader, we have a lone hostile approaching the Aphrodites. It's coming in twelve o'clock level and *Thrasher* says it may be a bomber. Have one of your flights deal with it and make sure they blow the hell out of it. I don't want that plane to have a chance at radioing its base."

Ever since they overtook the drones, the last of the *Pursuer*'s Corsairs gave them a wide berth. The flights would occasionally weave across them to make a quick inspection but, for the most part, they stayed well out to either side of the formation.

"*Pursuer* leader to Everest flight, probable German bomber approaching your position, twelve o'clock level. Intercept and shoot it down, don't play with it. Blow it apart."

The Corsairs on the extreme left accelerated and pulled ahead of the loose formation. The flight split into its constituent pairs and spread apart; freeing themselves for combat. They did not jettison their external tanks and would not if their contact did turn out to be a bomber. After two minutes at their ever increasing airspeed, a dark silhouette appeared in front of them.

"Everest leader to Everest three, target identified, it is a bomber. Swing in behind me and string out for a line astern attack. We're not going to give this one a chance."

The second pair of fighters S-turned onto the lead

282

element's tail and like them, they broke up and the wing man trailed back. Their target was a Heinkel 111, light blue with a green, swirled camouflage pattern; about a thousand feet below them. It did indeed look to be on an anti-submarine patrol; the last thing its crew probably expected to see was a half-mile long train of Royal Navy Corsairs.

Neither were they prepared for such an attack. Its pilot had just toggled the depth charges when Everest lead opened fire. He caught the Heinkel in the right side of its fuselage and wing root, killing most of the crew while they were still breaking out the defensive machine guns and attempting to radio an alert. As soon as he swung away, Everest two opened up.

His burst hammered the same general area, tearing at the right engine until its propeller ground to a halt. No smoke or flames erupted and apart from the dead propeller, the bomber appeared undamaged. But in the first seconds of Everest three's pass, it dipped its left wing and exploded. Most of the fuselage was consumed by the blast and the wings folded against each other and fell toward the Norwegian Sea.

"Mother ship lead, this is *Thrasher*. The bomber is gone, your fighters splashed it and they are returning to escort your second flight. We have just recorded the liftoff of aircraft from the Alta Airfield. Two, three, four aircraft in two pairs. They are joining into a flight and they are climbing fast. You appear to be their target and we estimate interception in fifteen minutes. Your second flight has not yet been detected."

"Okay, *Thrasher*, keep us posted on the progress of the interceptors and we'll deal with them. Mother ship one to *Pursuer* leader, there's a flight of German fighters airborne over Alta. They're probably coming after us so prepare for combat and alert the Aphrodite escort to descend to approach altitude. Lacey to Aphrodite controller, Andy, take full control of your drone and dive it to one thousand feet. Time to get off your butt and work. Mother ship one to mother ship flight, dive your Aphrodites to approach altitude."

At three thousand feet, the drones and their escorts would have become visible on the shorter-range, fighter director radar at a distance of forty-five miles. The unmanned Fortresses wavered as their human controllers took over from the auto pilot systems. Carefully, their noses tipped under the horizon line and the bombers slid the two thousand feet to their approach altitude of one thousand. Their escorts followed them down, gingerly drawing closer to the explosive-laden aircraft in the process.

"Controller to pilot, I got the drone at a thousand feet. Colonel, how long will it be before we start our runs?"

"They will begin in less than twenty minutes but you know the procedure. You will have to orbit until your time comes and in your case, that may mean a half-hour."

"Yeah, I know. You shoulda let me make that pick, 'cause I feel real lucky today."

"Mother ship lead, this is *Thrasher*. The Germans are above fifteen thousand feet. No more planes have followed them out of Alta or the Banak airfield. They obviously think you're just a recon ship and you don't warrant any further action. In the next four minutes, they will close to visual range."

"Mother ship one to *Thrasher*, give me a heading and a distance and I'll have the Corsairs pounce on them."

Bradley's flight moved to handle them. They climbed slightly and jumped ahead of the closely packed formation. At what Bradley considered a safe enough distance, he ordered the rest of Able flight to jettison drop tanks.

Each Corsair released a single, dark blue cylinder from its underbelly pylon. As the tanks tumbled away wildly, the Royal Navy fighters rolled onto their backs and dove, plummeting toward a barely visible set of specks far in front of and below the formation they had to guard.

"Red Falcon one to Alta base. We are closing on the intruder's position and I think we have him spotted. Whatever he is, he's big. I think we have two or even more airplanes here. Wait a moment, we have more. Enemy fighters! Break formation, enemy fighters!"

The Messerschmitts had been able to gather and maintain a neat, correct formation throughout their steep, emergency climb; until the descending Corsairs were spotted. Now the blue and black-green fighters flew apart; not even the wing men elected to remain by their leaders.

Bradley locked his sights on what was the commander of the flight. Red Falcon one was in a high-angle of climb and banking steeply to enter a turn. For a few seconds he exposed the undersides of his '109 to attack. In that amount of time, more than a dozen pounds of armor-piercing and high-explosive shells were sprayed by Bradley's six wing guns.

Not all of them struck the Messerschmitt, but enough penetrated its unprotected belly to sever the oil, coolant, hydraulic fluid and fuel lines. None of their tanks or reservoirs had to be ruptured; whatever the lines held was sufficient to rend the fuselage center-section with an explosion. The burning fighter snapped on its back and fell. Several miles later, a more powerful explosion disintegrated what remained of Red Falcon one.

His wing man fared a little better. At least he managed to bail out of his doomed aircraft, after Bradley's own wing man poured a long burst into his engine. The second pair of Me-109s lasted longer. Only the leader was hit in the first pass, though with the wing man in a headlong retreat, there was no one to protect him as the Corsairs bottomed out and came climbing back.

"Red Falcon three to Alta base. We have been attacked by Corsair fighters of the Royal Navy. The intruders must be carrier-based aircraft, not some reconnaissance plane. My ship has been damaged and I will try to return to base but the Corsairs are after me."

"*Pursuer* leader to Able three, don't bother with the cripple. Take care of his wing man instead."

Red Falcon three was hardly in the condition to give anyone much of a fight. The hits he took had cut the hyraulic lines and pierced the reservoir. With pressure ebbing away, the main landing gear wheels were creeping out of their wells and reducing airspeed when the Messerschmitt's pilot thought he could least afford it. But the ascending Corsairs zoomed past him and closed on the last, intact, Me-109.

Even here there was no fight. Eager to escape, the wing man was fleeing to the imagined safety of the Norwegian coast. In a level, flat-out run, he was an easy target for the Corsairs; who were overtaking him with a one hundred mile an hour edge in speed. A quick, well-placed burst exploded his engine; blowing parts through the cowling before the Messerschmitt itself tumbled out of control. High above their fourth victim, higher than their original altitude, the Corsairs ended their climb and re-grouped.

"Able three to *Pursuer* leader, why did you order us to leave that other '109 alone? He would've been easy."

"Because I don't want you wasting ammunition and fuel chasing down a cripple. There'll be time to do that later. The Germans know we're here and that we're Royal Navy fighters and shooting him down won't change it. They probably think we're some carrier strike on a target-of-opportunity rhubarb. Things will be getting hot again, don't worry about it."

A false calm descended as Bradley returned to the formation. No other aircraft were in the sky, beyond the B-17s and his squadron. Yet everyone in those planes knew how the Luftwaffe was now racing to arm, fuel and launch a more powerful challenge at them. The Alta airfield responded to their threat with a desperate, high-pitched flurry of activity.

The handful of fighters that were ready to go had to be manned and put through their pre-start and takeoff checks. More were being pushed out of hangars, though with empty gun breeches and fuel tanks, they would take much longer to prepare. Pilots as well had to be suited-up and briefed; it all took time.

"Mother ship lead, this is *Thrasher*. We have aircraft airborne over Alta. Eight, ten, twelve aircraft and more are rising. They are assembling into squadron-strength units but not into larger formations. At least two squadrons are being scrambled. The first, with twelve aircraft, is climbing after you. They're moving fast and we estimate they will reach your altitude in six to eight minutes. Currently you are thirty miles from Sor Iya Island."

"We read you, *Thrasher*, we will begin our attack in five minutes. Keep an eye on those Germans and let us know immediately if any of them are going after our second flight. Mother ship one to mother ship two. Alert your controller, Frank, standby to launch Aphrodite."

The stark, barren terrain of North Norway spread out before them. Wrinkled with mountains, the land was colored white and gray; no green, no vegetation or any other signs of life were visible. Not even the towns or any of the military installations everyone knew were there. The coastline was cut, fragmented, by countless dark fingers of water. One penetrated farther inland than any of the others; it even had auxiliary inlets branching off it—Alten Fjord.

"Mother ship two to mother ship one, we're ready to launch, Colonel. Just give us the word."

"Okay, Frank, standby. Mother ship one to *Pursuer* leader, you might as well loosen up your formation, you'll be going into battle any minute now. Alert the Aphrodite escort and tell them to get ready for our first run. Lacey to controller, standby to turn drone to the left. Lacey to gunners, man your weapons but do not test fire them until I tell you to."

From the corner of his eye, Lacey could see his flight engineer appear and climb onto the bicycle-like seat underneath the top turret. He unlocked and armed the machine guns, activated the power controls and switched on the gun sight. To test his station, he swung the turret and elevated the guns. On his wing men, Lacey could see their chin and top turrets being traversed. The ball turrets and tail guns were beyond his view, but he knew they had also been manned.

"Charles, where will we go?" Constance asked, as

she and Cox watched the gunners turn their attention to their weapons. "Should we stay here?"

"No, the waist section may be roomier but it's the radio compartment that has the most armour protection," he said, "while it will be cramped, it will also be safe."

"Mother ship one to mother ship two, launch your Aphrodite and good luck, Frank. Mother ship one to mother ship three. If this first run is successful, Vince, we will change to the alternate target, the Alta Air Base."

The attack commenced with the departure of the right hand drone. As it dove to its final altitude, the robot Fortress accelerated ahead of its sister ships. Following it was one of the formation's two Corsair flights. For now they held back and sat on the B-17's tail. Until the islands guarding Alten Fjord's entrance appeared, they would jump in front of the Aphrodite and silence any anti-aircraft guns in place along the fjord.

"Mother ship two to mother ship one, she's away, Colonel. Altitude, about two hundred feet. The nose gunner has it in sight, the escorts too and he says he can see ships down the length of the fjord. Looks like it'll be a hot time there as well."

"Mother ship lead, this is *Thrasher*. The first ship of your second flight is two minutes from the outer islands. That first squadron of interceptors is at eighteen thousand feet. The second squadron has formed, with sixteen aircraft, and there are signs of a third squadron taking off."

"Everyone wants to tell me something," Lacey noted. "I never knew I could be so popular. Mother ship one to *Pursuer* leader, Germans at eighteen thousand, squadron strength. Deal with them as you wish, warn the flights you're leaving behind that we're going to start circling. Mother ship one to mother ship flight, bank left, we're going to hold our position here. Mother ship three, alert your controller, I'll be doing the same with mine."

"*Pursuer* leader to Able and Baker flights, break formation and follow me. Enemy at angels eighteen, squadron strength. Charlie and David flights, remain with the bombers and be ready, they're going to start circling."

The Corsair flights split into two equal groups. The trailing and left hand flights stayed behind while the other two fanned out; first in front of, then increasingly to one side of the B-17s as Lacey initiated a wide, gentle turn. Only Baker flight's four aircraft had to jettison drop tanks. The necessary action delayed the start of their dives for a few seconds, allowing Bradley's flight to plunge far ahead of them.

Four and a half miles below, the two uncommitted Aphrodites started to circle in much the same manner as their mother ships. Their maneuvers weren't nearly as smooth but they kept their station, with their last group of escort fighters trailing some distance back.

"Mother ship two to mother ship one, Davis says he can see those outer islands on his monitor screen. He'll fly the route you told him to, everything is go."

Massive and jagged, Sor Iya appeared on the left; the much smaller islands of Silden and Loppa were on the right. Somewhere along Silden's shoreline, lay the wreckage of Catalina M-Mother; beyond the bodies of its crew, the Germans had removed nothing.

The B-17 had a channel miles wide through which to pass, this much at least would be easy. The Corsairs sitting on its tail jettisoned tanks then jumped in front of the bomber. Because of their rugged nature, the outer islands possessed no defences; only the mine fields sown in the surrounding waters. The Corsairs would have no targets until the inner islands and the actual mouth of Alten Fjord were reached.

"Lacey to Cox, I want you to come forward to the nose section. I'd like you to take a look at these warships in the fjord. The nose gunner says some of them look strange."

"All right, Dennis, understood. I'll come forward and have a go at identifying them," Cox responded, before he unplugged his intercom lead. "I don't care which Air Force they're from, Air Force-types are all the same when it comes to naval identification. They think every destroyer is a battleship. I'll be back in a minute, Connie."

"Be careful, Charles," she warned. "Remember, that position is awfully exposed."

"*Pursuer* leader to Able flight, fan out wide, this time every aircraft counts. Smash their formation open."

The four Corsairs spread apart so the entire squadron of ascending Messerschmitts could be engaged. The Germans came expecting to encounter fighters and not some lone reconnaissance plane. Their formation was a loose, thinly held arrangement ready for combat. Unlike their brothers, they were not going to be surprised; still, they would be not much better at defending themselves.

Bradley took on the lead flight alone. Instead of trying to shoot down just one aircraft out of the four, he kicked his rudder as he opened fire and sprayed them all with fifty caliber shells. None of the planes that he hit was seriously damaged but they all knew they had been. The Messerschmitts wavered for a moment, then broke ranks. In turn they caused the flights on either side of them to scatter; before any of the Me-109s got off a good burst and almost before any were badly hit.

Only one out of the dozen came away stricken, streaming a long plume of coolant. The dark blue Corsairs charged through the dispersing, lighter colored fighters and continued past them. They did not turn back to press their attack, they had other targets to tackle.

Several thousand feet farther on down was the second squadron. The opportunity to rout them both was too good to pass up.

"*Pursuer* leader to Able flight, we're going to use an old Luftwaffe tactic on the Luftwaffe. A diving attack on one formation after another. I hear they use it on the Americans, let's see how it works on them."

"Everest leader to Everest flight, target dead ahead. Looks like a fleet torpedo boat. My wing man and I will handle it. Everest three, you watch for other targets."

Everest flight was by now far in front of the lead Aphrodite. Nearly a mile in front of it; deep inside the inner island chain while the bomber itself was just entering the same narrow channel they were using. Everest leader and his wing man broke to the left and descended to the water's surface. Their target lay anchored close to Stjernoy Island, so positioned that it blocked most of the channel.

A fleet torpedo boat was as large as a destroyer though it didn't have a destroyer's main guns. Instead it had bank after bank of torpedo tubes as its primary weapons. The only guns were in the anti-aircraft batteries and, according to the day's orders, were to be manned. But they weren't.

The Corsairs came in at the same height as the main deck. They started firing a hundred yards out and maintained the barrage until they dipped their wings and pulled away. From one end to the other they had raked the ship, concentrating mostly on the superstructure. The anti-aircraft batteries weren't really damaged but the radar masts and optical gun directors had been destroyed. Those crew members unfortunate enough to be caught in the open were dead, so too were some of the ones inside the ship; especially those on the bridge. When the survivors finally got around to sounding general quarters, the Aphrodite was passing overhead.

"*Pursuer* leader to Charlie flight, peel off and join us. I want to even up the odds a bit. *Pursuer* leader to Baker leader, how's it going with you?"

"You can scratch another Jerry. We caught them trying to regroup, I don't think they'll be doing that again. Save us some of those other M.E.s, we're coming to join you."

Caught off-guard by the sudden appearance of Royal Navy fighters so early, the second squadron of Messerschmitts began to break up without a shot being fired. Just the first flight remained intact; its leader opening up on Bradley at the same instant he opened up on him.

The Me-109's slow-firing, 30-mm and 13-mm cannons were no match for the Corsair's six wing guns in a head-on pass. Hits sparkled all over the German's propeller and cowling. In moments smoke came curling out the engine access panels and the Messerschmitt was slewing violently; causing the rest of the flight to disperse.

The Corsairs left one other ship of the squadron fatally damaged. Together with the leader, it plunged toward the mountainous coastline below. One splashed into the water, the other fireballed on the top of a peak. No parachute blossomed from either.

After four miles of near transonic descent, Bradley hauled back on his throttle and control stick. Able flight followed suit; the quartet of whistling fighters pulled their noses up and leaped for the sky. The momentum they had gathered sent the Corsairs rocketing for a mile before the pace started to slacken. Then, all that was needed was just a little more power to keep the climb going.

"Here, sir, you will need these to see them from this altitude." The nose gunner handed to Cox a pair of binoculars. Every nose and tail gunner in the mother ships had been given a pair, so they could follow the progress of the drones. Cox laid down on the chin turret controls while the gunner crouched beside him. He gazed through the clear, flat, bomb aiming panel and would have had an unobstructed field of view; if it weren't for the gun sight. "Here, let me swing that out of the way for you, sir. Can you see the ships now?"

"Yes, they're visible to the naked eye," said Cox, "though I will require these to see any detail. There seems to be quite a number, more than a half dozen in all."

"The Nazis have one ship in each of the channels between the inner islands. Then they stationed one where all the channels come together and three more down the length of Alten Fjord. That makes seven altogether. When Christiansen bought it, he didn't report that many."

"I know, but he went down weeks ago when *Frederick* was still working up. Now, with her one day away from raising anchor, the Germans want to make sure that no attack damages or cripples her. What we're seeing is probably their full deployment and which of these ships do you claim looks so strange?"

"Well, the first is that ship anchored where all the channels meet. There are so many guns on it."

Cox followed the gunner's outstretched finger and locked the binoculars on a tiny, gray form far below. To the naked eye, it was no bigger than a large grain of rice. Under magnification however, it grew large enough for surface detail to be discerned.

"It's one of their Z-class destroyers," Cox said at last, keeping the binoculars trained on it. "She's been rebuilt into an anti-aircraft ship. Most of her main guns were stripped away to make room for the extra batteries. Ships like her are used to escort coastal convoys. They're good at repelling air attacks but not this time. I can see her being strafed by our fighters. This is bloody marvelous, I can't tell you how long I've wanted to see a German warship receive such a pounding."

"Me as well, sir," the gunner admitted. "I watched those planes hit the first ship back in the channel. It is most satisfying, especially when it occurs in your country's home waters."

"I can guess; what others do you want me to look at?"

"The ship in the middle of Alten Fjord, I think it's larger than all the rest."

Cox found it easily; in part because the gunner was right. It was the largest ship guarding the fjord.

"It's been damaged," he noted, "though not by the Corsairs. They haven't gone that far yet. It looks like she was torpedoed amidships or rammed by another ship. Wait a minute. She's carrying two triple-gun turrets aft and one forward. And that large funnel she has . . . My God, that's no destroyer. That's a cruiser! She's the *Leipzig!* Cox to pilot, there's a light cruiser guarding the fjord. Dennis, you have to warn those fighters down there. Tell them to attack en masse. It's the only way they'll have a chance to knock her out."

The elements of the flight had taken turns plastering the block ships, now they joined forces for a group assault. The Corsairs arranged themselves in a loose, line abreast formation. Each was spaced so their combined firepower could be spread over the *Leipzig*'s entire length.

"Lacey to Cox, Frank Atkinson wants to know if there's anything his controller can do to avoid the cruiser. Right now, Lieutenant Davis is flying the drone on the far side of the fjord. He's trying to get as much distance between his plane and the ship."

"In those narrow waters, that's the worst action he could take. He'll give them a side profile and with a Fortress, that's a very big target. Tell him to fly straight at the cruiser. A head-on silhouette is the smallest target he can present and you have no idea how unnerving it is, to have a plane fly right at you."

"Baker leader to *Pursuer* leader, there are two Jerries on your tail. A thousand feet or more below you but they're climbing fast. They may overtake you."

Bradley and his flight were almost back at their original altitude. They had managed to use their zoom-climb to its best effect. By nearly twisting his head off, Bradley was able to get a quick glance at the '109s.

"*Pursuer* leader to Able flight, we have a couple of Germans coming after us. They're some distance behind, so I'll relax my order against maneuvers just this once. Standby to make a hammerhead turn."

When Bradley pulled his Corsair vertical, the others did likewise. He gave the rudder a violent kick as he threw the joy stick around the cockpit. All four aircraft stalled at the same time and swung from standing on their tails to standing on their noses.

"Everest leader to Everest flight, cruiser ahead. Open fire when I do, let's make it good."

Unlike the ships before it, the *Leipzig* was not going to be caught unprepared; though the alert did sound at the last possible moment. Her anti-aircraft guns, even the main and secondary guns were manned. If the torpedo tubes could have been used, they would have been brought into play as well.

As ordered, the flight opened fire in unison. Some two dozen fifty caliber machine guns swept the *Leipzig*'s deck with a hurricane of shells. Nothing and no one who was unprotected, survived it. This went especially for the crews in the exposed anti-aircraft mounts. All the 20 and 37-mm batteries were silenced, save for a few on the right hand side of the cruiser.

They had been protected by the superstructure and managed to exact a small amount of revenge. The Corsairs had to break ranks and climb so they wouldn't collide with the ship's mast and funnel. As they roared overhead, the remaining guns caught Everest three in a cross fire.

"I've been hit! Everest lead, I've been hit. My hydraulic pressure is falling. So's my oil pressure and all the temperatures are rising. I don't think I can make it back to the ship."

"Stay with us as long as you can, Everest three. Then pull up and bail out. Good luck, mate."

With the loss of oil, the engine began to run rough, shaking the aircraft and, in the final stages, almost shaking itself off its mounts. The riddled, oil stained Corsair held its slot in the formation until the laboring Double Wasp gave every sign of seizing. Its last moments of life were used to haul the fighter into a high loop. At the top, with his plane on its back, the pilot pushed away the canopy and tumbled out.

As soon as he cleared the rudder, Everest three popped his chute. He was still in range of the *Leipzig*'s guns and felt sure they would fire at him but none did. Instead they were being hastily trained on another target; the lead Aphrodite.

Only the main and secondary guns could be brought to bear, since they were the only ones to weather the attack intact. The three triple-gunned turrets salvoed first. Their six-inch shells splashed down beside and behind the oncoming Fortress. The four-inch secondary guns unleashed a steadier stream of fire though they were no more successful. By the time the main weapons let go their second barrage, the bomber had cut the distance in half. By the third, it was less than a hundred yards away.

The shells landed closer to the surface-skimming B-17 than in the previous two salvoes. Eight geysered in front of and under it; the ninth exploded in the number one engine nacelle.

The cowling, the Wright Cyclone radial and the propeller, still turning, were blown off the wing as one unit. Davis knew his aircraft had been hit from the way his instruments reacted though he didn't know where—not until another member of the crew told him.

"Nose gunner to controller, they shot up the drone's number one engine! I think it will crash, do something!"

Davis had to and since there appeared little chance that the Aphrodite could continue to its target, the next best would have to do.

The Fortress first dipped then reared and flew sideways after the engine was lost. Finally it managed to straighten out, approximately, and tried to return to its original altitude. But the distance that remained was not enough and the bomber was still descending when it rammed the *Leipzig;* just behind the funnel.

Lightly armored, the plane alone almost sliced the cruiser in half before the torpex it carried exploded. The resulting blast consumed the entire aft section of the ship. While it had no bunker oil on board, the stocks of ammunition added to the power of the blast; which could be seen and felt for miles.

"What the hell was that! *Pursuer* leader to mother ship one, have you sunk the target already?"

Bradley had just finished destroying one of the two Messerschmitts tailing him, Able three got the other, when a bright flash commanded his attention. So did the shock wave which followed. In fact, every aircraft over Alten Fjord took notice of what happened below.

"Mother ship one to *Pursuer* leader, no, that wasn't our target. Cox says it was the cruiser *Leipzig*. It was towed here to be part of the fjord defences. It crippled our Aphrodite, which we in turn crashed into the ship. There's probably not much left of her. Mother ship one to Everest leader, can you see anything of the cruiser?"

"Nothing now, the forecastle and the bridge area survived but hey, it sank already. There's absolutely nothing left, not even any flotsam and no survivors. The only guy in the water is one of our men. He was hit just a minute before the ship disappeared."

"Baker leader to *Pursuer* leader, the Jerries are breaking combat and diving for the fjord. It's going to be a sticky time down there."

"Jesus Christ, if they find the other drones," Lacey said, mostly to himself. "Mother ship one to *Pursuer* leader, take your squadron after them. That includes this flight escorting us. The Aphrodites will need them more than we do. At least we got a few guns."

The last Corsairs to guard the mother ships toggled their tanks and peeled away. The departure left the B-17s at the mercy of their own defences and whether or not the Germans would decide to intercept them.

"Mother ship lead, this is *Thrasher*, we are going to have to submerge. A German minesweeper and E-boats have entered our area. We'll surface once they depart but we can't help you until then. Our last sweep shows all aircraft heading to the Alten Fjord area, that includes the third squadron of interceptors. We only have the first half of your other squadron on the screen. They will reach your position in ten minutes, good luck. This is *Thrasher*, signing off."

"Hold on a minute, *Thrasher*, what's their altitude? *Thrasher*, what is their altitude? Answer damn it!"

"Dennis? What's happening?" asked Cox, with the cruiser gone, there was no longer a reason for him to stay in the nose; so it was back to the cockpit.

"Your silent service has really gone silent," Lacey noted. "Your submarine had to crash dive. Which means there's no more radar coverage. We won't know what the Germans are doing or even our own fighters, unless we ask."

"Yes, I'm sure the Germans will tell you if you ask them nicely. Do you have any idea what's happening?"

"Some, they're swarming into Alten Fjord. I don't dare send another drone down it. Not until Bradley clears them. If he can at all."

"What about Rotherham?"

"Still enroute," Lacey answered. "The sub reported that half of his squadron was on the way. But I don't know if it's the high group to protect us or the low group. I hope it's the low, Bradley needs all the help he can get."

"And what about us?"

"We're on our own. We and our drones will have to orbit out here. At least until we see which way the battle is going."

Alten Fjord became a hornet's nest. The remaining planes of Everest flight had to fight their way out. If it weren't for the intervention of arriving Corsairs, they would have been slaughtered. The battle raged mostly above Alten Fjord; with Bradley repeatedly ordering his pilots to break combat when they were drawn down into the ganglia of narrow channels.

"Get the hell out of there, Charlie lead! Go to war emergency and pull away. You don't have the room to maneuver. Haul your ass, now!"

When the throttle was pushed through its safety wire, it activated the water injection system; boosting the Double Wasp radial to its maximum rated output. The result was almost like adding another engine. The Corsair would emit a trail of bluish haze and jump forward like a frightened deer. Though it could only be maintained for five minutes, the result was startling. Especially to the pilot of a Messerschmitt who thought he had the upper hand in the duel. There were a few however, who did not obey the order.

"Able four, break combat now! Somebody go down there and help him, before he has his ass shot off!"

Able four got more than his ass shot off. The Messerschmitt's cannon fire walked across his rear fuselage and through the cockpit. Pilotless, the Corsair had only to spiral a few hundred feet to hit the water and disintegrate. Those who did obey, and escaped, headed out to sea. Not all of their pursuers bothered or had the ability to follow them but

301

enough did to draw off the last remaining fighters not committed to the battle.

"Mother ship two to mother ship one, our Aphrodites just lost their escort. Colonel, they're sitting ducks now for sure. Request permission to leave formation and join them."

"Request denied, mother ship two, we need you here to provide for our defence. There's a whole squadron of fighters down there. They'll defend the Aphrodites."

"They can hardly defend themselves, Colonel. Two have gone down already and help won't reach them for a couple of minutes. In air combat that's an eternity. I'm not really needed here, my Aphrodite is gone. It's you and Vince that're important now. I sure hate to disobey your orders but I have to. See you later, when all the Aphrodites have been launched. 'Bye, Colonel."

"Mother ship one to mother ship two, you get back in your position. This isn't a time for grandstanding! You're taking too big of a risk, Frank. You get back here or I'll personally tear those funny leaves off your shoulders!"

It was too late. Atkinson had departed, breaking away cleanly and putting his Fortress into the steepest dive it could structurally take. Short of shooting him down, there was no way Lacey could stop his wing man.

"That's the angriest I've ever seen you with your men," Cox observed. "Will you really demote him?"

"Yes, then write him up for a Distinguished Flying Cross," Lacey admitted, "if he lives through this stunt."

"Tail gunner to pilot, we have company. Fighters rising, six o'clock low. I count twelve and they have to be Nazis. They don't look anything like Corsairs."

"Could that be the third squadron *Thrasher* warned us about?" Cox asked.

"No, Bradley's engaging them. This has to be a fourth squadron. I hope it's all the Germans can launch for now. It's six to one odds as it is. Pilot to crew, gunners prepare your weapons. Standby for attack."

"I believe I should return to the radio compartment."

"That won't be necessary, Charlie. It's really no safer back there than up here and it's best not to have a lot of running around during an attack. Frank told me that. Frank. Pilot to crew, can anybody see what's happened to Atkinson's ship?"

At the maximum diving speed, it took about a minute for Atkinson to reach the same altitude as the remaining drones. He did not find them alone. A single Messerschmitt was cautiously circling them. Staying beyond the range of guns that didn't exist.

"Pilot to crew, we got a Kraut to nail. Top turret, chin turret, get ready to fire!"

Like a four-engined, thirty-ton fighter, the B-17 pounced on the German with all the forward guns it could bring to bear firing. They caught the '109 in a web of tracers it could not escape from. Even the ball turret joined in as the Fortress passed overhead. The final blow was delivered by the turbulence the giant created. It slapped the burning Messerschmitt into an unrecoverable spin. The fighter broke up before reaching the sea.

"Score one for our side!" shouted Atkinson. "Now let's go back and see if the drones have been damaged."

"Mother ship one to mother ship three, the enemy is splitting into two groups. One with eight aircraft, the other with four. Standby for attack."

The orbiting Fortresses soon proved to be a difficult target to properly assault. The Me-109s kept trying to position themselves for a head-on pass, the classic Luftwaffe tactic, only to have the bombers slide away each time.

"After all those missions over North Africa and Italy, it's a great feeling to fly another way than straight and level. Hey, Colonel, you think these Krauts will get frustrated and leave?"

"No, more like frustrated and reckless. And they may have reached that stage. Here they come, three o'clock high!"

The larger group finally elected to make a beam attack instead; hoping that the four-to-one ratio would mean no one aircraft could be singled out. It didn't exactly work that way.

As they approached, the lead flight jumped too far in front of the other, allowing the top turrets and right waist guns to concentrate first on them and then on the second flight. The ball turrets and left waist guns were waiting for the Messerschmitts as they dove away and succeeded in exploding one from the lead flight.

"Hey, my guys got one, did you see it, Colonel?"

"What do you mean your gunners? It was my top turret that got him smoking first. Try your luck with the other group, looks like they're going to do a head-on pass. Standby to jinx your ship."

Once the fighters had committed themselves, the B-17s began to yaw from side to side; spoiling their aim. But the speed of their approach enabled them to escape. Neither the cheek guns and the chin turrets, nor the top turrets and the tail guns, managed to score any significant hits.

"That first group is splitting into its separate flights. That means they can attack us from three different directions, Colonel. Have you heard anything out of Frank?"

"Not yet, I hope the insubordinate s-o-b hasn't been shot down. Mother ship one to mother ship two, what's going on down there, Frank. Report in."

"Hey, Colonel, glad you're seeing it my way. We nailed a Kraut and we just finished looking over the Aphrodites. Yours has a few bullet holes in it, Colonel. These two are spread so far apart, it's going to be difficult guarding them but we'll do it. How's it going up there?"

"We have a gaggle of M.E.s after us but we're holding them off. We sure could use you."

"If you're holding them off you don't need me. There's a couple of M.E.s snooping around here, in fact a lot of them. Gotta go, 'bye, Colonel."

There were five of them, at different altitudes and distances though all were coming from the same general direction. And they were all drawing toward the Aphrodites. Farther in the distance could be seen some Corsairs but they wouldn't be arriving for a long time.

Atkinson peeled away from Lacey's drone and flew out to challenge them. While he didn't catch the Messerschmitts by surprise, he did at least disrupt their approach. The first two broke completely and ran back to Norway; preferring to engage Royal Navy fighters over a four-engined bomber, charging them like an enraged bull. The rest easily sidestepped the less maneuverable Fortress to attack the other, more docile, ones.

"God damn it! They're not getting those ships!" Atkinson stormed, watching the Me-109s pass him by. "Pilot to crew, standby for a turn."

The Boeing giant stood on its left wing as he made the course change. It was violent enough to throw

305

some gunners away from their stations and not all guns opened fire once the bomber was righted. Fortunately, the trio of fighters swarmed after the same Aphrodite. Capollini's.

Again the unmanned ship was approached warily, the Messerschmitts being cautious of the guns it did not have. When they realized it was turretless, and therefore probably defenceless, their mood became more belligerent and they swung in for an easy kill.

"Mother ship two to mother ship one, my controller has fighters on his monitor. You better tell your guys to get his plane out of there."

Two of the Messerschmitts dove underneath the Aphrodite. Even if they did believe it was unarmed, they still weren't going to take any chances. Atkinson decided to take them on; hoping that the other German wouldn't attack at the same time.

As he dove under the robot's nose, they came up under its tail. All forward guns on his Fortress opened fire on the two fighters. One staggered from direct hits immediately but the other managed to start a line of cannon shells walking down the Aphrodite's belly. Then it evaporated in a searing flash.

From twenty-five thousand feet, it looked like a giant star shell going off. Though Lacey tried at once to contact Atkinson, everyone knew it would be in vain.

"Frank. Frank," repeated Capollini, "I told you you took too any risks. Why couldn't you listen, just this once?"

"Give it up, Dennis, they're gone," Cox advised, putting out his hand to cover the microphone. "That was a very brave man. No matter how foolish you considered him, he had to do what he felt was right."

"They were all brave men," said Lacey, "Davis and

all those Norwegians who volunteered to join us . . .''

"Top turret to pilot, fighters coming in! Seven o'clock high!"

Not everyone's attention was seized by the distant explosion. One flight of Messerschmitts took advantage of the momentary letdown in the bombers' defences and pounced on them. Diving in from the left, they snapped out a series of short bursts and scarcely received any return fire. Both Fortresses were hit, along their wings, tails and fuselages. Shouts and warning cries swamped the intercom, though one voice came through quite clearly.

"Charles, help me, please!"

Oh, God, no, thought Cox, as he tore out his intercom lead and made a grab for his oxygen tank. Lacey also made a grab and caught Cox by the shoulder.

"That was Connie's voice I just heard!" he shouted. "What the hell's going on here? Is she on board?"

"I . . . I, I'll tell you later," Cox replied, slipping out of Lacey's grip and squeezing past the top turret gunner.

In the bomb bay, he saw holes in the fuselage skin, even in the upper set of ferry tanks, though they posed no danger. The tanks were long empty. In the radio compartment it was much the same. The fuselage was rent open, only here there were bodies.

The radio operator was slumped over his desk and Martinez lay partly on the floor; partly in Constance's lap. She had his flight jacket open and was trying to stop his bleeding when Cox appeared.

"Constance, thank God you're safe," he said, kneeling beside her. "If you had been killed I . . . How is he?"

"Still alive and still conscious, I think. I don't know about the wireless operator. Some shells came through the side and exploded. Lieutenant Martinez threw himself over his controls and then fell to the floor."

"Oh no, the drone." Cox leaned over Martinez and shook him gently. "Lieutenant. Lieutenant, what about the drone? The Aphrodite, man, what did you do to it?"

Martinez was only half-conscious and it took a little more urging to stir him.

"My side hurts," he whispered at last. "Yeah, Commander, I hear ya. I put the drone on auto-pilot. She's heading out to sea. You should slow her down. Oh God, give me something for the pain."

Cox rose and removed the first aid kit from the compartment's aft bulkhead. He passed it to Constance as he stepped around her and took the empty controller's seat. He needed just a few moments to switch off the auto-pilot, ease back the throttles and reactivate it. Lastly, Cox went over to the radio operator and slid him to the floor.

"He's still alive but he's in worse condition than Mister Martinez. Looks like the radios are still working."

"Charles, it's Dennis. He's calling for you to report in."

"I don't see why you can't tell him, he knows you're on board," Cox informed her, locating the intercom terminal she was hooked into. "I'm here, Dennis. Lieutenant Martinez and the wireless man have been wounded. Yes, she's here too, she'll explain why she's here later. Right now she's administering a morphine injection to Martinez. Lord, no . . ."

As he glanced down at Constance, he caught sight

of a trail of blood staining her jacket. From its location, Cox knew it couldn't be caused by Martinez.

". . . There's something wrong here, Dennis. I'll have to handle it. No, the drone's all right, it's currently heading out to sea. Could you send us some men to help with the wounded?"

"Sorry, I wish I could," Lacey admitted, "but those fighters are still out there and I need all the gunners that I have. Fix up Andy as best you can, he's got to fly that drone."

The moment the conversation ended, Cox was back by Constance's side. Why he didn't see the blood stain before, and realize its source, he couldn't understand. When he moved in close enough, Cox confirmed that it was Constance who was bleeding and that it came from under her oxygen mask. A quick glance and he located a small, crescent-shaped hole in the side of her mask.

"Charles, I need that to breathe!" she exclaimed, as Cox undid the straps which held it to her face. Her entire left cheek was smeared with blood. A small wound matching the hole in the mask was under the cheek bone itself. Exposed to the high-altitude, sub-zero air, the thin film of blood started to freeze before Cox could use a cotton ball to wipe it away.

"Here," he said, placing another directly over the wound. "Hold this in place while I find some tape. With all that shrapnel flying about the place, I should've known you'd be hit. It's a miracle you weren't seriously wounded."

"I know it isn't serious. So why do you want to treat it?"

"Because later it could be. What if this blood were to get into your oxygen line and freeze? You could be in trouble then. There, this should stop it. Now let's

309

put your mask back on and tend to the others."

"Pilot to crew, Germans two o'clock high!" Lacey shouted then ducked as the Messerschmitts came through the barrage of defensive fire and dove past him. "That'll be the last attack for a little while, until those bastards regroup. Maybe now I can talk with our escort. Mother ship one to *Pursuer* leader, can you tell me what happened down there? I want to know especially about my wing man."

"I'm sorry, Colonel, he's gone. The man you sent to protect the Aphrodites, went up with that last one."

"I didn't order him down," Lacey corrected. "He . . . He, volunteered. What about the planes responsible for it?"

"They went up too, all three of them. At least your loss helped reduce the odds we're facing here a bit. I have two Corsairs guiding the last Aphrodite. Why's it flying out to sea?"

"We've had some trouble up here but don't worry, we'll have it all figured out soon enough."

"Tail gunner to pilot, I have a second squadron of fighters approaching us. They are coming in fast."

"Christ, just what we need. More trouble."

"Wait a minute, Colonel. We are heading toward Norway," the co-pilot indicated, "which means that new squadron is coming out of the west. And if it is out of the west, then those fighters should be . . ."

"Mother ship one. Mother ship one, this is *Ravager* leader. Sorry for the late arrival but we'll make it up to you. Hold your position and we'll drive off those mosquitoes around you."

Unlike Bradley's, Rotherham's Corsairs wore blue and green mottled camouflage and the more traditional British insignia. He brought with him only half of his squadron, the rest were at that moment joining battle over Alten Fjord. The mere sight of the fresh Royal Navy fighters caused the Luftwaffe to break combat in each area. And since Rotherham's squadron was composed of experienced instructors, not green pilots, a full rout was accomplished in a matter of minutes.

"God damn, isn't that a beautiful sight," Capollini remarked, watching the last Messerschmitts flee. "Look, they just got another one. The way those guys are flying, we'll be the only planes up here in another thirty seconds. What'll we do, Colonel?"

"Do a one-eighty turn and catch that last drone. Standby, Mother ship two, making left turn, now."

With their edge in airspeed, the mother ships were soon on top of the sole, remaining Aphrodite. By then, Cox had a report for Lacey on Martinez.

"I'm sorry, Dennis, but with shock, the blood loss and the morphine we've given him, Lieutenant Martinez is simply not able to fly the drone. Couldn't we hand it over to Mister Capollini?"

"That's out of the question. We don't have the time or the gear to make such a transfer. If Andy can't fly it, you'll have to, Charlie."

"Could I have a second to think about this?"

"Okay but don't take too long. I don't know how long those Corsairs can keep the Luftwaffe at bay."

"Constance, you know more about this equipment than I do," said Cox, pointing at the console. "You fly the ship."

"Charles, you have to be joking. I may know the technical details but I've never worked the controls. You have, the Lieutenant showed you how, you told me he did. While I can help you, it's in your hands now. Remember what your father told you? Well this is the best chance you'll ever have to sink a battleship. Take it, Charles, take it."

"C'mon back there, have you made up your mind yet?" Lacey asked. "I've told Bradley and Rotherham to take care of the last flak boats and to provide the drone with an escort. We can't wait, are you ready, Charlie?"

"Probably as ready as I'll ever be," Cox replied, sitting in the controller's chair. "Auto-pilot, off. Increasing drone's airspeed, standby to put this ship about."

The two B-17s swung a hundred and eighty degrees again and settled on course for Norway. Four miles below, the Aphrodite duplicated the maneuver; sliding a little as it came out of the turn. The Corsairs hovering over it were soon joined by a second pair; then an entire flight turned up and took position in front of the unmanned Fortress.

"Just follow that lead flight, Charlie," Lacey advised, "they'll guide you through the islands. You don't have to worry about getting lost. Just keep that plane in the air."

In minutes, the outlines of Sor Iya and the other outer islands appeared on the monitor screen. The Corsairs made it easy to thread the channels between them and the later, inner chain of islands. When the mouth of Alten Fjord came on the screen, Cox could see the last of the Kriegsmarine destroyers being strafed. Apart from that distant activity, the fjord was quiet and the ships near its entrance were silent. Only once did a threat arise.

"*Pursuer* leader to all aircraft, there's an M.E. breaking into the fjord. Stop him, now!"

A pair of Rotherham's Corsairs pounced on the Messerschmitt as it came over Alten Fjord's north wall. Their dozen machine guns fired in unison, almost disintegrating its fuselage with hundreds of shells. The Me-109 skidded and cartwheeled into the water; sending up a plume of spray visible on Cox's screen. Moments later, he saw the Brattholm Islands slide by on the left. He was now less than four miles from Kaa Fjord's entrance.

"Lacey to controller, those Corsairs will be leaving you now. From here on in, you're on your own. The town of Alta should be in the center of your screen. Kaa Fjord will be off to the left."

The lead flight peeled out of his view, followed quickly by the fighters sitting on the drone's tail. Alta was in the center of the monitor but the mouth of Kaa Fjord did not appear until the last moment; when Alten's southern wall fell away. Cox immediately throttled back and tilted the pencil-sized joy stick to the right.

The image on the monitor screen streaked and blurred as it moved. Nothing was recognizable and Cox switched over to the flight instruments to complete the turn.

"Charles, watch the screen," Constance urged.

"You watch the screen! That jumble will give me vertigo! Tell me when it clears."

"There, it's cleared. My God, Charles, look at it!"

It was a remarkably undetailed shot, just a squat shape with a stacked, temple-like spire on top. No other details could be seen on the *Frederick the Great*, not until the muzzle flashes started. Cox pushed the throttles to the gate stops and left them there. He worked the joy stick with both hands, held it firmly and concentrated on the monitor. He ignored all the instruments and other controls, what it showed become his whole world.

"Go, Charlie, go!" shouted Lacey. "Don't blink your eyes when it's ready to hit or you'll miss the whole damn ship!"

The fifteen-inch main guns fired as well as the

smaller weapons; for the first and only time in anger. B turret's salvo hurled past the Fortress and out of Kaa Fjord itself, striking Alten Fjord's far wall. A turret's salvo hit the water in front of it, creating twin geysers of spray. The descending bomber flew through the brief shower with no effect.

Shore based flak batteries and *Frederick*'s four-inch and six-inch guns kept the Fortress bracketed with a steady barrage of tracers and shell bursts. Clouds of shrapnel battered it and random hits by the lighter anti-aircraft guns sparkled along its fuselage and tail; but nothing in the storm found a vital spot or hammered at one area long enough to cause any serious damage.

In its last seconds of flight, the Aphrodite dropped a hundred feet; it was barely half that distance off the deck when it swept over the bows. The propeller blades were scraping the roof of B turret when the dive came to an end.

The B-17 tore through the ship's superstructure below the bridge. Its wings were severed at the moment of impact; the tail fin and stabilizers were sheared away an instant later. Only the fuselage plunged into the battleship, smashing through the deck levels and armoured bulkheads until it was buried deep inside *Frederick*'s bowels. It was some-where underneath the massive, single funnel by the time the detonators had completed their firing sequences.

Twelve and a half tons of torpex vaporized in a single, titanic flash. The *Frederick the Great*, all fifty thousand tons of her, shuddered from the initial blast, then split apart. The flash had found and ignited the ship's six thousand, five hundred tons of bunker oil, the thirty-six thousand gallons of gasoline for the V-1s and the fully loaded ammunition magazines.

Almost the entire superstructure was consumed by the newly spawned fireball. Only B turret escaped the inferno; blown off its mounting and thrown high into the air. Like the shells it had just fired, the two hundred and fifty ton turret hurtled out of Kaa Fjord; tumbling end over end. It landed on its roof, creating a fountain of spray like an exploding depth charge.

The growing fireball covered the rest of the battleship and spread to engulf the service boats moored alongside. An almost visible shock wave preceded it across the fjord, destroying virtually every shore-based flak battery, flattening their sand bag revetments, scattering their crews, even uprooting some of the anti-aircraft guns and burying others under landslides.

Outside of Kaa Fjord, the shock wave quickly weakened. Still, it was strong enough to shatter most of the windows in Alta and toss around the fighters milling overhead. The fireball itself threatened to grow beyond the narrow confines of Kaa Fjord, only to dissipate and burn out at the last moment.

A brief rain of twisted, blackened battleship parts fell from the sky as a dark mushroom cloud formed. It rose to ten thousand feet in under a minute. Eventually, it would reach the altitude of the mother ships. When the roiling, angry waters of Kaa Fjord subsided, little remained beyond the hull of a capsized service boat. The others had all been sunk, as were the floats for the anti-torpedo nets. Of the battleship's eight hundred and twenty foot long hull, just its clipper bow and stern were intact.

Trapped air pockets kept them afloat for a little while. Finally, the stern section rolled to one side and sank. The bows slid beneath the surface with a loud gurgle and the hiss of escaping air. The *Frederick the Great* was dead.

"Jesus Christ. Jesus H. Christ," said Capollini, "that thing went up like a fucking volcano. If only Frank could've been around to see it. That was the best damn fireworks display I've ever seen."

"Yes, I wish he could've been around too," Lacey added, "but at least it's given him one hell of a send-off. Mother ship one to *Pursuer* and *Ravager* leaders. Gather your charges and let's get the hell out of here. The Germans are too stunned to do anything now but that won't last forever."

"Charles, it's over," said Constance, hugging Cox. "I can't believe it, it's really over. When do you think I may see Dennis?"

"Not for a little while," he replied, "not until we are well out to sea and the threat of interception is gone."

"Do you think he will be angry with me?"

"No doubt. He is, after all, in love with you. That however, is the least of your problems. What you should really be worried about is that I'm still angry with you. And as your commanding officer, I can take action against you. Rest assured that I shall make the punishment fit the crime."

CLASSIFICATION: MOST SECRET
WARNING:

To: The Board of Sea Lords—The Admiralty.

On November twelve, forces under the command of this officer, successfully carried out their planned attack on the missile-battleship *Frederick the Great,* as it lay in its anchorage at Kaa Fjord. In spite of a fierce defence put up by the Luftwaffe and the Kriegsmarine, a remotely piloted B-17 bomber was flown into the ship just forward of its bridge.

This direct hit totally destroyed the *Frederick the Great.* Only her bows, part of her stern and B turret, which was thrown clear by the tremendous explosion, are left. No one who was on board the ship survived and the Germans also lost the light cruiser *Leipzig* with all hands, 25 Me-109 fighters and 1 He-111 bomber. Our own losses were 6 Corsair fighters, 1 B-17 mother ship and all three B-17 drones.

The combined Fleet Air Arm/U.S. Army Air Force/Royal Air Force unit performed splendidly and its members fully deserve the awards they are now receiving. We should not underestimate the importance of what they've done.

Intercepted Enigma radio traffic indicates that the *Frederick the Great*'s planned sortie would have coincided with a large-scale offensive on the western front. Together, these two operations would have dealt us a death blow. Whether or not the Germans will proceed with the land offensive remains to be seen. By the first or second week in December, we should know.

In any event, the Third Reich is far from defeated and the threat it poses to all Allied nations will not end until the European conflict does. We have not yet heard from its Luftwaffe, though any threat it has should be discovered soon. The Americans assigned to my unit were recently reassigned to the Enemy Aircraft Evaluation Unit, based at the Patuxent River, Naval Test Centre in Maryland. They will keep in close touch with us; especially since my former aide and intelligence interpreter, Sub-Leftenant Constance Smythe, has now been assigned to the Royal Navy liaison office in Washington D.C.

I have the honour to be, Sir,
Your Obedient Servant,
Leftenant-Commander
Charles Wilfrid Cox R.N.
Intelligence Division
Leader of the Enemy Threat Evaluation Team.

MORE EXCITING WESTERNS FROM ZEBRA!

THE GUNN SERIES BY JORY SHERMAN

GUNN #12: THE WIDOW-MAKER   (987, $2.25)
Gunn offers to help the lovely ladies of Luna Creek when
the ruthless Widow-maker gang kills off their husbands.
It's hard work, but the rewards are mounting!

GUNN #13: ARIZONA HARDCASE   (1039, $2.25)
When a crafty outlaw threatens the lives of some lovely
females, Gunn's temper gets mean and hot—and he's got
no choice but to shoot it off!

GUNN #14: THE BUFF RUNNERS   (1093, $2.25)
Gunn runs into two hell-raising sisters caught in the middle
of a buffalo hunter's feud. He hires out his sharpshooting
skills—and doubles their fun!

THE BOLT SERIES BY CORT MARTIN

BOLT #6: TOMBSTONE HONEYPOT   (1009, $2.25)
In Tombstone, Bolt meets up with luscious Honey
Carberry who tricks him into her beehive. But Bolt has a
stinger of his own!

BOLT #7: RAWHIDE WOMAN   (1057, $2.25)
Rawhide Kate's on the lookout for the man who killed her
family. And when Bolt snatches the opportunity to come to
Kate's rescue, she learns how to handle a tricky gun!

BOLT #8: HARD IN THE SADDLE   (1095, $2.25)
When masked men clean him of his cash, Bolt's left in a
tight spot with a luscious lady. He pursues the gang—and
enjoys a long, hard ride on the way!

*Available wherever paperbacks are sold, or order direct from the
Publisher. Send cover price plus 50¢ per copy for mailing and
handling to Zebra Books, 475 Park Avenue South, New York,
N.Y. 10016. DO NOT SEND CASH.*